AND I LOVE HER STILL

PAMELA DEAN

Cover art by: Michelle Morhaime of Lost Marbles Designs

Cabin drawing based on artwork by: Virginia Wright

Edited by: Deborah Dove

Re-edited and proofread by: Laurie Starmer

ISBN 979-8-9913924-0-2 (paperback)

ISBN 979-8-9913924-1-9 (digital)

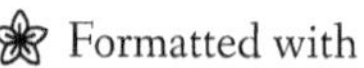 Formatted with Vellum

AND I LOVE HER STILL

CONTENTS

A NOTE FROM THE AUTHOR

The Modoc National Forest is nestled in the northeast corner of California, with small towns like Adin, Canby, Lookout, and Alturas. While these are very real places, my description of them is mostly fictional. The book of Cowboy Poetry featured throughout this book is entirely fictional as well.

This story takes place in 1988. Some of the choices the characters make are based on the timeframe in which they lived. I care about your mental health, so please be aware there are things in this story that you might find upsetting. You can find content warnings on my website. (Content warnings do contain spoilers)

www.pameladeanauthor.com

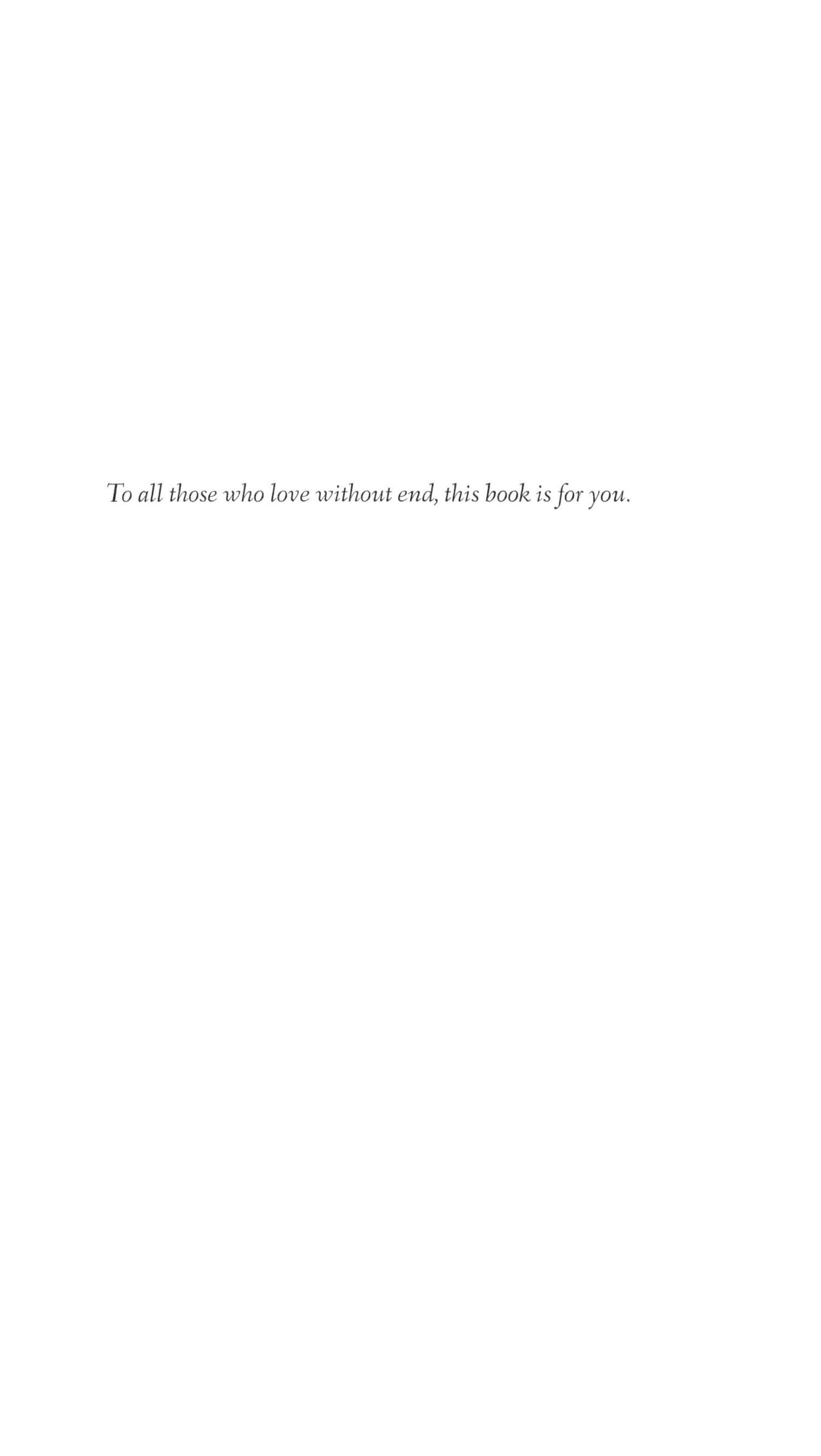

To all those who love without end, this book is for you.

COWBOY POETRY

BEYOND THE FENCE LINE ~PUBLISHED 1950

The flat expanse
before me
The hills that rise
pull me
Climbing to the top
bears me
~By M.S 1914

ONE

KENNY

Modoc National Forest
Adin, California 1988

"Kenny! Hurry it up. We leave in ten," Captain Henderson yells from inside the engine bay.

"Almost finished! Why don't you check on the rest of the crew instead of yelling at me? I put my red bag up top an hour ago. I'm busy restocking compartment D," I say, then mutter under my breath, "I know how much that matters."

I shove another roll of toilet paper into the already full compartment and slam the lid shut, twisting the lock in place.

"Ryan is fucking around in the office. If you're done with that, see if you can't hurry him along," the captain says, wiping his brow with his red bandana.

"I'm not going to babysit him. I've told you that. If he can't figure his shit out on his own, then he doesn't deserve to be here. Do you know how many people were trying to get to this station?" I say as I stand defiantly in front of the engine, hands on my hips.

I have my long, brown hair pulled back into two tight French braids and am wearing my bright pink bandana. It is my favorite one. I'm wearing my new White's, my boot of choice, the government-issued green Nomex pants, and our custom black T-shirt with our engine logo. Luke designed it last year, and it is pretty badass. We all really like it. I've never been a super curvy girl, and the sturdy running bra I wear at work helps keep things in check. My legs and arms are muscular, and my stomach is showing a slight six-pack. Luke teased me and told me it was a few cans short still, but I'm happy with my progress.

So far, this year's fire season has been a lot easier with all the training I did in the offseason. Climbing hills with my web gear and saw didn't slow me down like it did last year, and I delighted in beating the rest of the crew to the top. I can barrel up the hill, easily passing most of the other guys. Our first fire this season was a small, half-acre at the top of a ridge. Another engine had been sent to assist, and I could see the judgy looks when I hopped out of the crew cab.

Once people work with me, they see what I can do, but before that, there's all sorts of eye-rolling and snickers. Especially when I put my chaps on and hoist my saw to my shoulder. They certainly don't expect me to be a sawyer.

Captain Henderson gives me that look I hate so much, the one that means "I really need your help" as he nods toward the office.

"Ugh. Fine. But if he is in there flirting with Bonnie again, I'm going to kick him right in his boys" I turn and pull open the back door to the ranger station.

Big Valley Ranger District is a small Forest Service station that has a fire crew, a brush disposal crew, a fire prevention truck, and other non-fire related Forest Service employees. The US Department of Forestry has fire engines to protect its natural resources but doesn't like to have actual fire stations, so we share our space with archeologists, biologists, and foresters.

This is my third year doing fire, but only my first as a full-time employee instead of just a seasonal firefighter. I'm going to go through the academy to become an engineer after this season, and I just got my AS degree in fire science and my EMT certification. I love this job so much. Most of the people I work with have become like family. Hell, all of them have except the new kid.

Ryan MacGrill is an idiot. He failed out of the testing process for CDF and came to the Forest Service with a big chip on his shoulder. Acting as if he knew everything and was better than everyone. He mentioned more than once on his first day at the station that he was just slumming with the green engines until a spot opened up in Southern California. Captain Henderson told me the truth about Ryan after having a few too many whiskey shots one night.

I can hear Ryan laughing as I walk down the hall. I knew he was at the front desk chatting up the receptionist. Bonnie is a pretty local girl, very sweet but really naive. It makes me uncomfortable how easily swayed Bonnie seems by anything Ryan says.

"Hey, Ryan. Captain said, we are leaving. Your red bag isn't loaded yet. Get moving, dude," I say as I walk past him. I'm not going to stop and wait for his response. I want to say goodbye to Neil and Rick and see if they will make sure the fire cat has food and water while we're all gone.

"Don't get your panties in a bunch, Kendra. I'll get my bag loaded as soon as I'm done talking to Bonnie," Ryan says.

Rolling my eyes I keep walking. No one calls me Kendra. I'm not even sure how he found out that is my real name. I have always gone by Kenny. My family, my friends, and my teachers call me Kenny. No one but him calls me Kendra, and it makes my skin crawl.

I stick my head into the Archeology office and smile at the boys. "Hey, we are just about ready to leave. You guys are going to feed Fred while we are gone, right?"

"Hey, Kenny. Yeah, Rick is going on a dig, but I'll be here the whole time. Food and water bowls still out back by the hose racks?" Neil asks.

"Yeah. Thanks, Neil. So, a new dig, huh, Rick? Where are you headed?" I lean against the doorframe and glance back out to the office catching Bonnie reach across the desk and ruffle Ryan's hair.

"It's on the edge of the Indian reservation. Well, it's on Forest Service land but close to the reservation. Anyway, they think the body is old, and they want us to go check out the area and see what else we can find." Rick sighs and shoves some papers into his work bag before standing up.

"Gross. Sounds like a fun time!" I say with a laugh.

"Yeah. It's probably just a regular dead body and not something cool like an ancient human. I swear my grad school friends are in fucking Egypt digging up pharaohs and I'm here in the woods identifying dead hunters. I'm living the dream." Rick attempts a smile, but it falls flat.

"You never know, Rick. Maybe it's a Sasquatch," I say, hiding my smile with my hand.

"Don't even joke about that. My God, woman. That is the dream. One day, mark my words, one day we will find him," Rick says, and Neil agrees, nodding his head vigorously. Then they both stand up and shift toward each other, doing some lame fist bump thing.

I love these two so much. They are actual real scientists, but they are also obsessed with Bigfoot and finding any proof he exists.

"Well, as soon as we get back, I'll buy you both a beer and you can tell me all about the body and how Fred did without us here. Watch that back leg of his. He was favoring it again," I say.

"Will do, Kenny. Hey, make sure you take that douche, Ryan, with you. We don't want him hanging around here." Neil winks at me, making me smile.

I'm about to turn around and yell at Ryan to get moving when I hear the engine siren chirp, followed by my captain on the bullhorn yelling last call for loading up.

"Shit. I gotta go. Bye, guys." I wave and turn, following Ryan out the back door.

Apparently, the siren did the job of prying him away from

Bonnie. He stops and grabs his bag out of his truck bed and climbs up the ladder of the engine to put his red bag with the rest. I have to wait for him because I sit by the door, while Ryan is in the middle. My good friend Luke has the other door. When Ryan started this season, he immediately assumed I would take the middle seat since I'm a little shorter and there is less legroom. He quickly learned that the new guy doesn't get to pick where he sits. I've been here two years, plus I'm the EMT. I need to be first out.

Ryan climbs in and makes a big deal about getting adjusted and comfortable before I feel like I can get in.

"You ready over there, Princess?" I ask, winking at Luke, who is already pulling out his novel. How he reads on these windy roads, I will never understand.

"I'm ready, Kenny. Got my inflight snacks, and my tray table is in the upright position. Please feel free to ignore me as I'm about to find out if Rochelle is indeed going to marry Bram or his stupid brother. I will be unavailable." Luke salutes me and smiles as he opens his book and becomes lost to the outside world.

"How about you, Ryan? Are you all set there?" I ask as nicely as I can.

"Yes, Kendra. I'm all set." Ryan pulls his bandana over his eyes. He sinks down as low as he can in the seat, his knees bumping against the partition.

I climb up into the crew cab and close my door. I bend forward into the front and say, "All ready. Where are we meeting the rest of the strike team?"

"Down the hill, probably at the rest stop by Redding," Captain Henderson replies, then begins his favorite argument with Chuck, our engineer. Every fucking time we go off forest, Ted starts before we even pull out of the station.

"So, Chuck, let's just say there was another shooter. I know you think it was Lee Harvey, but you really aren't taking all of my theories into account."

I roll my eyes and lean back in my seat. It isn't long before I close my eyes, trying to get some rest. It's a good habit since I'm never sure what lies ahead. We are being sent to a fire that, at last check, was over three hundred acres. They only have about 25 percent containment, so they started calling in more resources. The fire is over in the Tahoe National Forest. It's an area I'm unfamiliar with, but Ted worked there when he first started. I know it is a similar elevation to here, and there are a lot of hills. I'm ready, grateful to have the distraction of a big fire.

I don't mind the little projects we do around the station or the medical calls we go on—they all make the job interesting—but going off-forest to a big fire is my favorite. Fire camp is so cool. I love everything about it. It is like camping with three hundred of your closest friends while also getting to cut down trees and hike. I mean, sure, there is the whole fire thing, and I'll never tell my mom this, but the fire is undeniably the best part.

I know my parents were worried when I told them about this opportunity, but after the first season they realized I was hooked. My dad was super excited about me getting to work with the chainsaw. He taught me how to use one when I was in high school. My aunt's property had a few trees that needed to be taken down, and since Uncle George had passed, there was no one to take care of it. My dad couldn't, and he didn't want to pay to have the tree service guys go up to the property. So he taught me. I was already using a lot of power tools for my woodworking, so the saw wasn't all that different.

I mentioned to Ted that I had a desire to get certified as a sawyer when I first started. He put me through all the training courses, and I quickly progressed to a level C sawyer, meaning I could cut down any size tree. It has become my favorite thing to do on a fire.

I let the gentle sway of the engine lull me to sleep, even though I can feel Ryan fidgeting next to me.

COWBOY POETRY

BEYOND THE FENCE LINE ~PUBLISHED 1950

Lost among the
Pines
Lost among the
Hay
Lost among the
Cattle
Lost and alone is
Me
~By M.S 1921

TWO

PATRICK

Well, fuck. This can't be right. No way there is a town out here.

I've pulled over so many times to check the map, it's taken twice as long as it should have. I've pulled onto Hwy 299 like the map said, and it should be a straight shot, but this highway also is called 139 for some odd reason. The first time I passed that sign, I had a minor heart attack. I'm probably not making the best decisions on the four hours of horrible sleep I had last night.

Leaving Seattle yesterday and driving as far as I could did not land me in a town with a hotel like I had envisioned. Since there is nothing out here, I slept in the parking lot of a campground in the back seat of my car, because I was dumb enough to believe I'd just be able to get a hotel room somewhere when I was tired. That is true in the civilized world; clearly, I've left that region.

So, here I am trying to find Adin, California, where I'm to go to the Frosty and ask for Jenny. She has the keys to my Great-Uncle Mitchell's house, which now belongs to me.

I'm still trying to process all of this. When I got the first letter from an attorney out of Alturas, I thought for sure it was a mistake and threw it away. I didn't know an Uncle Mitchell or remember either of my parents ever talking about him, so it was probably a different Patrick Smith they were after. A week later I received another letter and a message on my answering machine asking me to please call back as soon as possible.

That phone call changed everything. So, I'm driving out to the middle of nowhere to take ownership of a ranch. I guess I have nothing better to do since I haven't been able to come up with one decent book proposal in over a year.

I've submitted nothing. Gone completely silent. Dropped off the radar. Now I'm probably going to be listed as a missing person since I just locked up my house in Seattle and walked away. Not like I had anyone to tell I was leaving. The guy at the corner coffee shop might miss my pen tapping. I think he was fond of my rhythm and the occasional pen toss I would throw in to keep him guessing. He stared at me a lot. He will probably miss me, but no one else will.

I'm not running away, I'm running towards something. That's what I'm telling myself at least.

The book series I wrote starring a dashing ex-military hero has done very well, but I feel kind of done with the mystery genre. I had some really great ideas, sold a shit ton of books, and even had a movie deal, so I should be super happy, but the thought of doing one more book with the very popular leading man, Kent Price, makes me want to shove my face into a wood chipper.

I used to love the guy. But now? I fucking hate him. Every new situation I think of for him has me pushing him under a moving train, or him falling face-first into a pile of ants. Pretty sure you aren't supposed to kill off the main character of your book, so I ended the series.

Maybe this diversion, attempting to find a town that may not actually exist, will spark something new in my writer's brain. I sure as hell wasn't finding it in Seattle.

Is that a sign? Oh shit!

Adin 64 miles.

I kinda want to stop and kiss that sign right on its numbers. I *am* going the right way! The end is near! Wait, that isn't a good thing to say. The road trip is almost over, and my new adventure awaits.

Fuck, I'm so lame.

An hour later I pull into "town." A few minutes ago, I was actually worried I wouldn't be able to find the Frosty, but like the attorney said, you can't miss it. Seriously, there are three buildings on this main street, which is also the highway, 299 or 139 or whatever. There is a big building that looks like it was built during the gold rush or something. It has a large wooden porch and two doors, one leading to the town store and the other the town bar. Seriously, the bar is called The Bar. The lettering is kind of faded too, like no one cares enough to retouch the paint. I hope it is actually open because I know tonight I'll need a drink.

Down the street a little bit is the Frosty, a run-down burger joint with a large cutout of a soft serve ice-cream cone. It looks like that sign is cared for a little more but still has seen better days. Next to that is a US Forest Service station with a sign that reads Big Valley Ranger District. There is another sign indicating Fire Danger Today High. Smokey the Bear is waving like he's trying to reassure you that while the forest may ignite soon, it's going to be okay.

Well hell, who am I to doubt a bear that knows how to put on jeans? Of course he couldn't figure out the shirt, but maybe he just wanted to show off his chest. That dude is jacked.

I park on the street in front of the Frosty and stretch my arms above my head, yawning and cracking my neck. Jesus, that was a long drive. Hopefully Uncle Mitchell's place is close by.

I walk up to the entrance only to be met with an unyielding door. There isn't a closed sign or anything, so I looked around. A small window with a shelf to the right of the door is open. Crossing to that, I lean on the ledge and wait. A girl pops up from behind the counter and screams when she sees me. She is holding a bunch of straws, and seeing me causes her to toss them in the air. They rain down on her, with more than one sticking in her hair.

"What the fuck, dude?! Could you not sneak up on me like that?" She pulls headphones off her ears and presses the button on her Walkman, stopping the tape.

"Sorry. I didn't mean to scare you. I was told to come here and ask for Jenny. Are you Jenny?" I ask.

"No, she went home for lunch. She should be back in an hour or so." She squints at me, then asks, "You want a burger or something?"

"Uh, sure. Can I get fries too? Oh wait, do you have milkshakes? I'd love one of those too." I rub my stomach with excitement. I haven't had a milkshake in ages.

"Sure. Yeah, I can do that. You can wait over there. I'll bring it out." The girl points to a couple of picnic tables in the gravel parking lot. She is still squinting at me, sizing me up. Probably wondering who the new guy in town is. That's me now, the new guy. I like it.

"Thanks. What do I owe you?"

"Eight fifty" she says over her shoulder.

She walks over and starts pulling out the burger fixings, so I put a ten dollar bill on the inside of her window, anchoring it with her Walkman.

"Keep the change" I wander over to the lovely outdoor seating area. Lovely might be a stretch. It is actually just two crooked picnic tables that have probably been here since the dinosaurs walked the earth. Part of the bench is broken off and is lying on the ground, and the top is decorated with all kinds of interesting carvings. Linda apparently gives good head, and if you want weed, you should look for someone named Dave.

Looking back at the restaurant I can see the girl bustling around the kitchen. I wonder if I will get a clean straw or one of the ones she just tossed on the floor or pulled from her hair. Best not to dwell on that.

Pulling my notebook out of my shirt pocket and slipping the pen from behind my ear, I jot down a few notes about the feeling of this one-street town. The rundown buildings, and the teenager that screamed when an actual customer graced her window. Hopefully my writer's block is going to get knocked loose here. I mean, if I want to keep writing, that is. I'm not sure that I do.

COWBOY POETRY

BEYOND THE FENCE LINE ~PUBLISHED 1950

Two by two they walk along
Sunset, sunrise, moon high, sun low
shoulder to shoulder
Two by two
~By M.S 1917

THREE
KENNY

"Kenny, you take Luke and Ryan and get up that hill. We need those trees along the ridge taken down. The hand crew is heading that way to cut line, but those scraggly ass trees are going to cause us a lot of problems. Get rid of them," Captain Henderson says, circling the area on the map with his finger, then pointing to the ridge behind us.

Ryan walks to the compartment that holds the chainsaw and twists the lock, popping the lid. I stop him before he can put his hands on my saw.

"Stop. I'll get it. I don't need your help," I snap, already irritated that I'm going to be stuck with this asshat for the next few days.

"Just trying to be useful," Ryan says, holding his hands up in a defensive pose.

I take a deep breath. "Listen, I like to get the saw out myself because it's part of my routine. I like to make sure I have everything. I don't grab my saw until I have everything else I need. I don't want you to pull it out because it fucks with my routine. Got it?"

"Whatever," Ryan says, looking around as if he is trying to find someone.

"Luke went to the bathroom. He should be back in a second, and then we can head out. You'll carry the extra fuel and the piss pump. Luke will have the wedges and the boy's axe." I pull everything I need, then hoist my Stihl 044 onto my shoulder just as Luke jogs over to us.

"Ready? I feel light as a feather now! Man. I mean, that was a good one. Probably I lost ten pounds. I'm ready to climb that hill," Luke says, smiling and pulling the axe and the bag of wedges from where I had laid them at my feet. He leans into the engine and pulls the already full bladder bag out and holds it out to Ryan.

"Okay, your faithful swamper and this grumpy guy over here are ready to go! Let's hit this," Luke says with a smile. The guy is chronically happy. I can't think of a time when I have seen him in a bad mood.

"I'm ready," I say and look over at a very sulky Ryan who has put the bladder bag backpack on. His helmet is still clean, with only one or two scuffs. I'm kind of surprised he didn't rub it in the dirt to make it look like he had more time on. I have buckled my chaps on and spun them backwards so they cover my ass and the back of my legs. I'll pull them to the front when I start to cut but wearing them this way is a lot cooler. The heavy Kevlar really holds in the heat, and hiking uphill doesn't need to be more miserable if it can be helped.

"Ready," Ryan snaps and sets off down the dirt road. He cuts in too soon, but I don't say anything. I keep walking, turning into the woods about twenty feet ahead of where he did. Luke is right behind me, whistling like one of the seven dwarfs and making me laugh.

"Fuck!" we can hear Ryan grumble as he makes his way back down to the road, then over to where we had gone up into the woods.

"Lots of boulders in this area. The captain told us where to turn to avoid them. Guess you were busy and didn't hear him. Or maybe you forgot to look for the flagging?" I say, trying not to laugh. I touch the blue and white striped tape that Chuck used to mark our path up.

The ground begins to rise beneath me, and I glance up. There is a pretty clear trail, probably made by deer and other animals. Ted and Chuck scouted this for us earlier when they drew the maps for the fire line. There are three snags at the top of the ridge that need to be felled. I lean into the hill and enjoy the burning feeling in my legs and lungs as I climb.

Everything falls away, and I'm able to focus on my breathing, the weight I carry, and the sound of my boots crunching through the underbrush and dirt.

I don't even realize I have pulled ahead of my team until I reach the top of the ridge and set my saw near a rock. Sitting, I take a long drink from my canteen while I wait. Luke acts like he will not make it, stopping and pretending to wheeze and cough, then powering past Ryan in a few strides. It is clearly pissing Ryan off, and nothing makes me happier.

While I wait for them to reach me, I quickly assess the situation. Luke is right next to me before I can complete my cursory assessment. He is really good at the safety aspect of this, and I always defer to his suggestions.

"You gonna aim for that clear area there?" He points, adding, "I'd stay away from that. It looks stable from up here, but when we passed that, I noticed that big tree on the ground is actually resting on a boulder. You hit that and it could snap back up." Luke is all business now.

"Yeah, thanks. Noticed that, too. I'm going to start with this one, then do the other outside one, leaving the middle tree for last. I don't like the way it looks. Reminds me of that tree that bucked back on Ted last year."

"Fuck yeah. That was scary. I thought I was going home without a head." Luke laughs, but I don't. That tree had a rotten core and fell before we were ready, almost knocking Luke to the ground. It reminded us that no matter how careful you are, this is dangerous work.

Ryan has made it to the top of the ridge and is walking around looking at the fire that is one ridge over. Since we were dispatched, it has jumped to about five hundred acres but has slowed a bit. Unfortunately, high winds are expected this afternoon, so things are about to get hairy. This line is important if the wind pushes the fire up and over the lower ridge.

"Ryan, can you come over here and tell me your escape route? I'm cutting this tree first." I rest my hand on the tree I'm starting with.

"I think I can handle it. Don't worry your pretty little head about me," Ryan says, dropping his pack at his feet.

"Need to know your plan, Ryan. I'm going to drop this tree there." I point to the clear area downhill. "Luke and I plan to go that way on the ridge because those lower branches could snap and bounce back up. I need you to either follow us or tell me your plan, because if I take you back to the engine with a branch through your neck, I'll probably get in trouble," I say, trying to sound lighthearted instead of angry.

"I'll follow Luke," Ryan says, staring up at the giant sang I'm about to knock down. "You sure you can handle that? I can take it down for you."

"Nah, I got it. Since you haven't finished your chainsaw certification yet, I can't really let you play." I pull my goggles off my helmet, letting them fall into place over my eyes, then yank my Kevlar chaps around to the front. Making quick work of the first tree, it drops exactly where I want it. I move to the second tree and do the same, yelling like before, "DOWN THE HILL."

Listening for the creaks and cracking, then the solid thud, the crash of the tree to the forest floor always brings a smile to my face. Even dealing with Ryan can't damper my spirits.

The middle snag proves to be just as difficult as I imagined when my back cut hits a knot first, kicking back the saw a little. I move over a touch, then sink into soft, rotten wood. I step back to reassess.

"It's rotten on this side, but I could feel firm wood through some of the back cut. I'm going to use some wedges on this side to make sure it falls over that way," I say more to myself than my team. I like to talk things through and make sure I have a solid plan. This tree has been dead for a long time, and the bark beetles have made it soft in the worst places. The soft patches are higher than my cuts and on the downhill side. I'm pretty sure this won't fall clean.

"I think we are going to end up with a barber's chair no matter what I do," I say, this time looking at Luke.

"Yeah, that's alright, Kenny. Let's just get it down, then we can clean it up after. Captain H radioed the crew is heading our way."

"Got it," I say and make quick work with the boy's axe, hammering my wedges in place. The pie cut on the back side is challenging, but I manage to get it done, and the tree falls where I expected. Luke lets out a pleased whoop and begins to clear the debris from the trail. I set my saw down as Luke and Ryan move a few branches out of the path where the hand crew will be coming.

I take the time to clean off my saw and inspect the chain. That knot was like hitting a rock, so I run my fingers along the chain, looking for where it hit. I use my file to smooth out the notch as best as I can. It isn't bad enough to warrant changing the entire chain, but I don't want to have it hang up on me later.

Ryan is watching me as he pulls a few smaller branches. It is clear he's still angry. Probably mad that I wouldn't let him take the saw. I really don't know how I'm going to get through the season with this idiot. It's one thing to doubt me before seeing my work, but I pride myself in always challenging the expectations people have of me. I know I'm good at my job. I don't need Ryan to think so.

"Hey, Luke, did you find out who Rochelle married?" I ask as we head west to meet up with the hand crew.

"Fuck yeah. She made the right choice and married Bram. That was a good book. I need to find a new source now that Mitchell is gone. Can't believe I won't have access to his books anymore. I'm going to have to go up to Alturas or over to Klamath Falls to the library," Luke says, shaking his head.

"Yeah, that really sucks. I'm going to miss that old coot. He cracked me up with all his stories about living in the "big city" that one year." I make air quotes, and Luke laughs.

"Yeah. On no planet is Susanville a big city. Although they have a Taco Bell, so that's something."

"How many books do you go through in a month?" I ask. Luke is always reading. If he isn't on a fire or hiking in the wilderness, he is reading. I'm pretty sure that most of his pack is weighted down with paperbacks.

"Hmm, I don't really know. Five, maybe? It depends on whether we get called out. Obviously, I don't have time until we get back to fire camp. I'm about to start a new one, the last of my Mitchell loans. It's the first in a series, so that bums me out. Mitchell had all of them, but wanted me to take only one at a time. This one is a mystery. The main character, Kent Price, is like a super-stud ex-military dude who solves crimes. I hope there are a few love interests thrown in. You know that's my favorite," Luke says with a wink.

"Only the first book? Man, that's cold. I guess he wanted to ensure you'd come back for a visit!" I say with a laugh.

"Fuck, that was never a problem. Although I made it easy on him with my love of books. With you, on the other hand, he had to get creative. Did you ever finish fixing those steps on the front of the house, like he asked?" Luke asks, and I immediately feel a pang of regret.

"Nah, I had to go down to Redding on my days off. Then, when I got back, I think it was the next day we got the call that he had fallen."

"You know there was nothing you could have done, right?" Luke stops me on the trail, grabbing my arm.

I take a deep breath and let it out. On a logical level, I know that is true, but I don't feel that way. I really liked Mitchell. Hell, everyone did. He was ninety-four years old, but it seemed to all of us he would live forever.

Rusty had been out at Mitchell's ranch moving the cattle into the pasture by the house and went in for some water. He saw Mitchell on the floor in the living room and called the Frosty. Ted and I were in the ambulance in seconds, flying out to his ranch, but by the time we got there Mitchell was already gone.

"Yeah, yeah. I know. I wonder what is going to happen to the place. Rusty moved the cattle over to his property after the funeral. I can't even go down that road. I used to run that way during my morning workout, but now it just makes me sad."

"I know what you mean. I miss that old dude," Luke says, wiping his face with his bandana.

"You are awfully quiet back there, Ryan. You okay?" I ask.

"Yep," he says, his voice thick with irritation.

I sigh and put a little more speed into my step. At least once we meet up with the hand crew, there will be more people to buffer Mr. Nasty Mood.

COWBOY POETRY

BEYOND THE FENCE LINE ~PUBLISHED 1950

Pieces of me
Among the pines
Among the fence line
Among the wheat
Among the wind
~By M.S 1917

FOUR
PATRICK

After what could only be described as the best burger of my life, the elusive Jenny finally returns to the Frosty.

She is a thin, wiry thing with hair that was probably blonde at some point. Now it's gray with streaks of white. Her face is wrinkled, but in the best way, like around her eyes and with smile lines that show she has led a life filled with laughter. She wears a pair of faded Wranglers and a button-up western shirt that is as colorful as a rainbow, if rainbows were as bright as acid trips. It's almost hard to look at; it's so intense. The pattern reminds me of the carpets in a casino in Vegas. She pulls a key ring from her back pocket, holding it out to me. I reach for it, but she holds onto the worn leather strap.

"He meant a lot to us. We all miss him terribly. You planning on living on the ranch, or are you going to sell?" she asks, looking me up and down.

"Um, to be honest, I haven't made any decisions about the property. I think I need to see it first, understand what kind of shape it's in. You know?" I say. I don't want to get into my plans with someone I've just met. Mostly because I don't know my plan, but that is beside the point.

"Well, Kenny never fixed the steps, so be careful if you go in the front door. Also, the cattle are over on Rusty's property, but he will move them back if that's what you want," Jenny says, finally letting the worn piece of brown leather go. She drops her gaze, trying to hide the tears forming.

"Cattle? Wait. Uncle Mitchell had a working ranch? He was ninety-four years old! I figured it was just a house on some land. Sorry, but the attorney was kind of vague about the situation." I'm feeling bad for not knowing even the most basic things about this man.

"He was down to about fifty head. Rusty did most of the work moving them from the higher mountain property down to the pasture area around the house. Mitchell did all the care though. He vaccinated them and fixed up their cuts and scrapes, helped birth a calf only a few days before he passed. He was still very much involved in things right up until the end." Her voice catches as she says that, and I smile at her.

"It's nice he had people around him who cared," I say, feeling like that is something you would say about an uncle. I really have no idea. I've been on my own for thirteen years. Both of my parents are gone, no brothers or sisters or cousins. It's just been me. Me and Kent Price, my leading man, my moneymaker. The guy I now can't stand.

"Well, there's a group of us here in town that will help out if you need anything. Mitchell was a fixture here. It hasn't been the same for the last two months. Ted and Kenny took it the hardest because they all played poker together every week, and Kenny was working on fixing all the things that were broken at the house."

"Well, I'd like to thank them. Are they around?" I ask.

"Nah, engine went off forest to a fire down on the Tahoe. Should be back in a week or so." Jenny shrugs and starts to walk away.

"Wait, Jenny! Where is the ranch?"

She points and says, "Out that way. Road W. You can't miss it. His mailbox is on the main road. It's the big blue one. The gravel driveway is a bit overgrown with weeds now, but you'll see the box."

She doesn't turn around again or wave; she just walks into the Frosty, disappearing with her grief in tow.

"You can't miss it seems to be the only way to give directions around here," I say to no one. I walk to my car and head out again on the main road, turning onto Road W. Within a few miles, the blue mailbox is there, just like Jenny said. The gravel driveway is almost hidden by the overgrown weeds and manzanita. I'll have to see if that Kenny guy would be willing to help me cut some of that back.

I drive slowly, looking around the property as I approach the main house. It's a simple structure, a typical ranch-style home. The porch has three steps that lead up to the front door. A nice planter box sits by the door. The flowers are all still alive, and I notice a watering can sitting to the side. There are two chairs on the porch with a small table between them.

I park my car and get out, looking around for any sign of this Rusty guy. Jenny mentioned that he had been coming out once a day to check on the place. He must've been watering the flowers. Preoccupied with my thoughts, I head up the front steps, immediately falling through the second stair.

"Shit! Oh, fuck, that hurt." I yank my leg out of the splintered wooden hole I had created. My dockers are ripped and stained with blood. The broken plank has a nail sticking out that's covered in my blood.

"Well, that's quite the welcome. Fuck, I probably have tetanus now, and I'm going to die here alone. Does tetanus give you lockjaw? Hell, my jaw feels tighter already. This is it. This is how I die," I say, again to no one.

I try to peer into the rip in my pants to see if I'm going to lose my leg, but cannot get a good look. I limp the rest of the way to the front door and fish the keys out of my pocket. Of course, it's the last key I try that finally opens the old, worn door.

The creak is quite satisfying as I push the heavy door open. I don't know what I expected to find when I entered the house, but I can tell you it's not what I see. The place is spotless. There's one pair of boots in the entryway, and a well-worn tan Carhart canvas jacket that hangs on a hook. To the left is the archway leading to the kitchen, but it's the room to the right that pulls me in.

Floor-to-ceiling wooden bookshelves line the entire room, and every inch is filled with books. A leather couch and one recliner take up the rest of the place, with the recliner positioned in the best spot in the room next to the fireplace. A floor lamp and a beautiful wooden table sit to the left of the chair. There is a pair of red-and-black, flannel-like slippers by the chair, and the coaster on the side table holds a whiskey glass with the last bit left untouched. The bottle next to it is almost empty, but there is a little left. I close my eyes and can imagine this man I didn't know taking up the space.

It's my kind of room. It smells like books and leather and maybe Old Spice. I think I would've liked Uncle Mitchell a lot.

The cool trickle of blood running down my leg pulls me from my thoughts, and I set out to find a bathroom and hopefully a Band-Aid.

After patching my wounded leg and realizing that I probably won't need to have it amputated, I go back to exploring the house. It's a three-bedroom, two-bath home with hardwood floors throughout. The front guest bathroom toilet has the lid off, and it looks like someone had been attempting to fix a problem. There are tools set neatly on a towel on the edge of the tub. I will soon find out that it's like that everywhere in the house; there were a lot of repairs or projects that weren't finished. Everything is at least orderly. Mitchell must've liked to keep things clean and neat.

The attorney said my great-uncle had never married and had no children. He had written his will up over twenty years ago, so I would have only been twelve years old. I wish my parents had talked about this man even once. And, for the millionth time, I wish I could talk to them again. I have so many questions.

I bring my bags in from my car and place them in the master bedroom. The bedding is folded neatly on the foot of the bed, so I remake it, pausing to try to remember if I was told where Mitchell died. Was it in here? The mattress looks clean enough, and glancing around, there's nothing out of place to indicate a fall. Just a little dust on the tops of the dressers. I open the drawers revealing everything neatly folded. Every drawer is the same way; nothing is out of place. It's unnerving to go through a stranger's life in this way.

I close the dresser drawer and head back to the living room. Something on the third shelf, right at eye level, catches my eye. A very familiar spine. Kent Price books two through twelve stare back at me. Huh. I wonder where the first book is. Glancing around the room for a clue to its whereabouts, I come up short, but I'm honored and surprised to see my books in his library. On the fireplace mantle, there is a leather-bound notebook. I flip it open to a list of names with book titles written next to them. There is a line drawn through each title with a date. Mitchell seemed to have been running his own lending library. I flip to another page and see the name Luke. The next four pages are filled with book titles Luke borrowed and returned, with the last entry being book one of my Kent Price series. Well, that was an easy mystery to solve.

If I ever get the chance to meet this Luke person, I'll have to ask if he wants the other books. If I stay here, I don't want that series in my library. I'd like to never have to look at those books again.

COWBOY POETRY

BEYOND THE FENCE LINE~PUBLISHED 1950

Howls and yelps
Float down the ridge
Chilling my blood
Rattling my nerves
Howls and yelps
Closer still
~By M.S 1918

FIVE

KENNY

I have never been so happy to see fire camp. Every inch of my body is tired. I think my pinky toe is going to fall off. Stupid new boots. The pair I wore for the last two seasons had just started to get comfortable, but I lost one of them somewhere between Adin and Chico last October. I should have checked the tailgate latch before heading out, but I was in a hurry to get home after a long season.

My dad needed help with a project he was doing for Mom while she was visiting her sister. I love how much he loves her. He is always trying to find ways to make her smile. My older sister went to college on the East Coast and recently got into a fancy art school, so we won't be seeing her anytime soon. That means all things family will land on my lap. I don't mind, but it does make this newest transition a bit challenging.

I won't be leaving in October to go home like I have the past two years. I'm going to stay on through the winter. Ted arranged for me to have a single-bedroom house on the grounds so at least I don't have to share with anyone this year.

Both my parents said they were happy for me, and they didn't need me to be around, but I worry that isn't true. I'm my dad's little buddy—his partner in crime and all home improvement projects. He taught me everything I know, and I'm grateful. I can fix almost anything and am pretty decent at things like hanging drywall and minor plumbing repairs, but I excel in woodworking projects.

Dad has been in a wheelchair since he was twenty years old. He and Mom were high school sweethearts. They've been together since their junior year and married the summer after they graduated.

In college, Dad was on a hunting trip with his buddies and had an accident on the way back into town. His spinal cord was damaged enough to make walking impossible, but it didn't remove all his feeling, so in a cruel twist of fate, he still has pain. He is the bravest person I know.

"You going to hit the showers before dinner?" Luke asks, stowing his gear in the engine compartment. I have finished cleaning my saw, and I wrap the chaps around the chain to protect it.

"Fuck yeah. I'm not even the same color I was an hour ago. I don't know how I manage to get like this. It's like I'm a soot magnet," I say with a chuckle. I put my saw away and shake out my shirt, watching the sawdust fall around my feet.

"It's probably all that lotion and shit girls put all over themselves. The soot and dirt stick to you. Maybe don't do that," Ryan suggests as he shoves his gear in the back of the engine.

"Gosh. Thanks, Ryan. I didn't think of that. You are so smart. It must be that giant man brain of yours that allows you to problem-solve that way, huh?" I say, letting the sarcasm do its work.

"Fuck off, Kendra." He slams the crew cab door and walks off towards his tent.

"He's a goddamn delight," Luke says, shaking his head. "Now go wash off all that girly lotion and shit so we can eat. You stink worse than me." He lifts his arm to take a sniff. "Oh, shit, nope. No, that horrible smell I have been experiencing is coming off of me. My bad."

I laugh and walk towards my tent, reaching in quickly to grab my small bag out of my red bag that holds my camp clothes and my shower stuff. I wave over my shoulder as I head to the temporary showers they set up in camp. Shower might be a stretch, it's a tent with a hose, but I'm not picky. I've never understood the guys who eat first. I mean, I'm hungry, but I don't want to eat while covered in layers of dirt and grime.

There are a few more girls on this fire than the last one, so I have to actually sit and wait on the bench for a stall to open up. Once it's my turn, I strip out of my fire clothes, hanging my bag. When I step into the stall, I'm delighting at the instant hot water that drenches me. Waiting until the water runs almost clear before attempting to wash my hair or use soap on my body, I let the water do most of the work. I shave my legs and bikini area, and armpits. It would probably be easier to let that go during fire season, but I just can't do it. I tried once and felt very uncomfortable.

As I wash my hair, I think about the fire and all we accomplished. The dozer line was doing a great job, and they had some air tanker drops that stopped the forward movement they were worried about. I took down countless trees today and bucked up several fallen ones to clear the path for the hand crew we are with. My hands are blistered and sore, but I feel amazing.

After using conditioner in my hair, I step out and smile at the girl who is waiting. "All yours. Enjoy. I'm a whole new woman."

She laughs and grabs her bag. Before she closes the curtain, she asks, "Hey, are you on engine four out of Adin?"

"Yeah." I stop and use my towel to wring out my hair. I want to get to dinner and pop a few Tylenol, but I don't want to be rude.

"Tell that prick you work with that the line isn't his personal pickup zone. Dude wouldn't leave me alone all day," the girl says.

"Fuck." I shake my head, knowing immediately who she means. "Yeah, he's an idiot. I'll talk to our captain. Sorry you had to deal with that."

She shrugs. "It is what it is. Most of the time I can discourage them by talking about my girlfriend, but this guy thought he might be invited to join us if you catch my drift."

"Ew. Yeah, he thinks pretty highly of himself. Probably thinks he can get you back on the other team." I laugh.

"No, thanks." She smiles and pulls the curtain shut.

I drop my bag at my tent and make my way over to the chow area. Luke is in line with his nose buried in a book already. I join him and tap his shoulder.

"I'm here. Not that you care, but I am," I say, pretending to be hurt.

"Hey, Kenny. Just a second. Man, this guy is good. Three pages in and I'm fucking hooked. Who knew I would like mystery books!" Luke says as he holds up a finger. I watch as his eyes dance over the page, rapidly scanning. It doesn't seem possible that he is actually reading that fast, but he is.

"Okay, done with that chapter. You all better?" Luke asks.

"God, yes. I'm back to my normal pinkish brown and my hair is no longer the texture of a twine rope. All is right with the world."

"You leaving it down? People might find out that you are actually a girl if they see your long hair," Luke says, tugging on my wet hair.

"I was going to braid it, but I have a bit of a headache and pulling it back tight makes that worse. I guess I'll just have to live danger-ously as a full-fledged woman," I joke.

Then, as if on cue, I hear, "Hey, Kenny! I almost didn't recognize you with all that hair! What's up, Luke Dog? Still reading up a storm?" Lyle Hamlin takes his place in line behind us, and Luke and I both turn and take turns hugging him.

"Hey, Lyle. It's great to see you! How's the wife?" I ask.

"Huge. She is due to pop any time now. I might be bugging out if I get the call. I'm hoping with the progress they made today, the crews will start getting thinned out and my strike team will go home," he says as he wipes his bandana down his face.

"What kind of piss-poor planning did you have getting your wife pregnant with a due date smack in the middle of fire season?" Luke says with a laugh.

"I don't know, man. It was really bad planning, for sure. I think she got pregnant when we came off that monthlong assignment. I hadn't seen her in like six weeks because before that fire, we were covering another station. Guess my little swimmers found their mark."

"Ew. No need for details, man." I hold up my hands, and Lyle laughs.

"Hey, I heard about Mitchell. I'm sorry," Lyle says, lowering his voice.

"Thanks," Luke and I say together, then Luke adds, "I miss him so much. He was such a cool guy."

"You were on the call?" Lyle asks me, and I nod.

"Yeah, he fell in his living room. Had poured his evening whiskey, even though it was only about four in the afternoon. He stood from his chair and just collapsed. We tried CPR, but we knew he was gone," I say. I'm inching along in the line as we finally get closer to the food.

"The world lost one of its best that day. If I have a boy, his middle name is going to be Mitchell," Lyle says, scuffing his boot along the ground.

"That's really sweet. Got a first name picked out? Kenny is a nice name," I say, poking him in the arm.

"I'm not naming my son a girl's name. Fuck that. It will be something manly like Jeb or Duke. Oh! Fucking Duke Mitchell! I love it. That's the winner." He pumps his fist in the air, and Luke and I laugh.

"God, I hope you have a girl," Luke says with a smile.

COWBOY POETRY

BEYOND THE FENCE LINE~PUBLISHED 1950

Wolf among the fold
Ember floats on high
Fist grips so tight
Coiled like a rattler
waiting
~By M.S 1919

PATRICK

After touring the inside of the house, I check out the backyard and the three outbuildings. There is a shed with some tools for yard work and a lawnmower. The other outbuilding seems to be supplies for the cattle and fencing, and the last one is a woodworking haven.

Slabs of already stained wood rest against a wall, and there is a paper taped to the workbench. It looks like plans for a bookshelf. I wish with every fiber of my being that I could finish those shelves, but I haven't ever really been a handy person.

I can use a hammer and most other tools, except for that weird wrench thing that has a screw in the middle. I never know which way to spin the stupid thing or how to lock it in place. Plus, I spent most of my teens and early twenties writing.

Twelve books in twelve years really took it out of me. Right in the middle of that series, I did a short novel spin-off of one of my favorite side characters, Mandy Love. She was the scientist my main character consulted whenever he got stumped on a case.

Mandy knew everything. She was smart and sassy and absolutely hated Kent. I needed him to be challenged in a way that the mysteries he was solving didn't. She provided all sorts of challenges. At all my book signings, the number one question was would Kent and Mandy ever get together. I wanted to scream, "God, no! The dude is a fucking tool, and Mandy knows that!" But my agent thought it would be best to play it coy. Her book gave her a solid backstory and a secret lover that I'm sure everyone assumed was Kent.

Spoiler: it was not.

I had more fun when I wrote that book than I had in a long time. Giving a female character a voice that was strong and confident made me feel challenged, interested, and invested.

She wasn't like any girl I knew in real life, and I really appreciated that about her. I wish I could do a whole series about her, but in book twelve I kind of sent her off into the sunset with her mystery lover revealed. Man, the fans were not happy with me. You just can't please everyone.

I head back into the house and realize I need to go into town for dinner or at least groceries. Someone kindly cleaned out the refrigerator and cupboards, so there is no food left in the house. The only alcohol left is approximately two fingers in Mitchell's whiskey bottle by his chair. There is a little sludge left in the glass, too. I don't have the heart to rinse it out, and I imagine his friends felt the same way. I walk out to my car and drive towards the street they call Town, hoping for food and a stiff drink.

The Frosty seems to be closed, with all the lights in the building turned off, so I drive a little farther down to the store-bar building. The grocery store is also closed, but the door to the bar is propped open, and I can hear music and laughter.

Well, at least I can get a drink. I toss my glasses on the dashboard and lock up before heading into the bar. It takes my eyes a minute to adjust, but I feel the slow smile spread across my face when they do. This place is amazing. It's exactly how you would picture a bar in a one-horse town. Old wooden floors, stained and gouged with years of use, beer and hard alcohol advertisements hang from the walls, and a pool table takes up prime real estate in the middle of the room.

There are booths along the wall that have red leather seats that have faded to almost a pink color. A jukebox stands in the corner playing what I assume is Merle Haggard. I don't really listen to country music, and that is the only artist's name I can think of. So in my mind, that is who it is.

The bartender is an older man with a faded tattoo on his forearm and a long, gray beard. He doesn't have a single hair on top of his head, not even a hint of hair, like that Mr. Clean guy. Well, except for the beard and the tattoo. He is definitely someone I would write as a side character for a book. Scary as shit to look at, but probably really nice.

"What the fuck are you looking at?" he growls at me, making me realize I'm standing in front of him, probably with a goofy smile on my face as I picture how I would describe him in a paragraph.

"Oh, sorry. Didn't mean to stare. I, um, I'm new in town and was hoping to get something to eat and um, a drink?" I ease onto the barstool in front of him.

He tosses a yellowed menu at me but doesn't smile.

"Cash only. I don't take checks," he says. He glares at me and runs his tongue across his top teeth.

"Got it. Not a problem. Um, what do you recommend?"

"I recommend you figure out what you want pretty quick. Jenny is leaving soon, and if she's already scraped the grill, she's gonna be pissed if you order the cheesesteak."

"Jenny? Like the Frosty Jenny? Oh! I know her," I say, happy to hear a familiar name.

The bartender just squints at me and, without turning his head, yells, "Jen, a friend of yours is here to see you."

Okay, so this is not one of those guys who looks scary and then is secretly nice. Nope, he's actually scary. Thankfully, Jenny pops out of the kitchen, wiping her hands on a towel.

"Oh, Patrick. How are you? Did you find the place okay?"

"Who is this guy?" the bartender barks with an unwavering glare. I can literally feel his eyes on me. I know what that means now. It's like they are pressing into my face.

"This is Mitchell's great-nephew. He took the keys today when he got into town. I sent him out there around lunchtime and never saw him again." She shrugs, then leans over closer to the bartender and whispers loudly, "Thought he got lost."

She winks at me, and I smile and say, "Yeah, I found it okay. Fell through that step you warned me about, but it seems like I won't lose my leg like I initially thought. It was just a scrape." I'm tempted to pull up my pant leg and show her my very impressive bandaging skills, but think better of it when the angry bartender grunts at me.

"You want a drink?" he asks.

"Yeah, whisky neat. Top-shelf please," I say, adding the please at the last minute because his eyes only got angrier with my order.

"Top-shelf? Oh, that's hilarious. You'll get what everyone else gets. Jack Daniels. Do you want some dinner? I haven't started to close down yet, but you got lucky. I normally try to be out of here by seven." Jenny leans on the counter and gives me a much-needed smile.

"Jack Daniels sounds great, and I heard something about a cheesesteak?" I ask since I couldn't really read the menu that was shoved at me. It's quite grimy and has what looks like blood on one corner. I gently push it away from me.

"Sure, darlin'. Coming right up. Rusty, be nice to Patrick while I go get his cheesesteak," Jenny says over her shoulder as she leaves the room.

"Wait, Rusty? You moved my uncle's cattle, right? Jenny mentioned you," I say, hoping his anger will dissipate some now that he knows who I am.

"You got a problem with me moving the cattle? I've done it for fifteen years now. You come into town one day and want to tell me how to do my fucking job?" Rusty says as he slams an empty whiskey glass down in front of me.

"Uh . . . no, sir. I'm grateful for all the cattle moving and other cattle-related things. I didn't even know my uncle had cattle, and well,"—I lean in like I'm trying to make my point—"I never had even a hamster growing up, so I don't know what I would have done with cows. In fact, if you want to keep them, I really—"

Rusty interrupts me by slamming another whiskey glass on the counter.

Without moving his gaze from my face, he reaches under the counter and grabs the bottle of Jack, pouring equal amounts into each glass. He slides one to me and takes the other, downing the half-glass in one gulp. Continuing to glare, he wipes the edge of his glass with his dirty rag and returns it to the rack. I smile nervously and may even titter.

Do I gulp mine or take leisurely sips like I normally do? Damn, I wish he would stop staring at me. My back is all sweaty now, and I feel like I can't breathe. I think a bead of sweat just rolled down my ass crack. That's going to show in these light-colored Dockers I am wearing. I shift in my chair, causing a loud, guttural noise that sounds like a fart. Oh God, that seemed to anger him more.

"That, um, that wasn't me. I mean, it was me. I moved on the stool. But that sound was the chair, not me farting. I mean, I didn't come into your fine establishment to fart or anything. I don't do that. I mean, I do, but I'm civilized about it, you know? Like I would have excused myself or something. I am not just going to rip one right here in front of you. Although sometimes it can't be helped, right? I mean, who among us hasn't had one sneak out? Or like you think it's going to be quiet, but it's not. I guess that is better than the silent but deadly ones, am I right? But no smell here," I say. Then, for some ungodly reason, I cup my hands and scoop air from my waist and fling it at him, saying, "See? No smell! It wasn't me."

I can't seem to stop myself, but thankfully, Jenny emerges from the kitchen with my dinner, and I take the plate and my drink and walk to a booth to regain some of my manhood.

Jesus, that was rough. I take a sip of the Jack, letting the drink coat my tattered nerves. I pull out my notebook and pen and make a few quick notes about the feel of the room.

The bar top where angry Rusty spends his time is stained with whiskey and the tears of townsfolk, I imagine. Perhaps the blood-stained menu was evidence of a late-night brawl? As much as I don't want to write mysteries anymore, my brain is wired to think that way. What I want more than anything is to write a love story. Something deep and timeless that has you both laughing and crying. It feels so elusive. I can't even come up with the bones of a character after Kent Price. It's like he sucked the life out of me.

I take another sip from my glass and lean back against the booth, glancing around the rest of the bar. One or two more people have come in since I sat down, and a new song is playing on the jukebox. An upbeat little number about boots and walking... I tap my pen on my chin and think about whether I should buy some boots. These shoes really weren't meant for outdoor, rugged work. My collection of Dockers isn't either. I need to reevaluate my wardrobe if I'm going to stay in this town, that is for certain.

A heavyset woman comes in through the door and yells, "Rusty! How they hanging, lover? You need to start pouring before my fat ass hits that stool or I'll climb right over the bar and give you that kiss I've been promising."

I snap my head to look at Rusty, expecting him to maybe just pull out a gun and shoot this crazy woman right on the spot. He just glares at her, takes a glass from the rack, and pours her a Bud Light from the tap.

"You are slow as shit, Veronica. You'll never get that kiss, and you know it. Jenny's still back there if you want something to eat," Rusty says without taking his glaring eyes off of Veronica.

"Nah, sugar. I'm good. I stopped in Alturas and ate. Just need my beer before heading home to the asshole I call my husband." Veronica settles in the stool that I had occupied, and the same awful noise occurs. I glance over to Rusty to see if he will say something, but he doesn't. Sadly, Veronica does not launch into a lengthy explanation about the chair making the noise. Instead, she just leans her head back and burps loudly.

"Christ, Veronica. Have some class," Rusty says, glaring at her.

"I got all kinds of class, Rusty. I just really needed to let that out. Riding around in that damn truck all day is doing a number on me." Veronica pounds on her enormous chest with a fist.

"They done with that clear-cut yet?" Rusty asks angrily.

Veronica probably answers, but I have lost interest. There is no character there; none I care to develop, at least. She is someone who could have played a role in my mysteries, someone that would have irritated the perfect Kent Price, but not someone for my next book. Whatever that will be. Could I write a love story? Maybe a comedy? Fuck, why are ideas so hard to come up with now?

It seems like this town will be good for my writing. A change of scenery, something totally different from my life back in Seattle. Yeah, this is what I need. I guess it's a good thing I don't have anything keeping me in Washington. I own my home there, and while it's nice, with views of the Sound, there is really nothing for me there anymore. Don't have a lot of friends, and my love life, if you could call it that, is in pieces. There isn't a person who would care that I'm gone. Not one. Especially not the woman I almost married.

COWBOY POETRY

BEYOND THE FENCE LINE~PUBLISHED 1950

Glinting in the late day
sun
Shine bright and sharp
Tangled with memories of those
who went on
by
~Author unknown, Discovered 1922

SEVEN
KENNY

We've been on this fire for only four days, and it looks like they are going to send us home. I hate that. I wouldn't mind staying for mop-up, but Ted said we got tapped to go. Ryan has been a little angry brat most of the time, so it will be nice to get away from him.

I walk down to the chow hall to find Ted and Chuck talking to the incident commander. The fire is held at five hundred acres, and they have already released the air tankers and helitack crews. They are sending most of the engines home today, keeping the hand crews and inmate crews for mop-up.

"You can pack up your tent, Kenny. We are heading out. Go ahead and get breakfast first. We aren't leaving for a few hours. If you see Luke and Ryan, tell them too. I have to go to the trailer and finish up some paperwork. Chuck is going to take the engine and fuel up after he eats," Ted says, then pats the IC on the back, letting him know he is ready.

"Damn, I was hoping we could stay," I say to Chuck.

"Yeah, me too. I tried, Kenny. Volunteered us every chance I got, but they were pretty set on clearing us out. Better get some grub." He motions to the short line for the food, then over to the opening of the tent where two or three hand crews are making their way in.

"Shit. Thanks." I bolt to the food line, grab my tray, and load it up before the influx of people. I find a quiet spot and plop my tray down, immediately digging into the bacon and eggs. The pancakes are weird and left a strange taste in my mouth yesterday, but like the fool I am, I got more today.

"Why do these pancakes make me regret my life?" Luke asks, settling in next to me. He has his plate piled high with the thick discs. He also has bacon, sausage, and eggs.

"Not sure. Maybe try the syrup? Not sure that will help, though. Are they chalky? Is that it? Why can't I put my finger on what's wrong with them?" I ask, poking the pancakes with my fork.

"No idea. I got five of them for some reason. They sat in my belly like a bunch of rocks yesterday. I also know I said I would not eat them again." Luke sighs, then adds, "But here we are." He cuts a bite off with his fork and shoves it in his mouth, wincing.

"Well, they are going to rumble in your tummy as we drive home. We are done. Chuck left to fuel up the engine, so once you're done with breakfast you can break camp. If you see Ryan, can you tell him? I'm going to find Lyle before we go," I say, pushing my eggs around. I'll settle for just eating the bacon for now.

"Oh, dude! He headed home at like three in the morning. His tent was right next to mine. His wife went into labor!" Luke says, smiling around his mouthful of pancakes. "God, these are horrible. How do you fuck up a pancake? And why can't I stop eating them?"

"I have no idea, Luke. Try putting the fork down?" I laugh, then ask, "She's in labor, huh? That's cool. I hope to God he has a little girl. He deserves that." I push back from the table. "I'm going to pack up, and I'll meet you over by the parking lot in an hour."

I smile and dump the contents of my tray in the trash and stack it with the other dirty ones. Glancing around for Ryan, I quickly give up and head to the tents. My first year I lost my tent in the sea of domes, so this year I tied a blue-and-white strip of fabric to the top pole. I spot it, but freeze when I realize my tent is moving. I walk slowly up to it, trying to be quiet, and stand with my hands on my hips as Ryan backs out of the door flap, holding my web gear in his hand.

"What do you have there?" I ask in the angriest voice I can muster.

"Shit!" Ryan says, dropping the belt at his feet.

"What the fuck are you doing in my tent, Ryan?" I ask, bending quickly to pick up my belt. My knife holder is unsnapped, and the pocketknife Mitchell gave me lies on the grass by Ryan's foot. He tried to cover it with his boot, but I had already seen it. I shove him hard, knocking him off balance, and swipe the knife up.

"I'm going to ask you one more time. What are you doing in my tent?" I step into his personal space, shoving him in the chest again. The girl I met the first day at the showers comes out of her tent a few feet away and walks up to stand next to me.

"Hey, fucker, she asked you a question. What are you doing?" the girl says, sounding even angrier than me.

"I was looking for you, Kendra. Chuck said we're leaving. I thought you might need help getting your stuff," Ryan stutters.

"Bullshit. You have no reason to be in her tent, you little prick."

"No need to be a bitch," he says, glaring at her. He must realize that she could kick his ass because he lets his shoulders drop a little. "See you at the parking lot, Kendra." He stomps off toward the chow hall.

"God, what a little asshole! I'm Meghan, by the way. I'm on a hand crew off the Shasta T."

"Kenny. Nice to meet you. Thanks for that. I have no idea why he would be taking my web gear." I check to make sure everything is still there, and slide my pocketknife into the holder, then snap the cover shut.

"You an EMT?" Meghan asks, pointing to the scissors I carry on my belt.

"Yeah, trying to prove my worth," I say with a laugh.

"Fuck right off with that. I heard you are lead sawyer! The guys on my crew were talking about how fucking rad Kenny was with the saw, and I thought they were developing a crush on another dude. It was you! You are a legend," Meghan says, holding out her hand.

I reach out and shake her hand, smiling. "Thanks, that's nice to hear. Got to be the best at everything, or they might find out I'm a girl." I wink and she laughs.

"I feel that in every inch of my body. My crew is pretty cool. I imagine someday in the future women will be more common here, but for now I'm honored to work with a badass like you," Meghan says.

"Thanks. Right back at ya. I don't know if I could do the hand crew thing. You guys hike for days! Do you like it?" I ask.

"Yep, I love it. The Shasta Trinity wasn't my first choice, but it's fine. My girlfriend lives in Redding, so I shouldn't complain." Meghan shrugs. "You better get in there and see if he touched any of your stuff. I'd report that shit as soon as possible. That guy is an asshole," Meghan adds, and I agree.

I say goodbye and duck into my tent, finding my red bag open and a few things pulled out. I've always been an overly neat and organized person, so I know I put all my dirty clothes in the mesh bag, and yet my sports bra from yesterday has been pulled out, as well as the cotton thong I wore. A chill runs up my spine at the thought of Ryan touching my underwear. I definitely need to talk to Ted about this.

I put all my stuff back and make it to the parking lot at the same time as Luke. Ryan is already there, sitting on his red bag. He nods hello, but doesn't try to talk to us. I feel my stomach turn and bile move up into my throat, but for some reason I can't speak. It's the first time I have ever felt this way, and I don't like it.

The drive back to the station is quiet. I spend most of the time staring out the window, trying to come up with the words to describe what happened when I found Ryan in my tent to Ted.

The asshole was one hundred percent in the wrong, but there is something about the line he crossed touching my underwear that makes me feel vulnerable instead of just angry. When I saw him with my web gear and my favorite knife, I was insulted and pissed, and ready for a fight. Why did that change when I knew he had touched my underwear? Why did I feel violated? It was just underwear; it wasn't me. It wasn't my body, but it seemed that way. My stomach twists, raw and exposed, those words bounce around my head and I hate it. I wish I could go back to being angry.

We pull into the station after dark, and after getting all our gear off the engine and checking on Fred the fire cat, I toss my bag in the bed of my truck and wave goodbye. I will talk to Ted later. No way I can do it tonight. I need to go home, take a shower, and hopefully drink until I fall asleep.

When I drive out onto the main road, I glance at the bar, noting all the usual cars and trucks in place. There is a comfort in the regularity of this town. No surprises, no change. As I turn my truck around to pull into the long driveway that leads up to my little house, I see a bright red BMW that I haven't seen before. I wonder whose car that is. Hopefully Jenny finally treated herself to something nice. She certainly deserves it.

As soon as I'm in my front door, I set my bag down in the laundry room. I should start a load now before heading to the kitchen, but instead I open the fridge and grab a Bud Light, popping the can open and taking a big pull. I yank my T-shirt off and sit to untie my boots. My feet sigh as I slip them off. I shed my Nomex pants and sit back down, wearing nothing but my black thong and black jogging bra. Not really comfortable on this scratchy couch but necessary. I reach over and turn on the fan, tipping my head back as the cool air hits my skin. I should probably take a shower before going to bed, but I just don't have the energy. Instead, I finish my beer and get another one before gathering my dirty clothes to take to the laundry room. I head to my room and pull my favorite T-shirt from my dresser. I grab the faded AC/DC concert T-shirt that is too big to wear as anything but a pajama shirt. It's my dad's, and he doesn't know that I stole it. I'm pretty sure he would be really mad if he knew. He loves this shirt.

I finish my beer and grab another before putting a frozen dinner in the microwave. Hopefully, sleep will come easily. My body is tired, but my mind is back at the tent, watching Ryan paw at my things.

COWBOY POETRY

BEYOND THE FENCE LINE~PUBLISHED 1950

Canby
Can it be?
Canby
Do you see me?
Do you know I want to flee?
Fear rising I'm all alone
Canby
Lost again
Oh
Canby
~By M.S 1923

EIGHT

PATRICK

I finally make it to the store when they are open.

They don't seem to have regular hours; they just open when they feel like it. I'm making notes to see if I can spot a pattern because I can't keep eating at the Frosty and The Bar. I've been here in this street called a town for a week now, and I'm starting to feel a little more settled out at Mitchell's ranch. I'm hoping to run into Ted and Kenny to thank them for all they did for my uncle and hopefully learn a little bit more about the man who left me this new life.

I grab some canned goods and chips before making my way to the freezer section. I'll need to get to a big town soon and do some actual shopping, but for now I can piece together a few meals with what is here. There is a young guy in work boots, green pants, and a black T-shirt digging through the frozen food, so I wait.

"Oh, sorry, man. You want to get in here?" he asks.

"I can wait. Not in any hurry, and you seem to be on a break from work." I motion to his uniform, and he shrugs.

"Just grabbing lunch before heading up to Alturas for some dumbass training. I haven't seen you around before. You new?" he asks.

"Yeah, just moved here. I'm Patrick," I say, extending my hand to him.

"Ryan. Nice to meet you," he says before turning back to grab a frozen burrito. "Well, I'm sure I'll see you around. I mean when I'm actually in town. I'm on the fire crew here and we never know when we will be called out, you know?" He juts his chin out like bad boys do, then actually runs his hand through his hair. It's short on the top and sides, but longer in the back.

This guy has grit. I should write a book about a firefighter. They seem cool. "How long have you been in fire, Ryan?" I ask.

"About a year. I'm waiting for a spot to open up with CDF, but need to stay busy so, you know, I agreed to help out the Forest Service for the season," he says, looking over his shoulder. I can hear a radio somewhere in the store, so the rest of his crew must be in here as well.

"Cool. I'll let you go. Maybe we can grab a beer or something sometime?" I say, trying to play it cool. Dudes like him don't like eager.

"Sure, sounds good. I usually go to The Bar and shoot some pool after work. I'm sure I'll see you," Ryan says before walking away. He has swagger, and not that I was staring at his ass, but I notice he has a can of chew in his back pocket. Of course he does. He is totally that kind of guy. Rugged, tough, manly.

Not super tall—he's shorter than me actually—but has to be about five foot ten. He is muscular, though, from what I can see. He has broad shoulders and big biceps, probably from all the hard labor he does. As my gaze travels down his arms, it snags on his freakishly small forearms and hands. If I wrote a leading man who fought fires, I would need to change that. Nothing freaks women out more than small, dainty hands on a man. Kent Price had big mitts and thick, muscular forearms. I know what is up.

I finish my shopping and make my way outside to my car. I will need to trade in the Beemer if I stay here through winter. No way my red beauty will make it in the snow. I need a truck, some work clothes, and more food than what I can get here at the general store. Looks like I'm going to be making a trip to one of the bigger towns and soon.

There is a lot of activity at the Forest Service station when I drive past. They must all be back from the fire. I can see a crew washing the engine and a few guys leaning against a green truck holding an orange cat. I should stop in and introduce myself to everyone, maybe see if I can find Ted and Kenny. I also want to find Luke, but no idea how to do that. I should've asked that Ryan guy if he knew him. This is such a small town, I'm sure he would at least have heard of him.

Pulling up to Uncle Mitchell's ranch, I realize this place is really starting to feel like home, even if I haven't done anything to make it mine. There is something about this Mitchell guy that makes me feel welcome. His things, the decor, and the large number of books he owned all tell a story about who he was. I'm getting a sense of him. Going through his things is still uncomfortable, but realistically I need to donate or dispose of his personal effects at some point.

The wild card for me in all of this is that cranky-ass bartender. I wonder what Mitchell thought of Rusty. Was Rusty mean to him as well? Is that just his nature? Time will tell. I plan on going to The Bar Friday night to soak up some of the local culture and see if anyone stands out as potential characters for my new book. I've made a few notes about Ryan—nothing too concrete, just my initial feelings about him. There isn't a full sense of a character yet, but I'm closer than I've been in a long time.

Being an author really heightens your senses to people. I can accurately describe someone's personality after only a few seconds with them. People are, for the most part, easy for me to read. Sometimes I get stumped or make assumptions that are not correct. Most recently Rusty. He is not at all like I suspected. One other person fooled me as well, but I'm trying not to think about her.

After putting away the few groceries I acquired, I walk over to the front door and kick off my Top-Siders. I've walked past these old ranch boots every day. If they don't fit me, I will put them in a dona-tion pile.

I sit on the bench in the entryway and slide one foot in. It's a little loose, but I'm not wearing socks. With thick wool socks they will fit better. Since you never try on just one boot, I put my foot into the other one. Immediately there is a hard crunchy thing pressing into my bare naked toes. I, of course, picture stepping on a beetle. My mouth opens in a not so silent scream as I fling my leg around to rid myself of the boot and the scorpion or rattlesnake that I've surely stepped on. Grabbing my foot, and expecting nothing more than a bloody stump, I sigh when I touch a warm, dry foot. Tipping the boot upside down, I prepare myself to run in the opposite direction from whatever falls out. A crumpled piece of paper drops on the ground, making me feel a little ridiculous. I glance around, grateful no one is here to witness my hysteria.

I slip on the boot again and sit to smooth out the paper, which appears to be a list of things around the house that need to be repaired. Next to each item there is a name. Most of them say Kenny, but next to an electrical issue in the cattle shed the note writer, presumably Mitchell, had written Rusty.

He had circled "finish bookcase for my bedroom," and there are initials by that: K.W.

K.W. was also next to "Fix leak in front bathroom. Toilet and sink."

I assume K.W. is Kenny. I really need to meet this guy. He must be the town handyman or something. I wonder if Kenny would know why the list was crumpled up and shoved in Mitchell's boot.

I take the boots off and set them back in the hallway, realizing there are probably socks in the dresser that would work. This leads to me trying on several pairs of jeans, which fit perfectly, and some of Uncle Mitchell's old shirts. He must have been exactly my build because I only find one or two shirts that are too short in the arms. At six foot two, I have pretty long arms and legs. I have been a runner for as long as I can remember, so I don't have a lot of extra weight on me.

I stand in the bedroom, looking at myself in the mirrored door of the closet. I'm having to imagine this man Mitchell because there are no pictures of him on the walls. My cursory look through the closets yesterday yielded no photo albums, but there's got to be a box with loose photos or something. He had to have some pictures of himself, right?

If he didn't, then perhaps someone in town will have a picture. This is my new mission. I really want to put a face to the name.

I wake up early the next morning, excited for it to be Friday. Not because I had a long week or work or anything. I have never had a job that made me punch a clock. No, I'm excited because Friday night at The Bar will most likely be a bonanza of good material for my creative brain. I grab my notebook and a cup of coffee before heading out to the front porch. The chairs out here make for a nice place to sit and write as I have my morning cup of joe. I call it that now since I'm a rancher.

I take notes on the smells of the morning dew on the tall grass and the rumble of a truck or two on County Road W. I'm making a note about the enormous grasshoppers when I catch something out of the corner of my eye.

The road is obscured from view because of all the weeds and overgrown bushes, but I'm sure I saw something. Waiting I see it again. I squint and shake my head because what I'm looking at doesn't make any sense.

There appears to be a person, possibly a woman, jumping up in the air with their hands above their heads like they are being mugged. They disappear from view and pop up again a few seconds later. This goes on for a few minutes, long enough for me to set my notebook down and creep down the steps. I haven't turned on any of the lights in the house, or the porch light, because I learned quickly that my porch time becomes a bug party if the lights are on.

Whoever was being rhythmically mugged didn't know I was here. I have on Mitchell's flannel slippers, so I don't want to venture too far down the gravel driveway, but I'm able to peer around a bush and see what is definitely a woman lying on the ground. I take off running toward her, wielding the only weapon I have—my trusty Bic pen. Ready to gouge out her attacker's eyes, or at the very least mark him for future identification, I hold it out in front of me.

My slippered feet are not allowing me to run at my normal speed or grace, and before I can reach the woman in distress, I go down hard when I trip over a fallen tree.

I lie in the gravel for a moment, trying to collect myself before continuing my effort to save the woman on the ground. Rolling onto my back, I squint up at a very angry-looking girl who is standing over me, hands on her hips.

"What the fuck are you doing out here? Do you have permission to be at Mitchell's ranch?" she asks, kicking at my shoulder with her sneaker.

"Um, yeah. I own the place," I say, but am interrupted before I can explain further.

"No, you don't. That's Mitchell's place." She jabs her finger toward the house to make sure I understand what she is talking about. "I know him, and you are not him," she says, kicking me again in the shoulder.

"First of all, stop kicking me. That hurts. I'm pretty sure I broke my leg falling over that tree limb. You don't need to kick a man while he's down. Oh, hey, that's where that saying came from! I am literally on the ground, and you are kicking me! Yeah, that is no good. I'm going to need you to stop doing that," I say, because while I was talking, she kicked me again.

"I asked you if you had permission to be out here. And how could you have tripped over a tree limb? There are no trees around here."

She looks around, then bends over and pulls a stick up off the ground. "This? Is this what you tripped over? Jesus. This is probably Rusty's cattle dog's chew toy. Fucking tree branch my ass. You're kind of ridiculous, you know that?" she says, then kicks me again for no reason.

"Stop that. Why are you kicking me?" I ask, getting a little angrier. I also sit up because lying down is really not helping my case.

She shrugs and kicks at me one more time for good measure; I assume.

"I'm Patrick. Mitchell was my great-uncle. He left me his ranch," I say, getting up and brushing off my sweatpants. I've lost one of the flannel slippers, so I'm forced to stand on the gravel with my very tender foot. The rocks are like tiny knives, but I brush it off.

"I'll have you know I was on my way to save you from whatever was happening a few minutes ago. Were you being mugged or stung by a bee or hornet? You were clearly in distress, and I was going to save you. Well, until I tripped and then there was all the kicking. I guess you don't really need me to save you. I'm the one that should be yelling for help! Help!" I say, waving my arms around, trying to make light of the situation.

Her eyes narrow, lips forma straight line and then she just glares at me.

Silent.

Angry.

Women like her always make me nervous. I hate silence, and angry silence makes my ass sweat.

She points to my long-lost slipper at the side of the road and says, "Those are Mitchell's favorite house slippers. He never wore those outside. Congrats on ruining them."

I'm just about to fire off a witty comeback, but she turns on her heels and starts to jog away, not looking back once.

That went well. She must be related to Rusty. She has the same charming disposition.

COWBOY POETRY

BEYOND THE FENCE LINE~PUBLISHED 1950

Captain Jack, lead us, free us
Captain Jack, protect us
Help us
Captain Jack, betrayed us
Killed us
~By M.S 1922

NINE
KENNY

The two-mile jog back to the station did nothing to dissipate my anger.

What an idiot.

How could someone as awesome as Mitchell have an ass like that in his family tree? Why on earth would he leave his ranch to someone like that? The dude can barely function from what I can tell. No way he can handle a cattle ranch. I wonder how long he's been here. I'm definitely going to ask Rusty about it tonight. Seems like he would probably know about this Patrick person. I can't believe he thought I was being mugged. Who the hell would be out on County Road W at six thirty in the morning to mug a person?

Hasn't he ever seen someone do a burpee before? For the last two years, I have run to Mitchell's ranch and stopped by his driveway to do twenty burpees, sometimes adding some squats or just regular push-ups. Then I jogged back to the station. It's a great workout, but I haven't done it since we lost Mitchell. There was something about what happened with Ryan that made me want to go out to the ranch this morning. I wanted to feel close to Mitchell again.

If he were alive, he would have been on his porch, drinking his black coffee. I would have stopped and talked to him, told him what happened, and he would have known just what to do. He would have probably tried to kick Ryan's ass for me, but he would have also known just the thing to say.

God, I miss him so much. I could talk to him about things I hadn't been able to tell anyone else in my life. He saw me. The real me. The me I had a hard time showing other people. Now there is some tall, handsome, professor-looking guy with deep blue eyes and jet-black hair taking up all the air out at the ranch. Jenny told me she was giving the keys to someone this month, but I guess I liked pretending it wasn't going to happen.

I reach the station and bend at my waist, breathing deeply. I pull up, stretch my arms above my head, and walk around, cooling off. I was going to go home and shower before getting into uniform, but Ted's truck is in the lot and I want to ask him for a private meeting before anyone else comes in.

"Ted?" I call, jogging over to him as he shuts his door.

"Hey, Kenny. Get your PT in already?"

"Yeah, ran out to the ranch. Hey, can I have a meeting with you today? In private?" I ask, sounding more nervous than I want.

"Sure. Everything okay?"

"Yeah, I'll explain later. Does nine work? The rest of the crew will be out doing their PT, so we can talk," I say.

"That works. See you then. Hey, when you get in, I need you to find a time to schedule that CPR class. Ryan and a few of the guys on the BD crew need to get certified." He walks into the office, and I follow behind.

"Of course. I noticed the master schedule on the desk in the garage. I'll find a time when those guys are all on shift at the same time and get it booked." I'm dreading teaching that CPR class, knowing Ryan will make it very uncomfortable.

Giving Ted a quick nod, I turn to jog off toward my house, passing Ryan as he pulls his truck into the lot. I keep my head down and run past him. It's easy to avoid the rest of the engine crew when I come back to work, busying myself in the back rolling hose and petting Fred. Once the crew heads out for their run, I make my way into the station to Ted's office. I knock on the doorjamb and say, "Ready, Captain?"

"Captain, huh? Better come in and close the door, Kenny," Ted says with a soft smile.

I step into his office and close the door. He has an old wooden chair next to his desk that he uses to put his feet up when he is in here writing reports. I brush off some of the dirt and sit.

Before I start I take a deep breath to settle my nerves. "I don't really know how to begin, but I need to tell you about something that Ryan did on the fire that made me really uncomfortable." Trying not to drop my gaze down at my hands, I focus on the wall just over his shoulder.

Ted puts his pen down and leans forward with a concerned expression on his face. "Was he unsafe when he was swamping for you? Luke made a comment about that. Ryan needs to let go of some of that ego. You are the best sawyer I've seen in a long time, and you could teach him a thing or two." Ted shakes his head.

"No, that's not it. Well, I mean, he argued with me when I asked for his escape route, and he didn't really pull his weight when it came to clearing limbs and stuff, but no, Ted. This was more of a...um-" I stop and swallow hard.

"I caught him coming out of my tent the morning we were bugging out," I say, forcing myself to look Ted in the eyes.

"He was in your tent? Why?" Ted sounds as confused as I felt that morning.

"I don't know. He had my web gear, and my pocketknife that Mitchell had given me had fallen out. Ryan tried to cover it with his boot, but I saw it and grabbed it and my web gear from him."

"What did he say?" Ted asks, folding his hands on his desk.

"He said he was trying to help me pack up since we were leaving soon."

"Well, I guess that could be true." He pauses and scratches his chin. "What if he felt bad for not helping on the line? I wouldn't worry about it too much, Kenny. I'm sure that is what he was doing." Ted leans back like the matter is settled.

"No, I doubt it, because when I went into my tent he had gone through my red bag," I say now with a higher pitch to my voice that I don't like.

"What? Now, how would you know that? My bag is always all spread out. We had been there for almost a week. Maybe you just think he went through it," Ted says, shaking his head. He's not being unkind, but I'm rattled that he is defending Ryan.

"No. He did. I keep all my dirty clothes in a mesh bag on the left side of my red bag. That mesh bag was pulled out and…" I stop suddenly, uncomfortable about describing this to my captain.

"What, Kenny?"

"Um, my underwear and bra were out, nothing else. I had two pairs of Nomex pants and shirts in there and socks, and those were still in the bag." This time I let my gaze fall, fighting the sense of shame that is rising in my chest.

"Well, that's not good. Okay. I will talk to him. Did anyone else see him?" Ted asks, grabbing his notepad.

"Yeah, a girl named Meghan who is on a hand crew out of the Shasta Trinity Forest. She yelled at Ryan when she heard me asking why he was in my tent. The first day we were on the fire, she told me that Ryan had been hitting on her all day on the line. She made it clear she wasn't interested in him, but he kept it up. I told her I would talk to you about it," I said.

"I see." He rubs his hand down his face. "Okay, Kenny. I will talk to him and hear his side of this. Hang tight and steer clear of him for a while until I can get some answers. Okay?" Ted leans back in his chair again.

"Sure, yeah, that works. Oh, and I can teach that CPR class on the third if we don't get called out. Do you want me to put a flyer up at the Frosty for the community or just teach those three guys?" I ask, grateful to change the subject.

"A flyer would be great. Put one at the store and The Bar too. I'd like to limit it to the first ten people since we only have that many dummies. Thanks for that suggestion." Ted stands, and I take that as my cue to leave.

"Oh, hey, Kenny. Can you take a look at the sprinkler line out front? Bonnie said the sprinkler is, as she said, 'all wonky,' and it's spraying the window." Ted smiles as he says that and shakes his head.

"Yeah, I'll go check on it now," I say, and leave his office. I stop at Neil and Rick's office, but they are out, indicated by a note taped to their door that says, "Gone looking for Bigfoot."

I head to the front desk to ask Bonnie to describe what is going on with the sprinklers. Apparently, it's only going through half of its cycle, hitting the window but not moving past, so the window frame is getting soggy.

I walk around to the side of the building, turn on the main valve, and watch as the sprinkler starts its normal path, then stops right at the window. Sure enough, it stalls out. Should be easy enough to fix. I head out to the garage and grab all the tools I will need, and get to work.

COWBOY POETRY

BEYOND THE FENCE LINE~PUBLISHED 1950

Way out west in the Warner Mountains
Was a place I longed to be
Where the rivers run long and free
The fish jump high and the deer feast
On sweet meadow grass
~Author unknown
date unknown

TEN

PATRICK

After nearly losing a foot and probably suffering a broken shoulder because of a crazy lady, I finished my project of going through each drawer and closet to find things I can use and things I can donate. I make sure to brush off the red-and-black flannel slippers because I do actually feel bad about wearing them on the gravel driveway.

I vow to never try to save a woman in distress, or perceived distress, again. Well, at least not that particular woman. She was angry. Beautiful but angry. Muscular like no woman I know, but mad as a polecat. I mean, that's the saying, but is a polecat really mad? Who knows? At least I learned what it was like to be kicked while I was down. I don't want to repeat that ever again, thank you very much.

I need lunch, and my shopping trip into town yesterday didn't really give me a wide variety of lunch options. I also really want another one of those milkshakes and, well, that is not something I can make here. I pull on a pair of shorts and a T-shirt of my own since Mitchell seemed to have only ever worn jeans, button-up shirts, and boots.

I pull into the Frosty's parking lot and hop out of my red BMW, heading to the window to order. That guy I saw at the store is in line ahead of me, so I tap him on the shoulder.

"Hey there! So we meet again!" I say cheerfully.

"Yep. Small town," he grumbles and turns his back to me.

"I guess you are right. It's not like there are a lot of options for lunch..." While I'm talking, he steps up to the window and orders, then steps to the side to wait.

I walk up for my turn and am pleased the teenager at the window doesn't scream in terror this time. She waves and smiles, asking what I want.

"The usual," I say with a huge grin. I have always wanted to say that.

Her face falls. "Don't do that. I can't keep track of everyone's orders," she says, sounding irritated.

"Right, of course. I would like a burger, fries, and a milkshake, and I will go wait over there," I say, pointing to the tables.

"No, you'll wait right there. I can't bring you your food when we are this busy!" the girl snaps.

"Oh, right. Got it." I pay and step aside next to my new friend, Ryan.

"What did you order?" I ask, leaning over like it will be a secret we will share.

"Food," Ryan barks.

"Bad day or something?" I try and match his somber tone by nodding my head like I know his troubles.

"You could say that. Fuck, speak of the bitch herself." Ryan uses his chin to point towards a woman who has walked up with another guy. They are both wearing the same uniform as Ryan, and the woman looks familiar.

"Hey! I know her! She's mean. She kicked me this morning. What's her name?" I ask, folding my arms over my chest more as protection than in irritation. I also take a step back, just to be safe.

"That is Kendra," he says, his voice dripping with hate. I have written that line in books before, but have never actually heard it in real life. It makes me a little uncomfortable, and to be honest, I think my balls retreated a bit.

"Kendra." I make a humming noise in my throat. "Okay, I will make a note to steer clear of her." I'm about to ask him about the guy she is with, but Ryan's food order is ready, and he grabs it and leaves.

When he stomps off, Kendra looks in my direction. She stops talking to her friend and glares at me.

Thankfully, before my ass can start sweating from her angry glare, my food order is ready too, and I make the very smart decision to eat somewhere else. I'll go back to the ranch where I'll be safe.

I spend the rest of the afternoon bagging up the donations I pulled and piling them into the front bedroom. There is nothing left in the drawers in that room or the closet, and seeing the clean space gives me a sense of accomplishment. I don't know if they have a charity around here that picks up clothing and bedding, but I will ask when I go to The Bar tonight. I plan on keeping most of the household things, because even if I keep my place in Seattle, I will stay here for a while. This place has everything I need and seems to have sparked some creativity in me. I haven't written anything yet, but I can feel it bubbling up like in the old days.

I let my thoughts drift to Ryan. I wonder if his hatred for that Kendra woman is actually brought on by unrequited love. That would be an interesting idea for a book, although a bit overused. If I write a romance book, I want the main character to sweep his heroine off her feet, not argue with her.

I never liked that about Kent Price. The guy never found love in my books because he was such an ass. I couldn't fathom a woman who could stand him for longer than a few dates, so I couldn't write her. I mean, he had women, don't get me wrong. There were lots of women who found their way into Kent Price's bed, but none of them stayed. It's the one thing that jerk and I have in common.

I make myself a simple meal and grab a fresh notebook and a new pen since I lost mine this morning during the battle of County Road W. I have waited until seven because I don't want to seem too eager showing up at the bar at five. What kind of loser does that? Someone who has no life or friends, that's who. While that does accurately describe me, I'd rather not have others see me that way.

Pulling onto the main street, which is also the whole town, I'm surprised to see a lot of cars parked in front of and next to The Bar. There are people sitting on the steps drinking and laughing, and I can hear music pouring from the open door. It reminds me of a frat party in college. Parking a ways down, I walk up, smiling at everyone and nodding hello. I'm regretting not getting here earlier to snag a table where I can sit and take notes about all these amazing characters.

I go inside and go straight to the bar to order my whiskey before looking around for a place to sit. The squeaky fart stool is open, no thank you, and one other stool at the other end of the bar. I make my way to that and sit down, happy to see Rusty glaring at everyone and not just me. Once he sets my glass down, he is forced to walk away and help other patrons, leaving me with a quick scowl. I'm not going to lie, it feels like a victory. That is until he comes back and yells at me.

"Hey! Have you talked to Kenny yet about finishing those projects out at the ranch? Bookcase in the master bedroom needs to be done, and the bathroom wasn't finished either," he says, leaning forward like I will fight him about these things.

"No, I, um, haven't had the pleasure of meeting Kenny yet. But I was hoping to ask him a few questions when I do finally get to meet him, so if he comes in tonight maybe you could growl at me and point? I can take it from there. No need for a formal introduction or anything. I can hold my own, you know?" I say, puffing out my chest.

"Jesus," he says, then points over my shoulder. "At the pool table. Good luck holding your own there, champ." He walks away, and I glance over to the pool table to see that blonde guy who was with the mean girl earlier and...oh crap. There's the shoulder kicking Kendra. Well, this should be fun, and by fun I mean in a terrifying way.

I fold my notebook and shove it into my back pocket, then tuck my pen behind my ear. I take my whiskey with me, hoping it makes me look a little more intimidating than the Bic pen behind my ear does.

I tap the blonde guy on the shoulder. "Hey, sorry to interrupt your game, but are you Kenny?"

He turns, looks me up and down, and smiles a slow, big smile. "Nah, I'm Luke, dude. Who are you?"

"Oh! You're Luke? I was looking for you too! Oh, this is lucky," I say, holding out my hand for Luke to shake. He just looks at my hand and laughs, then does like a weird fist bump thing that I totally screw up.

He reminds me of that character Jeff Spicoli, from the movie Fast Times at Ridgemont High. His eyes are bloodshot, and he seems to have a permanent lazy grin.

"You were looking for me, dude? You with the government or something?" Luke asks through half-closed eyes. The smile never wavers, though.

"No, I'm Patrick Smith," I say.

But before I can say I'm Mitchell's nephew, Luke says, "No shit? For real man? Like Patrick Smith, the author? Fuck, no way. It's you! Hang on." He bends down, pulling a backpack out from under the pool table. Digging around, he finally pulls out an old copy of my first book. Luke flips to the back, finding my picture, and holds it up to my face, comparing the two. That picture is about thirteen years old, but it's obviously still me.

"Fuck, dude, you are in this book. You are in this book and in the bar. That is so fucking trippy. Right, Kenny?" He turns and smiles at Kenny. I whip my head around, expecting to see a new guy who has walked up to join the game, but I am met with the glare of Kendra, who is silently chalking her cue stick while clearly wishing I was dead.

When Kenny doesn't respond, Luke says, "Oh, man. I'm so rude. I'm sorry. Kenny, this is Patrick Smith. Patrick writes fucking books, man. Like good books too. Not gonna lie. I'm burning through this first book, and I'm mad about it."

"Wait. Why exactly?" I say, confused. I glance over at Kendra to see her still staring at me, but now she isn't as angry. Her face has relaxed a touch, like learning I'm an author has changed her opinion of me. Huh.

"Dude. I know there are eleven more in this series, but my good friend who loaned me the book only gave me this one, and he died, man. He fucking died, and I miss him so goddamn much," Luke says.

His smile fades at that, and he grabs his beer off the pool table and shouts into the air, "To Mitchell!" and the entire bar responds, "To Mitchell!" And they all take a drink. I do as well, overwhelmed by this new development.

"Well, listen, Luke. I, um, I can get you the other books because I —" I'm cut off by Veronica stomping into the bar and yelling at Rusty to get her drink ready. The same exchange that occurred the first time I was here goes down again, and the conversations around us turn to laughter and people betting if Rusty will ever end up kissing Veronica.

Kenny leans over the pool table and calls her shot, easily making it with the expert jab of her cue. She hit two more before finally missing and letting Luke have his turn. Luke misses the ball and loses his grip on the cue stick, shooting it across the room. He falls over a bit, clutching the side of the table and laughing.

"Damn it, Luke. How about next time you wait till after pool before you toke up," Kenny says with a shake of her head, but she doesn't seem mad.

"Sorry, I just wasn't expecting to have an author staring at me tonight. It's kind of freaking me out." He looks at me, then back at Kenny. "Can we get a booth or something? I need to sit. You know you were going to kick my ass anyway," Luke says. He picks his stick up off the floor and sets it on the table.

Kenny nods and sets hers down as well. They grab their beers and walk off towards the back of the bar, so I return to my empty barstool to think about what just happened.

Kendra is Kenny? The shoulder-kicking, angry woman is the

handyman? Handywoman? Handy person? Well, damn. This will not make things easy. I can see their booth from my stool and notice Luke and Kenny sitting across from each other. I wonder if they are a couple. It doesn't seem like it from their body language, but of course Luke is seriously stoned so who knows what they are like when he is not in the stratosphere.

I take some notes about him. He is probably about six feet. I'm guessing he was a swimmer in high school because he has that kind of build. He has what they call dirty-blonde hair that is wavy and hangs just past his shoulders. His Grateful Dead tie-dye shirt and shorts have seen better days. He has on a pair of cheap flip-flops, and his feet look like he spends most of his life barefoot. He has a great smile and an even better laugh. Whatever Kenny is saying to him is really cracking him up. Of course everyone is funny when you are that high, but it's nice to imagine there is another side to her besides angry kicker.

I tap my pen on my chin and stare at Kenny or Kendra. I wonder which she prefers. Maybe only her good friends call her Kenny. I don't want to get kicked again, so I'll play it safe and just call her Kendra.

Interesting is a good word for her, that's for sure. Now that she isn't standing over me kicking me, I can see how very pretty she is. She has long, dark-brown hair that she seems to only wear in braids. At least that is my assumption, since I have only ever seen her with her hair like that. She has dark-brown eyes and a bunch of freckles across her nose and cheeks. She is tanned, like someone who works outside for a living, and damn, is she fit.

She's wearing a pair of cutoff jean shorts that show off her very muscular thighs. I'm not going to lie. When she bent over the pool table to take a shot, I felt things. Her ass is absolute perfection, and her arms are very toned. She wears a simple white T-shirt that hugs her chest and stops a little short of the top of her shorts, giving me an occasional glimpse of a very flat, firm stomach. I bet she could bounce a quarter off that thing.

I try to think back to the women I have been with over the years, and I can say with confidence not one of them looked like Kenny. I can't even imagine what she would look like naked. Jesus, now I'm imagining what she would look like naked. That's a dangerous road that I'd rather not drive down.

Despite her terrible personality, I find myself wanting to go talk to her more. I'm apparently shallow and easily swayed by a girl with muscles. Who knew? I wonder if Kent Price would have liked her. Nah, he would have been jealous of how she commands attention. Kent always wanted every eye on him. God, I'm glad that series is done. I hope my next book can be about someone nice. Is nice interesting? Would the public like a story about a good person who is just looking for a life partner?

I really like the vibe up here. I think these are people who want to find happiness with real people and not made-up fictional characters that are clearly assholes.

COWBOY POETRY

BEYOND THE FENCE LINE~PUBLISHED 1950

Meadow foam
And owls hoot
Yellow butter daisies
Warm sun finds my face as
Lichen winds around the trunk
Tethering it to the earth
I am happy
I am home
-By M.S 1918

ELEVEN
KENNY

"I'm telling you he deserved every single kick," I say to Luke, who has not stopped laughing since I told him that Patrick is the one I met this morning out at Mitchell's ranch.

"I'm just picturing it," he says, waving his hand in front of his face, then doubling over laughing again.

"It was pretty funny, I guess. He said he thought I was being mugged. I was doing fucking burpees, Luke." Chuckling, I shake my head. Patrick is staring at me from across the bar, but I don't even glance his way. Let him stare. I had a shit day, and sitting here with my friend is exactly what I need. Well, this and a few more beers, and maybe some shots.

After fixing the sprinkler, which turned into an all-day project thanks to the faulty riser and a leaky pipe, I got called into the captain's office and was told that after speaking to Ryan, he was just going to assume it was a misunderstanding and leave us to work out our differences.

Ryan acted like a fucking asshole for the rest of the day, making me regret having the conversation with Ted. I asked Ted if he talked to Meghan, and he said they were still off forest but he would follow up with her when he could. I had to remind myself more than once that I love this job; I love this town, and I'm here for the long haul. Ryan is like a gnat, buzzing around and pissing me off, but not a long-term problem. I can deal with anything for one season.

"So," Luke says, after finally catching his breath, "is he living out there now? That's fucking weird. I don't know if I like that."

I glance over at Patrick, who is scribbling something in a note-book. Rusty is wiping down a glass and glaring at him. I can't hear the exchange, but Patrick must have asked for another drink because Rusty snatches up the empty glass and pours some whiskey in it, then pours one for himself. He glares at Patrick while he throws back his half a glass. I've seen him do that a few times over the years, and I've never understood it. Of course, I don't really understand Rusty. He is a surly bastard. Never once have I seen him smile, but he was pretty good to Mitchell from what I've heard, so I guess it all evens out.

I turn back to Luke, who has slid down in the booth so he can put his troll feet up on the bench next to me. I knock them down and say, "Dude, no. We have talked about this. Get your hooves away from me."

"Come on, Kenny. They aren't that bad," he says as he tries again.

"I told you, Golem, they are. Keep them away from me." I swat at him, and he relents.

"Do you think he will want the cattle back? Do you think he could handle them? Rusty doesn't seem to like him," Luke says. He can't see the bar from where he is sitting, but he guessed what I'm seeing.

"No, he doesn't, but really, who does Rusty like?" I ask.

"He fucking loves me," Luke says with a grin.

"Yeah, because you bring him weed. That is the only reason," I say, and Luke shrugs.

"I'm going to get more beer. You want something?" Luke stands on wobbly legs.

"Sure. Whatever is fine," I say, then add, "See if you can get some pretzels or something. You need food."

"Sure thing, boss lady." Luke gives me a two-finger Boy Scout salute, then giggles and walks away.

I go back to watching Patrick write in his notebook and tap his pen on his ridiculously chiseled chin. Why does he have to be so damn good-looking? He has Mitchell's eyes, and he is roughly the same build. I'll have to pull my photo album from last year when I finished the bookcase in the living room. I made Mitchell stand by the fireplace and I took his picture, much to his dismay. After I told him I wanted to show my dad the finished project, that softened him right up. He met my mom and dad once when they came up for a barbecue with the engine crew. Of course, my parents loved him. Everyone did. Now, there was Ryan and a few other new crew members who had never met Mitchell. It was like a divide in time for me. Before and after. The afters would never know what they were missing.

Luke comes back balancing two beers, two shots, and no pretzels. Damn it.

A few hours and several shots and beers later, the bar crowd has shifted from the it's Friday night, let's have a drink crowd to the it's the weekend, let's get shit-faced crowd. Since I'm still here and rather drunk, I guess I fit that last category. Luke and I are playing another round of pool, and I am, of course, kicking his ass. I also might be losing, but at least I look good doing it. I feel good too. Someone with great taste has been feeding the jukebox quarters all night, and I sway along to a few of my favorite Eagles songs. Occasionally I remember it's my turn, or I tell Luke it's his. No idea if either is true.

Hank Williams Jr.'s song "Family Tradition" comes on, and the whole bar cheers and starts to sing. This is Luke's favorite because it talks about getting stoned. We all yell the callback lines "to get drunk" or to "get stoned" in all the right spots. I notice Patrick still on his barstool, just watching us. Well, watching me. He has a nice little smile on his face, and when the part of the song comes on asking why he must live out the songs he wrote, I yell, "To get laid!" while looking right at him. I may have even done a little finger gun thingy at him. Who knows? I'm drunk. Happy, but drunk.

The next song that comes on is a favorite of mine, a slower song by Kenny Rogers and Sheena Easton called "We've Got Tonight." I start to sway and sing along, and Luke grabs my hand and pulls me in, placing his other hand on my back. Luke sings the girl parts loudly and off-key while I, of course, carry Kenny's lines. We did this all last year too, and it always makes us laugh. I'm a terrible singer. Like, really, fucking horrible. Luke is just as awful, but the bar always cheers for us, and we bow like we have performed at the GRAMMYs.

After the song, I stagger to the bar and plop onto the empty seat next to Patrick, who has finally put away his notebook and has tucked his pen behind his ear. He is drinking water now, probably something I should consider in the near future.

"You're a really terrible singer," he says, raising his water glass to me.

"Thank you so much," I slur. "I'm quite proud of my accomplishments." That makes me pause. "Wow, a mint sounds great right now. No, I want watermelon. Fuck, that sounds good. I like melons. I have melons, Patrick. Did you know that? Allow me to introduce you. These are my melons," I say, then grab my boobs and give them a squeeze. I'm not wearing my running bra, and I'm showing the girls off in this T-shirt. They look pretty darn good if I do say so myself.

"Um. They do," Patrick says nervously.

"What?" I ask, glancing up at him while still holding my boobs.

"They, um, do look good in that shirt," he says, and I notice him lick his lips. He looks nervous and a little sweaty.

"Fuck. Did I say that part out loud about my boobs looking good?"

"Yes, and you are still holding them if you are wondering," he says, pointing at my hands.

"Well, shit, would you look at that?" I glance down.

I give them another little squeeze for good measure, then let them go and sigh. "That's probably the most action I'll get all summer. Thanks for bearing witness." A little hiccup escapes my lips; at least, I think it came from me.

"Do you work tomorrow?" He asks, and I shake my head.

"Nope. Neither does my good buddy Luke. You know who is working on a Saturday? That fuckwad Ryan. I fucking hate him. He's a fuckwad. A dipshit. A ball sack. Wait, no, I like ball sacks. He's not that. Those are nice, squishy, warm. I like to roll them in my palm, you know? Play with them, maybe tug on them? Bury my face in them, perhaps give 'em a lick... I'm sorry I said he was a ball sack. He is none of those good things."

Patrick shifts in his chair. He seems very uncomfortable. I should ask him about that.

"You seem uncomfortable, Mr. Patrick Author. Why?" I tap my chin with my finger, trying to appear scholarly like he had earlier. I cross my legs to really drive home the scholar vibe I'm going for, and I fall right off my stool.

He reaches to grab me as I fall and ends up punching me in the eye. I guess I deserved that after all the kicking. Oh my God, the kicking. My laughter causes me to fall into him, probably the laughter and not the fact that the room is no longer straight.

"Shit, I am so sorry, Kendra," he says.

I pull back a little and stare up into his very blurry face. "Don't fucking call me that. My name is Kenny, not Kendra. Only fuckwads call me Kendra. Are you a fuckwad, Mr. Patrick?" I ask, clutching the front of his T-shirt.

Rusty appears out of nowhere, and I let out a yelp. I've been thrown out of The Bar one other time, and I think that time I was more sober.

"Hi, Rusty, ole pal. How's it hanging?" I say, trying to straighten up. He does not seem happy. His usual scowl is there but now it's a blurry scowl. That can't be good.

"Um, she was just leaving. What's the damage?" Patrick asks as he points to his drinks and me. Rusty barks out a number, and Patrick drops some cash on the bar before grabbing me by the elbow, leading me to the door.

"Wait! My good buddy Luke! Luke? Luke? Where are you, Luke? I am your father…" My spot-on impersonation causes me to bend forward in uncontrollable laughter.

"Jesus," Patrick says as he leads me outside. The cool air feels amazing, and I lean back, taking a deep breath in. Patrick steps behind me, guiding me by my shoulders down the wooden steps and out onto the street.

"I'm not even going to ask where you parked because there is no way you are driving tonight."

"I drove my feet. I'm like Fred Flintstone. Or Wilma. Wait, I like Betty better. Betty better. That's hard to say. Betty better. But I do. Betty is bodacious. She's better. Wilma is awful. I mean, she had to put up with Fred, and that probably made her uptight, but Betty? She is awesome." I pause and take a breath because this is a difficult conversation to have. "Better, you know?" Resting my hands on my hips, I wonder why Patrick is talking about the Flintstones so much. He's weird.

"Um. Okay. You walked here? Where do you live?"

I was ready for this question. I even have an answer. "In a house!" I say proudly.

"Okay, great. Where is it?" He looks around.

"No clue. It was here earlier. It must have gotten tired and went home," I say. I'm getting tired. I need to lie down. This grass looks nice. Maybe I'll just take a little nap and my house will come back. I flop on the ground and make some grass angels because that is what one does, then close my eyes and fall blissfully to sleep.

COWBOY POETRY

BEYOND THE FENCE LINE~ PUBLISHED 1950

Whiskey on my lips
Beer around the fire
Stew in the pot
Cattle in the field
She's on my mind
She lights me up
Nothing feeds my soul
Like the love she offers
~By M.S 1919

TWELVE

PATRICK

Well, hell. Now what?

There is a very drunk woman passed out on the grass in front of me. Her "good buddy Luke" wandered off somewhere, and I don't know what to do. I look around the empty street and down at Kenny-not-Kendra because I'm definitely not a fuckwad.

There is no other choice since I can't leave her here on the grass for the night. I bend down and pick her up, intending to carry her like a baby—you know, under the knees and arms—but she wraps her arms around my neck and buries her face into my shoulder.

Okay, that will work too, I guess. Her breath is hot on my neck, and it's making me feel all kinds of uncomfortable things. I carry her across the street to my car and brace her against it while I fish out my keys. I somehow manage to open the door and I set her gently in the passenger seat. At least that is what I'm going to tell her happened. I actually hit her head on the doorjamb and dropped her like a lead balloon onto the seat. I think she whimpered.

Oh god. I'm going to get arrested for kidnapping and maybe murder when she dies of the head injury I inflicted. Why am I putting a drunk woman in my car? I should have left her on the grass.

I mean, what would really happen in this town? A deer or a moose would probably step on her. Do they have moose here? I bet they do. It seems like that kind of town.

I sigh heavily and walk to the driver's side. Maybe if I drive around the few streets that have houses, one will have a sign in the front yard that says, "Kenny lives here!"

While this is my dream, it seems unlikely, so I decide to go back to the ranch. There are two extra bedrooms there. I'll put her in one of those rooms and she'll wake up in the morning and I can take her home. Thoughts roll through my head of the last time I shared a house with a woman, and I have to remind myself this is nothing like that. Kenny is not Tricia.

The quick drive out to the ranch is quiet except for the soft snoring sound that is coming from Kenny. I hope that isn't a sign of a brain bleed or something. Pulling into the gravel driveway, my mind drifts to how I had imagined Kenny as my handyman savior. Every time I saw something that needed to be done around here, I told myself that I'd ask Kenny to handle it. In my mind, Kenny was a tool-belt-wearing, Santa-Claus-looking, older man who always had butterscotch in his pocket. He'd tell stories of the old days while he stared off into the distance, all while fixing the leaky toilet.

I might be having a midlife crisis.

Thank God I left the lights on in the house. I knew I'd be coming in late, and I didn't want to fumble around in the dark. I might have also been afraid a cougar or bear would assume my darkened house was a cave.

The front steps still have a huge gaping death hole, so I carry Kenny carefully over to the side entrance that leads straight into the kitchen.

She stirs in my arms but doesn't wake. She isn't heavy, but man, she is solid. I stop myself again from imagining what she would look like naked. I would never take advantage of a drunk woman. Not that she would be interested in me when she is sober. Although she did that finger gun thingy at me when she sang a provocative line to a song. It's been so long since I've had a normal interaction with a woman, I can admit I'm a little confused. All in one day she went from kicking me to saying she wanted to sleep with me? Is that even right?

I push the door to the spare bedroom open a little wider with my foot so I won't hit her head on the doorjamb again. Listen, it's not my fault. It's not like I carry women around all the time. The doorways in this place seem unusually narrow. I have also never been known for my grace, but we don't need to get into that.

I walk to the bed and this time manage to set her down gently. As I pull off her tennis shoes and socks, it occurs to me she might get cold so I grab a blanket from the closet. I'm not about to attempt to get her under the covers; that seems too intimate. No, this way she will wake up in the morning and realize I touched her as little as possible.

She will probably have one hell of a headache when she wakes up, so I go to the kitchen and get a glass of water and some aspirin to put by her bed. When I return, I see she has spread out like a starfish and is snoring lightly. God, she is adorable. Her shirt has pulled up a little, and I can see her very flat stomach and what looks like a tattoo. Writing curving along her hip, from where I'm standing I can't make out what it says. I'm not about to investigate. My luck, she would wake up and think I was trying to take advantage of her.

I whisper good night and make my way to my room. Shedding my clothes as soon as I close the door, I crawl under the covers and fall asleep quickly. Dreams of the dark-haired starfish in the next room fill my mind and whisper to my soul.

I wake at the same time I always do, no matter where I am or what I have done the night before. I'm awake at six. Sighing, I rub my face, recalling that Kenny is here. Just a wall separating us. I squeeze my eyes shut and pinch the bridge of my nose. There is no reason to be thinking about her, picturing her. There is certainly no reason to touch myself while doing either of those things.

I pull my running shorts on and head out to the kitchen. After making a full pot of coffee, I take a cup out to the porch, like I've been doing since my first day here. I try not to think about the girl in the spare bedroom who slept wild and free and drank like a sailor on leave.

The morning feels different. It's muggy, with the air thick and warm. I can hear the insects buzzing already in the tall grass, and clouds are gathering at the bottom of the foothills. I'm grateful I didn't pull on a T-shirt since it's already uncomfortably warm.

Looking toward the road, I realize I will have to either ask Kenny for help or cut all those weeds back myself. It's getting a little out of control, and I like the idea of sitting on my porch and watching the occasional car drive by. Or maybe even seeing a pretty girl out for her morning run and other exercise-related things that are definitely not being mugged. I don't like the fact that she called me ridiculous when I tripped over the tree branch, or "stick" as she called it. It was a little emasculating when she held up what I had actually tripped over.

I admit I tend to exaggerate, but I blame my author brain. The same brain that got me published at twenty years old and has made me a very rich man at only thirty-two.

Not everyone appreciates my descriptive nature, however. Teachers in high school thought I was distracted or lazy when, really, I was trapped in my own little world.

What I could create in my mind would always hold my attention more than the reality around me. After my parent's death, I retreated even more. I'm aware of that now. At the time, however, it was how I survived. Kent Price saved me until he destroyed me.

My thoughts drift to Kenny, with her long, dark braids. What would her hair look like if she set it free? Is it soft and silky? Why am I picturing running my fingers through it or wrapping it around my hand? I need to pull myself together, not picture pulling Kenny's hair.

Would she like that?

Jesus. I have problems.

Stop, Patrick. Stop thinking about her.

Of course I don't. I attempt to think about her differently, not naked beneath me. She has dark brown eyes that are almost black, but I bet when the sun hits them, they have more depth. There are probably flecks of lighter brown scattered throughout, like the freckles that cover her nose and cheeks. Her features are a contradiction: sweet and innocent with a touch of sin. I wonder how I would write her. Would I let the audience know right away that she had a softer side, or would I let that slowly emerge? Is she intelligent or a hard worker?

Mandy Love was a simple character with clearly defined goals. For me, she was easy to write and enjoyable to know. So far, Kenny has been anything but easy to know. She is complex. Beautiful. Stunning, really, and that thought keeps returning no matter how much I try to stop it.

"Morning," a gravelly voice says from behind me.

I turn to find a very disheveled Kenny clutching a coffee cup.

"Hope you don't mind," she says, gesturing to her cup.

"Not at all. Care to join me?" I expect her to say no, but she nods and sits in the empty chair next to me.

"Mitchell and I would sit out here sometimes. He liked to start and end his day here," she says quietly.

"I can see why. I've only been here a short time, and it's already my favorite place on the property." I steal a glance at her and have to stifle a laugh. Half of one of her braids has come undone, and it's sticking out at an unimaginable angle. She has sheet creases on her cheek and neck. I can't be sure since I don't want to stare too long, but I think she has some grass stuck to her face.

"I found the water and the aspirin you left for me last night. Thank you," she says, wiping her face with her hand. She feels the grass and rubs her face a bit more, then feels up to her hair and sighs.

"I hope I don't need to apologize for anything," she says, peering over at me. I notice her eyes linger on my bare chest and arms.

"Nope. You just didn't know where your house was, and you thought sleeping on the grass in front of the Frosty was a good idea," I say with a chuckle.

"Oh, God." She puts her cup down, then buries her face in her hands. After a moment, she reaches up and pulls the remaining hair tie from her braid and flips her head upside down, running her fingers through and untangling what is left of her braids. She flips back up and puts the hair tie around her wrist, her hands reaching to smooth the last of the strays.

Her hair is so much longer than I thought it would be, and it's thick. Without even trying, she looks so pretty. All that dark hair spilling over her shoulders and down her back like a chocolate water-fall. She has long bangs that frame her face perfectly. Her hair looks so soft, and my fingers itch to touch it, but I remember how fond she is of kicking me, so I don't risk reaching out.

"Well, I'm sorry for making you deal with my drunk ass last night," she says finally. It seems like that was hard for her to say.

"Not a problem," I say, trying to seem unaffected by the little hair show she just put on.

"See, I just moved into a house on the grounds this season. Last year I lived in the barracks. I know where those are. My new house? Not so much, apparently. Luke must've met up with Zia."

"Zia?"

"Yeah, a local girl from over on the Indian reservation by Lookout. They have been on and off for about two years. Her family isn't too fond of the surfer boy," she says with a laugh.

"Ah. Well, I didn't notice him leaving, but I was trying to prevent you from getting kicked out. Rusty seemed intent on that."

"Well, wouldn't have been the first time," she says with a shrug, then looks around and adds, "We are going to get some weather today. I bet Ted is already in the engine waiting." She stands and stretches her long body, then touches her head.

"Did I fall or something? I seem to have a small bump on my head." She is rubbing a spot on the left side. I start to sweat.

"Hmm, not that I remember," I lie, hoping she won't remember me slamming her into the car door or the doors in the house.

"Well, thanks for the coffee. I'm going to get my shoes, then do the walk of shame back to my house." She turns to leave.

"Wait. You don't need to go just yet, do you?" I watch as her eyes travel the length of my body. It feels good that she is seeing me upright and not ridiculous, and I don't want it to end.

"I really do." She nods toward the horizon. "Those clouds mean thunderstorms, and that means lightning strikes. We are going to get called out for sure." She turns and walks into the house, so I follow.

"But you said you were off today." God, that sounded desperate. Hopefully, hopefully she didn't notice.

"Yeah, on days like this they cancel time off. All part of the job." She set her cup in the sink and bent to get the soap out from under the cabinet.

"Just leave it, Kenny. I'll get it later," I say, placing my hand on her arm. She stares at the connection, then up to my face, letting her eyes rest on my lips before jumping up to my eyes. There is a crackle in the air that I hope isn't an impending lightning strike. My gaze drops to her mouth as I lick my lips nervously. I realize I'm still touching her, so I pull my hand away from her arm letting my fingers trail slightly over her soft skin.

Clearing my throat to break up whatever the hell just happened, I say, "I'll give you a ride. You don't need to walk five miles into town."

"It's two, but okay. I'd probably end up barfing in the bushes, and I'd rather not start my day that way."

I go into my room to get a shirt, shoes, and my keys and come out to find her in the hall gently running her fingers over Mitchell's Carhart jacket.

"I miss him so much," she says, then adds, "You look like him, you know? You have his eyes."

I don't know what to say to that, so I just smile and reach past her for the door. I'm not ready to admit I know nothing about Mitchell except what I have learned since arriving. Not to someone like her, who clearly loved him.

"Do you think you can tell me where you live now?" I ask when we reach the car.

"Yeah, you're going to laugh at how close I was to being home last night. At least next time you can just steer me to my porch and leave me."

"Next time?" I sputter.

"Well, yeah. Fire season just started, and that fuckwad Ryan is bound to piss me off to the point of angry drinking at least a few more times. Luke is easily distracted, so it looks like you are my new drinking buddy. Congrats."

"Okay. Well then, I guess that is better than a swift kick in the ass. I wonder if that is how that saying got started? Someone kicks you a lot, then offers a less horrible way to hang out, and you're like sure." I say, more to myself than to her.

She doesn't talk the rest of the short drive into town, so neither do I, but when we reach the ranger station she points to the right and says, "It's up here. Just at the end of the drive. See? I can see my house from the Frosty in the daytime. I must have been pretty trashed last night." She laughs and shakes her head.

After she climbs out of my car, she leans into the window and says, "Thanks for last night, and for the ride this morning, Patrick. I appreciate it." She starts to walk away but turns back, pausing before she adds, "Sorry I kicked you."

As she walks up to her front door, I let my eyes follow that spectacular ass all the way into the house. Damn, I might have a little crush on this girl.

COWBOY POETRY

BEYOND THE FENCE LINE~PUBLISHED 1950

Electric pulses ripping air
Shatters trees
dreams
me
A million pieces
Shattered soul
Shattered me
~By M.S 1920

THIRTEEN

KENNY

Holy hell.

How is it possible that I got that drunk last night? I pull off my shorts and T-shirt and unhook my bra. Glancing down at my breasts, there's a vague memory of holding them last night. Damn. Did I do that? Oh God. I think I did. I think I felt myself up in front of Patrick.

Jesus.

He should have left me on the grass. I'm going to kill Luke when I see him.

I'm stepping out of the shower when I notice how dark it has gotten. The clouds have come in, and it won't be long before we start seeing down strikes. I pull on my fire gear and grab a breakfast burrito from the freezer, popping it in the microwave. I try to slip my foot into my boot, but I'm a little wobbly, so I sit and lace them up. The microwave dings at the same time as the phone rings.

"Hello?" I say, grabbing some paper towels for my makeshift plate. Ted barks at me loud and quick. His words are like tiny knives directly into my brain, but I can't be a baby about a little hangover right now. "Yeah, I figured. I'm on my way. Did you get a hold of Luke? Try Zia's. Yeah, pretty sure he's there. Okay, see you soon."

I hang up and grab my backpack off the floor. It isn't even eight yet. This is going to be quite a day, made worse by me being hungover. Cutting line and barfing is really not my favorite combination. Sadly this won't be the first time.

When I make it to the station, the engine has pulled out, idling, and Ted is standing talking to Neil and Ryan.

"Hey, thanks for coming down so quickly. They already dispatched the Canby engine, so we are on deck. Down strikes are hitting all over up by Alturas with a few small fires called in by the spotters," Ted says, and I nod, tossing my bag in the back of the engine.

His eyes narrow as his gaze studies my face. "You get in a fight last night at The Bar?"

"What? No, not that I remember. Why?" I ask, lightly touching my face.

"You've got a little bit of a bruise there by your eye," Ted says with a chuckle.

I touch the area, and it's tender. I also have two mystery bumps on the left side of my head. "I got into some kind of trouble last night, but the last thing I remember is kicking Luke's ass at pool."

"Nice," Neil says, adding, "I'm coming with you guys if Luke doesn't make it in. He'll get stuck with the BD crew, or he can go out with the fire prevention truck."

"Oh, okay. Did you get ahold of him, Ted?" I squint at Ted. Fuck it's bright out here.

"Yeah. He sounded like he might still be a little intoxicated, so we will see if he drags himself in. We can't wait for him, especially if he has to find a ride back from the reservation." Ted finishes that thought, a call comes in over the loudspeaker dispatching engine four to a fire.

Everyone hustles to the engine and Chuck hits the sirens as soon as we get to the main road. Ted's checking the map and telling Chuck the fastest route to get to the coordinates given by the lookout. Lightning struck a single tree, and it's burning but hasn't spread. Lookout told dispatch it appeared to be an area with a lot of dead trees, meaning if there is any wind, those embers are going to light 'em up.

The burrito I had for breakfast is sitting like a rock in my stomach, and sweat is forming on my upper lip and the back of my neck. I can feel Ryan staring at me, so I turn to face him.

"Can I help you?"

"Just making sure you aren't going to puke on me. You are about as yellow as your fire shirt." He scoots closer to Neil, who laughs.

"Fuck, girl, you do look bad. How about you roll down the window, or drink some water or something," Neil suggests.

"I'm fine," I lie. The urge to close my eyes and rest is strong, but the motion of the engine would be too much. I can feel all five hundred gallons of water we have in the tank sloshing around with every corner we take. It's like I'm in there instead of buckled in the crew cab.

I need to sweat this out. I've been in this position before, and a little exercise and possibly donating my stomach contents to a private little manzanita bush somewhere, and I will be golden.

Thankfully, the fire isn't more than about twenty minutes from the station. The problem is, it's at the top of an old clear-cut lot. I get out and glance up, watching the fire dance around the top of one single tree like a sad little birthday candle.

"Think we can just, I don't know, let it burn out?" Chuck asks, squinting up at the tree.

"Possibly, but if the winds pick up and it jumps to that grove there, we will be in a world of hurt," Ted says, hands on his hips.

I take the opportunity to duck behind the engine and barf. That makes me feel a whole lot better, except for the nasty taste in my mouth. A quick swish of my mouth with some water from my canteen and I'm ready to face this fire. I thought I had been stealthy, but when I come back to get my chainsaw, Ryan is standing by the engine. His arms are crossed over his chest, and he is smirking at me.

"Rather unprofessional of you, don't you think, Kendra?" He says it in such a condescending way that I want to punch him.

"Mind your own damn business." I stomp off towards Ted and Chuck.

"So, what's the game plan here, Captain?" I ask, trying to sound chipper.

"Well, Kenny, this might sound crazy, but we are going to have you climb to the top of that ridge and cut that flaming tree down," he says with a chuckle. "Ryan will bring the piss pump and take care of the fire once the tree is down, and Neil will be your swamper."

"Cool. Okay. Let me grab my saw." I turn to find Ryan holding my chainsaw out to me.

"Here ya go. Thought I'd help you out since you are sick and all."

"I told you not to touch my saw, Ryan." I grab it from him and set it down before going back to the engine to clear my head. There's a system I use, a way of doing things so I know I have what I need. I close my eyes and take a deep breath.

I open the compartment where my chainsaw is kept and find the bag with the wedges. I set that down, and pull out the chaps Ryan discarded when he grabbed my saw. Neil comes up, puts his hand on my shoulder, and asks quietly, "Are you good? I can bring that tree down if you need me to. I'm certified."

"Thanks, Neil. I'm fine. It's not the tree." I blow out a frustrated breath. "I like to do things a certain way, and Ryan knows that. He's just fucking with me," I explain.

"Okay, run through it with me. Talk it out," Neil says, and I glance over my shoulder. Ryan, Ted, and Chuck are standing off by the path, discussing which trail is the fastest route up.

I take another deep breath and say, "Okay, I grabbed my bag. I checked for the boy's axe and wedges." Pointing, I say, "There's the extra fuel can and my saw and my chaps. You are taking the wedges and axe, and Ryan will carry the fuel. I have my saw." Saying it out loud feels silly, but it also grounds me. It's not a complicated thing, but I did this when I first learned how to use the saw. I had a pattern of grabbing this, then that. Muscle memory telling me I had done what I needed, and I had all my tools.

"Thanks, Neil. I'm ready." I lift my chainsaw to my shoulder and head over to the rest of the team. Ryan, who already has on the bladder bag, grabs the fuel can and charges up the hill ahead of us, probably determined to beat me for once. I don't care. It's obvious the fire is still contained to that one tree, and the wind hasn't picked up. I hang back and talk with Neil as we climb the hill, asking about his latest Sasquatch hunt and getting filled in on Rich's dig. It turns out it was just a hunter, and digging around the area where the body had been located yielded only some Coors Light cans and a moldy Playboy magazine.

I set my saw down and pull my chaps to the front, taking my time to adjust them. With my hands on my hips, I glance up at the tree. Of course, the fire has almost burned itself out in the time it took for us to get up here, but whatever.

I make my assessments and plan where I will drop it. Neil clears some brush that is above us, making our escape route a little safer. Ryan stands around trying to act like that run up the hill didn't just kick his ass. He's not fooling anyone with his nostrils flaring like an angry bull.

"Glad you were here early to watch this fire burn out, Ryan. That's great," I say, but before he can answer, I pull the chain on my saw and make the back cut. This tree isn't dead and feels nice and firm, so my pie cut goes easy and I yell, "DOWN THE HILL," and drop her right where I planned.

"Nice one, Kenny. You make it look easy," Neil says as we watch Ryan scramble down with the bladder bag to put water on what's left of the fire.

"Want me to chop that up a bit?" Neil asks, pointing to the downed tree.

I shrug. "Sure. Let him feel like he's the one who put out the fire, though. His ego is fragile."

I clean the saw and refuel, then pull my chaps around. While Ryan and Neil are busy, my stomach decides it would be a good idea to barf one more time while no one is looking.

Heading down the hill, I can hear dispatch sending our engine to a fire that is growing rapidly. Timber Mountain lookout called it in about an hour ago, and it's already taking up a lot of resources. At only eleven a.m., there have been over fifty down strikes on the Modoc. This is going to be a long day.

By two that afternoon, all hell has broken loose. The lookout on Timber Mountain has to be evacuated, and they are calling in strike teams from all over California. We even have air tankers out of Redding and Reno dumping the pink stuff, but the fire is showing no signs of slowing down.

We've been sent to an area where a new growth plantation is being threatened. Ted is barking orders, wanting a running attack along the edge of a flank that is slow-growing. I grab my hard line and move to the back. Ryan is arguing with Neil, saying he will take the front.

As soon as the engine pulls away, I try to kick my nozzle open, but it won't budge. All the fine dirt from the road must have jammed it up. I keep trying as the engine begins to move faster. Ryan is doing a shit job on his end because there is nothing but flame passing me as I continue to struggle.

The damn nozzle finally kicks free, and a burst of water catches me off guard. I stumble a little but regain my footing just as I hear Ted calling off the running attack over the radio. Great. That was a waste of time.

The pumps on the engine shut down, and I hurry over, pushing the button to wind back my hose. I climb to the top of the engine and pull the hose packs, tossing them down to Neil and Ryan, who hook up to the pump. Slipping on a pack, I run ahead, ready to meet Neil when his pack runs out. We connect the two hoses and then I go on until my pack runs out. I glance around for Ryan and find him at the pumps talking to Chuck, arm resting against the engine like he has all the time in the world.

"Fuck," I grumble and jog back to the engine. "This only works if everyone is pulling their weight, Ryan. Get your ass out there."

I grab another pack and go to the end of my line, connecting the new hose quickly. We are closer to the fire now, but really need an additional fifty feet of hose. That's when I realize why Ryan stalled. He wanted the fucking nozzle. He knew if he was middle pack, he wouldn't get the nozzle, and he wouldn't get to squirt water. What a fucking baby.

I glare at him as he jogs up to me and connects his line, then pulls out the last fifty. He stops and gives the hand signal to Chuck, who turns on the pumps. Ryan lays the water down low at the base of the fire, knocking it down quickly. I walk the line, checking the connections, and make my way back to the engine. Neil has joined Ryan and is helping him, so I take the opportunity to climb back up and check the rest of the packs. We have three left, so we could move further if we needed. I drop them over the edge and wait to see what Chuck and Ted want, pissed off that it wasn't Ryan who we couldn't reach today. I wonder where Luke ended up.

At six o'clock we're dispatched to a spot fire that is starting to gain some ground. We met up with a water tender, so we are running with a full tank again. I wish I could say the same for myself. We ate some meals we keep on the engine, and I had one of my granola bars, but my stomach is still pissed off at me.

Ted says he is taking Ryan with him up the hill to start on a hand line and asks me and Neil to grab the saw and join them.

The helicopters and tankers have been grounded due to low visibility, so it's up to the engines and hand crews to make some headway. The good thing is that the winds have died down, and the temperature has dropped. This helps the fire lay down a little, giving us time to work.

Neil and I meet Ted and Ryan at the top of the hill, and Ted points out a few trees he wants me to take down. There has been some logging done in this area, and they did a shitty job of cleaning up. There are slash piles taller than me everywhere and quite a few trees that are in our firebreak.

I get everything ready and make my way down the line, dropping one tree after another until I have only two more to go. Ryan's above me talking to Neil, and he's pointing at something. Neil shakes his head. Of course, I can't hear shit with my headphones on, and my goggles are covered in sawdust. I take my bandana and wipe them as best as I can, then make my back cut. Out of the corner of my eye, I catch movement and hear a muffled yell of "Watch out!"

A three-foot-long, thick tree stump from the logging job has come loose and is barreling right toward me. My chainsaw is still running so I ditch it, flicking the kill switch as I do. I dive off to the side, landing hard on my knee as the stump takes a bounce over the top of me. If I hadn't moved when I did, I'd be wearing that log like a shirt.

I yank my headphones and goggles off and stand up, looking up the hill to see Neil charging toward me.

"Fuck, Kenny! Are you okay? That thing almost hit you!" He grabs me, looking me up and down, then he pulls me into him and wraps his arms around me.

I push at him and say, "I'm fine. I'm fine. Let go." I turn and watch Ryan calmly walk back up the ridge and disappear along the line.

When we pull back into the station two days later at eleven a.m., I'm quiet. That had been a rough couple of days, and I know I need sleep before I say anything. I'm pretty sure Ryan knocked that log loose. Also, pretty sure I screwed up my knee. It's hot and swollen, but I keep that to myself.

We pull all the hose and our packs and ready the engine for the next fire before heading home. I sling my backpack over my shoulder and walk up the hill to my house, fighting the tears that are forming with each step.

As soon as I'm inside, I let the tears fall as I sink into my kitchen chair. I try to pull my pant leg up, but I'm not able to because of the swelling. I take off my boots and stand, peeling the filthy Nomex pants down my legs. My left leg is twice the size of my right, and there is a deep purple bruise below my kneecap. I knew I had been stabbed by a tree branch when I went down, but that part doesn't seem too bad. There is only a little blood there. I strip the rest of the way down and make my way to the bathroom, where I gently step into the shower. I let the water wash away the dirt, grime, and my tears.

I have no way to prove Ryan sent that log my way, but I will go to my deathbed knowing he did. When I get out of the shower, I grab a towel off the rack, wrapping my body as best as I can. Quickly running a comb through my hair is the most I can do. No way I have the energy to braid it. I limp back out to the kitchen and pull out a bag of frozen peas, then struggle to the couch. I've just sat down and put the vegetables in place when my front door opens and Patrick sticks his head in.

"Hello? Kenny? You in here?"

"On the couch." I lift a hand and wave.

"Oh, there you are!" he says, then notices I'm only in a towel. "Oh, look at you. I'm sorry. This is a bad time. I saw the engine come in and I was at the Frosty and Jenny said you would probably be hungry, but you don't seem hungry. You seem wet. I mean showered. I don't know if you are wet. Like you are just sitting there, probably not thinking sexy things, you know. You look tired and I should..." His voice trails off as I watch his eyes move down my body to my legs. More specifically, to my left knee.

"Holy shit, Kenny! What happened? Are you okay?" Patrick sets the bag of food on the coffee table and moves to the couch.

"Yeah, I fell. I'm okay. I was just going to ice it for a little," I say, trying to play it off. The bag of peas slips, and I bend forward and grab it.

"Looks like it hurts." He gently places his hand over my kneecap. His hand feels cool, and I know it's because my knee is on fire.

"Jesus, Kenny. Here, let me help," Patrick says, taking the bag of peas from me. He places it gently on my knee, then stands and goes into the kitchen, finding a glass and filling it with water.

I can hear him opening cupboards, so I say, "Advil is in the bathroom, Patrick."

"Okay," he yells back and comes in with a pillow from my bed, a glass of cold water, and four Advil. He helps me get situated as best as he can, but we both realize how difficult it is to elevate my knee while I'm wearing only a towel. I'm pretty sure I flashed him, but he was a gentleman and didn't even flinch.

"Where are your clothes? I can bring you a T-shirt or something. Do you want some panties?" he asks.

"Panties? What am I? Eight?" I laugh, but he doesn't. "Sure, Patrick. In my top drawer, you will find my underwear. The black cotton thong on top will be fine unless you prefer white?" I ask in a deadpan.

He blinks a few times and stares at my towel-clad body. "Um, I prefer red if you are really asking my preference, so I will look for that. Tank top okay or do you want a T-shirt?" he asks, and I laugh.

"Okay, red it is. You're full of surprises, aren't you?" When he smiles, I continue, "Yeah, there are tank tops in the middle drawer. Oh and some shorts would be nice. I mean, I don't want to kill the mood, but this couch was made from discarded barbed wire." Now it's Patrick's turn to laugh, but he nods and goes to my room to find my clothes.

I lean over and pull the brown bag off the coffee table, delighted to find a hamburger and some French fries.

He comes back holding my clothes and sees me digging in. He blurts out, "I drank your milkshake on the way over here. Sorry. It was my second one today, too. I have no control."

"Interesting combination," I say, looking at the red thong and black tank top.

He shrugs. "I'll give you the shorts once you tell me which ones. I didn't know if you'd want denim or these little cotton ones that look like bike shorts." He holds up both pairs, then shrugs again and just tosses both of them to me.

"Thanks. Want to wait in the kitchen while I get dressed?"

"Not really. I'd rather stand here, but now that I say that it sounds super creepy. Also, I thought that was only in my head, but based on the way you are looking at me, I said all that out loud." He pauses and swipes his hand down his face. "Sure. I will wait in the kitchen." Patrick disappears until I tell him it's safe to return.

He eases down next to me on the edge of the couch, and repositions the bag of peas again. "You should see a doctor. That bruising looks bad."

"Yeah, I know. If it's still like this tomorrow, I'll go. I fell on it pretty hard, so that bruise is probably just from the impact. I don't think I tore anything."

"Okay. Well, I'm sure you know best. Can I get you anything else?"

"No. I mean, you can sit and hang out if you want, but like, whatever," I say, trying to sound cool. For some reason, having him sitting this close is making my stomach all fluttery. Not like when I was hung-over, this is better.

"Sure. If you don't mind, I actually have some questions for you."

I motion for him to get comfortable, so he moves back a bit. "Oh, this is rough. What kind of upholstery is this? Tumbleweed?" he asks, and I snicker.

"Probably. It's government issued so whatever is cheapest." I shrug, lean back into the couch, and say, "Okay Patrick, what do you want to know?"

"So many things. I need to cut the weeds and bushes down in the front of the house, and I saw a lawn mower and weed whacker in the shed, but," he pauses, then says, "Now don't judge me."

"I would never," I say with a small smile.

"Okay, I've never used either of those. Like ever. I've seen people on TV mowing and whacking all the weeds, but I lived in an apartment with my parents growing up, then the dorms in college, then a condo with only a balcony. I was wondering if you could show me how to start them and also use them in a way that won't cause me to lose an arm or leg. Or an eye. I enjoy being able to see."

"I can totally help you with that, and it sounds like you have a good reason for not knowing how to use that equipment. I mean, just because you are a man doesn't mean you just know what to do with a lawn mower. Why do people assume that kind of shit? Like, I had to learn how to do all the stuff I do, not because I'm a girl, but because everyone has to learn, you know?"

"Exactly! Thank you for that," he says, sighing, and then he smiles that big, beautiful smile Mitchell had. Although my stomach never swooped at Mitchell.

I nod and can't help but smile back. He is actually kind of adorable. Bumbling professor kind of cute. I mean, looks-wise, he is a hot professor type. Dark hair and brilliant blue eyes. He is tall and lean but surprisingly muscular. I definitely noticed how muscular he is when we were sitting on the porch and he was only in his running shorts.

"Okay, so my next question is about the cattle. Rusty said he can bring them back if I want them, but I know nothing about cows. I never had animals growing up. Dad was allergic, and well, we lived in apartments. So, how do I tell Rusty he can just have the cows? That guy hates me, and even though I would be giving him cattle, I feel like he would take offense to that."

"Oh, he for sure would take offense. You can't just give him the cattle. They are like eight hundred to a thousand dollars a head! How many are there?" I ask.

"I think he said fifty? Or maybe Jenny told me there were fifty. I don't know. I just know I have had nightmares about cattle running through the house and I'm trying to feed them, but I don't know what the fuck they eat, and they won't sit at the table, and they keep breaking shit." He shakes his head. He has really given this some thought.

"Yeah, if you offer Rusty fifty thousand dollars of cattle for free, he will punch you right in the face. Don't do that," I say, then think about it for a while.

"Maybe you could offer them at a discount, or you could ask if he would help you take them to market. Ask that first. I think he has a pretty solid herd, so he might want one or two more, but not all of them. I'm just guessing though, based on conversations I had with Mitchell last year. Rusty scares the crap out of me," I say.

"Really?" Patrick lets out a noise like air escaping a tire. "Oh, thank God. I thought it was just me. He makes my ass sweat. Every time I see him, I can just feel myself getting all sweaty," he says, rubbing his hands down his face.

I laugh and fight off a yawn. "Sorry. I didn't get any sleep last night. We went from fire to fire. I'm only home because we have to be off shift for eight hours now."

When I yawn again, Patrick starts to stand up, but I put my hand on his arm and say, "You can stay. I don't need to sleep." I fight the urge to curl my fingers around his muscular forearms.

"Why? Because you are a vampire? Everyone needs to sleep, Kenny." He goes to stand again, and I hold onto his arm, not wanting him to leave. This time my thumb moves gently over his skin.

"No, I want to stay up until at least seven tonight. I'm not going back on the engine because I have to teach a CPR class tomorrow. Ted didn't want me to cancel it since so many people from the community signed up. Luke will take my spot on the engine since he was with Zia and missed all the fires. Ted was pissed, so I get a break today and then an easy day tomorrow. Probably for the best, with my knee all banged up." I finally let my hand slide off his arm.

Patrick relaxes into the couch and nods. "Okay, if you're sure. I can keep you awake. I tend to ramble on quite easily about things, so I'm sure we can find things to talk about. I do have more questions about the ranch if you're up for it?" he asks, turning a little on the couch to face me. He reaches for my legs and drapes them across his lap, raising an eyebrow at me like he's asking if it's okay.

I smile. "Lay it on me." I adjust myself too. My knee really hurts, but the ice pack and the Advil are starting to help. Too bad I don't have some whiskey.

Patrick asks a bunch of questions about the property and the house. He has a few questions I can't answer, but I tell him who in town he can ask, and that makes him happy.

We transition pretty easily to other topics, but mostly he asks me questions and gives short answers about his own life. We talk about our parents, and I share with him about my dad's spinal cord injury in college and my mom being an art teacher. He shares that his parents are both deceased but doesn't explain how, just that he was only nineteen when he lost them. He was in his second year of college. I can tell he doesn't want to talk about it, so I don't press.

"Do you have any siblings?" he asks, and I nod.

"Yeah, my sister Stephanie. She's two years older than me and lives on the East Coast. She got into some fancy art school out there."

"Wow, you two are both very talented. Your parents must be so proud," Patrick says, and I'm caught off guard. I thought he was going to say how different we were, meaning "your sister is really girly, and you are such a tomboy." I've heard it so much growing up, but that isn't what he said. My eyebrows bunch together as I run his statement through my head again.

"What? Did I say something wrong, Kenny?"

"No, just the opposite. Most people like to point out how different I am from my sister. They don't see my skills as talent, more like I'm a tomboy or a freak or something."

"Nah, you're a complex and very interesting person. Your skills and abilities don't define you; they enhance you," he says, and I feel my eyes well up instantly at those words.

"Crap, I'm sorry, Kenny! What did I say now? I didn't mean to make you cry." Patrick grabs my hand and squeezes it.

"It's okay. I guess I'm emotional since I'm so tired. Mitchell said that exact thing to me last year." I take a deep breath to settle the odd sensation I have in my chest.

"Uncle Mitchell thought you were a complex and interesting person?" he asks.

"No," I laugh. "I mean, maybe, but he said the thing about my skills enhancing who I am, not defining me."

"Well, it seems like he was a wise old dude," Patrick says, and he keeps his hand on mine for a moment longer. It's warm and comforting, and I like it a whole lot.

When he moves his hand back, I try to hide my disappointment. It seems like he was careful not to touch my legs, so of course, I wonder what it would feel like if he had. I close my eyes while he talks about his drive out here from Seattle. He has a very nice voice, and when he laughs, it's like a deep rumble from his chest. I wonder what he does for exercise, since he is clearly very fit.

I kind of thought someone who wrote books for a living would be soft. I have only ever dated guys who had manual labor jobs. Well, except for that one blind date I had right after I graduated from high school. That guy worked at a bank or was it a grocery store? I can't remember, but man, he was high-maintenance. He was not at all my type.

Not that I really know what my type is. I have wondered about that a lot lately. After I turned twenty-six and my mom asked if I ever thought of having a boyfriend or a girlfriend (because that's how open-minded Mom is), I realized I haven't had the best track record with my dating life.

COWBOY POETRY

BEYOND THE FENCE LINE~ PUBLISHED 1950

Lay me down
In the tall summer grass
With the brook babbling
Near
Press your lips
to mine, pull me close, hold me
Near
Can you feel my heart beating fast
as you draw me in my
Dear
~By M.S 1919

I trace my finger over the words lightly, hoping not to wake her.

She fell asleep during a story I was telling about trying to find this small town. Once I realized she had dozed off, I sat very still, unsure what to do. If I move her legs to stand up, I will wake her. Her tank top has lifted a little, and by her right hip I can make out the words I saw when she was at the ranch.

"And I love her still..." is written in beautiful script, and I feel the sadness held within those words. Did she lose someone? Does her heart break when she sees these words, or do they tether her to the love she felt? I hope it was a bridge to healing, a lifeline to that person.

She stirs at my touch and blinks a few times. My hand freezes, my fingers guilty in their path.

"It's from my favorite poem," she says, and closes her eyes again. I watch her for a bit, not speaking, and I almost miss the tear slide down her cheek.

"I'd love to hear the whole thing someday," I say softly.

Without hesitation, she recites the entire poem and looks at me when she says the last line, "and I love her still."

"That's beautiful. Who wrote that?" I ask, letting my thumb trace over the line of script again, now allowing my arm to rest on her stomach.

"Mitchell. He wrote a lot of poems, but that one was my favorite. I got the tattoo the day we lost him. Got in my truck and drove straight to Redding and stopped at the first place I could find."

I'm not sure what to say. The knowledge that my uncle was a poet hits me hard for some reason, and I rub my chest while my lungs struggle to inflate.

"I've been spending a lot of time feeling sorry for myself lately," I admit to myself and to her when I can finally speak.

"Why?" she asks, tipping her head up again to look me in the eye.

"Because I never knew him, and all I will ever get are other people's memories. It's like hand-me-down clothes, you know? They never fit quite right, and they aren't what I would have chosen. But that memory, the fact that he was a writer too? That fills a piece of my heart. Thank you," I say, and she smiles soft and sweet. My breath catches at the sight, my heart doing a little dance in my chest.

"You didn't know him at all, did you?" she asks, and I shake my head.

"Well, I only had two years with him, but I can tell you without hesitation he was a good man."

"It seems that way." My sigh escapes without permission.

"He showed me his poetry when I was building the bookshelves in the living room," she explains, and my eyes go wide.

"You built those? Kenny, they are beautiful!"

"Thanks. We spent a lot of time measuring out his collection of books so the shelves would be custom for each series, and he would be able to easily see what was missing or out of place. The bottom right side is where he kept his poetry. His work is published in one of those books. I can't remember the title right now, but I can show you sometime," she says.

"I'd like that very much," I say. I haven't stopped tracing the words with my thumb. Her skin feels so soft and warm.

"That feels nice," she whispers, then asks, "Why are you doing that?"

"Because you are letting me," I answer honestly.

"I like it. You have been really nice to me, and I'm not sure I deserve it," she says, placing her hand over mine. Her hand is rough, the calloused parts of her palm and fingers brushing against my skin.

"You don't think you deserve kindness?" My gaze drifts from her hand up to her face.

"Not from you. I kicked you the first time I met you, then I made you responsible for my safety when I was drunk off my ass. I also remember grabbing my boobs in front of you," she says as she lightly rubs her thumb across the back of my hand.

I laugh at that. "Oh, your memory is coming back to you!"

"Sadly. That's a memory I could do without." She winces a little.

"Well, it was my favorite part of the evening," I say with a wink, then add, "It was better than when you started talking about ball sacks."

"What?" Her eyes fly open wide and she goes completely still.

I trap her fingers with mine and say, "Yeah, you told me how much you like them, what you like to do to them. It wasn't a conversation I was ready to have with you."

Her mouth falls open a little as the prettiest shade of pink dances across her cheeks. "Okay, well that's it for me. I'm just going to close my eyes, and hopefully I will stop breathing, and I will just float up to heaven." She covers her face with her hands.

I pull them away and look into those dark brown eyes. I smile and lightly trace my fingers over her cheek.

"Please don't be embarrassed, Kenny. You are a breath of fresh air. I have met no one quite like you." I fight the urge to trace her lips with my thumb, but I let it dance dangerously close.

She sits up and pulls her legs off my lap, wincing a little when she bends her knee. "I haven't ever met a guy like you, Patrick. Most of the guys I know are, well...rough and kind of shallow. I mean, Luke isn't. He's got depth, but he numbs it with pot so much that I sometimes forget that about him." She's rambling like she's nervous, and she is rubbing her hands on her thighs.

"Well, I don't know if this is out of line, but I would really like to ask you out on a date. Would that be okay?" I say, reaching for her hand. I miss the connection we shared over the past few hours. Since we sat down, we have been touching, and I want to get that back.

"You want to take me on a date? Where?"

"I...um...well, I hadn't thought of that. I mean I guess we could go to the Frosty or see if Jenny would make us something nice at The Bar. What I would really like to do is cook you a meal out at the ranch, but I need to go to a real store and get some groceries. I was thinking about going this weekend, but I have a CPR class to take tomorrow. I hear the instructor is really cute."

"You signed up for the class?" I'm relieved to see her smile as she asks.

"Yep. Back when I thought Kenny was an older Santa-Claus-looking dude who would ride in on a reindeer and save me from all my troubles," I say, and she laughs like I wasn't serious.

"Well, Tuesday and Wednesday are my regular days off, and I really need to go down the hill too, so maybe we could have a grocery-getting date?" she says shyly.

"That sounds perfect. Sorry I didn't let you sleep. It's close to seven now, so I should head home. Hopefully, you'll be able to get some more sleep tonight." I stand and help pull her up, but don't step back because I want to be in her space, breathe her air. My body craves this closeness with her.

She looks up at me with those deep, dark eyes. I reach up to tuck her hair behind her ear, and as my finger caresses the pulse point, she closes her eyes and leans into my hand. Holding her face, I try to calm my racing heart. I want to kiss her so badly, but I'm still struggling with what I want from this.

I was hurt by someone who loved the idea of me, but the real me?

Not so much. I'm not sure my heart can take it, but maybe if I take it slow. I give in to my temptation when she opens her eyes and looks at me. Bending, I inch my face closer to hers, savoring her soft breath on my lips. You only ever get one first kiss with a person, and I want it to be perfect. I like that she hasn't closed her eyes again. She is watching me, mesmerized like I am, her gaze flicking from my lips then back up to my eyes. I move my hand to her waist and pull her in a little closer, and just as I'm about to press my lips to hers, Luke walks in the front door.

"Kenny! What's up, dude? Oh, fuck. Sorry, man," he says as he tosses a bag of chips on the table. Kenny steps back and wipes her hands on her legs nervously. Her face is flushed and the same color is spreading down her chest.

"Why are there peas on the coffee table? That's a really weird snack. You smoking pot without me?" Luke asks.

"No, dipshit. I was using it for an ice pack," Kenny says, motioning to her knee.

"Oh, yeah, that makes more sense. Ted said you took a fall. You okay?" He bends at the waist to look at her knee. "That's a wicked bruise," he says, then looks up at me. "Hi, Patrick. Want some chips?"

"Uh, thanks, Luke, but I was just about to head out. I'll see you tomorrow at the class, okay, Kenny?" I say, trying to hide my disappointment about being interrupted.

"Yeah, sure. I'll walk you out." Kenny steps gingerly as she tests out her knee. We walk the few feet to her front door, and she pulls it open.

"Thanks for lunch and for keeping me company. I really enjoyed it," she says.

"Me too. I'm glad we got past the kicking me thing. You are a lot more fun to be around when I'm not lying down with you above me," I say, trying to make a joke, but then picture her above me, wearing only that red thong. My mouth goes dry, and I lick my lips. "I meant..." I start, but she just laughs and pushes me out the door.

"See you tomorrow, Patrick," she says with a smile, then she shuts the door.

The drive back to the ranch goes by too fast, and I'm not ready to be in the house alone, so instead of turning into the driveway, I keep going on County Road W, letting the twists and turns of the road smooth out the stress that is coursing through my veins.

Kenny consumes my mind, so I pull my car over and get out. The sun is low on the horizon, and the sky is clear. Climbing onto the hood of my car, I lean back against the windshield. I sit there until the sun slips behind the mountains and the stars begin to peek out. I watch as the darkness spreads across the sky, each star popping out as if it's breaking free. It takes my breath away. There are no city lights around me, so the night sky is able to show me its true self.

There is a thick band of stars that streak across the sky, and I realize I'm seeing the Milky Way. I'm thirty-two years old and have only seen that in textbooks. Shaking my head, I marvel at how beautiful it is out here. Words swirl in my head, and I can see why Mitchell wrote poetry.

Bright like I had never seen
leading me to you
The arch of the Milky Way
mirrored in the soft curve
of your hip.
I trace my fingers along the path
leading me to you

I say it over and over, committing it to memory, not wanting to get up and find the notebook I have in my car. I have an unrealistic fear that if I look away, the sky will return to the one I knew before. Dull, with only a light scattering of stars and a cityscape below.

Dull is a perfect way to describe how I was feeling in Seattle. My life has changed so much since coming here, and I'm seeing things more clearly. Not just the brilliant night sky, but all things. I can see how Tricia sucked me in, and I can see why it didn't work. I think part of me knew from the first date it wasn't right, but I was winding down the Kent Price series and I was panicking about being alone.

Tricia was a fan. I met her at a book signing. I believed her when she acted interested in me. She wasn't. She was interested in Kent Price and believed I was just like him. For a while, I had tried to be like him for her, but I saw all the things about him I didn't like. It was the undoing of my relationship with him.

I swore after I kicked her out of my house that I would never get involved with a fan again. In book twelve, Last Tango, Kent Price has a wild night of sex with a suspect in his case. His life began to mirror my own, and it messed with my reality. Tricia loved it and told all her friends that she was Tammy in the book. It made my stomach tighten, but my editor loved the scenes and liked that Kent was having some different fun in his last book. When Tricia called me Kent during sex, I stopped and looked at her. "What did you say?" I asked her.

"You heard me. Don't stop now. I'm so close. Kent, you know how I like it," Tricia had said breathlessly.

She wasn't delusional. She didn't think I was actually my character, but I realized then that she wished I was more like him. I pulled out of her, tossed the condom in the trash can, and went to take a shower, locking the door behind me.

We had a big fight when I came back to the bedroom, and she told me she was tired of my "silly ways" and liked it better when I was manly like Kent. She thought if I could write a character like that, then surely there was a part of me that was like him. It wasn't the first time someone had said I wasn't manly. Perhaps that is why I wrote Kent the way I did, because he was so opposite from me. He never needed help with things like mowing a lawn, and he sure as hell wouldn't have tripped over a stick. Fuck.

These comparisons are why I hate Kent Price. Without knowing it at the time, I had written a character that embodied all that I wished I was, all that I had been told I should be. Tricia didn't love me; she loved what she thought I was capable of. I almost asked her to marry me out of my desperate need to be with someone, to have someone in my life who cared about me. I'm so grateful I didn't settle for that false kind of love.

I think about the poem that Kenny recited. The love in those few lines is deeper than I have ever experienced. I want to write books about that kind of love. My brain had been so blocked when I was living in Seattle, but here I'm beginning to feel an awakening.

COWBOY POETRY

BEYOND THE FENCE LINE~ PUBLISHED 1950

Ranch hand
Rough and blistered
Turns soft when it's held in yours
Never let me go
Hold me in the soft ways
Where I am yours and you are
Mine
~By M.S 1920

I walk around the engine bay where I am teaching a CPR class. Everyone is , practicing what I've taught them. My knee is a lot better today, with only a little swelling. The bruise looks bad still, but that's okay.

I ask the class if there were any questions about what we had just learned. Patrick has a lot of questions; we like to call what-ifs. I answer some that are realistic scenarios, but he really goes off the deep end pretty quickly, creating problems I'm very sure will never happen. So I move the class onto the hands-on portion after Patrick makes me promise to answer some of his concerns privately.

With any other guy, I would assume that is a line. I truly believe he wants to spend at least another hour going over ways people could stop breathing. What it must be like in his brain.

"Ryan, you need to slow down the compressions a little and try not to go quite so deep. See how Regina is doing it? That is the perfect depth," I say, using a technique I appreciated in my EMT class. Our instructor always pointed to a student to model what he was after. It boosted our confidence in a way that him showing us wouldn't have.

Regina beams and Ryan grumbles, but when he thinks I'm not looking, he adjusts his technique to match hers. I observe everyone doing single-person and two-person CPR and administer the written test, pleased that everyone passes. I hand out the cards and thank everyone for coming.

I wish I could always have that many other people around when I have to interact with Ryan. Crowds seem to defuse his anger toward me. I give him his card first so I can be done dealing with him for the day, and I'm sure he appreciates that.

Patrick comes over and asks me if I would come out to the ranch after we are done cleaning up.

"We? Patrick, you don't have to help me clean up. It's fine. You can go get a milkshake or something. I won't be too long. I just need to wipe down the dummies and give all the paperwork to Ted. It will only take me about half an hour."

"Are you sure? I'm not going to lie to you, Kenny. I was going to insist on helping, but then you mentioned a milkshake and now that's all I can think about," Patrick says as he rubs his stomach.

I laugh. "Yeah, go. It's fine." He gives my hand a little squeeze and takes off for the Frosty. He is so adorable. I love how honest he is. I also like how he is never trying to one-up the next guy. Like, he just is who he is. It's nice.

I line the dummies up so I can start cleaning each one. Pulling the removable mouthpieces off to let them soak in the disinfectant, I make quick work of it. Since the class was held out here in the engine bay, cleanup is fairly easy. Right outside, past the engine, is a place where I can rinse out the masks with a hose. There are two people over by the fire prevention truck, that from my quick glance I'm pretty sure is Ryan and Bonnie. I'm not positive it's them until I'm coming back in and I hear him talking.

"You want to sneak out tonight? I can show you all the mouth-to-mouth I learned."

I roll my eyes so hard I'm surprised they don't fall out of my head. He is so gross. What did he mean "sneak out"? Does Bonnie still live at home with her parents, or something? How old is she? Jesus. I know Ryan is twenty-one, but now that I think about it, I don't think I have ever seen Bonnie out at The Bar.

"I can't. Remember? My dad is still pretty mad about me coming in late the other night. I told him I was having car trouble like you said, but he started asking questions, and I don't think I answered them right," Bonnie says.

"Damn, baby, you must not love me like you said you do if you are going to leave me desperate," Ryan says in a gross baby voice.

"No! I do love you. I do. I just don't know how to sneak out without getting into trouble, you know? Why can't we do something before my curfew?" Bonnie asks.

"Well, I was hoping to take you up to do some stargazing. We can't do that if the sun is out, now can we?" Ryan says, and Bonnie giggles. Ryan must have whispered something in her ear because she says, "Okay, I'll meet you in front of the station at nine. You'll bring the condoms though, right? You can't forget like last time."

I see red. What a fucking asshole. Bonnie has to be underage. What a douchebag. I finish rinsing the masks and take the paperwork into the office to put on Ted's desk. Marge is at the copier, and it occurs to me I could stop and say hi, possibly get more information about Bonnie. I purposely slow my steps to catch her eye.

"Oh hi Kenny, how'd the class go?"

"Fantastic. Everyone passed. I was coming in to drop off the paperwork on Ted's desk." I glance over my shoulder before saying, "I was hoping to see Bonnie in class. You should encourage her to sign up next time!"

"Oh, she took CPR in her health class last year. She's certified!" Marge feeds paper into the side of the copier like she could do it in her sleep.

"That's nice. Did she take it at the community college over in Susanville?" I ask.

"Goodness no. She's only seventeen. It was her health class at

Modoc High. She will be a senior this year. She wants to go to college in Susanville, though when she graduates."

"Well, I hope she does," I say, fighting the urge to run outside and punch Ryan right in his twig and berries.

After I put the papers on Ted's desk, I'm heading back outside as Bonnie is coming in. She is rubbing her neck where Ryan had been trying to leave his mark. My anger rises, but I don't want to take it out on her.

"Put some ice on that before it gets worse," I say with a smile, and she nods. She turns left to go into the break-room, and I suddenly can't decide if I should follow her or go kick Ryan's ass.

I choose Ryan.

When I storm into the engine bay and look around, he isn't here. I go around the back of the building, without finding him. When I walk to the front the taillights of his truck are all I see as he turns onto 299. I have never been so angry in all my life. It's one thing to be an asshole, but to mess around with an underage girl? What the fuck is wrong with him?

As I stomp back to the engine bay my eyes narrow. I need to do something. I growl and kick a trash can that is by Chuck's desk. The can smashes against the wall, making a satisfying sound, so I kick it again and again until it's dented and useless.

I wish I had done the same to Ryan. He is already useless, but he could use a few dents. I put my hands on my hips and take some deep breaths, trying to calm down. My head falls back, as I squeeze my eyes shut. My heart is racing and my stomach twists a little. I take a deep breath, then one more and it seems to help. My head drops as I formulate a plan.

"Do you feel any better?"

I snap my eyes open and glance over at Patrick. Damn. I didn't hear him come in. "Yeah. Sorry. I—" I start, but he interrupts me.

"Don't apologize. You're allowed to have emotions. That trash can must have really pissed you off. I'm sure it deserved everything you gave it."

"It did. It thinks that women are there just to please it, and really, it needs to have its tiny dick ripped off," I say, apparently still furious. My deep breathing wore off quickly.

"Okay, that's a lot of information about the trash can. Did you see the trash can hurt someone?" he asks.

"No."

"Did the trash can confide in you that it wanted to hurt someone and you felt the need to stop it?" he asks.

"No."

"Okay, one last question, and I want you to answer honestly, okay?" he asks, and I nod.

"Did you picture a certain person while you were drop-kicking the trash can?"

"Yes." My lips roll in, holding back the smile that is trying to escape.

"Was it me?" he squeaks, and I laugh.

"God, no."

"Okay, phew. I feel better. There is no way you could have known this, but I went and got a milkshake like you suggested, then I got you one because you did a great job teaching that class, and well, let's be honest, I am a kiss ass. But I drank the milkshake I got for you on the way back to the station. I threw the empty cup into the can by the shed. I'm so embarrassed," his words coming out in a rush.

"Wow." I put my hands to my mouth to hide the huge smile I have on my face.

"I know." He shakes his head. "I have a problem. I'm looking into Milkshakes Anonymous. They have a chapter in Alturas, but I'm not sure how to get there. Is that south of here or north?"

"Thank you."

"For what? Drinking your milkshake? If that's what makes you happy, I am your guy!" he says with a smile.

"No, for helping me calm down without treating me like a hysterical female."

He shrugs. "Sure. I bet you will do the same for me someday, and by someday, I mean later today when we go over all the ways in which a person can stop breathing." He holds his arms open, motioning me in with his hands.

I walk reluctantly into him, and he wraps his long arms around me, resting his chin on my head.

"It's okay to be angry." He makes a little humming sound before saying, "I prefer you kicking a trash can to drinking your weight in beer when you are mad, but if beer is what you need now and then, I'll be there."

He kisses the top of my head and squeezes me a little. He smells like Old Spice. Like Mitchell. I pull back a little and ask, "Are you using Mitchell's Old Spice?"

He smiles and says, "Yes. Isn't it amazing? Pretty sure the bottle he had is older than I am. There's a rash everywhere it has touched me, but I can't seem to stop spraying it on my body."

I tuck my head into his chest and laugh harder than I have in a long time.

When I finally compose myself, Patrick helps me put the CPR dummies away, making comments about how it's like putting a body in a body bag and how I should have failed the entire class because no one survived. My stomach hurts from laughing this much, something I didn't think was possible only a little while ago.

When we are all done, he asks some questions about the engine bay, and that leads us out to the engine where I show him what I ride around in while at work. He doesn't comment when I show him the chainsaw I use and explain what a sawyer and a swamper do. He just nods, as if doing this job makes perfect sense to him. My heart swells a little; I can't lie. It reminds me so much of my conversations with Mitchell. Honest questions about the job, not how I can possibly do it since I'm just a girl. Mitchell never questioned my skills or my job. He just appreciated me. It's the first time since his death that I don't miss him so much that it hurts. Because talking to Patrick, I've got a piece of him back.

"Why are you looking at me like that?" Patrick asks, cocking his head to the right.

"Like how?" I ask, knowing exactly what I was doing.

"Like you are comparing me to someone," he says, and he sounds sad.

"You are perceptive. I was doing that. I was thinking how you are just like your great-uncle Mitchell. Even if you didn't know him, you are a lot alike."

I see his shoulders relax, and he smiles. "Really? That's a nice compliment. I know how much he meant to you. I like you can see him in me."

"Mitchell was the only other person besides my parents who thought my job made sense for me. He never asked me why a girl was trying to do this man's job, you know? He just wanted to hear about my day, all the stories about the trees I had to take down, or the crashes we responded to. I wonder if he wished he could've been a firefighter instead of a rancher?"

"Nah, he was a poet. He wouldn't have wanted your job. I bet he just appreciated your passion. I could hear it when you were telling me about the engine. It's just parts and pieces to me, you know? Compartments filled with things and a water tank, but that isn't how you see it. It's a representation of you, an extension," he says.

"What do you mean?" I ask, feeling as if someone has stolen the air from my lungs.

"Tough looking on the outside, each compartment filled with something useful. Tools that help those in need, tools that help you do your job. When people see it coming, they know it's going to be okay. You are going to make it all okay." He goes on, "The crew cab where you sit is like the center of you. Where you can pull back, talk with Luke, and go over the day. It's safe. Comfortable," he says as he shrugs.

"I never thought of it like that," I say quietly.

"That is how my brain works. I can't help it."

"I like your brain," I say, grabbing his hand.

"Yeah? Well, good, my brain has a lot of questions for you. Are you ready to go out to the ranch?" he asks.

"Yeah," I say, and we walk out hand in hand.

COWBOY POETRY

UNPUBLISHED WORK

Bright like I had never seen
 leading me to you
The arch of the Milky Way
 mirrored in the soft curve
of your hip.
I trace my fingers along the path
leading me to you
~by Patrick Smith 1988

I'm so excited to have Kenny all to myself for a few hours. Watching her all day teaching the CPR class solidified my feelings. I need to see where this will go. If there is no connection, so be it. I will file away all the things that are awesome about Kenny and develop a character based on her at a later date, because I know I will always want a piece of her in my life, in my heart.

I'm curious about what happened when I was on my milkshake run, but I'm sure she will tell me when she's ready. Now, however, I just want to spend time with her.

As soon as I pull into the driveway of the ranch, Kenny starts laughing.

"You aren't going to waste any time, are you?" she says, pointing to the grass patch in front of the porch.

"Nope. I need to know Kenny," I say and jump out of my car. She follows and puts her hands on her hips, looking down at the lawn mower I had pulled out.

I had unearthed a really old push mower I planned on using someday, but for now I want to master the engine-powered one.

"Okay, well, the first thing we need to do is make you familiar with all the parts and what they do. I could show you how to pull the cord and you'd be off, but you need to be able to problem-solve if the mower stops working."

"See, this is why I hired you," I say, gesturing to the sky. "You know what I need!"

She laughs again and steps into my open arms, then reaches up and pulls me down to her, gently pressing her lips to mine. Her kiss is light, sweet, the kind that questions...wonders.

I don't react at first because I had plans for our first kiss, and it wasn't in the front yard of the ranch flanked by a lawn mower. But her lips, oh God, her lips. Soft and full, pulling me under, lifting me up. I grab her around the waist and pull her closer, pleased when she comes easily to me and lets out a little moan.

This kiss quickly becomes more demanding, and I tip her head back a little, taking charge. She is more perfect than I could have pictured. It's as though I have been away a long time, and I'm finally in view of my home. Warmth, comfort, and belonging are all within reach with this kiss.

She pulls away first, breathing heavily, and says, "That is what I needed. I hope that's okay."

"More than okay. It was long overdue. I was trying to plan the perfect place, the perfect way to kiss you," I admit.

"You were? You thought about that?"

"Ever since the night at The Bar. I'd like to say it was since the first time I saw you, but let's be honest with each other. You were a little scary." I bend down and kiss her again. Her lips taste like vanilla mint, and I know at that moment I never want to stop kissing her.

"I'm glad you aren't afraid of me anymore," she says, pulling back from our embrace. Looking up at me, she says, "Now that we have gotten that first kiss out of the way, let's mow this wild patch before lions and tigers move in."

"Solid plan, Kenny. I'm ready," I say, trying to calm my racing heart. Is she as affected as I am? It doesn't seem like it. That kiss made the whole earth shift. My knees went wobbly, and my stomach erupted with a hundred butterflies. Also, and most importantly, because I'm a man after all, I got very hard very quickly. I wait until she bends to check the fuel in the mower to adjust myself, hoping she doesn't notice the situation I have going on in my shorts.

After a very fascinating lesson about how lawn mowers work and where not to stick your fingers or toes, I'm finally able to pull the cord and hear the glorious sound of the engine. My nostrils are immediately filled with the smell of cut grass mixed with gas and oil. It's oddly pleasing.

Kenny stands back and watches me make strips back and forth, cutting the knee-high grass down to a respectable length. When I get to the edge of the grass where the weeds and manzanita bushes start, I stop and kill the engine. She jogs over and pats me on the back.

"What did you think of your first lawn-mowing experience?"

"It was fucking amazing," I say with a huge smile on my face. I mean it. That was the best thing I've done in a long time, maybe ever.

"Well, it bodes well for you that you enjoyed it, because you will need to do that once a week until winter. Now let's talk about how to handle this stuff here, because the lawn mower can't take it." She motions to the tangle in front of us.

Hours later, we limp into the house. Well, I limp. Kenny seems fine. I have blisters on my hands that are actually bigger than my hands. We found a pair of Mitchell's leather gloves once I could no longer grip the rake, but the damage had been done. I might lose both hands. I told Kenny this, but she disagreed.

"Thank you for helping me with all of that, Kenny," I say from the couch. She is helping me out of my boots because I have lost the ability to bend my body.

"Sure thing, Patrick. I really should have kept the yard up after Mitchell passed. It would have probably made me feel better to come out here," she says.

She stands and takes the boots back to their spot by the front door. Seeing them there under the coat reminds me of the crumpled paper I found.

"Hey, when I first got here, and I tried on those boots, I found a balled-up list in the left one. Do you know why it was in there?"

"A list?" she asks, and I explain what it was.

"Oh, yeah. I must've dropped it. After we did CPR on him for a while, Ted was told it was time to call it. He was on the phone with the hospital out of Fall River Mills. The doctors said because of his age and all, we just needed to stop." Kenny takes a breath, then continues, "Ted called the time of death, and the first thing I saw was the list Mitchell and I made of all the things he wanted fixed. It pissed me off that I wasn't going to be able to finish it, and I crumpled it up. I thought it was in my hand when I went out onto the porch to wait for the coroner. I guess I dropped it. That's weird that it landed in his boot. I didn't know what happened to it."

"Yeah, I thought it was a scorpion or a very large beetle," I say, and she laughs, hopefully thinking I'm kidding.

"Of course you did," she says. She looks down at me, and a small smile crosses her lips. She climbs onto my lap, straddling me. I put my hands on her hips, holding her in place. My head drops back onto the couch. "How are you not tired? We worked on the front yard for eight hours straight. I can barely lift my arms."

"Patrick, that took us two hours." Her eyes dance with delight. My stomach flips seeing the look on her face. No one has ever looked at me like that.

"Oh. I thought it was three days. Seriously, I'm out of shape if that kicked my ass." I let my eyes fall closed because I'm afraid she will notice the emotions boiling up in me.

"You were just using different muscles, that's all. Your body will adapt," she says as she traces my face with her fingers.

"I hope so. I would like to be able to put my arms around you again," I say, keeping my eyes closed. It's so nice to have her touching me, I hope she never stops.

"I would like that too," she says, as she leans forward and gently kisses my lips. I let my hands move up from her hips to her back, pulling her closer. This time I'm sure she knows what she is doing to me since she is sitting right on my lap. Not like I can do anything about it; her kisses, her touch affect me that much. Her breathing changes, and her kisses become more urgent. I slide my hands up her back then down to her hips, allowing them to curl around. With each pass, I graze the side of each breast with a feather-light touch. I want to explore all of her, but I'm not sure exactly what she wants.

"God, that feels so good, Patrick," she says as her hips move a little, slightly rocking into me. Her gaze finds mine as she rolls herself against me, her mouth finding mine again, eager, lips open, pliant.

Oh.

I know what she wants. The journey my hands are taking stops, and I pull back from her kiss. "You have the most incredible body I have ever seen or touched, Kenny. I mean that. You are so beautiful." I slowly put my hands under her shirt, questioning if this is what she wants as I let my fingers dance along her flat stomach. She nods and, wasting no time, reaches down, pulling her shirt off, exposing her tan, muscular body. She is wearing a running bra that doesn't unhook from what I can tell, so I pull the straps off her shoulders and tug it down. I don't move, I can't. The most perfect breasts I have ever seen in my entire life are right in front of me. She leans forward to kiss me again, and I stop her.

"Wait, I'm not done looking at you. God, Kenny." I lift my hands, hovering near her, but I don't touch yet. "You are like a work of art. I've never seen such beautifully defined muscles on a woman."

"Patrick," she says, and it sounds as if she is pleading.

I gently cup each of her perfect breasts and let the weight of them rest in my hands. I give them a squeeze like she did at the bar, and she laughs.

"It's so much better when you do that," she says.

My thumbs trace slowly up to her nipples and softly graze them. She arches into my hands and reaches up, pulling her hair out of the ponytail she has worn all day. Seeing that brown, silky hair cascade over her shoulders makes me crazy. I take a sharp breath and lean forward, opening my mouth on her nipple. My tongue dances across the hardened peak, and I enjoy the instant moan that erupts from her lips. I have imagined this moment more than once, but it's better than I thought it could be, and I don't know how to stop.

I kiss along each breast and up to her neck, then find her mouth again as she tugs at my shirt. We break the kiss long enough to rid myself of my T-shirt, and she presses herself against me. The warmth of her skin on mine is almost too much for me, and I let out what can only be described as a growl.

"You like that?" she asks, giggling softly into my ear. She bites the tender lobe, and I swear stars explode before my eyes.

"I like it so much. It's not enough. I need more. I want all of you," I say and kiss her again and again, swallowing her moans as I match her hip movements with mine. Our hands roam over each other, frantic to learn. Lifting myself up, I turn us, flipping her quickly onto her back. This new position allows me to take advantage of exploring her breasts again with my hands, then my tongue and lips. I kiss my way down her stomach, marveling at the definition, the strength. When the top of the tattoo peeks out, I pull roughly at her shorts to expose it. I run my tongue along the words needing to taste her.

Gasping, her fingers thrust into my hair, tugging lightly. My control is slipping, and it seems like hers is too. Forcing myself to slowly kiss my way back up her body, I stop to enjoy each breast. I pull back, hovering above her, afraid to lay my weight on her.

If I allow that contact, my brain will short-circuit and my desire will take over. I take some deep breaths, trying to calm myself, but she has other plans.

While I'm trying to settle my racing heart, she wraps her legs around me, pulling me down onto her. She arches up and moans when she feels how hard I am. My hips decide one or two little thrusts would be okay, and before I know it, we are both grinding on each other, seeking release.

God, the sounds she is making, her breaths on my neck, her kisses … I feel like I can't breathe without her. Like I can get lost in her, that I'll be lost without her.

Shit.

"Kenny, wait. I think we should stop," I say, instantly hating myself for suggesting such a thing.

"What? Why?" she asks, confused.

"I don't want our first time to be like this." I close my eyes tightly and open them again, finding her gaze and locking onto those deep brown eyes. "I want to take you out on a proper date. I want to cook you a meal, feed you, nourish you. Then I want to drive out to see the stars, lay you on a blanket under the Milky Way, and show you what you do to me. I want you to feel every inch of me as I claim you under a sky that looks like promises. I want you to feel my heart beating out of my chest, like it is now, but with nothing between us but the wind. I want to feel the heat of your body as you fall apart beneath me and watch your eyes when you see me do the same."

The words come out before I can stop them, and a moment of panic grips me as I see what looks like fear flash through her eyes.

I hang my head and close my eyes. Damn. Too much, Patrick. Too much, too soon.

She takes my chin with her hand and lifts it so she can see my face. I see the sweet pink in her cheeks, the fullness of her lips, and a gleam in her eyes.

"I think that sounds like an amazing evening, Patrick. I would love to do that," she says and pulls me down for a soft and sensual kiss. Her lips reassure me with each pass, with every swipe of her tongue against mine.

Relief floods my heart, and I smile against her lips.

"I found the best spot the other night. It's not too far from here. I'll show you. Soon, I promise," I say.

"I'm looking forward to it."

COWBOY POETRY

BEYOND THE FENCE LINE~PUBLISHED 1950

The road that winds away from home
Feels longer than the return
The cattle know the drive to high
Is longer than the drive back
home
~By M.S 1945

SEVENTEEN
KENNY

Standing on my little porch, I watch him drive away. My head is spinning with all that happened and all he said. I have had men in my life, even a long-term boyfriend while I was in college. No one has ever made me feel like that. No one made my heart race or my resolve fade so quickly.

If he hadn't stopped what was happening on the couch in Mitchell's living room, I would have crossed a line. Let's be honest here; I was ready to hurl myself naked across that line like I was in the naked Olympics.

I lost all sense of myself. My breaths felt as though they were connected to his; my body melted into his fingers with every touch, every kiss. I found myself getting lost. When he told me about his plans for a date with me, I was stunned. I'm not used to men who speak from their hearts. It's a language I'm unfamiliar with, but one I've discovered I want to hear more of. He is so genuinely unafraid to speak what he feels. It's refreshing.

We talked for a while after deciding to take the physical thing a little slower. I learned more about his home in Seattle, and by home I mean literally his house. He didn't speak of friends or family that he had left behind. It seems like he got a letter from Mitchell's attorney, then got in the car the next day to drive here.

Patrick dropped me off back at my house, and we made plans for him to come back tomorrow to pick me up for our Redding shopping trip. So, once I could no longer see the cute red BMW, I went inside and sat at my kitchen table to make a list of all the things I needed. It has been over a month since I have made it down the hill, and I'm out of a lot of essentials.

I'm grateful my knee is on the mend. The bruise isn't as bad as the first day, and the swelling has come way down. I think the impact, then inability to rest afterward, made it seem like more of a problem. Patrick asked me about it once during the CPR class, and I noticed Ryan looking over to see what I would say. Even if I were still hurting as badly as the day I came home, I wouldn't admit it within earshot of that asshole.

When I finish my list, I rub my eyes and check the clock. It's after eleven. I'm beat. I strip off my clothes, throw on a T-shirt, then climb into bed and fall fast asleep.

A horrible ringing sound rattles my brain, and I roll over to glance at the clock. It's only six. Moaning, I stumble out of bed and into the kitchen where the phone hangs on the wall.

"Hello?" I mumble while rubbing my eyes.

"Kenny! Going to need you to get in here as quick as you can. We are heading out at seven. There is a big fire down on the Cleveland National Forest. We are meeting the strike team at nine," Ted says.

"Down by LA? Wow! Okay. Be there in ten."

The excitement of going off forest fills me with adrenaline, and I run to take a quick shower. I braid my long hair and grab my backpack, shoving my Walkman, extra batteries, a book, and some more snacks in for the long ride. I should've borrowed a book from Mitchell's place when I was out there with Patrick. Glancing down at the table and see the list I made. Damn. I was supposed to go shopping today with Patrick, then have that amazingly romantic date.

Well, that's disappointing. I hope he will understand and still want to get together when I get back. I scribble a quick note on the bottom of the list and tape it to my front door.

I probably could have called out to the ranch, but I don't have a lot of time. I glance at my watch and jog down the hill to the station. Ryan is just pulling up in his truck. He isn't living at the barracks, but I don't know any more than that. I wonder if he and Bonnie got together last night. I also wonder if I should say something to Ted.

Without the distraction of all the regular staff at the office, we get our stuff together quickly and are on the road a little before seven. Luke hasn't pulled a book out yet, and I look over at him, wondering what is going on.

He is staring at Ryan with a smirk. "Saw you and Cindy at The Bar," he says. "Looked like you two were getting along well."

"Fuck, yeah. She is such a babe. Thanks for introducing us," Ryan says.

"She asked me to introduce you. That shit wasn't my idea," Luke replies, shaking his head.

"Dude, she was good to go after one beer. We didn't even make it back to her place before her lips were all over my cock. I had to pull my truck over so I didn't crash. It was crazy. As soon as the truck was in park, she was straddling me in the driver's seat. I barely had time to lay the seat back before she started riding me. She couldn't wait to have all I could give her." Ryan is leaning over like he is sharing a secret with his bro, but he's loud enough for me to hear.

"Dude, I don't need all the details," Luke says.

Ryan just shrugs. "Figured you were wondering what all that noise was since we were parked in front of your place. My truck was rocking!"

"Gross. No, I was at The Bar. Glad now I stayed there as long as I did. But, uh, yeah. That's Cindy for ya. She's a real go-getter, that girl," Luke says with a chuckle.

He bends forward and grabs his book from his pack, then salutes Ryan and disappears into his novel.

Ryan, not taking the hint, leans back in his seat with a satisfied smile and says, "She was a firecracker, and not clingy at all. When we were done, she was on her way, and I was able to meet up with a date I had at nine. It was a perfect evening, being a doubleheader and all." Ryan winks and jabs his elbow at Luke, who just glares at him and goes back to reading.

"Does it bother Bonnie when you fuck other girls?" I ask before I can stop myself.

"Why would Bonnie care what I do? It's not like I'm seeing her," Ryan says, eyeing me suspiciously.

I realize then that I only know about them because I had overheard them. Ryan doesn't know I was by the trucks when he was making his plans with Bonnie.

Shit.

"Well, I just kind of figured since you are always sniffing around her desk," I say.

"She's just a kid, Kendra. Jesus," Ryan scoffs.

I roll my eyes at him, knowing I can't call him out on his bullshit. God, I hate him. I'm sure Bonnie believes she is in love with this douchebag. Hell, at seventeen I was sure I was going to meet Donny Osmond and as soon as he took one look at me, he and I would be married. Okay, well that was a bit ridiculous, but I did imagine I would get to meet him. I'm not sure why I was so confident in that since I grew up ten hours away from Los Angeles. I went to Disneyland exactly two times as a teenager, and neither time did I run into any Osmonds, but the dream lived on.

I close my eyes and try to rest like I do on every trip, but I'm too agitated.

"Fuck. Seriously? No! Ugh," Luke is muttering.

"You okay over there, Luke?" I ask, leaning forward.

"Damn it, no. I finished Kent Price, A Man on a Mission, and it ended on a fucking cliffhanger! I should have asked that Patrick dude for book two," Luke says, putting his head in his hands.

"I have a book with me, not book two, but still something. Want to trade?" I ask, reaching my hand out for Patrick's book.

"Sure," Luke sighs. "I packed a few other books, but I'm always open to suggestions. What did you bring?"

"A Stephen King novel called Misery. My dad said it was great, but I haven't started it yet."

"Oh! I wanted to read that! Fuck yeah, I'll trade you!" Luke hands over the book that Patrick wrote. My fingers itch to flip to the back page so I can stare at his picture. I dig into my backpack and pull out the book for Luke.

"I'll need that back when you are done. At Thanksgiving my dad is going to want a rundown of what I thought."

"No problem. I might finish it before we get to the fire," Luke says with a shrug, and I laugh.

I hold the Kent Price novel to my chest and close my eyes. I wonder what the appropriate amount of time would be for me to open the book to the About the Author page.

Now. Now seems like the appropriate time. I flip to the back of the book and read the passage below his picture.

It states that he lived in Seattle and had recently lost his parents, causing him to delve into the world of fiction. Kent was born from grief, but also from the fond memories he had of his father and grandfather, who had served in the military.

There was a little blurb about the fact that he was only twenty years old and still attending University of the Pacific. He was getting his degree in geography.

Huh. That isn't at all what I expected. I figured he majored in English, or at least creative writing or something. I wonder why he picked geography as a degree, and what kind of career would that provide, anyway? Was he going to make maps? From the story he told about coming to Adin, it seemed like the Thomas Guide was not a friend but a foe.

I run my finger across the black-and-white picture. He looks so young in it. His cheeks look a little fuller than they are now, and his hair is cut very short. He is smiling, but it doesn't quite reach his eyes. I wonder if the photographer captured the pain he was feeling. The pain of knowing that his parents would never see their son's book in print. It had to be there then, and I'm sure it's there still.

I have so many questions about why he started writing when he did. Why didn't I ask more when we talked the other night? I know I tried, but he was very good at deflecting and asking me about my family or my childhood. I should have been more persistent.

As we get farther away from Adin, a heaviness settles in my chest. It's a dull ache that makes it hard to catch my breath. This is the first time since starting this job that I've felt divided. My heart is in two places, and I don't like the feeling one bit.

I pinch my eyes closed and try to think about what lies ahead. The terrain we will encounter, and the strike team we will be with. I picture the long, hard days of work I have in front of me, grateful for the challenge. I must have dozed off because the sound of the air brakes on the engine startle me awake. Patrick's book is clutched to my chest, and I bet I had my mouth open because my throat is dry.

I quickly tuck the book into my backpack and climb out of the truck, stretching my arms above my head. I catch Ryan watching me, but he looks away and heads toward the bathroom before I can say anything.

Luke comes up to me and asks where we are going. "Have you ever been to the Cleveland?"

"No, I think the farthest south I have been is the Stanislaus. You remember that fire where Chuck got food poisoning?" I say with a snicker.

"Fuck, that was awful. Yeah, I remember." Luke laughs out loud, and I see Ryan by the picnic tables flicking his chew can. A lot of guys in fire use chew, and even a few girls I've met. I think it's revolting. I'm glad Luke isn't into it.

I watch as Ryan pinches a big wad and stuffs it into his lower lip, making it jut out. He closes the can and tucks it into his back pocket while his face contorts as he tries to get the tobacco right where he wants it.

How can Bonnie find that attractive? How can she see him as

anything other than a complete tool? He is everything I hate in a man.

"Why are you glaring at Ryan like that?" Luke asks after looking over his shoulder to see what has caught my gaze.

"I'm just hoping he doesn't keep that wad in when we load up. I hate the smell."

"Oh, fuck yeah, me too. I thought maybe you were mad about Cindy," Luke says.

"Why would I be mad? She can do whatever she wants."

"Yeah, but last year you were the one she went crying to when everyone was judging her about her choices."

"Well, you can lead a horse to water, but you can't make it stop humping everything in a pair of Wranglers," I say, making Luke snort.

Ryan looks over at us and then turns his head to spit. He pushes off the table and walks away, heading back toward the bathrooms.

"How are things with Zia?"

"Really fucking good. Dude, her dad actually talked to me the other day! I'm wearing him down with my charm, Kenny," he says, beaming.

"I knew you would. That's great. Hey, can I ask you a question?"

"Sure, man. What's up?"

"Do you miss her when we go off like this? I mean, when we get called out, do you sometimes wish..." I trail off, unable to complete the sentence.

"All the time, Kenny. I love my job, but that doesn't mean I enjoy being away from my girl. I'm lucky that she's pretty chill about it. There are lots of people who break up during fire season, or because of it, you know? The hours are long, and the assignments are unpredictable. Everything gets put on hold for six months out of the year. Relationships don't always survive that." He pauses, looking at me with questions dancing across his face. His smile spreads with the realization, and he asks, "Kenny, are you seeing someone?"

"Maybe. I don't know. We were supposed to go out on a date

tonight. That obviously isn't going to happen now," I say, trying to laugh it off, but Luke doesn't buy it.

"Oh, man, that sucks. First date put on hold? Rough, dude, rough. But hey, if he's worth it, he will wait around. I assume he knows what you do for a living?" Luke asks, and I nod.

"Ugh, it was just moving along really well, and I was excited to see him tonight. What if he just got caught up in the moment and that spark fades by the time we get back?" I say quietly.

"Nah, I don't think that will happen. You're a fucking catch. Is this anyone I know?" Luke asks, wiggling his eyebrows at me. I'm sure he knows, but I appreciate him pretending he doesn't.

"Not ready to talk about that, but when I am, you will be the first I'll tell."

"Okay, but if it's Rusty, I'm probably going to have a heart attack. Just letting you know so you can get the paddles ready," Luke says, slapping me on the back.

"No. Definitely not Rusty. I better hit the bathroom before we go. See you back here."

Luke and I get back to the engine at the same time as Chuck and Ted. Ryan is leaning against the crew cab, arms folded across his chest. He turns his head to the side and spits, narrowly missing my boot. I look up and glare at him.

"We are heading out, Ryan. Take that dip out before you load up. I'm not about to let you stink up the engine for the next eight hours with that shit. And if I ever find a spit cup in my engine, you'll be scrubbing the whole damn thing down with a toothbrush," Chuck says, crossing his enormous arms over his barrel chest. He stares Ryan down; no one moving.

Ryan kicks off the engine, then sucks hard on the wad one last time before hooking his finger in his lip. He swipes out a black lump and flicks it onto the pavement, where it lands with a wet plop. Wiping his finger on his pants, he smiles a big toothy grin at Chuck. He has black flecks of chew stuck between his teeth, and he knows it.

"Sure thing, boss," Ryan says with a little salute. He opens the door and climbs in, and I wait for him to get buckled before taking my spot by the door.

As soon as we are back out on the freeway, I pull the book out of my pack. Maybe since I can't be with Patrick, I can get to know him in this way, through his words and characters.

I turn to page one and take a breath, settling in. Just like Luke said, by page three I'm hooked. This Kent dude is tough but relatable. About four hours into the story, Kent is trailing a suspect and ends up meeting a beautiful woman in the process. I read Patrick's description of her, and my heart drops into my stomach.

SHE TURNED, her blonde hair fluttering like a field of daffodils on a breezy day. Her eyes were bluer than any summer sky. Her long, dainty fingers curled around her wineglass, and Kent was mesmerized by the long, red nails that adorned each finger. Her lips were painted the same color, and he wondered how long it would take to kiss that color right off her.

When he approached, she smiled, her white teeth perfect against her plump, full lips. Her voice was light and crisp and reminded him of bells ringing on a far-off hill.

Her gauzy, floral-print dress clung to her curves like he imagined himself doing. He could picture how soft she would feel pressed up against him. He must know what that would feel like; he must know what those lips taste like. Putting aside his goal of finding Fernando, he set his martini on the table and reached out for her hand...

I CLOSE the book and let out a sad puff of air. Is that what Patrick finds attractive? That woman was soft and feminine and had a voice like bells, for fuck's sake. Jesus. How would he describe me? My voice is not like bells on a faraway hill. My curves are more like a straightaway, and I usually have dirt under my very stubby fingernails. I also never drink wine. Beer and whiskey are my go-to drinks, and tequila if I'm in a mood. Wine? Gross.

I have worn dresses; never ones that could be described as gauzy, but still. There were exactly two occasions, and both times people came up to me asking why I was so dressed up. One of those times was at my own graduation, for fuck's sake. I had just wanted to try something different, to look special or extra pretty. I didn't account for the fact that people had only ever seen me in worn jeans and T-shirts. Hell, a sweater is fancy for me. I just don't know how to be girly and frilly or feminine.

I lean forward, shove the book into my backpack, and pull out my Walkman. Music is a lot less anxiety-inducing. I pop in my favorite Alan Jackson tape and lean back into the seat, closing my eyes.

COWBOY POETRY

UNPUBLISHED WORK

The delicate curve of her body
Dances through my mind
The way she's moving entices me
Drags me under, makes me wonder
Her strength, her power, excite me
I yield to her wishes, I give in to her
My needs are her desires
 and I want
Her
~By Patrick Smith 1988

EIGHTEEN

PATRICK

Well, damn. I reread the note I found taped to her front door again, hoping somehow I had misunderstood.

> Patrick,
>
> Sorry, I had to go off-forest for a fire. Not sure when we will be back. I will try to call out to the ranch when we get to camp. I'm sad about missing our first date. I hope we can make it work when I get back,
>
> Kenny

OKAY, well, I'm not sure if she left me this list so I could get what she needed in Redding, or if this was the only paper she could find on short notice. I turn the doorknob to her house and find it unlocked. I peek my head in and look around. She is definitely gone. Would it be creepy to go in and maybe steal a T-shirt of hers so I can have something that smells like her?

Yes. Fuck, of course, that is creepy.

Jesus, pull it together.

I take a deep breath and close the door again. I'm developing a little more than a crush on this girl. Last night was incredible. She was incredible. She was smart and funny and so fucking beautiful. I've never known such a confident woman. It was refreshing and overwhelming and hell, I don't know what. But now she is gone, off being a badass somewhere.

I fold the list up and put it in my pocket, deciding that I can get all the nonperishable things on her list and just put them in her house for her. When she gets back, she will appreciate my thoughtfulness, and I will get to take her on that date.

Or she will realize that I'm a needy fuck and she will move on. Maybe she'll talk to that Luke guy and he'll tell her to steer clear of me because I ended my first book with a cliffhanger. Who does that? I mean, what if they hadn't asked me to write the second book? I was just going to leave people wondering who stole Kent Price's notebook and, for the love of God, why would someone steal that since it was all in an indecipherable code? Yeah, that's all kinds of arrogant and messed up. I can admit that now; I was twenty, and all of those things. Very arrogant and sure that my series would be a hit, even if only the first book had been published.

I drive down the hill and into the bustling city of Redding, California. I'm in search of many things, but the first thing I needed to do is trade in this BMW for a truck. Something with four-wheel drive, because according to Kenny, it does snow up in the northeastern corner of California. Plus, if I'm a ranch owner, I need a truck. I might need to haul something someday. Like hay.

I'm picturing myself with a truck bed full of hay when the salesperson approaches. I might as well have a sign on my shirt that says SELL ME AN OVERPRICED TRUCK because that is what happens.

I leave the car lot with way too much truck and find a grocery store where I can finish my shopping. Kenny is out of a lot of things like paper towels and toilet paper, so I load up my cart with her needs and mine.

It's like I've been stranded on a desert island when I see the huge cheese selection in the Albertsons grocery store. More cheese than I can possibly eat makes it into my cart. When presented with that many choices, you can panic or be practical. I, of course, panic.

After buying all the cheese, I stop by Mervyn's to pick up some new bedding. Mitchell didn't have very discriminating taste in sheets, and the thought of laying Kenny's perfect body on two hundred thread count sheets is unbearable.

Not that this is a guaranteed thing, but I want to be ready if it does become a possibility. That thought leads me to remember that I don't have any condoms with me. They probably have them at the general store in Adin, but I don't really want my sex life to be public knowledge.

I find a perfect comforter and matching sheets and grab some new pillows as well. Mitchell's hadn't been terribly uncomfortable, but they had an odd smell about them, kind of a mix of mothballs and sinus infection breath. I hate to judge the old guy, but I'm ready for some fresh-smelling pillows.

Shoving all of my purchases into the back seat of the truck, I can see the appeal of these bigger vehicles. The truck bed is filled with ice chests containing all my perishables and all the things Kenny needed. There was no way this stuff would've fit in the BMW.

It's good to help Kenny out in this way since she has done so much for me. Even if it might be a while before she knows how helpful I am. I can wait. Right? It's not like there is another choice. I just really enjoyed having her around, and now I'm going to be on my own again.

I wonder if she has gotten to the fire yet. She didn't say where they were going, so she could still be driving. I stopped and picked up an answering machine at the mall because the thought of missing her calls made my stomach hurt. I hated that when I got back to the ranch tonight, I wouldn't know if I had already missed her call.

The drive back up the hill, is peaceful and enlightening. The tall pines lining the highway give way to wide open spaces reminds me of stumbling out of the darkness and into the light. My mind wanders to Kenny and the way she has captivated me in such a short time. She has become the bright spot in my recent darkness. That's cliche, but true. My thoughts jump to the other women I've known over the years. Tricia was the only other one who shared a piece of my heart. Most of them just shared my bed.

By the third Kent Price book, I was getting recognized and approached by women who wanted a famous author claim them. It was intoxicating to have their attention and their bodies. I guess that's why I was so mad at myself for letting Tricia in. I knew better, but I allowed myself to believe she wanted me.

Kenny has never even read my books. Hell, she didn't know I was an author; she just thought I was trespassing on her friend's ranch. I try to picture the friendship between a tough as nails twenty-six-year-old and a ninety-four-year-old poet/rancher. What did they talk about? I feel an old familiar pang of regret at not knowing him, not having my own memories of him.

Pulling up to the ranch, my memory snags on that book of poetry Kenny told me about. I can't turn back the clock, but I can peek back into the past through his words. Quickly putting away all the things I had purchased, Kenny's things get moved to the cab of the truck so they won't be out in the open overnight. Last thing I do is set up the answering machine with a clever outgoing message.Once all that is complete I go to find the poetry book in Mitchell's library.

Kenny said they were on the lower right-hand side, and that is exactly where I find them. He had several books of poetry, so it takes me a while to locate his published works. The brown, leather-bound book, called Cowboy Poetry: Beyond the Fence Line, contains lots of Mitchell's poems. I pour over them, each one touching me deeply. This man had loved and lost. That had shaped him, defined him, but it did not destroy him. The poem that is Kenny's favorite makes my breath catch when I discover it.

And I love her still

I loved her first
I love her still
I loved her fierce
I love her still
I loved her in the morning,
the day, the night
I loved her in her anger,
her joy, and her fear.
I loved her at her end
and
I love her still

~By M.S 1920

I FLIP THROUGH THE PAGES, looking for a poem that was written after that, because that must be when he lost her. Every bit of me wishes that there was more than just a year listed. There are so many questions that I have, and I can see why this poem spoke to Kenny.

I imagine knowing Mitchell like she did would've added another layer that I will never quite understand.

Standing, I hold the book to my chest and glance over at the recliner where his almost empty glass of whiskey still remains. The bottle that sits next to the glass has at least two fingers left. I pour the whiskey into the glass, then pick it up and reposition it so the label of the bottle faces me. Almost right, but something is missing. Snapping my fingers, I return his slippers to beside the chair and set the book of cowboy poetry on the seat, open to his heartbreaking love poem. Perfect. Now all I need is my camera. Excited about my idea, I hurry to my room and grab it off the dresser. It's time to honor who he was and capture his memory.

A few adjustments need to be made, like turning on the lamp that sits on the handmade wooden table, moving the glass of whiskey closer and arranging his slippers to be more in front of the chair. I take several pictures until I am satisfied that I've captured the essence of Mitchell Smith.

Overwhelmed and caught up in the moment, I raise the whiskey and toast the man I will never know.

I swallow the amber liquid, and while it's a symbolically nice gesture, dust and a sludge of some kind has settled in the glass. I hadn't paid attention to that when I poured the last shot, since I was focused on getting a good picture. Swallow again, I must say, it has left a rather unpleasant aftertaste. I cough and sputter and wonder about the choice I just made.

Oh God.

Is that a hair?

Do I have a dead man's hair in my mouth?

I start frantically trying to find the hair with my fingers but keep coming up empty with every sweep. The realization that I will have to swallow the hair hits me like a slap in the face. I freeze in place, slobber on my hands and running down my chin. I take another tentative swallow and understand immediately why cats make that god-awful noise when they have a hairball.

I sprint to the kitchen and thrust my face under the faucet, trying to flush out the evil hair. I take a gulp and swallow before it occurs to me I should have swished and spit.

Always swish and spit, Patrick. Damn it. You know this.

Oh God.

I have a dead man's hair in my stomach now. This is the end of me. The dust-covered sludge I ingested seems to still coat my tongue. At that moment, I unfortunately remember a television show that I once watched that said dust is actually dead skin cells.

Jesus.

I have Mitchell's hair and skin in my mouth and stomach. I have basically eaten my dead uncle. The involuntary cat removing a hairball sound returns, and I hang my head over the kitchen sink, praying that God will just come and tap me out. He will say, "You had a good run, Patrick, but the hair and skin cells were just too much for you." And I will nod and agree, then maybe he'll give me a milkshake and a hug.

There is a strange noise coming from over my shoulder, and I assume it's St. Michael's bells. Or St. Peter? Who is the patron saint of accidentally ingesting your dead uncle? I slowly realize that a phone is ringing and snap my head up. Drool and probably some tears run down my face as I dive for the ancient, avocado-colored, wall-mounted phone that is next to the kitchen door.

"Hello?" I croak out, channeling Mitchell from beyond the grave, I'm sure.

"Patrick?" a female voice asks.

"Yes." I cough and hack like a twenty-pack-a-day smoker.

"Patrick, are you okay? This is Kenny."

"Hi!" I rasp.

"Um, did I catch you at a bad time?" she asks.

"No!" I clear my throat and try again. "No, sorry. I may have accidentally ingested Uncle Mitchell. He was caught in my throat. I think I have dislodged him now. Oh God. He's gone. Oh!" I feel a wave of euphoria when I no longer have the tickle of a dead man's hair in my throat. It's like no joy I had ever felt.

"Patrick? Did you say you ate Mitchell? It's kind of loud here. Why would you do that?" she asks, clearly concerned.

"Well, not on purpose. I drank the whiskey."

"The whiskey by his chair?" she asks.

"Yes, I read his poems and then I wanted to honor him, so I took some pictures. It was a whole touching thing, really. You had to be here, but then I got caught up in the moment and I toasted him with the whiskey and drank it."

"Oh. Wow. Okay. How was it?"

"At first, it wasn't bad. I mean old and a bit dusty and Kenny?" I say, lowering my voice in shame.

"Yeah?"

"There was a hair, Kenny. An old man's hair," I croak.

"Oh God," she says, and I can hear her cover her laugh.

"Yeah. I couldn't get it out. It just danced around in my throat like it was hanging on for dear life, his life. That was his last go-round. Oh God." A whimper escapes me.

"You said you ate him!" She isn't hiding her laughter now.

"Well, the dust, Kenny. Dust had formed a protective layer over the whiskey sludge. I poured in that last shot from the bottle, you know? Listen, that sludge, the dust, was in all certainty his skin. Skin and hair. That is what I drank." I wipe my hand down my face, wishing God really had tapped me out.

"I'm surprised that you survived that, Patrick, but why on earth would you drink that?" she asks, regaining some control of her laughter.

"There wasn't much thought that went into it, and to be honest, I didn't look too closely at it. I just threw it back like a shot," I say, pulling out a chair by the table. The phone has a long cord that has been twisted and pulled over the years, creating a tangled mess. I wrap the cord around my finger while I listen to her laugh. It's a beautiful sound.

"Well, I'm sorry I had to leave. I was really looking forward to stargazing with you," Kenny says.

"We will go when you get back. It's totally okay. Can I ask where you are, or is it top secret?" I say, mostly joking.

"We are down by Los Angeles on the Cleveland National Forest. It's a huge fire. I think at last check it was over two thousand acres, and it's still growing. We are teaming up with a strike team tomorrow and will be out all day. Might not be coming back to fire camp, so I can't guarantee I can call again."

"I understand. Sounds exciting. Do you sleep in a tent when you are out on assignments like this?" I ask.

"Yeah, we do. Sometimes we are in big camps, sometimes it's just a small team of us far away from the main camp. I think that is the plan for tomorrow. We are meeting up with some smoke jumpers and a hand crew. I'm lead sawyer, meaning I cut down the big trees, remember? So I get to do a lot of that tomorrow," Kenny says.

"God, that's hot," I say before I can stop myself.

"Literally," she says with a laugh.

"Oh, right. No, I meant you. You have got to be the sexiest woman I have ever known," I say.

"I'm glad you find my job sexy. I thought you would think…" Kenny trails off.

"What? You thought I wouldn't be turned on by the fact that you can cut down a tree? Fuck, Kenny. I'm so hard right now," I say.

She laughs and I smile, feeling like maybe it was a good thing God let me live through the hair incident.

We talk for almost an hour, and I finally tell her to go get some sleep. She informs me that Mitchell's ashes are in a wooden box on the bookshelf and tells me to be careful not to accidentally snort him or anything. I'll be taping the box shut as soon as I locate it.

COWBOY POETRY
UNPUBLISHED WORK

Metal and leather
dust and grit
gas and oil
Beautiful
stunning power that pulls
tugs
until I surrender
And I will
again and again
~By Patrick Smith 1988

NINETEEN

KENNY

Three weeks.

This fire has kicked my ass for three weeks and it's still not out. The thing is a beast and refused to be knocked down until yesterday when it rained. God was like, "Okay, I got this. I'll help a little."

Whatever. At least there is a line all the way around it now, and it's listed as eighty percent contained with expected full containment today or tomorrow. I don't think I have ever worked so hard in all my life.

I rest my forehead against the shower wall as the water runs over the top of my head. Looking down at my body, I can see bruises in various stages—some dark purple, some a sickly greenish-yellow color. I haven't shaved my legs in a week and a half because my only shower has been jumping in the creek to rinse off. We have only come back into camp twice, so I haven't bothered to call Patrick. I'm so tired I probably wouldn't be very good company. I turn my head, pressing my cheek against the wall, and think about the past week, marveling I haven't killed Ryan.

He has been extra obnoxious this whole time because we were teamed up with some guys from CDF. Apparently; he has friends, and they are just as big douchebags as he is. Actually, that doesn't surprise me at all. No normal guy would like someone as idiotic as Ryan.

I swear I saw him leaning on his shovel more times than he was slinging dirt. The guy is a fucking wimp and cuts the line for like ten minutes, then finds a way to take a break by sticking some chew in or taking a piss. He's lazy, and one day I got so angry I laid into him in front of his buddies.

All that got me was a bunch of assholes talking about me behind my back, but loud enough for me to hear. It was lovely. Luke even yelled at him, and he never yells at anyone.

We were all tired and hungry, so when we were sent back to fire camp, I stayed quiet, not wanting to cause any more problems. The ride back was quick, and after Chuck and Ted told us what to expect over the next couple of days, we were released to clean our gear and set up our tents again. I pulled my saw out and went to work, grateful I had kept up on the maintenance in the field even when I was exhausted. It didn't take long for the saw to be ready for use, so I stowed it in its compartment in the engine.

I pulled my backpack out of the crew cab and picked up my red bag and tent, lugging all of it over to the grassy area where the tents were pitched. I set up at record speed, then hit the shower, where I planned on staying for at least an hour.

So here I am, rolling my head to the side, letting the hot water hit a new part of my neck. I finally decide I should wash my hair and make my way to the chow hall. My stomach isn't going to tolerate the lack of food much longer.

After giving my hair a good scrub, I shut the water off and step out of the shower area. I dry off and pull on a pair of shorts and a T-shirt. I lack clean clothes and know that is on my list of things to do tomorrow. We're getting three whole days off. We'll stay here in camp, but we won't be sent out on the line. We can rest. I can't fucking wait.

I grab a plate and load it full of whatever they are feeding us. I don't even know, I'm that tired. Luke comes and sits with me, but neither of us says much. When he is finished, Luke pushes his plate out of the way and lays his head on the table.

"Even my ears are tired. I don't mean like I can't listen anymore, you know? I mean, my actual ears. I can't move, not sure how I'm still breathing," Luke says into the table.

"Same," I say, taking the last bite of my meal. This is the first meal in a week that I have eaten at an actual table, and I can't tell you what it is. How sad.

Luke stands and waves over his shoulder at me as he walks off toward the showers. I'm so glad I did that already. Now, I'm going to find my tent, strip out of these clothes, and sleep like the dead. I hadn't bothered to braid my hair after my shower because the thought of holding my arms above my head for even a second sounded awful.

I pull the scrunchy off my wrist and gather my hair up into a ponytail, twisting it to make a bun of sorts on top of my head. It's heavenly to have it off my neck. A loud satisfied sigh escapes my lips as a breeze hits me.

"That's so fucking hot, baby. I like it when you make those sounds," a male voice says behind me. A chill dances up my spine because I recognize that voice.

Damn.

I turn slowly around and stare into the eyes of the last person I want to see.

"Jeff. Thought you quit fire," I say, then turn and continue to walk away. Just like old times, he grabs my arm and turns me toward him a little too rough for my liking. I yank my arm away and glare at him.

"Damn, woman. Settle down. Just saying hello." Jeff puts his hands up and steps back.

"Well, hello and bye. I'm beat, been out on the line for over a week. Catch you around." I walk off before he can say another word. God, I really don't want to see him. Why is he even here? He didn't do fire last year; he quit because his father wanted him to come back

East and help with their family store. I was happy about that, happy to never see that asswipe again.

I make it to my tent and unzip it quickly, ducking in and closing myself into my own little oasis. Yanking off my T-shirt, I slip on the tank top I sleep in. My uncomfortable denim shorts are next to go, traded for my soft pajama shorts. As soon as I get my sleeping bag unrolled, I see a shadow cross in front of my tent. I hold my breath.

"Kenny? Where'd you go? I thought we could catch up a bit. Kenny? Fuck, how did she disappear so fast?"

I continue to lie as still as a dead man until I hear Jeff on the other side of the large grassy area talking to someone else. I let my breath out slowly. Damn it. Is he on an engine crew? Hand crew? I didn't look at his crew shirt long enough to even see if he was still with the Forest Service. I just wanted out of there.

Jeff is the one thing I regret about my first year in fire. I would like to pretend I hadn't made such a horrible mistake, and that is a lot easier when he isn't around. It's just embarrassing. I'm beyond grateful that Luke never brought it up. We have all made bad choices, right? That was Jeff. A bad fucking choice. He didn't break my heart; he didn't even hurt my feelings. I shouldn't have been with him even once, let alone the ten or so times it happened. He was on the engine with me the first year I did fire. We met in college, and we both thought it was funny that we ended up at the same place for our first year.

For me, fire was going to be a career. For Jeff, it was just something to do for extra money during the summer. He didn't take it seriously at all and kind of made fun of me because I did. He wasn't even remotely my type—not in looks, not in personality. I had never even considered dating him in college, nor him me.

During work hours we were professional, but for some reason, when we had some alcohol in us, clothes were an optional thing. Also, being upright. We became more horizontal friends. I swore to myself that I would never get involved with anyone in fire because I was afraid it would appear I was only doing the job to meet a man.

After the first drunken night, I told Jeff it couldn't happen again, and yet it always seemed to. I was away from home for the first time, doing a job that was challenging, and I guess I enjoyed having his attention. I've known guys that had fuck buddies, and I do not judge them.

I do, however, judge myself.

Harshly.

That's probably why Luke thought I would be mad about Cindy hooking up with Ryan. When she came to me last year crying about her reputation, I shared with her my questionable choices with Jeff. I wanted her to understand that we all make mistakes. It seemed like she was understanding my reasons for doing it, and the many more reasons I had for not doing that ever again.

I shouldn't blame Jeff or dislike him as much as I do. It isn't his fault I view our interactions the way I do. I just wanted to be taken seriously, and I was afraid if I had developed a relationship with someone on my crew I would be seen in a different light. I wonder if Ted and Chuck ever knew. God, I hope not.

That would be very embarrassing. As I lie here thinking about it, it occurs to me that Jeff probably never felt that way. He didn't have to worry if people thought he was sleeping his way into a job. Life is so unfair. It's like I constantly need to know more, to be the best. I can never complain, never say it's too hard, absolutely never cry. That was something I decided on my first day. If I lose an arm, I'll just be like that Black Knight guy on Monty Python's Holy Grail. Totally fine. Yep. Not bleeding at all.

Ugh.

That's why having fun and sleeping with Jeff felt like such a bad idea. It was a betrayal of who I wanted to be. Well, who I wanted to be seen as.

I close my eyes and roll over, hoping sleep will just take me away from the uncomfortable knot that has formed in my stomach. I toss and turn for all of three seconds. Apparently, I'm way too tired to be kept awake, even with regret.

The sun beating on the side of my tent didn't wake me, the sprinkler that I had set up by didn't wake me, and the fucking backup bell of every engine that has ever been made didn't wake me. Nope, I slept through breakfast and woke an hour before lunch. Considering I crawled into my tent at six o'clock last night, this is incredible.

I stretch and groan at the pain that lives in every muscle I own, including my ears. Fuck. How? Luke was right. Why are my ears tired?

I roll over onto my stomach and unzip the window flap so I can peer out. There are some people taking down their tents, while others are stumbling in after a long shift on the line. I can see Luke stretched out under a tree with the book I loaned him tucked under his leg. He is out cold, sleeping like he isn't surrounded by fifty other people. I smile. He probably got up early wanting to read, then fell asleep because we've worked way too much. He did a great job swamping for me. Stupid manzanita brush. I will take felling pine trees any day over sawing my way through that shit. I'm sure that's where all my bruises came from. It was like hacking away at a never-ending sticker patch.

We fell into a good rhythm and made a lot of progress before we got relieved, but man, that was tough. I think I had dreams of cutting a branch only to have it grow right back.

I rub my hands over my face and stand as best as I can in my tent. I grab the clothes I wore for dinner last night and change, then climb out of my tent and head over to Luke to wake him up for lunch. His head rests on the big root of the oak tree like it's a feather pillow. I swear this guy could sleep anywhere.

"Luke. Dude. Wake up. Let's get lunch," I say, kicking at his boot.

"Five more minutes, Mom," he says without opening his eyes.

"Come on. I slept through breakfast. I'm hungry," I whine.

"Damn it, Kenny." His eyes pop open and he says, "I was having a dream about Zia."

"Sorry. I'm sure you can pick back up later. You need food."

"True." He stands and tucks the book under his arm.

We walk toward the chow hall, and I glance around, wondering if Jeff is still in camp. Because Luke is some kind of wizard, he says, "He left. Went back to San Diego with his engine."

"Who?" I ask, trying to play dumb

"Your fuck buddy, Jeff." Luke turns to me with a smirk.

"Right. So you saw him too?"

"Yeah, he found me when I came out of the shower. He asked if I knew which tent was yours, and of course, I lied and said no," Luke grabs a plate and hands it to me.

"Thanks," I say. Damn, this is embarrassing.

"You know I don't judge you. Why does it bother you so much that you guys hooked up? It's not like you were hung up on him, you were just having fun. Cut yourself some slack, Kenny." Luke reaches over and gently pushes me on the shoulder.

"Yeah, I guess." I blow out a breath, then say, "I just wish I hadn't, you know? I feel like..." I trail off.

"I get it," Luke says with a smile. "Hey, I'm almost done with that book you loaned me. What did you think of that Kent Price book?"

"Oh, I haven't read much more. Seriously, I fell asleep last night as soon as my head hit the ground. I'll read it today when I'm doing my laundry."

"Yeah, I'm going to ask Patrick if I can get book two as soon as we get back. I should just ask for the entire series," Luke says.

"You better just get one book at a time. I know you, and you'll try to read them straight through."

"True," Luke says with a chuckle.

Luke and I eat lunch, then I head back to my tent and gather my laundry and make my way to the local laundromat that is about a block from here. This is the biggest fire camp I have been to, not that I have been around much to enjoy it. The camp is set up at the fairgrounds, so there are real showers, a huge indoor chow hall, and a really nice grassy area for our tents. I have been sleeping on sticks and rocks while out on the fire line, so the soft grass is amazing.

I grab the book from my bag and open to where I left off. Kent and the girl had just had some pretty exciting sex on the balcony of the party where they met. He was a fast talker and was able to charm her out of her underwear in record time. None of his lines would have worked on me. I mean, I don't really fall for that kind of stuff. I think back to the night at the ranch when I was willing to do whatever Patrick wanted, and I realize it wasn't because he told me I was "beautiful like a Hawaiian sunset" or whatever.

We had just talked, learned about each other, and it felt so right. His hands on me had been like a drug. It wasn't like that with Jeff or Tommy, my college boyfriend. It wasn't like that with anyone else I fooled around with.

Patrick was the one to pull back that night, not me. That isn't something this Kent Price guy would do. He is all about the conquest, the score. I set the book down and go to switch over my clothes into the dryer. I've never known anyone who writes books, just Mitchell and his poems. I know the story behind most of his poems because he and I talked about them. It was obvious how badly he hurt when he lost Helen. He had loved her so much my heart ached at his story. It was too much. His poetry was a window into his soul. I knew him better after reading them.

Is that how it works with fiction writers? I mean, his books must reflect some part of his personality, right? Kent Price, the aggressive guy who gets what he wants, then moves on. Crap. What have I gotten myself into? I don't want to be someone's conquest. I haven't really given my love life much thought in the past year, since I've been so focused on firefighting and learning all I can. I didn't intend to date anyone, but then that stupid, handsome, bumbling professor Patrick came into town with his adorable questions and mild hysteria. God, he is ridiculous and cute.

I sigh and plop back down, picking up the book. I can't believe he wrote eleven more of these. How? How does someone come up with so many fresh ideas? He must have a very good imagination. Mitchell owned all of these, and he knew his great-nephew wrote them. I wonder why he never mentioned that. I feel like he was pretty open with me, although, come to think of it, he only told me about Helen. He didn't really talk about his family. I think Rusty mentioned Mitchell had a brother once, but he passed away. I think when you make it to ninety-four there aren't many people still alive who you knew growing up, family or otherwise.

I force myself to focus on the book in my lap.

"KENT RAN *his fingers across her cheek and stared down into her sleeping face. She was the key. He knew that now. Fernando wouldn't get away this time. He climbed out of bed and ripped a page out of the phone book, scrawling a message to her. She would learn soon enough who he really was, but hopefully Fernando would be in jail before that ever happened. He could protect her if he left now.*"

MY EYES ARE heavy from reading, even though it wasn't very long. I'm still exhausted from the past week, I guess. Setting the book down, I get my clothes from the dryer. Once everything is folded and back in my laundry bag, I hoist it over my shoulder. I'm looking down when I walk out, so I don't see Ryan, who is coming in. We hit shoulder to shoulder, and I glance up to apologize.

"Fuck, Kendra. Watch where you are going," he snaps.

"Sorry. I didn't see you. Don't get your panties in a bunch."

"Fuck off," he hisses, and I walk on. He isn't worth it. Not today, not ever.

Once I'm back in my tent, I put my laundry away and tuck the book under my sleeping bag. Really wish I could finish it, but my eyes can't take it. I need to do something else for a while. Luke seems like an excellent distraction, so I set off in search of him. He's easy to locate with his tall frame and blonde hair. He's by the payphone talking to Zia, I assume. I sigh and take the other open one, dialing the number for the ranch.

I don't know what to say, but it will be nice to hear his voice again. Maybe this doesn't have to be weird. Maybe I'm creating problems where they don't exist.

"Hello, this is Patrick Smith, the new owner of the Smith Ranch. If you are calling about the cattle, I'm aware they have gotten loose, and I'm working with Rusty to fix the situation. If this is Kenny, hi. I, um, hope you are okay. I miss having you around. Okay, well, leave a mess—" The answering machine cuts him off with its loud beep.

I almost hang up but feel bad. How long has that been his outgoing message?

"Hey Patrick, it's me, Kenny. Sorry I couldn't call. This fire has been kicking our asses. I'm fine. Not sure when we are getting released. I hope you were able to catch the cattle. I bet Rusty was real friendly about all that. Well, shoot. I'll try to call later." When I hang up, I see Luke smiling at me, arms folded across his chest.

"Well, well, well... Now why would you be calling Patrick? That is a very interesting development. Did something happen after that night I walked in on you almost kissing?" His eyebrows are doing a wonderful impression of dancing caterpillars. "Would you care to fill me in on those details, or will I need to get you a few beers first?" He has a very big, stupid smile plastered across his face.

"Beer. Definitely. Wait, is that even an option?" I ask, looking around.

"Yep, there's a bar a few streets over. Come on. I might have a story or two for you about our favorite author," Luke says, linking his arm with mine and leading me to the neighborhood bar.

COWBOY POETRY
UNPUBLISHED WORK

Leather creak and saddle squeaks
Angers the old man
My body reeks
My aches and pains
Angers the old man
There is no joy out here in the brush
Cattle wander, cattle lost
All seem to
Anger the old man
~By Patrick Smith 1988

TWENTY
PATRICK

When Rusty told me we would, and I quote, "Ride at dawn," I thought he meant in his truck or mine. Nope. He meant ride horses.

Actual horses.

Jesus.

Did I mention that I have never even owned a hamster? I had exactly one friend growing up that had a dog, and to be honest, it wasn't much of a dog. It was a one-eyed chihuahua that had a thyroid problem and a goiter that was as big as its head. That's not the kind of dog you pet, or even want to look at. It still creeps into my nightmares more than I want to admit.

I got a call a week ago, or two weeks after Kenny left, because that is how I see time now. The cattle that were on Mitchell's property up in the high country (wherever that was) had broken through the fence line and were roaming onto BLM land. I tried to tell the person on the phone that whoever this BLM person was, he could just have my cattle since they were already on his property. I got a quick lesson in a few things. One, it's the Bureau of Land Management, and they did not want my cattle, nor do they want my cattle wandering around on their property. They also said that if they have to round them up, they will fine me. Actual money.

I made my way into town as quickly as I could and told Rusty my problem. I expected him to blame me or be mad, but he just told me the ride at dawn thing and walked back into the kitchen. So I went home and set my alarm for before dawn, and I'm sitting on my front porch when Rusty rides up on one horse, leading another by the reins.

I stand and wipe my very sweaty hands on my jeans. Thankfully, I have on jeans and boots and one of Mitchell's shirts, because if I had been in my shorts and Top-Siders, Rusty probably would have shot me.

"I'm going to go grab some barbed wire and a few things we will need to fix the fence. You stay here with the horses. Don't walk behind them unless you want to get kicked in the face." Rusty climbs down and drops the reins, and the horses wander over to my nicely mowed grass and begin to help themselves.

Well, this is about to be the most interesting day of my life, or the last day. Maybe both. I watch the very large horses grazing on the grass and try to psych myself up for the inevitable. I'm going to be sitting on one of those monsters soon.

Rusty comes up and drops a leather bag at my feet. I look up at him expectantly, but he doesn't say anything. He walks over to the horses with the things he retrieved from the cattle shed. There's a length of barbed wire coiled tightly that he wraps a piece of leather around before adding it to the bag on his horse, then pulls out some tools from his back pocket and does the same thing with them. He looks up at me with his narrowed eyes, and I freeze. My balls decide that being inside my body again is a good thing and my ass is sweating like I'm on fire. The reality is only a second or two pass before he speaks, but a part of me realizes I will not survive this excursion if his glances cause that reaction.

"Go pack. You can use that saddlebag. We will be gone about a week," Rusty says.

"Okay. Sure. A week? Like seven days? Where are we staying?" I ask, somehow finding the nerve.

"Out under the stars. Well, one night at the cabin, but mostly outside. Mitchell has a bedroll in the front hall closet. Grab that and maybe two shirts. Shouldn't be cold at night." Rusty closes his saddlebag and leaves to fill his canteen and hopefully mine.

I go inside filled with apprehension and more than a little terror, but oddly also a little bit of excitement. This is so far out of my comfort zone I feel like I need to grab a passport. A deep breath helps calm my nerves a bit as I grab a few things, including a couple of pens and my notebook. God, I'm really doing this. I'm really going out on a cattle drive. I'm a cowboy. It's like I'm Wyatt Earp. Might as well change my name to Patrick Wyatt. Has a nice ring to it.

I mosey back out to the front yard where my trusty steed is waiting. I wonder what his name is. His? Maybe it's a she. Why did I assume the horse was a boy? Damn, that is probably a rookie move. If I can get through this without Rusty killing me, it will be a miracle.

In my excitement to pack and leave, I forgot to change my outgoing message, but it should be fine. At least Kenny will know I'm thinking about her. I really do hope she is okay. I said that, right?

Now, days later, as I lie here under the stars on a bedroll that smells like mothballs (and sadly, sinus infection breath), I'm amazed to still be alive. Neither Rusty nor that demon horse have managed to kill me in the four days since we left the ranch. I only fell off my horse (Penny is her name, and she was born from the devil himself) twice. Once was my fault. I assumed I would need a lot more force to get myself up and into the saddle. This wasn't true, and I launched myself over the horse, not unlike Mary Lou Retton in the 1984 Olympics. I, however, did not stick the landing.

The second time Penny decided she was done having me on her back, she tried to drown me. She waded into a river, which Rusty called a creek later just to irritate me, and started splashing around. I had no idea horses did such a thing, and I may have let go of the reins, falling on my ass in the shallow end. Rusty had an asthma attack after laughing so hard, but I'm going to let that go. He's been surprisingly not murderous toward me. He has actually taught me a lot.

The first and most important thing I learned from Rusty is that Rusty doesn't like it when you talk or breathe. Also, the way I sit on top of the horse is super annoying. I think the way I screamed when the horses broke into a sprint, or "trot" as he called it, also made him angry.

The stars above me right now kind of make up for all of it. The long days in the saddle, and watching Rusty work with the cattle, moving his horse in such a way that communicates to the cows that they should go in a different direction. It is a language all its own, one I'm sure I will never understand.

I am, however, starting to understand these stars. Their brightness, quiet, still, and constant, fills a part of me I didn't know was empty. I have fallen asleep easily each night; the fatigue of the day taking over as soon as I lie down. Tonight is different. I might be getting used to the routine, or maybe the stars are brighter tonight.

I wonder if Kenny is working right now. I wish I had been able to talk to her before I came up here. At least we will have a lot to talk about once she comes back home. I will tell her how I rustled cattle, mended fences, and ate by an actual campfire. I will leave out my experience with tobacco. No one needs to know about that. My only hope is that Rusty was so disgusted by my attempt to "enjoy a dip," as he called it, that he will never speak of it.

I didn't know that one could empty the contents of one's stomach in such a violent manner. I also didn't know that barfing on a fire "ruined it forever" and a whole new fire would have to be built. See the things I'm learning?

I close my eyes and picture Kenny next to me, holding me and kissing me. She also has a milkshake from the Frosty in her hands.

I think I'm going a little crazy out here.

We have been out on the trail for five days now, and I haven't seen the cabin Rusty mentioned when we started this journey. I'm starting to think there isn't a cabin, and he just said that to make me hopeful. The next day when we saddle up again, I look around at the sagebrush and rocks and wonder how much of this land belongs to Mitchell. Is all this his? We have stopped several times to fix sections of fencing that are sagging or have completely come undone. No wonder the cattle got out.

I wonder how often this kind of maintenance needs to be done. Had Mitchell been doing this, or was it all up to Rusty? I know he has his own land and cattle to worry about. I don't like that he has doubled his responsibility just because my uncle passed away.

I wish I already knew how to do this. I take a deep breath and try to remember what Kenny said about the lawn mower. This is something I could learn. I shouldn't just be expected to know these things because I'm a guy. Watching this sixty-something-year-old man for the last few days has made me feel like I'm missing a few things to hold the title of "man." I bet if I ask Rusty, he will tell me all the things I'm doing wrong—starting with not being able to handle tobacco and probably ending with my ridiculous walk.

My legs have stopped speaking to me, and I don't really have the ability to bring my knees together anymore. He thinks I'm trying to, as he puts it, "walk like a cowboy." That isn't it at all. I'm just trying to live my life and hope that my balls drop back down where they belong.

We haven't seen any more wayward cows since the second day. Rusty managed to get them all back on the ranch land, then we spent a whole day moving them away from the fence line and toward where Rusty originally thought they were. I've had more questions than I expected, and it's because I'm having second thoughts about selling the cattle.

When I saw them for the first time, something shifted in my soul. This is what my great-uncle did. This was a part of who he was, and what he left me. We were both writers. Maybe we could both be ranchers? Why am I so willing to give up before I even try? I could learn things. For example, I learned how to mow a lawn, how to sit on a horse when it really didn't want me on its back, and I learned how to make Rusty smile. Well, that has only happened once and hasn't been replicated, but I'm nothing but hopeful now.

So as we ride along checking the fence line, a real thing by the way, I think about ways I can learn to be a cattle rancher. Rusty doesn't seem opposed to showing me how to do things like reattaching the barbed wire. I mean, he only grunted when I stood near him; he didn't shove me away. That is a start, right?

The land rises beneath us, and I realize we have been on this ridge before. Looking around, I recognize the spot where the cattle broke through onto the BLM land. I swivel my head and am pleased to see the tall pines mixing with the lower sagebrush. Rusty stops his horse and waits for me to come alongside. I'm starting to think like a cowboy. Not going to lie, I enjoy it.

"What's next?" I ask.

"We are heading down this ridge to the cabin." He points to the left, where a small trail winds down the ridge into a valley.

"Lead the way," I say, pulling back on the reins to move out of the way. Penny is getting used to me, and I have to brag here: I think she might actually like me now.

Rusty grunts, his primary form of communication, and leads his horse down the trail. I follow behind him and marvel at how the vegetation can change so much in such a short time. On the higher ridges there is nothing but bushes, dead grasses, and stickers that like to hitch a ride on anything that walks past. As we drop into this valley, there are pine trees and green grass, different manzanita bushes and flowers. Lots and lots of wildflowers run along in a winding pattern, and I realize as we approach they are following a creek. God, it's beautiful.

Rusty stops at the stream and hops off his horse, so I do the same. He pulls the saddle and reins off, and I watch as he slaps his horse on the rump. That must be his signal, because she wanders off into the meadow.

"Are we taking a break?" I ask, sliding my saddle off Penny and setting it next to where Rusty put his. I've learned that if I do exactly what he does, he wants to punch me less.

"The cabin is right through those trees. The horses will get a drink and eat here," Rusty says.

I look to where he pointed and can just make out the small, wood-framed cabin. It's tucked among some pine trees with a wide dirt patch surrounding it. My whole body seems to react to the sight of it. I feel my heart skip, and I take a breath before clearing my throat. "Did Mitchell come here a lot?" I ask.

"Yeah. He did. This was the main house on the property until about 1950. He moved into town, into the house you live in now, around that time. Still came up here though. He loved it here." Rusty sighs, and I try to close my mouth. That is the most I have ever heard him say. It's like seeing a wild animal up close. I don't want to spook him and have him run off, so I just nod. I hold off on the thousands of questions I instantly had.

We walk along in silence, and I look back to where we left the horses, wondering if they will run off, leaving us stranded here. Rusty doesn't seem to be worried, so I take a breath and wait for him to unlock the cabin.

"I'm surprised it's locked. People in town never lock up," I say, looking over his shoulder as he releases the padlock holding the front door secure.

"We didn't lock up until a bunch of hunters decided to use the place as their personal hotel. They did a lot of damage, so Mitchell put the padlocks on. There are keys in the kitchen drawer at the ranch house if you want to come up here on your own," he says, again going over his yearly word count.

"I'd never be able to find this on my own," I say with a laugh, and Rusty raises his eyebrow.

"Just take the dirt road," he says, pointing to the wide dirt road that appears behind the cabin. "It takes about half an hour by truck. The turnoff is marked with black-and-white fire flagging. Just off County Road W." Rusty pushes the door open and goes in to open the only window I can see, allowing a breeze to flow through the small cabin.

I follow Rusty in and look around. I have never been in a real log cabin, and man, it does not disappoint. The logs that make up the walls are flat with the chinking smooth and flush with each log. It's incredible, and I want so badly to run my hand along the wood, but there is too much to take in. I almost don't know where to look first.

The far wall holds a fireplace that looks both too big for the space and perfect. It actually looks like the cabin has been built around it, like someone built the best fireplace in the world, then added a house. It's made of a light color rock and has a hand-hewn wooden mantle.

I feel a stirring, a sense of something, pride maybe. I don't know how to describe the feeling I'm having. It's a connection to my family, something I have been missing. I set my bag down and walk over to the fireplace, immediately reaching out to touch the cool stone, then run my hand along the mantle. I turn to ask Rusty a question only to find him staring at me, arms crossed over his chest.

"What?" I ask, afraid I have overstepped.

"Mitchell used to do that. First thing when he walked in, he went straight to that fireplace." Rusty shakes his head, then walks to where I'm standing.

"Except this is what he was after." He places his hand on the stone just under the mantle on the right side. He traces his finger over what looks like writing, stepping back so I can see.

A crude heart has been carved in the stone with the initials M.S. and H.L. then the year 1915. Under the heart are five lines, but they stop.

1920. When he lost her. I know, or at least I think I know based on his poetry. I'm not sure what I can ask, but I know if I don't at least try for some information, I will regret it.

"Mitchell and H.L., do you mind if I ask what her name was?" I ask.

"Helen," Rusty says. He walks over to the area that serves as a kitchen and reaches up to some shelves, pulling down two glasses and a bottle of whiskey. He pours some for us and rejoins me by the fireplace. Handing me a glass, he raises his and says, "To love that cannot be lost, even when God himself interferes."

I raise my glass and take a quick glance for any hairs or dust, then drink. Rusty traces his finger over Mitchell's initials, then Helen's.

"They only had five years together?" I ask.

"Nah, they knew each other for longer than that, but I don't think they knew what they had was love. Not at first, you know?" Rusty says, raising an eyebrow at me.

Mentally crossing my fingers, I ask, "How did you come to be friends with Mitchell?" I hope he will answer the one question that has been on my mind this whole trip. Hell, it has been on my mind since I met Rusty.

"Mitchell and my father were best friends growing up. My father was killed in a logging accident the year I was born, the same year Mitchell lost Helen," Rusty says, letting his hand finally drop to his side.

"So your mom and Mitchell..." I start, but Rusty shakes his head.

"Oh, right, sorry," I say.

"Everyone thought that was the story. You aren't the only one. No, my momma never got over losing Pop, and Mitchell never got over losing Helen. I guess Mom and him were friends of sorts, but mostly he and I just did stuff. We were as close as could be." Rusty wipes his hand down his face and says, "I'm going to go check on the horses. We can stay here tonight or ride back down the dirt road. It won't take more than an hour or so. Up to you."

He walks out, leaving me in this room that held so much love and sorrow. A bridge to the past has been laid out, welcoming me to come and explore. My head is filled with a sudden flurry of words, jumbling and tumbling, fighting to find a pattern. I sink onto the couch and finish the rest of the whiskey. Leaning back and closing my eyes, I try to let my mind settle. Allowing the words to take over, I retrace them again and again until they are mine.

Helen

Not enough time to know you
Not enough love to show you
How do I breathe without you
How do I carry on
When you held my heart in your hand
as you left.

I WIPE my eyes as I stare up at the ceiling. I can't stay here, not yet. Standing, I take my glass to the sink, setting it next to Rusty's. Heading out to find him, I plan on letting him know I would rather head back down to the ranch house. I glance around at the small space, hoping that someday I'll know more about the love that these two shared. It feels like a love story that needs to be told.

What kind of man was my great-uncle Mitchell? This man who took on his best friend's son and treated him as what? A son? A friend? All while grieving the loss of his Helen? There are so many questions that swim around in my head and my heart. I'm going to need a few days to let the questions lead me to what is most important. I don't think Rusty is ever going to be an open book, so if I only get to turn a few pages, they better be good.

Rusty seems relieved that I want to go, but as we get closer to town, his surly mood returns. I decide that it was the cabin's magical qualities that had him opening up and talking to me. There were a lot of emotions there, and I know it will be a great place to write someday, but I want to be home. I miss my bed, running water, and toilets. I also miss food that hasn't been pulled from Rusty's saddlebag. I crave food that requires refrigeration and possibly a beer. Oh, God. An ice-cold beer sounds like actual heaven.

Of course, I'm not letting myself think about the real reason I'm eager to get home. I wonder for the millionth time if she is back, or if I will at least have a message on my machine when I return. I don't know her that well, but I sure miss her. I miss her confidence, her humor. Turning in the saddle, I glance back down the road.

I wonder how many times Mitchell traveled this road with Helen. Not as many as he did without her, that's for sure. He had been twenty-six years old when he lost her, and twenty-one when he knew he loved her. Five years. Why hadn't they married? That seems unusual for the time, for this place. I mean, even now in 1988, this place tucked in the corner of Northern California seems lost in time.

The logging and cattle ranching lifestyle doesn't seem to keep pace with the rest of the world, and that is what makes up the economy up here. Life here is slow and peaceful and has quickly started to feel like home. It gave me pause, a little, when I thought about staying up at the cabin. The words that came to my mind were that I wanted to go home. I didn't mean Seattle. That hadn't been my home even when I lived there. To be honest,I haven't felt like any place was home since I lost my parents. They were home.

I was in my second year of college when they crossed the double-yellow line on a rain-slicked road, removing a word from my vocabulary.

Parents.

Gone, just like that. They would never read my finished book. They had seen the birth of Kent Price, knew my ideas about a series, but they were long gone when the first book went to print. Kent, at first, held their place. The place where people were proud of me and said things about how talented and creative I was. People's expressions at my first book signing were burned forever into my mind, mingling and confusing me. Pride. Awe. Wonder.

It's addicting, intoxicating. In my grief and loss, it was the only thing that kept me alive. That had me wondering again: what kept Mitchell going? Was it his poetry? Was it Rusty? If that was the case, and I'm almost positive it was, why on earth did he leave the ranch to me and not him? There are so many things I don't understand. So many questions that need to be answered.

COWBOY POETRY

UNPUBLISHED WORK

Rusty wire wound tight
Rusty nails driven deep
Rusted over time
Reminding me
You've always been here
Even when you left
~By M.S 1944
Discovered 1988

I've never been so happy to see a blinking light in my life.

I stand over the answering machine for a long time before I hit play. God, I want so badly for it to be from her that I almost can't do it. The immediate relief that hits me when I hear Kenny's voice is unbelievable. I have to listen to the message a few times to really absorb what she said.

She said she would try to call later, but that was a week ago, and there are no new messages after that one. I try not to worry, to understand that she is doing what she loves. A lot has happened in the last week. I have blisters and sore muscles. I slept on the ground, rode a horse, touched a cow, and mended a fence. Kenny will probably not even recognize me. To be honest, I don't recognize myself. I have never gone a week without shaving. What grew on my face couldn't really be considered a beard, but it's the closest I have ever come. Just running my hand over my face, I would have told you I have a nice, thick growth of hair. Finally seeing it in the mirror is a bit of a punch to the gut.

My "mustache" doesn't quite reach the hair on my chin, so it looks like I had two different ideas that never gelled into one. My facial hair is like I started to write a mystery book but ended with a biography of some random person no one actually knows. The hair on the sides of my face sticks straight out and grows in weird patches, like I have mange. One side has grown longer than the other, making me wonder if that's normal.

The stuff on my upper lip doesn't even have the decency to cover the whole thing. The center bit has zero hair. None, not even a stray. It's as if a caterpillar had a fight with its mate and they agreed to go their separate ways.

I bet this is why Rusty was so irritated with me. He has a majestic, long, white beard that makes him look like a fucking wizard. I looked like Wolfman Jack's stunt double after a fire.

Damn it.

After I shower and rinse off, I shave. Seeing my soft, smooth skin again brings me a little sadness. I'm not even man enough to grow a decent mustache. I can try again, and maybe it won't look like a cartoon villain, but that seems unlikely. Pulling on a pair of shorts and an old T-shirt, I head into the kitchen to make something to eat. That ice-cold beer is waiting, as well as more than a few different kinds of cheese. I make my mom's famous baked macaroni and cheese with a breadcrumb crust and put it in the oven to cook. I take my beer into the living room and sink into the recliner, kicking my feet up. There is no television here at the ranch, and I haven't really missed it. When I first got here, I thought about getting one, but the more time that has gone by, the more I realize I don't miss it. I've just taken a long pull from my beer when I hear the strangled ring of the phone in the kitchen. God, it makes an awful noise. I really should have picked up a new phone when I was down in Redding.

I slam down the footrest of the recliner and run to the kitchen to answer the phone.

"Hello?" I'm breathless not from the quick jog, but because it might be her.

"Patrick?" a female voice asks.

"Kenny? Is that you?"

"Yeah. Hey!" she says, over the loud music in the background.

"Where are you?" I pull the kitchen chair over to sit. My legs are still angry with all the horse riding I did.

"Oh, we are still down in LA at that fire, but I'm on my day off, so Luke and I hit the bar. I can't believe I caught you at home!" she says.

"I'm glad you did. I just got in a few hours ago. Rusty and I were gone about a week."

"Did you get all your cattle back?"

"Yeah, the fence was down, and once we got them back over onto Mitchell's land, Rusty showed me how to repair it. Kenny, I rode a horse," I say, pride bubbling up in my chest.

"What? It sounded like you said you rode a horse. There is no way that is what you said." She laughs and I can almost picture her.

"No, that's what I said! I did! I rode a horse for like six days! I'm a cowboy now, Kenny. You won't recognize me when you get back."

"Wow. Well, I'm impressed. Rusty didn't kill you?" She asks because she knows the truth. He hates me just as much as he hates everyone.

"Nope. I lived. It's the thing I'm most proud of now." She laughs, the sound filling my heart with something I don't recognize. I reach up and rub at my chest.

"Well, I'm impressed, Patrick. Really impressed."

"Thanks. Hey, um, any idea when you'll be back?"

"I wish I knew. This fire is fully contained, meaning they have a line all the way around it and they've been releasing resources all day, but—" she says, and I interrupt her.

"Why is there always a but?"

"Yeah sorry, Ted said we might get sent to a station down here to cover for a week or so. I'll be able to call more often if that happens. Unless we get sent to another fire from that station. I guess I really don't have any solid information yet. Everything changes so much from minute to minute."

There are whoops and hollers from the other patrons in the bar, and Kenny laughs and yells back, "Fuck off!"

"What's happening?" I ask.

"Oh, they were just giving me a hard time about something that happened on the line the other day. It's nothing." She puts her hand over the mouthpiece and cusses at someone. It sounds like she said they couldn't cut a line in kindergarten, so that's why camels were brown.

What?

"Sorry about that. These guys are fucking idiots." She laughs and my stomach twists.

"Are you the only girl there?" I ask, hating myself instantly.

"Um, no. There are a few other chicks here at the bar tonight, and on the fire there have been a lot. Why?"

"Just curious. I don't really know that much about what you do. Hey, Kenny? I'm really glad you called," I tell her, not wanting to end on a weird note.

"I'm glad you were home. I guess I should go. It's getting more crowded in here and I probably won't be able to hear you for much longer," she says, then adds, "Oh hey, I read your first Kent Price novel. It was good!"

"Oh? You read that? Okay. Glad you liked it," I say, using my book signing voice.

"Yeah, well, okay. I'll try to call later this week or something," Kenny says.

"Okay, thanks again for calling. I already said that, but it was really great to hear your voice."

"You too."

"Bye, Kenny."

"Bye, Patrick."

The oven timer goes off as I hang up the phone, and I pull out my dinner, almost wishing that I hadn't answered the phone. Why did that feel so awful? I rub my hands over my face hard, trying to rid myself of the uncomfortable feeling I have. I take only a few bites when the phone rings again.

"Hello?" I say, half hoping it's her, but also hoping it isn't.

"Patrick Smith?" a male voice asks.

"Yeah, this is me," I answer, hoping to God the cattle haven't broken free again. My ass needs a rest.

"This is Thomas, Martin's assistant. He was hoping to schedule a meeting with you."

"Oh? Well, I'm not in town. I guess you know that since you called me here. Wait, how did you get this number?" I ask.

"Martin spoke with the attorney, and he shared the number where you are staying. Martin was hoping to meet on Wednesday at the office. Does that give you enough time?" Thomas asks.

"Um, yeah. I guess I can do that. I hadn't really planned on coming back to Seattle, but yeah. Okay."

"Great. I will put you in for eleven. Thank you." Thomas hangs up before I can answer. Well, damn.

If I have to go back, I might as well get all my stuff and list the condo for sale. I really don't want to live there anymore, and even if I decide not to stay here, I don't want to go back there. The thought of doing that drive again has me groaning, and I finish my mac and cheese, then grab another beer from the fridge. There has to be an airport somewhere around here, right? That will be the first thing I'll ask tomorrow when I go into town.

I had a horrible night's sleep. It's like the mattress suddenly realized its original owner was no longer here and it decided to rebel. I got poked by a spring that came through the worn top, and I had to scissor-kick myself out of the Mitchell-shaped hole I slept in. A groan is forced out as I sit up. I have a really nice king-size bed at my condo. I will definitely bring that back. Come to think of it, I really like all of my furniture, and some of this stuff is probably original to the house. I will need to rent a truck or hire someone to drive all my stuff here. That. That is the winner. I don't care how much it costs. I'm not making that drive again.

After breakfast, I climb into my truck, grateful for a different kind of horsepower, and head into town to ask about an airport. I can't help but glance over as I pass the ranger station. She isn't there, but my heart still wants to see her.

God, was I as awkward as I thought on that phone call last night? I guess I pictured our phone calls being some deeply romantic thing where she was leaning against the phone booth wall with a row of dimes ready so the call didn't drop. The rain beating against the glass doors would create an ambiance as I told her how much I had missed her. Instead, there was honky-tonk country music and yelling drunk men in the background. She didn't seem to want to talk, or maybe it really was getting loud in there.

I groan again and pull my truck over in front of the Frosty. They don't open till eleven, but sometimes Jenny is here early getting things ready. Today is one of those days, and I smile as I rap on the window with my knuckles. She looks up and smiles back, walking to unlock the door.

"I'm glad you're back! Did you guys get the cattle all back where they belong?" she asks, waving me in.

"Yep. I only fell off Penny twice, and I think I was kind of helpful a few times when Rusty was mending the fence." I beam at her.

"Nice job, Patrick." She pats my arm, and I feel like she just handed me an award for best cowboy. I really am a ridiculous person.

"Sorry to bother you, I bet you are trying to get ready for your day. I just have a quick question."

"Honey, you aren't bothering me. What do you need?" Jenny says kindly.

"Well, I need to go back to Seattle," I say, watching her face fall.

"Oh. I thought you were staying. Well, that's a damn shame." She shakes her head.

"No, I just have to go get the rest of my things, and I have a meeting with my agent."

"Really?" Her eyes go wide and a smile reappears on her face.

"Yeah, I like it here." My face splits into a big and genuine smile that feels foreign. I really do like it here. I feel at home.

"Okay, good. How can I help then?"

"Is there an airport near here? I really don't want to make that drive again."

"Sure is. I even know a pilot who might take you to Seattle," Jenny says with a little chuckle.

"Wait, what? No, that's not what I meant. I mean, like a big airport. You know?" I say nervously, picturing some terrifying one-propeller airplane that would most likely kill me.

"There is a big airport in Reno, about three hours from here, or down in Sacramento. Or you can just let Rusty take you. Up to you, sweetheart," Jenny says, raising one shoulder in a shrug.

My eyes go wide, and my mouth drops open as I ask, "Rusty?"

"Yeah, he's a pilot, has his own plane. I've flown with him a lot. He's quite good unless he's been drinking. Don't fly with him if he's already started on the whiskey," she says, looking at me with big, wide eyes like I gave her.

"Oh, right. Well, that does sound horrible. No, I don't want to bother Rusty, sober or not." I shake my head as I say that to really drive the point home.

"Patrick, I was teasing. He's never flown drunk. Hell, I don't even think he's ridden a horse drunk. He's down at the bar talking with Jimmy. Go ask him."

"Who's Jimmy?" I ask.

"Oh, that's right, you haven't met him. He and his wife were on a little vacation when you got here. Jimmy owns The Bar. Rusty was just helping him out while he was away. Now that Jimmy and Sandra are back, Rusty will be itching to do something. The man gets intolerable when he's bored. Really, you'd be doing the whole town a favor."

"Do you mean to tell me what I've been seeing is a happy Rusty?" I ask, allowing my face to show my genuine horror.

"Yep. He was downright cheerful getting to sling drinks at the bar. He usually works there one or two nights a week when Jimmy needs a break, but for the past two years he has taken over for a month or more while Sandra and Jimmy travel," Jenny says with a smile.

"And now he will be grumpy with nothing to do?" I ask for clarification.

"Yep. Let me ask you, was he almost pleasant out on the ride? You know, talking and stuff?" Jenny asks.

"Yes. It was a little unsettling," I admit.

"That is where he is happiest. Those are my favorite times with him. He needs to be busy, and if he's working outside fixing things, riding his horse? Well, that's just the best place he can be. Second to that is when he's flying," Jenny says.

I don't know what to say, so I just blink at her. She is serious. She wants me to ask Rusty to fly me to Seattle. Well, damn.

"Go on and ask him. I got work to do around here, and if you stick around much longer, I'll make you clean out the fryer."

"Okay. I'll go. Thanks, Jenny. I guess I'll ask him, and when he punches me in the face, I'll call the Reno airport and get the flights to Seattle." I smile and wave before heading back out the door.

I walk down to The Bar, happy to see the door propped open. The smell of cigar smoke and men laughing drifts out the door. I pause, unsure how to approach Rusty with such a big favor.

"I'm sure you'll meet him soon enough. Spitting image of Mitchell, just so you know. I about had a heart attack the first time I saw him," Rusty says.

"He a good kid?" a male voice I presume belongs to Jimmy asks.

"Yeah, I didn't want to think so, but he seems to be. Doesn't know shit about cattle or anything, but he's trying," Rusty answers.

I freeze. I can't walk in now right after they have been talking about me. Crap. I'll just stand here and wait a few minutes. Hopefully, they will move on to another topic, and I can wander in as if I hadn't overheard Rusty say something nice about me.

I let my breathing go shallow and pray that I won't have to sneeze or anything. Jimmy seems to have a thousand questions about me and the ranch, and Rusty is like an old lady at the hair salon. Gossiping about all things me, including the night I saved Kenny from getting kicked out.

"Oh, hell, I'd pay money to see that! I bet Kenny could kick his ass. I saw the engine from Canby at the station. Are Ted and the crew off on a fire?" Jimmy asks.

"Yeah, 'bout a month gone now. Not sure when they'll be back. Zia's pop said he heard they might be gone another month," Rusty says.

"Damn, I bet he's glad to be rid of that Luke kid. That boy is smitten with Zia. I half expected him to show up this year with a ring."

The two men start to laugh, and I take that as my opportunity to walk in.

"Rusty? You in here?" I ask as I look around, letting my eyes adjust to the dark room.

"Yep. Whatcha need?" Rusty says, not turning around.

I walk up to the bar and stick out my hand to the man who I assume is Jimmy.

"Hi. I'm Patrick. I don't believe we've met."

"Well, butter my butt and call me a biscuit. You do look like Mitchell," Jimmy says. He doesn't extend his hand, so I slowly lower mine and wipe it on my shorts.

"I'm his great-nephew, Patrick. You are?"

"Looking at a ghost. Jesus. How old are you?" he asks, squinting at me.

"Um, thirty-two," I say, looking over at Rusty like he might help me with this.

"Yeah, that's about right. Damn," Jimmy says, then turns to Rusty and asks, "Isn't that about the age Wallace was when he left?"

"Nah, he was like twenty-eight when he got that job offer."

"Wallace Smith? My grandfather? You knew him?" I ask, stunned.

"Well, yeah. He grew up here, just like Mitchell. Didn't you know that?" Jimmy asks, his eyes narrowing again.

"No. I didn't know about Mitchell at all until he passed away. I was pretty little when my grandpa died. My dad didn't talk about him too much, just shared a few things about Grandpa's military service." I've been feeling ashamed about my lack of family history knowledge since I got that letter from the attorney.

"Your parents died about, what, ten years ago?" Jimmy asks, surprising me.

"I think it's coming up on thirteen years now," I say.

"Right, well, I'm sorry about that. Your dad came here a few times when he was little. He was a good kid. Mitchell really liked him even though he was Wallace's son," Jimmy says, and Rusty laughs.

"Did my grandpa and Mitchell not get along?" I ask, sitting down at the bar.

Jimmy and Rusty both shrug.

"As well as two stubborn mules could, I guess. I think Mitchell was mad that Wallace chose to leave the valley. So much had happened, and I always thought Wallace just wanted an out. So when that construction company out of San Francisco came up here looking for workers, he jumped on it. Never even asked Mitchell what he thought," Jimmy said.

I glance over at Rusty to see what he thinks of all of this, but he just takes a drink of his coffee. I turn back to Jimmy and say, "Wallace met my grandmother in San Francisco. They lived there for years. My dad grew up there and probably would have stayed forever if he hadn't gone to college up north and met my mom."

"Yep, that's how I heard it. Mitchell was sad that your pop didn't want to move up here and work on the ranch. He asked him a few times over the years, and your dad always shot him down," Jimmy explains.

"Wow. I had no idea. I wish my parents had brought me up here, or even talked about Mitchell. I hate that I can't ask them," I say, looking at my hands, which I've placed on the bar.

"Can I get you a coffee or something?" Jimmy asks.

"Sure, that sounds great."

Jimmy pours me a cup of coffee and slides it over in front of me, watching me with curiosity.

"So you have no memory of coming up here then?" he asks, and I think I catch Rusty slowly shaking his head.

"I came here? To Adin? No, I don't remember that."

Rusty chimes in, "Well, you were only about two years old. Your mom and dad were on their way back from the city, and they came up here with you. It was the only time Mitchell got to see you."

"Oh, God, I wish I knew that. There are a few boxes of pictures in my condo back in Seattle. I'll look through them and see if there are any from that trip." As I say that it reminds me of my purpose for being here, and I turned to Rusty.

"Hey, um, Jenny said I should ask you, but please don't feel obligated or anything, I mean you can punch me if you want, or I can just not ask," I blurt out, as that trickle of sweat start its journey to my ass crack.

"What?" Rusty barks out as Jimmy laughs.

"Jenny said you might be able to fly me to Seattle?" I say and hold my breath.

"Sure. When?" he says with a little shrug. Like I asked him to pass the sugar.

I blink.

"What? Really?" I ask.

"Well, you've kind of made it impossible for me to say no since you asked my wife about it," Rusty says.

"Your wife?" I stammer.

Rusty shrugs and Jimmy laughs again, just as Jenny comes walking in. She strides over and wraps one arm over Rusty's shoulder, giving him a little squeeze and a kiss on the cheek. Then she says, "Did he ask you yet? You'll take him, right? I'd like to go too if we can get Jessica to watch the Frosty for a few days. How long will you need to be gone, Patrick?" she asks.

"I have to meet with my agent on Wednesday. I think it will take me a few days to gather my stuff into boxes and hire a moving company."

Rusty interrupts, "So you are moving all your stuff here? That mean you are staying?"

"Well, yeah, that is the plan. I just sort of got in the car and drove here when the attorney called. I wasn't sure what it would be like or anything. Now that I have been here, I know I want to stay," I say. My stomach hurts. I decided to stay a while ago, but a lot of information was thrown at me in the last few minutes.

Rusty looks at Jenny and smiles. An actual smile, like he has teeth I have never seen before. He leans in and gives her a kiss right on her lips, and I feel like I might pass out. All I had thought I knew about this man is dissolving right in front of me.

"We can leave tomorrow. That way you'll have a day before your meeting. Does that work?" Rusty asks.

"Yes. That works. Rusty, I'm so grateful for this. I'll pay you. I mean, I don't expect you to do this for free, should have probably led with that. God, how rude of me. I will totally pay you."

Jenny covers her mouth with her hand to hide a laugh. She nudges Rusty with her elbow, nodding her head towards me.

Rusty sighs, "You can pay for the gas. We will leave at eight. I'll come by the ranch and get you."

"Okay. Wow. Thank you so much. I really appreciate this. I mean, I really, really appreciate it. So much," I say in a rush.

"Don't mention it. Go pack," Jenny says, then she turns to Rusty and tells him, "The fryer has gone to shit again. Come take a peek at it before I shoot it with a rifle?"

He laughs, as Jimmy wanders off into the kitchen leaving me to wonder when this alternate reality started. What if I fell on my head while we were out on the range?

Clouds soft
and puffy
Floating, twisting
below me
Above me
Beside me
As I scream
~by Patrick Smith 1988

TWENTY-TWO
PATRICK

I'll be walking back to Adin, since I'm never getting in an airplane with that lunatic again. I've lost all respect for Jenny too since she laughed so hard at my terror that I swear she peed her pants. There is nothing funny about a grown man screaming like a twelve-year-old girl. I know because I have been telling both Rusty and Jenny this for the last half hour. They disagree.

My agent was kind enough to get a rental car for us at the airport, so I drove to my condo with Rusty and Jenny in the back seat snickering like children. Their giggles get worse every time I try to explain why I screamed, so I just stop. Bunch of jerks.

I pull into the parking garage and grab my bag from the trunk, waiting for them to do the same. Jenny stands on her tiptoes and pulls me down so she can kiss my cheek. I almost accepted this as an apology, but she burst into laughter again. She is waving her hand in front of her face, trying to stop laughing, which is better than a doubled-over Rusty, but still. Come on.

With my anger still bubbling up inside me, I stomp up to the elevator and almost shut the doors on them, but I'm not an asshole. Even if I really wish I could be. Damn it.

When I get off the elevator, I reluctantly wait for them to follow before leading them down the hall to my door. It's so strange to be here, and even stranger with Jenny and Rusty. I kind of assumed they never left the valley, like trees rooted in place or something. Apparently, after returning from World War II, Rusty did two things: he bought an airplane so he could keep flying, and he married Jenny. They've flown all over, taking small vacations when they can. I have to give it to Jenny; she is brave as shit. She didn't even flinch when Rusty let the plane drop into what I will forever describe as a death spiral. He swears we just hit some turbulence. I don't believe it for even a second.

As I open the door to my condo, I let out a sigh, knowing I won't be able to stay mad at them, especially since they'll be staying here for the next few days.

"The guest room is the first door on the left in that hallway. There is a bathroom across from it," I say, dropping my keys on the table by the door.

Jenny steps in first and makes a whistling sound, with Rusty right behind her. He runs his hand over his beard and gives me a look I'm unfamiliar with seeing on his face. His gaze dances around the room, taking in every part of my condo, of who I used to be. He gives a slight shake of his head before taking the bags to the guest room.

Jenny turns to me and says, "This is a very nice place, Patrick. Are you sure you want to sell it?"

I glance around at what I can see of my three-thousand-square-foot condo and shrug. The top floor of this building is just me and an elderly couple next door. They have either gone on an extended vacation or died. I never see them, and since I didn't smell anything bad over the last year, I assume the vacation thing. It was lonely here. After Tricia messed with my head, this place seemed even less like home. The black leather couches and glass coffee tables feel so impersonal now. Those couches are comfortable as fuck though, so I'll be bringing them back to the ranch. The coffee tables and all the art and decorations will probably be sold. I didn't even pick them, so I'm not attached. Well, except for the painting in my bedroom. I want that. I actually missed it, as odd as that sounds.

"Yes, I want to sell. This didn't seem like home when I was living here, and it sure as hell doesn't seem like home now. Now that I know what that's like." It's hard to meet her eyes as I say that, so I inspect my shoes instead.

Jenny squeezes my arm just as Rusty comes back out. He is holding a small wooden bowl that was on the nightstand in the guest room.

"Where did you get this?" Rusty asks, his voice filled with anger.

"Um, I think it was in my parents' stuff. I'm not sure where they got it. It looked old and handmade, so I kept it. Why?" I ask.

"It was handmade. I made it," he pauses and ran his hand over his bald head. "I made it in high school and gave it to Mitchell for..." His voice trails off, and I see his head dip a little before he looks up at me.

"Would it be alright if I took this back?" Rusty asks in the most pained voice I've ever heard.

"Of course. Please. I just thought it was interesting. It clearly means something to you. It's beautiful that you made that for him. Like I said, I'm not sure how it ended up in my parents' things." Watching his pained expression I add, "I'm sorry."

Rusty lets out a breath that he didn't seem to know he was holding in. He shakes his head and tilts his face toward the ceiling. "Thought this was gone forever. I looked for it at the house after Mitchell died. I thought he threw it away."

Jenny moves over to him and puts her hand on his back. She rubs up and down rhythmically and smiles gently at him until he looks her in the eyes. A small smile cross his lips, and he nods. I marvel at their connection, the way he looks at her, as if she were his entire world.

"I told you he didn't thrown it away." Her voice is so soft and kind that it makes my eyes sting a little. I swallow and glance away, wanting to give them privacy.

"Yeah, okay," Rusty says in a small voice that again makes me feel like I'm intruding. Needing to be somewhere else, I go into the kitchen and open the window that runs along the wall. The sea breeze coming off the Sound hits me and makes me remember the one thing I like about this place. The views are incredible.

After a few moments, I duck back into the living room and quietly walk past them, grabbing my bag. Once in my bedroom, I glance at the painting above my bed. Soft pastels swirl around the edges of the canvas, with a blue streak curving through the middle. There are greens and browns that've always reminded me of trees, but this is an abstract. My mother hadn't painted any other way. It's as if she wanted the viewer to decide what she had created. I remember begging her to tell me what this was to her, but she never did. All I knew was that this was her favorite piece. It had been my father's favorite as well, and while it would probably sell for a lot of money, like the rest of her paintings had, it's priceless to me. I would never sell it.

I flop back onto my bed and sigh. Oh, yeah, I've missed this too. Jesus, was it always this soft? I may never get up, but as I close my eyes, I'm immediately thinking of all the things that need to be done in the next few days. Sleep will have to wait. I head back out to the main room where Rusty and Jenny are talking.

"Do you need the car, or can Jenny and I take it? I want to go down to get some seafood for lunch," Rusty says.

"Rusty, that is rude. Patrick, would you like to go to lunch with us?" Jenny says.

Laughing, I say, "No, that's okay. There's a lot of things to do around here. I won't need the car today at all, and just for a little tomorrow for my meeting with my agent. Have fun exploring Seattle. The doorman should be able to point you to a good place for lunch."

"No need. I've been here before," Rusty says as he grabs Jenny's hand, leading her out of the condo. I will never get over this new layer of Rusty. If I'm being honest, it kind of freaks me out.

I walk down the hall and into my office, chosen because it's the smallest of the bedrooms and it faces the Sound. I like to open the windows and let the city noises that bounce off the buildings on their way up to me. My desk faces the window, so more than one scene in Kent's exciting adventures was based on what I saw. I sink into the chair in front of my trusty old typewriter, running my fingers along the cold, black keys. God, I love the feel of the divots of each letter on the pads of my fingers. Memories of sitting, poised to write, fill my mind.My eyes close as I let my fingers hover above them, the dance of anticipation of what was coming. There were times when I didn't know what was about to happen to Kent. My fingers knew, though, and they would fly across the keys, desperate to get the story out. I would read as I wrote, amazed at the twists and turns, never really knowing where they came from.

Taking a piece of paper from the waiting stack, I tuck it in the back, twisting the knob to pull it through like I've done thousands of times before. I tab over and let my fingers hover, waiting to see if they have a story to tell.

TWO MONTHS GONE
    From field to sea
    Lost without you
    Lost in me
    Who am I here?
    These walls no longer know
    The sea doesn't recognize my face
    The Sound doesn't remember my ears
    The fields know
    I will return.

I PAUSE and let out a breath. Another poem. It's all there is lately. They come out easily and sometimes wake me up. There are several pages in my notebook back at the ranch that carry words from my soul. I know what Martin is going to ask me tomorrow. What am I working on, and when will it be done?

I never minded these meetings during my Kent Price years. That guy had a lot of stories to tell me. I just sat and typed them out. Now? I have ideas, sure. Solid plots? No. Strong characters? Maybe. I want to write about Mitchell and Helen, but can I? Can I embellish something like that, taking the bones of a genuine love story and pulling flesh and blood from nowhere? Does that diminish what they had?

I also want to understand what happened between Mitchell and my grandfather. I stand and walk to the closet where I keep all the bank boxes filled with pictures and family papers. It doesn't feel right to go through them now. To be honest, it didn't feel right when I cleaned out my parents' home either. I wonder if it never will? After their death, I didn't throw away a single piece of paper, afraid I would miss something important. Of course, there were plans to go through each box, and then my life as an author took off, and I never even opened the boxes.

When I get to the kitchen, I pull open the junk drawer, grab the phone book and a pen before walking to the table with both. My cordless phone sits on the counter, and I notice my answering machine says there are three messages. I've been in Adin for over two months, and I only have three messages. I hit play listening to the first message for someone named Rick, who had oranges for sale apparently, and this guy Phil wanted two crates. The next message is a political campaign to which I donated money five years ago, and the last one is Martin, who forgot I had left.

My stomach is tight, and my eyes burn a little. I try to take a deep breath, but it's as if my throat is trapped in someone's grip and they are squeezing. Jesus, I'm so fucking tired of being alone, so tired of no one missing me. No one wondering if I'm okay. Fuck. I didn't realize how depressing this would be.

I grab the cordless and move back to the table to start the process of finding a moving company. Once I book a company, I go through each room and write down the things I want to take to my new place and another list of the things I want to donate or sell.

There is no concept of the day moving along outside my windows until I hear Jenny and Rusty come in. I glance at the clock on the wall, and my eyes grow wide. It's eight o'clock at night, and I have eaten nothing since we left Adin this morning.

"I brought you some clam chowder in one of those bread bowls. It's still hot, so come sit and eat," Jenny says, walking to the table with a plastic bag. She sets the bag down, then goes to the cupboard next to the sink and pulls out a plate, then finds my glasses. She pours some water for me and brings both over to the table and sets them down.

"Thank you. I didn't realize it had gotten so late, didn't eat lunch or dinner." I rub my eyes, noticing for the first time how heavy they are.

"Your Uncle Mitchell was the same way. If he had a project he was working on, we always made sure to pop in with some sort of food for him. He would just forget to eat."

I smile. I enjoy hearing how Mitchell and I are the same. It makes me feel connected to my family again. Occasionally, I would run into someone who knew my parents, but they would just say something generic, like it wasn't the same without them around. I didn't have anyone to tell me my eyes were just like my dad's or that I had my mother's creative mind. I had to remember those things on my own, and filling up your own bucket isn't always easy. Especially since my bucket is full of holes.

"Thank you for that," I say to Jenny. Rusty has said nothing since he came in. He is just leaning against the counter with his arms folded across his chest while staring at me. I'm getting used to it since it seems to be how he interacts with most people.

I pull out the takeout container and let the wonderful smell of warm sourdough bread and clam chowder fill my nose. Okay, the view and the food. Those things I miss. I dig in and don't speak until every last crumb is gone. I wipe my mouth with the paper napkin that came from the restaurant. How Rusty knew to go to this little local secret is a mystery to me. It's the best place to get fish and chips and clam chowder in all of Seattle.

I lean back in my chair and pat my stomach, smiling. "Thank you so much. God, I didn't realize how hungry I was. I have to say, when I was writing, I had to set food by the typewriter before I would start for the day, or I would have forgotten to eat."

Rusty grunts and comes to sit at the table with Jenny and me. His stare bores into me until the familiar bead of sweat forms. He clears his throat and glances at Jenny before saying, "Mitchell liked to write out at the cabin, said that is where he was close to Helen and Wallace. He missed them both terribly, right up until the day he died."

I freeze. I have so many things I want to ask him, but I'll wait to see what he volunteers.

"They were like the three amigos, you know? Helen and Wallace were in the same grade, two years younger than Mitchell, but the three of them went everywhere together. Helen was a tough gal, not unlike our Kenny. I think that is why Mitchell took such a shine to her. Helen could do anything the boys could do, and sometimes she could do stuff they couldn't. The cattle weren't afraid of her, so she could get them to come up for the branding like they were getting a treat." Rusty shakes his head and lets a little smile dance across his face.

"The way he talked about them always made me wish I had known them. Wallace came back once, but I was only eight so I don't remember very much of him, but it's like I knew him from the stories Mitchell would tell and, of course, the poems he wrote," Rusty says, and I see Jenny reach her hand under the table. I assume she is rubbing his leg because he tips his head and smiles at her.

Letting out a sigh, he continues, "There should be a box of poetry somewhere in the house. I remember he sent some in to that book company when they were compiling poems for their cowboy poetry book."

"I've seen that book, but I haven't found a box of poetry. I will be sure to look for that."

"Well, it's got to be there somewhere. I'd love to read them again if you come across them."

I can't help but ask; the words tumble out before I can stop them. "Did you ever write?" He just shakes his head no.

"You and your uncle have a gift, honey. Not everyone can make the words all line up and paint a picture the way you can. I can barely leave a note for the repair guy. I mean, I can write, but he never seems to understand what I want done!" Jenny says with a laugh.

"That's because the last note you left him said, 'The fucking thing won't work,' Jenny! You should have told him that the heating coil had gone out. He can't read your goddamn mind," Rusty says with more kindness than I have ever heard from him.

"Was your dad a writer too, Patrick?" Jenny asks after giving Rusty a playful shove.

"No, my mom was an artist, but my dad was more of a numbers guy. He got a lot of joy from his accounting firm. It was a mystery to me and Mom."

"Oh, what kind of art did your mother like to do? What was her medium?" Jenny asks.

"She was a painter mostly, but sometimes she would sculpt with clay. I think painting was her therapy," I say, remembering my mom in her studio covered in paint and laughing as her paintbrush told stories across the canvas.

"Do you have any of her paintings?" Jenny asks.

"I have several in storage, but I have one here at the condo that I love. Do you want to see it?" I ask.

"Yes!" Jenny says, and Rusty surprises me by nodding his head too.

I stand and lead them down the hall to my room. When I turn on the light, I step aside so they can come in. I motion to the large canvas above my bed, and Jenny gasps.

"The cabin! Oh my God. It's beautiful." She covers her mouth with her hands and takes a small step forward. I look at Rusty. His eyes have gone wide and his mouth drops open a bit. He reaches up and touches the corner of his eye, then wipes his fingers on his jeans.

"That's a damn fine painting," he says with a crack in his normally gruff voice.

"The cabin?" I ask and tilt my head to look at the painting that has hung above our fireplace in my home for as long as I can remember. There are no clear lines, just blurs of colors: greens and blues and browns, pastels around the edges. I have seen this painting a thousand times and thought I saw trees. Never until this moment have I seen what it really is.

"Holy shit. It *is* the cabin." I cover my mouth like Jenny did. My heart thumps like it's going to beat out of my chest, and I lean against my dresser so I won't sink to the floor.

"How did I not see that?" I ask no one, but Rusty answers.

"Because you weren't seeing it through her eyes. You hadn't ever been there, so you wouldn't have known. Jenny and I have both seen the cabin like this, with tears in our eyes making the entire scene blur, blending the colors into a mess before the clarity comes. This is what the cabin looks like through eyes that know the pain and the joy that love can bring."

Well, hell, Rusty.

He is a poet.

We all sit in silence, looking at the canvas and letting it tell the story my mother wrote so long ago. I step forward and look at her signature on the bottom. Next to her name is the date 1958. I turn to Rusty and ask, "Didn't Jimmy say I came to Adin when I was two? That is when she painted this. Maybe after we came home?"

"Must be," Rusty said.

Jenny walks over and puts her arm around me, pulling my body toward her. She is quite a bit shorter than me; her head coming up to just below my shoulder, but she is strong and determined. I duck down and let her hug me.

"I'm glad we came with you, Patrick. There are too many memories here for one man to carry," she says, and I'm betting she doesn't mean all the boxes.

After a fitful night's sleep, I'm on my way to see my agent, Martin. The drive over is quick, and once I park, my feet remember where to go without having to give it much thought. Martin and I met with my first book, and for a while, he was my only friend. I learned later, around book six, that we were just business partners. That realization hurt at the time, but now I understand the boundaries are necessary. For example, it would be hard to tell my friend I have no new ideas, but the asshole business guy? It will be easy to tell him. I should just cut him loose and admit I won't be writing anymore. He has other clients. He will be fine without me. It seems that all of Seattle is fine without me.

"Patrick! It's so good to see you! Come in, have a seat." Thomas greets me the second the elevator doors open.

"Hello, Thomas. It's nice to see you too," I say. I wonder if I really feel that way or if it's just reflex to say that shit? Rusty doesn't say things he doesn't mean, and I bet Mitchell didn't either. I need to work on that.

"Martin is on a call, but should be finished shortly. You can sit out here, and he will buzz me when he's ready for you," Thomas says, walking to the coffee pot set up behind his desk. The bookshelf doubles as a snack and drink cart, and I think about how Thomas is like an airline attendant, but he never gets to travel. He just offers coffee and tea to people here in this tiny office. He doesn't even have a window. What a horrible job. I tug at the collar of my shirt, suddenly very claustrophobic for Thomas. I decline the coffee, so Thomas sits down at his desk and folds his hands to wait.

I hear the intercom buzz because I'm sitting literally one foot away from the desk in what Thomas calls his office. Our knees are almost touching, and when he stands to tell me Martin will see me now, I have to fight off a sarcastic comment. His life is bad enough without my snark.

When I walk through the door, Martin is sitting at his desk, hands folded in front of him. He has a slight smile on his face, and his black hair is slicked back with so much gel I imagine he would be flammable. He wears a nice suit, but it isn't nicer than the ones I own. I wonder if he has other clients besides me?

"Patrick! You made it! How was the flight? Did you come in from Reno?" he asks as he gestures for me to sit.

"No, I flew right out of Adin. A friend, well, no, a person I met has a plane and he and his wife brought me here," I say. I glance over my shoulder, half afraid Rusty heard me call him a friend.

"I see. How nice. Listen, I won't take up too much of your time. I just wanted to tell you the publisher is waiting for your next big submission. Where are we at on that?" Martin asks, and I shift in my chair.

"Um, I don't have an answer to that, Martin."

"Still hammering out the kinks? Understandable. I'm excited to see what wonderful series has been swirling around in that brain of yours. I'm sure it will be just as good as your Kent Price stuff. When can I tell them it will be ready for the editor?"

"Well, I don't know that either. I have been working on stuff, obviously," I lie. "But I have also started to work on some poetry." I say this a little easier because that is true.

"Poetry? Like 'roses are red, violets are blue' kind of poetry?" Martin asks. He cocks his head to the side, trying to tell if I'm kidding, I guess.

"No, no. My poems don't rhyme," I start, but he interrupts me.

"Well, you're not very good at it then. Poems rhyme, Patrick." He pauses, his eyes lighting up. "Oh! Like, there was a man from Nantucket, his dick was so long he could..." Martin says.

"No! I'm not writing anything like that. More like about love and frustration and sometimes terrifying experiences on airplanes or horses."

He stares at me blankly, and since I have never been good at awkward silences, I say, "Like this, 'Hair so black, slick with oil tells the story.'" I stop myself because this will not end well for Martin. Instead, I just blink at him like a fucking owl.

Martin rubs his hands over his face. "So you want to go from writing a kick-ass tough guy series to writing poetry? Make it make sense to me."

"Well, I don't know that I can. Listen, when I write fiction, it's like I'm listening to someone else, but when I write poems, I'm listening to myself. I want to hear what I have to say," I say with a little one-shoulder shrug.

Martin just stares at me.

The silence creeps into the room, coating everything. I feel like I can't breathe. Is it hot in here?

"Well, I also have started a book about a rancher who may have robbed a bank or something because he has too much money and no one can explain his riches, and the train that was carrying gold bars goes right through his property, and it keeps getting robbed," I say in a rush of words that make no sense to me at all. I look at Martin, a big smile slowly spreading across his face.

"Jesus, Patrick!" He laughs and tips his head back to look at the ceiling, then slowly lowers his gaze to me.

"That is fucking genius. Why didn't you start with that? You scared the crap out of me!" Martin laughs again loudly.

All I can do is smile sheepishly and nod.

"So we talking like a month or two?" Martin asks.

"I need six months. I want to get the second book started before I turn in the first, and I'm still working on it. On the first one. About the rancher. Who robbed a train apparently," I say with my eyes wide. I might throw up.

Martin just smiles. "Okay, I'm sure the publisher will be as excited as I am right now. You can send over the first book for edits, and we can just hold off on publishing it till the second is done if you want," he says, and I shake my head so violently I think I knock a filling loose.

"No, nope, no thank you. I want to finish both books. That's all there is: two books. Not a twelve-book series. No. Nope. Just two. About a rancher, train robber maybe," I say. Martin has cocked his head at me like he is trying to figure out when exactly I lost my mind.

"Well, if that is all, I'm going to head out. I have a lot to do to get ready for the moving company. You have my new phone number, but let me give you my address."

I write:

Smith Ranch
County Road W
Adin, California

I slide the paper over to him, he looks at it, then at me.

"What's the street number?"

"There isn't one. The post office knows where it is. Trust me," I say.

"Shit, how small is this town?" Martin asks. He finally takes the paper and tucks it into my file, but he keeps a squinty eye on me the whole time.

"I think the total population is like two hundred and fifty people, but I could be wrong. The town is actually a street, well, the highway." A huge smile spreads across my face as I add, "It's amazing."

"Okay. Well, please never make me come there," Martin says, and I immediately think of Rusty punching him right in the face. I would actually like to see that.

"Wouldn't dream of it. I'm selling my condo. I've already contacted an agent, so if you know of anyone who wants it, better tell them now. Imagine it will go quickly," I say.

"Selling? You can't be serious? You aren't moving to that tiny town for good, are you?" Martin asks.

Nodding, I say, "I love it there. I'm connected to my family there, connected to myself."

"Who is she?" Martin asks with a smirk.

"What?"

"The girl? Who is she? I can't imagine a one-street town is capable of holding your interest for very long, Patrick, so there must be a girl." He leans forward, and I want to punch him right in the face.

I could be like Rusty. I can feel it.

"No girl. I've met some interesting people there, but no girl," I say. Not sure how convincing I sound, but I haven't talked to Kenny since she called me from that loud bar and I was awkward and weird. I may never hear from her again. Why mention her?

"Okay. If you say so, Patrick. Well, I will call the publisher and let them know where we are at." Martin stands as if the meeting is over, so I stand too.

"Will you mention the poetry?" I ask hopefully.

"No. God no," Martin says with a laugh.

My shoulders slump. I want to write poetry, and then I had some jackass idea of a robbing rancher. Fuck. I drive back to the condo in a foul mood.

COWBOY POETRY

BEYOND THE FENCE LINE~PUBLISHED 1950

Betrayed by your presence
But worse by your absence
Why did you have to go
To leave me here alone
My heart is under the old oak tree
But my soul has gone to the city
~By MS 1922

This station is ridiculous.

I can't find anything. Their hose rack holds only around three lengths of hose, and I swear it almost collapsed when we laid out one hundred feet of our one-inch hose. The engine bay door is broken, so it stays up all the time, according to the district ranger. That's lame. I got a ladder out and checked the rollers, finding a stick wedged into the gear. It took a bit, but I was able to free it. I pulled the garage door shut triumphantly and looked at it, letting the smile take over my face.

"Fucking rad, Kenny!" Luke says. He slaps me on the back. "I knew you could fix it."

"It was a stick, Luke. Anyone who looked could have fixed it," I say. God, I'm bored. I called Patrick when I got here two days ago, but all I got was his answering machine. He hasn't changed the message, so I assume he's been busy. I left a message with the number here, but he hasn't called. He probably won't call. Why would he? He likes girls who laugh like bells on hills and have daffodils for hair, or something like that. I rub my eyes. I want to go home, want to see him so I can find out if the spark we had is still there.

"Ted said that there is a project list we can check out if you want to tackle something else." Luke raises an eyebrow at me.

"Sure. I can't stand this sitting around shit."

"Everyone can tell. Come on," Luke says, waving me up the wooden stairs in the engine bay. They have a makeshift office loft thing that looks like kids who failed wood shop in high school built it.

"Can I rebuild this?" I ask, shaking the railing.

"Probably, but look. There is a pump out by this creek that they haven't been able to fix, and it's causing problems for the campsite nearby. Let's tell Ted we want to work on that so we can get the fuck out of this station."

"Okay, that seems like a plan. You go find Ted and Chuck, and I'll look at the notes and see if I can tell what tools we should bring. Have you seen Ryan?"

"Yeah. He is in the ranger station talking to the field biologist," Luke says, waggling his eyebrows at me.

"Of course he is. Jesus." I shake my head and grab the notebook, trying to decipher what the captain meant when he described the problem with the pump.

We spend the rest of the day out of the station at various campgrounds because it took all of twenty minutes for Ted and me to fix the broken pump. They have some nice places to tent camp, but it isn't like home. There are no tall pines like I'm used to, but there are some pretty areas. When we pull back into the station, the district ranger is out front talking to the captain of the engine that belongs here.

They've been released, so that means we can finally head home. I'm so fucking happy I want to scream, but I hold back. Chuck turns in his seat and says, "You little fuckers have exactly ten minutes to grab your shit or I leave without you."

Ryan, Luke, and I scramble out of the engine and run to the barracks to get our things. I guess I'm not the only one eager to get home.

We pull out of the gas station on the edge of town just as the sun is going down. It's about a fourteen-hour drive in the engine back to Adin, so Ted says we will go as far as we can, then either stay in a hotel or camp somewhere so Chuck can sleep. I'm almost tempted to let Ryan sit by the window so I can talk to Luke, but I know if I do that even once I will have to kick his ass to get my seat back.

I finished Kent Price, A Man on a Mission, and I don't have the energy to start Misery. The last set of batteries for my Walkman died about an hour into our trip, so I can't even listen to music. I sigh and close my eyes.

Chuck and Ted decide to trade off driving and power home, so I'm very disoriented to wake up in Adin as we pull into the station. I slept, but not well, so pulling my red bag down and grabbing my personal backpack is a monumental task. I head up the hill to my house and unpack the second I walk in the door. Probably should start a load of laundry before I take a shower, so I open the closet doors that hide the washer and dryer and smile when I see a new box of laundry soap that has a note taped to the front.

KENNY,
> I hope this brand is okay. I think it smells nice.
> Patrick

I STAND THERE FOR A SECOND, turning slowly around, looking back into the kitchen. On my table and counters are all the things I put on my list. Canned goods and cereal, a twelve-pack of Coke, and a bottle of Jack. Patrick has written little notes on almost all the items, explaining why he picked it or that he was thinking of me. My hands go involuntarily to my face. Tears are streaming down my cheeks, and it isn't like I'm sad, really, more just overwhelmed. I glance at the clock and see it's not too early to call, so I dial Patrick's number out at the ranch.

Damn, still getting the answering machine. I leave a message telling him we're back, and I thank him for buying all the stuff on my list.

I open the fridge and laugh when I see his note.

KENNY,

Milk doesn't last because it's not as strong as you. You could kick milk's ass.

Patrick

P.S. I'll take you shopping when you get home.

GOD, he is the biggest dork.

After getting all my clothes washed and repacked into my red bag, I haul it back down to the station and put it on top of the engine. I notice Luke's bag is already back in place, too. He is like me in that way; he can't rest until his shit is in order. My stomach rumbles, so instead of going in to chat with everyone, I walk down to the Frosty for a burger.

Jessica is at the window and looks very stressed, so I approach cautiously with a smile and say, "Hey! How are you?"

"I'm fucking losing my mind if you must know. Aunt Jenny and Uncle Rusty took that Patrick guy back to Seattle, and I'm stuck here trying to run this damn place by myself! That stupid fryer is acting up again, so don't order anything like French fries or the chicken unless you want to see me cry," Jessica says. She is leaning on the window ledge and has pulled her pencil out from behind her ear. She taps the pad in front of her. "So? What will you be having?"

"What do you mean they took Patrick back to Seattle?" I ask, feeling a knot form in my stomach.

She shrugs and says, "He wanted to go, so Uncle Rusty flew him."

"Oh, well. He must be coming back because he has his cute little red BMW here. He wouldn't leave that," I say more to myself than her, but she chimes in, saying he sold the car.

"Well, crap."

"Want a burger or something?" she asks, clearly bored with this conversation.

"Um, sure. Yeah. When are your aunt and uncle coming back?" I ask, and she just shrugs again.

I wander off to wait for my burger and try not to cry. How could he just leave without saying goodbye? Was I gone that long? Jesus, I mean, I guess it's been like six weeks, but who does that?

Luke comes up and sits on the picnic table next to me. He says nothing, so neither do I. I just stare at my feet. I don't realize that I'm crying until I feel a tear drop onto my foot. Luke puts his arm around me and says, "I know. I can't believe he's gone either. I really liked him. Like a lot."

"Me too," I say and tip my head back, trying to get the tears to stop.

"Well, from what I hear, he will be happier there. They have the things he needs, stuff we couldn't give him here," Luke says. I look up at him, and he is rubbing the back of his neck.

"I guess. I just wish I could have said goodbye, you know? Like why would he just leave without saying goodbye or leaving a note or something?" I choke out.

"That's funny, Kenny. Like a note that says, 'Sorry, I need more. Peace out, man?'" Luke says with a chuckle.

"Well, sure. I mean, it's just fucking rude to leave without telling people who care about you that you are leaving!" The anger rises in my chest. I turn to Luke and say, "What a fucking asshole. I thought I meant something to him. Jesus, I thought we were going to have that date when I came back, and instead I find out he needs stuff we can't give him here. What the fuck is that?" I say, although it comes out as more of a yell than I intended.

"Wait, what?" Luke asks, looking very confused.

"Patrick needs more than we can give him here? Is that what he said? Because we were gone? It wasn't my fault, Luke. I couldn't just come back because I missed him. This is my job, you know? Fuck that guy if he can't handle it."

Luke cuts me off by grabbing my shoulders and staring at me. "Kenny," he says. "What the fuck are you talking about?"

"Patrick went back to Seattle because I wasn't enough," I say, and my throat closes up like I swallowed a bite that was too big.

"Um, okay. Wow. I didn't know he had left. That is unexpected," Luke says, scratching his head.

"What?" I'm very confused. "What are you talking about then?"

"Fred the fire cat. He went to live with Bonnie's grandma down in Fall River Mills. He got sick while we were away, and I guess he has diabetes or something and needs medicine all the time. They said he also needs to be an indoor cat now, so Bonnie's grandma said she would take him. I thought that is why you were upset," Luke explains.

"Fred is gone too? This is the worst fucking day ever."

Luke puts his arm around me and leans his head against mine. After a minute, he says, "Want to get drunk at The Bar tonight? We don't have to work tomorrow."

"Fuck yeah. Thanks, Luke."

"Anything for you, Kenny. Plus, Zia is out of town and I have nothing else to do tonight," Luke says, ducking away from me like I'm going to hit him. I just laugh.

THE SUN HITS my face and I blink several times, then moan at the pain in my head. Fuck, I must have drank the entire bar last night. I force myself to open my eyes and am grateful to see I'm in my own bed, but that just makes me sad all over again because the last time I got that drunk at The Bar, I woke up out at the ranch.

My head hurts. My heart hurts more. Why didn't he tell me he was leaving? I drag myself out of bed and find Luke passed out on my couch. He's scrunched up like an inchworm with his ass in the air and his face smashed into the very rough cushion. If my head didn't hurt so much, I would laugh. Instead, I get some Advil and a big glass of water. I head in to take a shower, hoping that the warm water will help with the headache.

Finally, feeling a little more human, I get dressed and go out to the living room, where I find Luke sitting up with his head in his hands.

Without looking up, he says, "What the fuck is this couch made of, Kenny? Is it steel wool? I'll bet you it's steel wool."

"Probably. Nothing but the best for us government workers, you know?"

Luke peers at me through his fingers and asks, "Where are you going at this ungodly hour?"

"It's eleven in the morning, Luke. I'm going to walk off this hangover, because there's no way I can just sit here," I say. I sit and pull on my running shoes, then stand and tell Luke to leave the door unlocked if he leaves.

I walk down the steps and out onto the little road that leads to the main street of town. Not even sure where I'm going, and I realize I don't really care where I end up, just need to walk. I need to think. I need answers.

Of course my feet take me straight to the ranch, and I'm not even a little surprised. There is a brand-new Ford truck in the driveway, and I wonder if Patrick sold the place while we were gone. The front yard is showing signs of needing a mow again, but I keep walking. It isn't his place anymore, and it isn't Mitchell's place anymore. Fuck. I take a few steps and empty my stomach into the bushes in front of the ranch house. My parting gift, I guess. I turn on my heels and head back to town, my heart ripped out of my chest with the little pieces scattering in the wind.

Fucking Seattle. What is so great about a big city? Sure, they probably have more than one restaurant there. I mean, that is something. They probably also have more than one bar, and I bet they even have real grocery stores. Chico, where my parents live, has all of those things, but you don't see me running there. I love it here. I feel at home in this stupid, small town. Why didn't he? Why wasn't I enough?

I've never been to Seattle. Maybe it *is* awesome. I bet all the girls are feminine, delicate, and fragile. They probably file their nails instead of a chain on a chainsaw. Maybe they wear dresses instead of Nomex, and maybe they don't smell like fucking gasoline all the time. For the first time in my life, I wish I were different, and it makes me so angry. Fuck Patrick. I don't need this shit.

I head back to my house and spend the rest of the day inside nursing my wounds. It's so hard to see all the sweet notes he left me and all the things he bought me. I'll have to ask Rusty for Patrick's address so I can send him a check. I'm not letting that asshole pay for anything for me. After I eat dinner, I put on my pajama shorts and a tank top and climb into bed. I don't want to read or watch television, so I just stare at the ceiling. When the wooden slats don't provide answers, I roll to my side and eventually fall asleep.

COWBOY POETRY

BEYOND THE FENCE LINE~PUBLISHED 1950

Home is only where you
lay your head
If your love is
no longer there
Home is where your boots rest
If your heart is gone away
Home is a word without meaning
If the people you love have left
~By M.S 1923

TWENTY-FOUR
PATRICK

"Put your head between your knees for Christ's sake. If you throw up in my airplane, I will kick your ass all the way to Sunday!" Rusty yells.

I shove my head down, creating a worse problem in the back of this tiny metal death trap he calls an airplane. Jenny is laughing her ass off again, and completely unhelpful. Closing my eyes, I think about how odd it is to have my knees cradling my head. Honestly, I didn't know I could get into this position, but more importantly, I'm not sure how I'll get out of this position. I'm stuck, like completely. I imagine this will not go over well with Rusty, who has been yelling at me nonstop for the last twenty minutes.

Jenny finally catches her breath and turns around in her seat, shifting, probably looking down at me. I imagine she is covering her mouth with her hand as she asks, "Patrick, are you feeling better?"

"Sure. Yes. I'm fine. I wasn't actually going to throw up, but this position seems to help because I can't see the mountains we almost crashed into," I say to the floor.

"Well, I'm glad. You really need to work on finding a more manly scream. I mean, come on," Jenny says, but I cut her off.

"Listen, I'm not having this argument again. There is no manly way to scream. I can't deepen my voice, Jenny. It comes from a place of terror. I don't have control over it," I say as I try to lift my head back up. I keep hitting the seat in front of me, which is occupied by a very angry Rusty. He grunts, so I stop. I mean, really, I don't want to bump the man who is flying the plane, right? Jesus. I should have rented a car. The drive isn't that bad. This is horrible. It's three hours of sheer terror.

As if Jenny can read my mind, she says, "We are almost back to Adin, Patrick, twenty minutes, tops.

"Okay, sure, the ground seems like a place I would like to be again. But slowly and landing, not crashing," I say to my new friend, the floorboards.

"I'm not going to crash the plane, you spineless ninny," Rusty grumbles.

All the gains I made with Rusty at the condo evaporated when we got back in the plane to go home. I guess I really hate flying. Who knew? Not me, that's for damn sure. Well, I like big airplanes; you know, where you can't see the pilot or his wife, who can't control her laughter. Also, the kind of airplanes that have a nice stewardess who offers me a Jack and Coke or a glass of wine. Yeah, those airplanes are nice. This? No, I don't like this.

When the wheels touch the ground, I say thank you to every deity known to mankind. Once Rusty gets out and slides his seat forward, I'm able to extricate myself easily. He is busy grabbing our bags, so I'm able to get out with a little bit of dignity. We walk to his truck, and I think about getting home and seeing if Kenny has called. I really miss her. If she hasn't called, I'll have to be okay with it, right? It's not like she has a lot of control over her job. I love that she has something she is so passionate about, and to be honest, her badass job is part of what is so appealing to me, but that doesn't mean I don't miss her. I've had six weeks to figure this all out; I've experienced a wide range of emotions. For one week, I decided I couldn't do this. It was too hard. That was after the weird bar phone call. I realized I was jealous, and that is not something I want to be.

Rusty stops his truck in the street, and I jump out and grab my bag from the bed of his truck, knocking on the side to let him know I'm done. He sticks a leathery, tanned arm out the window and waves as they drive off. It occurs to me I have no idea where he and Jenny live.

I walk down the gravel driveway, my chest getting lighter with every step. Seeing the house and my new truck makes me feel like I've been pulled back to the surface. I can breathe again.

Once inside, I set my bags down, going straight for my answering machine. The red blinking light makes my heart skips a beat. Six messages! I have been gone a week and there are six messages! See? This is why I love it here. I press play and Kenny's sweet voice tells me she is at a station a little north of where they had been on that big fire. They are covering for the engine crew that is normally stationed there. She rattles off a phone number, and I write it down, excited at the prospect of calling her. There is another call right after that where she says she was checking in, and it makes me smile. The next two messages are from people about the cattle, but nothing I can't handle. There's another from Kenny saying she is back in Adin. My heart leaps out of my chest. The timestamp was yesterday. She got home yesterday. I'm grabbing my keys when the last three messages play.

"Patrick, it's me. Shh, Luke. I'm talking to Patrick. No, his machine, fucker. Okay, I'm back. I can't believe you left without saying goodbye. I think that's really shitty. You're really shitty. I have melons I was going to share with you. You know? I have great melons, and now you'll never know. That's on you. You can tell everyone you blew it with the girl with the great—"

The machine cuts her off, and I blink. What? That was Kenny, and she sounded very drunk.

There are two more messages, and I hold my breath as they play.

"Fucking machine cut me off, Patrick. Like you did. You cut off my feelings for you like a cheap-ass answering machine. You have no answers. Why do they call these answering machines when they only cause more questions? Like why did you leave?" Kenny's voice is quiet as she says that last bit, the phone clanging on the receiver before the dial tone finishes the call.

Well, hell. That's not good. She must think I left for good. I grab my keys and am about to run to my truck when the phone rings. I dive to answer it.

"Hello?"

"Patrick? You made it back! I was going to leave you a message, but this is even better!" Martin says.

My shoulders droop, and I rub my hand down my face. "Hey, Martin. Yeah, just got in."

"Well, I wanted to tell you I pitched your idea to the publisher, and they can't wait! They are so excited to read your western. I told them you could have the book to them by the end of the month. I know you said you needed more time, but they are giving you an advance, so I don't want to leave them twisting in the wind."

"An advance?" I ask, feeling as if I have been punched in the gut. That means they liked that stupid idea enough to pay me before even reading one page. Jesus. Do they have no standards?

"Yeah, and it's a good one. I sent over the contract; take a look at it and sign it. Once I get it back to them, they will put the check in the mail. Let's get this going, okay?" Martin says. I know that if I make money, he makes money, and really that is all there is, but man, it doesn't feel good. Like at all.

"Sure, Martin, sure. Hey, I, um, was actually on my way out. I gotta go. I'll let you know when the contract arrives." The phone is back on the cradle before he can even answer.

I run at full speed toward my truck, and in my mind, I hop on the hood and slide across to the driver's side door. In reality, I trip, almost face-planting into the passenger-side door. I right myself and take a deep breath.

Calm the fuck down, Patrick.

I walk over and open the door to my beautiful new truck. When I sit behind the wheel, it occurs to me that none of this would be happening without Mitchell. Why hadn't my parents ever talked about him? Why had my parents taken that wooden bowl from here? I shake my head, trying to focus on my main problem—getting Kenny back.

Just as I pull onto Hwy 299, or 139, or Main Street, or whatever the fuck they call it, I see the green fire engine going code three away from me.

Oh, hell no. No, I refuse to wait even one more minute. I press my foot to the floor, making the truck lurch a little, and I speed off, code two and a half after the girl I love. It's romantic as fuck, and I want to grab my pen and write down what I'm feeling, but it's a lot harder to keep up with the engine than I thought it would be. The big engine slows, then turns onto a logging road, kicking up a cloud of dust bigger than the tornado that took Dorothy to Oz. I yelp and slam on my brakes, having to wait for the cloud to settle before I can move on.

Once it's clear, I follow at a more respectable distance. A man in the passenger seat is looking back at me, and I imagine it isn't every day they have a tail. I don't care. I'm going to talk to Kenny if it's the last thing I do.

The engine pulls up next to a campground, and all four doors fly open. I think I see Kenny leap out, pulling a red medical bag from a compartment. She takes off in a run following the man who had been glaring at me in the mirror. I park and get out, hurrying to follow where they went.

There is a small group of people standing around a clearing next to a tent. A woman in tears is talking to the angry mirror man, and another man with his hands on his head is pacing back and forth. I can hear Kenny shouting, and I stop.

"I need the splint, Ryan!" she yells, then in a calmer voice she says, "Hey, it's okay. Look at me. It's not that bad. I'm not going to hurt you if I can help it, okay? Listen, your arm is definitely broken, so I'm going to put a splint on it, and then it won't hurt so bad, okay? You need to breathe."

Ryan is digging through the medical bag, and I bet Kenny is getting pissed. "Luke, you get it. It's on the bottom. Pull that stuff over. Yeah, that's it. Okay, I need those wraps too. Okay, thanks." Her voice is steady now.

I search for Kenny, keeping my gaze high so I can't see whoever she was helping, because I don't have the strongest stomach. I step closer to the circle of people, looking at the woman I assume is the kid's mom. She has very puffy eyes, and it's clear she has been crying. A man, possibly the dad, is still walking around with his hands on his head. He is cursing and taking deep breaths.

A vehicle pulls up, I turn around in time to see a teenage boy run towards us. "I told 'em, Ma. Oh man, they drove so fast. I couldn't keep up. Is she okay? Is Tammy okay?"

"I'm okay," a little voice comes from the middle of the circle.

"She's fine. I'm just about done with the splint, then you are going to drive her slowly to Alturas, okay?" Kenny finishes the wrap she placed around the splint, as she stands up she looks at the teenager. Her gaze darts around to the others before she adds, "You drive her. You are the only one who's sober."

"Yes, ma'am. I can do that. Tammy, you ready to go?" the boy asks.

A girl no more than eight stands up with Kenny's help, and I catch sight of her arm. Even through the splint, the deformity in the forearm is obvious. Her hand, like the rest of her, is covered in dirt, but her fingers are pale.

"I told her not to climb that fucking tree. I told her, but she doesn't listen. She never listens," the man who has been walking around finally says. His wife, I guess, walks over to him and rubs his back, and they both watch as the teenager walks the girl over to the car and buckles her into the front seat. He closes the door, the top of her brown hair barely visible through the window.

"I'll be back later," he says, climbing in. He starts the car, flips it around, and drives away back down the dirt road.

Kenny kneels down and starts gathering her medical supplies, putting them back in her bag. Luke and Ryan are talking to some people who made up the circle of adults around the poor little girl with the broken arm.

Before she can see me, I walk toward the engine to wait. My idea of coming here suddenly feels selfish and a little ridiculous. I sit on the bumper of the engine and wait, listening to the excuses, reasons, and pain pouring out of the little girl's parents' mouths. I put my head in my hands and sigh.

"Patrick?" a soft voice says with the thump of a bag hitting the dirt.

I look up into her beautiful face a small smile tugging at my lips. "Hey, Kenny."

"What? Wait." She looks back over her shoulder at the people in the campsite.

"Are you here with them?" she asks, thumbing over her shoulder.

"No, I followed your engine," I explain.

"Why? How? You're in Seattle," she says, and I see the confusion dance across her face along with something else. A memory maybe? Her mouth drops open, and then she hangs her head. Yep, I bet she is remembering the message she left me.

"I didn't leave for good, Kenny. I had to go to take care of some things, like selling my condo and meeting with my agent." When I stand and push off from the bumper, I want so badly to wrap her in my arms. I don't.

"Oh. Right. I thought..." she says, then stops.

"Yeah. I know."

"You left. You went to Seattle. Rusty flew you home," she says, still trying to reconcile me standing in front of her with what she had thought was true.

"He did. He brought me here. I mean, after he took me to Seattle. Hey, Kenny?"

"Yeah?" she says, her brows furrowed as if she is still very confused.

"Never fly with Rusty. I mean, if you can help it. I guess if he was taking you to a hospital or something, it would be okay, but for fun, or to get somewhere? Don't do it."

She laughs a big, hearty laugh that makes my whole body light up with joy, but then she claps her hand over her mouth.

"What?" I ask, and she just shakes her head and looks down.

"Hey, Patrick! What are you doing here?" Luke comes walking up with Ryan close behind.

"Hey, Luke. I came to talk to Kenny," I say, stepping a little closer. It's taking all I have not to grab her, let everyone know she is mine.

"Cool, man, cool. I knew you wouldn't just leave," Luke says.

Ryan grunts at me, then climbs into the engine. Man, he really is a fuckwad. I catch Kenny rolling her eyes in annoyance before she bends to pick up her medical bag. She opens a compartment on the side of the engine and replaces the bag before letting the door slam shut.

"I work till six. Want to maybe meet at The Bar or something?" Kenny asks.

Two men walk up just then, and since they are wearing the same clothes as Kenny, I assume they are also on the engine crew. An immense man with black and silver hair and the widest mustache I have ever seen stops and puts his hand on Kenny's shoulder. The gesture is protective and fatherly, and I immediately like him.

"You alright, Kenny?" His gaze darts from her to me, then back.

"Yeah, I am." She smiles wide. "Ted, this is Patrick. Mitchell's great-nephew."

The large walrus of a man drops his hand from her shoulder and extends it to me.

"Well, it's about time. I have heard a lot about you. Damn, you do look like Mitchell," Ted says, then adds, "Nice to meet you, son. This is Chuck. He's our engineer."

A tall, thin man reaches his hand out to shake mine, and I enthusiastically meet his and pump it up and down.

"Chuck and Ted. It's so nice to put faces to your names. I have heard a lot about you both."

"Why are you here? Were you camping next to these yahoos?" Chuck asks, looking over his shoulder at the family. They have settled down a bit. A few of them have sat back down around the campfire, the father with a beer in his hand.

"God no. No, I followed you. I wanted to see Kenny," I say, then realize how that might be a problem for her. Hell, this is her job, and I'm chasing her down? Jesus. Not my best choice.

Ted and Chuck look at each other and laugh.

"Yeah, she has that effect on people. Are you all done seeing her? We need to go into Alturas and make sure that little girl and her brother made it to the hospital and also stop by the sheriff's office to see if he can't come put the fear of God into this drunk ass family," Ted says.

"Oh, yeah. I'm good. I saw her. She is still just as beautiful as I remembered." I say the words before I can even think about them, and Kenny's cheeks flame red with embarrassment.

"Okay then. Well, I guess that's it for me," Kenny says, and she turns on her heels and climbs into the engine. She shuts the door, and I swear I hear her groan.

"It was nice to meet you both. I won't make a habit of following her around. I promise," I say.

Chuck laughs. "I think you should. I don't think I have ever seen Kenny blush. That was pretty funny." He shakes my hand and climbs into the engine. Ted hangs back, looking me up and down. He folds his arms across his chest and stares the way Rusty does.

"You going to sell the ranch?" he asks, and I shake my head.

"No, sir. I love it here. I'm staying."

"Fair enough. See you around then." He claps his huge hand on my shoulder before walking to the engine. The engine roars to life, and I hear the siren chirp a little before they drive off. I wander back to my truck and get in, driving back to Adin happier than I have been in a long time.

As soon as I get back to the ranch, I call Kenny's place and leave a message, telling her I will meet her at The Bar at seven. I'm so excited I can barely stand it. All thoughts of my earlier conversation with Martin have left my brain, replaced with that incredible, powerful, confident woman. She is intoxicating, and I'm not even a little bit embarrassed about being under her spell.

I take a shower and force myself to eat something for dinner, then drive into town so I can get to The Bar before she does. I park my truck and am walking in when I catch someone coming down the street toward me. My brain can't quite figure out what I'm seeing, so I pause and blink. Then I rub my eyes and blink some more. What the hell am I looking at?

COWBOY POETRY

UNPUBLISHED WORK

Strength, beauty
Grace and fire
Scar my heart
Light my soul
Control my mind
~by Patrick Smith 1988

Jesus. How on God's green earth do women walk in these things? I tug at my dress because, for some reason, walking makes the whole thing ride up. I stop and smooth my hair out of my face, breathing hard like I climbed to the top of a clear-cut block instead of walking down the street.

Fuck.

That's what I look like, a streetwalker. Oh my god. Why? Why did I think wearing a dress and actual heels would be a good idea? I haven't worn heels since my eighth-grade graduation, and they were probably only an inch high, not these skyscrapers. Damn it.

I wobble along trying not to seem like a drunk giraffe as I make my way to The Bar. I hope to get there early so I can be perched on a barstool or at a booth seductively waiting for Patrick. But now, I'm stumbling down this stupid pothole-ridden street that has no side-walks, just gravel. Thankfully, I don't see the little red BMW, so maybe he isn't here yet.

My hope dies in my chest, because when I glance up, Patrick is on the front steps of The Bar, watching me attempt to walk toward him. Raising my hand to wave, he cocks his head at me as if he's thinking, "What the hell is that?"

Shit.

I manage to make it to the steps of The Bar without falling on my ass, and I smooth my dress down and smile up at him. He's frozen in place, staring at me. Not like, "Wow, check out this hot girl I asked out on a date." Nope. More like "What the hell did I just witness?"

My gaze darts to the stairs, then down at my feet, then up at Patrick. Fuck it. I pull off the stupid shoes and hold them in one hand as I walk up the steps. I smile as best as I can and say, "Hello, Patrick."

"Hi, Kenny. You look..." He trails off as his eyes roam over my skintight black dress. It's shorter than the denim shorts I normally wear, but I have nice legs, so that's something I guess.

"I look?" I ask, running my hand down the front of my dress again nervously.

"Different," he says.

"Different?" I ask. Huh. That's not what a girl wants to hear.

"I mean, wow. God, you are so gorgeous, but I didn't think you wore dresses and heels. I mean, wow," he says. It seems like he is backpedaling, realizing he has been gawking at me.

"Well, I thought I'd dress up, you know, for our date," I say. God, I am a complete asshole. He is wearing a pair of khaki shorts and a T-shirt. He has on his tan Top-Siders. I look like I'm going to stand on a street corner to pay for my next fix. The heat rises in my chest and face as I go up in flames.

He glances down at his clothes as if he's realizing what I'd been thinking.

"Shit, Kenny. I didn't mean for... Oh, man. I really...I didn't..." He rubs his hand down his face, then looks up at me and swallows hard. "Sorry. I should've dressed up. I was just so excited to see you, I wasn't thinking."

"Oh, sure, no, that's okay. I don't need you to be all dressed up," I say, flapping my hand through the air.

"Are you sure? I can go back to the ranch and change. I brought one of my nice suits back from Seattle."

"No. God no, don't do that. Let's sit. I'll be more comfortable if we just sit," I say. I glance around and sigh a little when I realize there are not very many cars out front. Patrick holds out his hand, and I take it with mine. We walk into the bar together, and he steers me over to a booth in the back. Once I'm seated, he asks what I want, and then he heads to the bar to get us drinks.

I set my shoes on the bench next to me and wish I could crawl inside them. I have never been so embarrassed in all my life. I put my face in my hands and take a couple of deep breaths, missing the fact that Patrick has returned. Instead of sitting across from me, he slides in next to me, nudging me with his hip. I move further in, allowing him to sit. He turns to me and puts his arm up on the seat behind me, cocking his head. His gaze fixed on my face.

"You are so beautiful, Kenny," he says. He tugs on a piece of my curled hair, and I try to smile.

"I guess I should have asked if we were dressing up. I wanted to look nice for you."

"You don't have to dress up like this for me, Kenny. You are beautiful in your jean shorts and T-shirts."

"I find that hard to believe," I say nervously. All the spark and romance that was there before with him has dissolved, replaced with anxiety and stress.

"Why? Kenny, you are the sexiest woman I have ever known," he says, running his finger down my shoulder. I drop my gaze, my chest is tight and uncomfortable.

When I don't answer or look up, he pushes the beer toward me and says, "Here, drink this, then we are going to get out of here. I want to show you something."

I take the beer and glance at him. He is smiling like a damn fool, and that makes me feel a little better. "We can leave and go somewhere else?" I ask.

"Yes. I have a place I want to show you. You may already know about it , but I want to take you there," he says. This time when he lets his finger trail down my arm, I shiver.

I smile at him, a little more settled and almost confident. Winking at him, I say, "Okay!" I lift the mug to my lips, tip it back, and with a few easy swallows, I finish the whole thing.

He blinks at me in amazement and something else I can't place. Tiny beads of sweat have formed on his upper lip, and he quickly wipes his hand over his mouth.

"Okay, well, that was... okay. I'm just going to... Huh. Yep, I'm going to finish my beer because you are ready to go. Okay? Yeah," he stammers.

I laugh and reach over to pat his leg with my hand, and as soon as I do, he traps my hand there. He isn't looking at me, he's staring ahead, taking deep, measured breaths. After a minute he takes a big gulp of his beer, finishing about a third of it, then quickly lets go of my hand and rubs his nose.

"Oh, man. How did you do that?" He thumps his chest. "I'm holding back the biggest burp, I really don't want to do that in front of you."

"Well, you open your throat and let it slide down," I say, honestly not meaning anything more than how to chug a beer. The expression on his face and the return of the upper lip sweat make me hear what I said.

"Oh, no. Not like that, Patrick. I'm sorry." I giggle at his pained expression.

"Jesus, woman. You can't say things like that while wearing that dress. Okay, wait. No, you can't say things like that ever." He reaches down and tries to adjust himself, but I can still see the bulge in his pants.

"You okay, Patrick?"

"Yep. We can't leave for a little bit, but yeah, I'll be okay. I, um can't get up, or stand rather. Getting up doesn't seem to be a problem for me at the moment. Don't mind me, I'll be over here thinking about baseball and toenails and the way hamster cages smell." He lifts his beer, taking a smaller sip.

"Right. Okay. Toenails, huh?"

"Yeah, not a fan. I mean, I like pretty toenails, but I remember when I was a kid my dad always had these crazy gross feet, and his toenails were beyond disgusting." He shakes his head, and a little shiver runs through him. "I'm not sure how my mother tolerated it. I have perfect foot hygiene, just so you know."

"Oh my God. Never let Luke near you with his flip-flops on. He has troll feet!" I say with a laugh.

"Good information to have." He nods appreciatively. "Luke's feet will help me tonight. I'm picturing them now. Not the incredibly sexy thing you said." He pauses, his gaze darting to me then away. "Damn it, I pictured the wrong thing."

"You're so funny. I doubt that is all it takes. Hearing me say something like I'm good at blow jobs shouldn't affect you that much. If that's how you took it, I mean. You know, because I don't have much of a gag reflex and I can open my throat," I say teasingly.

Patrick lets out a deep groan and puts his head in his hands. I laugh, and he peers at me through his fingers. "You are really mean. I haven't seen you in six weeks, you show up in a dress that makes me want to rethink the whole taking it slow conversation I had been practicing, and then you say things, Kenny. You can't say those kinds of things to me," Patrick says with a strangled sound.

If I weren't wearing this stupid dress, I would have crawled over the top of him and pulled him out of the booth. Instead, I have to sit and wait for him to finish his beer and for things to deflate a little. I reach and grab his beer, chugging the rest of it, and set it next to my empty glass.

"There, now we can talk about feet," I say as I fold my hands on the table.

"I think I'm good. Quick, let's go before you say something else that makes me lose my mind."

He slides out of the booth, and holds out his hand to me. I scoot rather ungracefully out and as I reach back for my shoes, Patrick has moved closer. When I stand he crowds me, placing his hands on my hips. He applies gentle pressure shifting me to face him. His right hand moves, sliding up my body, trailing his fingers gently past my ribs, ghosting over the side of my breast. The fingers of his left hand curl in on my hip holding me in place. My breath catches as his thumb grazes across my shoulder, painfully slow. My throat has gone Sahara Desert dry. My tounge slips out and I wet my lips as his fingers continue their journey. He stares into my eyes as his hand cups my face, tipping my chin up to where he wants me. My breathing stops completely as he bends and kisses me softly on my lips.

A sigh escapes me without warning, and I blame the thousands of butterflies that took flight in my stomach. Patrick pulls back and looks into my eyes again, tracing his thumb across my cheek.

"I feel the same way, Kenny. I'm so glad you're home," he says. He interlaces our fingers and walks toward the door with me, a stumbling mess behind him.

"I'm right here," he says, walking to a brand-new white Ford pickup truck.

"This is yours?" I ask, and he nods.

"Oh, you sold the BMW because you got a truck," I say, slapping my forehead with my hand.

"Yeah, I couldn't drive little red around here in the snow, and besides, Kenny, I'm a cowboy now. Cowboys drive trucks," he says as he opens my door.God, Patrick is so adorable. I bark out a laugh that has a lot behind it, stopping myself again quickly. This time as I tamp down the hearty laugh, I attempt a giggle. Thanks to chugging two beers, however, my giggle is laced with a small and very unladylike burp. My eyes grow wide, and my cheeks flush.

Patrick cocks his head at me but doesn't say anything. He just closes my door and walks around to the driver's side. When he gets in and closes the door, he turns to me before starting the truck. He stares at me, narrowing his eyes.

"What?" I ask. He is making me nervous.

"Why are you wearing a dress, Kenny?"

"I told you. I wanted to look nice for our date," I say.

"Okay, but why a dress? Is that something you normally wear?" he asks, and I shake my head as I chew on my lower lip.

"Okay, and one more thing, if you don't mind?" He has his eyebrow cocked, making him appear like a handsome attorney questioning a witness.

"Um, no. Sure. What do you want to know?" I ask, tugging at the dress that is far too short when I sit down. No one sits down in the dressing room, do they? Nope. You also don't walk in the dressing room. Then you end up with a dress that only looks good if you stand completely still. Maybe they can bury me in this dress.

"Why are you different?" Patrick asks. He turns in his seat so that he is facing me.

My nerves shoot through me like lightning, twisting my stomach. "Different? Like how?" I say, wiping my hair out of my face.

"I can't put my finger on it exactly, but like the dress, and you aren't giving me a hard time. Well, except for the whole thing about being able to open your throat," he says, and I stifle a laugh.

"That!" he yells, causing me to jump a little. "Why aren't you laughing?"

"I am. I laughed." It's probably best not to look at him, so I fiddle with the hem of my dress again.

"No, it's different. Why?"

I sigh, the realization that I'm not good at this smacking me in the face. I can't keep this up. It isn't me, and it will never be me, no matter how hard I try. I blurt out, "I can't wear dresses or heels or laugh like bells."

"Bells?" His eyebrows scrunch together in confusion.

"Yeah, like bells on a faraway hill." I wave my hand through the air. "I don't laugh like that, Patrick, and my hair doesn't look like daffodils."

"Daffodils? Kenny, I'm so confused. Did I ever tell you I wished you had flowers for hair?" Patrick is shaking his head, trying to make sense of my craziness. Good fucking luck, dude.

"No. But in your book, the first one. The women that Kent Price falls for are...well, they are not me." My voice comes out smaller than normal.

"Jesus, Kenny." He wipes a hand down his face.

"Well, I wanted to at least try, Patrick, if that is what you find attractive." I swallow hard. "But I can't do it. I wear boots. I smell like a chainsaw most days, and my lips have never been the color of my nails, and if they are, please call the hospital." The honesty is making me feel a little more myself.

Patrick slowly turns and lowers his head onto his steering wheel. His shoulders start to shake, and he draws his hands through his hair as he lifts his head. He wipes his eyes, then looks at me with shoulders still silently shaking.

"Why are you laughing at me?" My voice pitches up like I'm whining so I squeeze my eyes shut and take a deep breath.

He presses his hand to his chest to settle his laughter, which has now become audible. "I'm sorry." He pauses and clears his throat. "It seems there is a lot you don't know about me, and the first thing is I'm not Kent Price. I fucking hate that guy."

"You hate him?" I ask, totally confused.

"Yeah, but Kenny? I need to be honest with you, I really don't want to talk about this right now."

He shifts in his seat and puts on his seatbelt. I do the same, still confused about what just happened.

He starts up the truck and turns to me. "I want to take you out to Mitchell's cabin. Have you ever been?"

"Mitchell has a cabin?"

A huge smile spread across his face, and he says, "Yes, Kenny. I can't wait to show you."

"Patrick?"

"Yeah?"

"Can we stop at my house? I really want out of this stupid dress."

Patrick nods with a wink and drives to my house without another word.

I still have my shoes in my hand as I run through the front door. The dress comes off and I toss it in the trash can on the way to my room. My favorite tank top and a pair of cut-off jean shorts replace that abomination of a dress. God, that is so much better. I can't believe how comfortable I am now. As I rush back to the door, I grab a scrunchy and slip it over my wrist. Wearing my flip-flops and a smile, I head back out to Patrick's truck.

"There's the girl I remember," he says as I climb into his truck.

"Yeah, I gotta say, I'm pretty fucking happy to be out of that dress."

"I thought about helping you out of that dress the minute I saw you tonight," Patrick says without looking over at me.

"Mr. Smith!" I tease.

"Well, I don't think it's fair for you to look that good without warning me. I mean, we can do the whole dress up and go to a nice dinner down in Redding or even go away for the weekend to Reno. I just need some warning so I don't make a fool of myself."

"So you did like the dress?" I ask.

"Kenny, you are beautiful in whatever you wear. The only reason I asked about it is because you seemed uncomfortable. I wouldn't care if you wore a paper bag. I'm really happy you're back and that I get to spend time with you again."

Patrick has turned onto County Road W but drives right past the ranch. I reach my hand over to him, and he tangles our fingers together, squeezing a little. After about fifteen minutes, we pull onto a dirt road, and Patrick lets go of my hand to push play on the tape deck. The Eagles start "Peaceful Easy Feeling," and I lean back in the seat and close my eyes. This night had started out so awkwardly, but as the Eagles sing about being a lover and a friend hope rises in my chest.

"Okay, here we are," Patrick says, slowing the truck. He pulls in next to a small cabin. When we get out, I can hear a creek off in the distance. The pine trees off in the distance make an impressive silhouette against the starlit sky. When a breeze whispers past I get a hint of wildflowers and wet mossy earth.

"This is beautiful." I walk to the front of the truck, meeting Patrick, who has his arms held open for me.

I step into him and sigh as he wraps me in his arms. He smells like Old Spice, and I pull back to gaze up at him. "Please tell me you bought your own bottle of Old Spice and you aren't still using that five-hundred-year-old bottle of Mitchell's."

He laughs and says, "I bought my own. I love it. It's timeless, and it's what cowboys wear. I did mention that I'm a cowboy now, right?" He pulls back a little, narrowing his eyes at me. "I think we glossed over that part of the conversation because you were wearing that dress, and then my truck was confusing for you." He points a finger at his chest and says, "I rode a horse, Kenny, and wrangled cattle."

He grabs me and pulls me back into his arms, as if having me even a few inches away is too much.

I fight off a laugh and ask, "Wrangled? Like you roped or something?"

"I sat on top of my horse at a safe distance while Rusty did all the things. He roped, made his horse do crazy back-and-forth things, yelled things like 'he-ya,' which has a lot of different meanings. One of them is 'cow, go that way.' It was amazing, and I was there for the whole thing."

I start to shake against his chest as he continues. I don't want to hurt his feelings since he is so excited for me to hear about his cowboy experiences, but he is just so ridiculous and adorable.

"Are you laughing at me, Kenny?" he asks into my hair.

"No. Nope. No, I don't laugh at cowboys, Patrick," I say, hiding my chuckle as best as I can.

He pushes me back gently, and takes my hand leading me to the cabin. He lights a Coleman lantern that is on the porch, and undoes the padlock on the door. As he holds the door open for me, I step inside the quaintest country cabin I've ever seen.

"Hang on. Let me light some candles. The generator I had delivered needs gas, and I haven't had a chance to do that yet, but there are a lot of candles." Patrick sets the lantern down and quickly lights about ten candles that are scattered throughout the room. The dancing flames make the cabin even more charming, and I stand frozen, imagining Mitchell here with Helen. This must have been the place he had told me about. I had no idea it was still here.

An enormous fireplace takes up one entire wall, as if the surrounding cabin was an afterthought. There is a small kitchen that is really just one counter and a sink. There are cabinets that flank the sink, but no overhead cabinets. Open shelving instead holds beautifully colorful plates and bowls. Because this place was Mitchell's, there is, of course, a shelf with alcohol and glasses. A doorway to the left seems to be a small closet or storage area, and there is another door that leads down a small hallway to what I assume is the bedroom.

"I'm having all my furniture shipped here from Seattle, and I think I'll take some pieces that are at the ranch house and bring them out here. Like Mitchell's recliner and his side table. I want to put those in front of the fireplace there." Patrick goes on to tell me the other ideas that he has, including building a bigger porch and a large window so he can see out to the creek. I squint around the room and take in what he is saying.

"I guess I should have brought you out here in the daytime. You can't really see all of it like this," he says.

"I love it. This place is amazing, Patrick."

He leads me over to the couch, and we both sit, hearing a crack as soon as our weight hits the frame. We both laugh.

"I guess I'll bring the couch from Mitchell's too."

He turns to me, pulling one knee up onto the couch. His gaze searches my face as he slips a lock of my hair behind my ear. When I sigh, he lets his hand linger on my cheek. I lean into his touch, my heart beating a mile a minute, I allow my heart to acknowledge how much I missed him.

I let out a breath and say, "I'm so happy to be here, Patrick. Can I tell you something?"

"Please." His voice is soft over my skin like a caress.

"I love my job," I start, and he interrupts me with a laugh.

"That is not what I thought you were going to say at all." He's still laughing.

"I wasn't finished!" I say, pushing him a little.

"Oh, then please continue." Moving his hand down to my thigh, he is rubbing small circles with his thumb, and I'm finding it very distracting.

"As I was saying, I love my job. I have gone off forest a few times, and I always enjoy the work. The new places, the different topography, and the excitement of a large fire camp." I look at him bathed in candlelight, and my heart skips. He is so handsome and funny, and talented, and it makes me feel small. I don't like feeling this way. I take a deep breath and blow it out.

"Okay," he says slowly, then adds, "These are not surprising things to me, Kenny. Why are you telling me this?"

"I just wanted you to understand that this time when I was gone, it wasn't the same." I glance down, watching his thumb lazily tracing circles. It's giving me chills, and the moment he notices, he flattens his hand over my inner thigh and glides it back and forth. He looks up at me questioningly, letting me take my time now.

"I missed…" I pause, not wanting to come across like a psycho since we have literally had no official dates or anything. "I missed being here."

"Yeah. I missed having you here. Why is that troubling to you, Kenny?" he asks, cocking his head to the side as if he really wants to understand why this is bothering me.

"Well, I'm not sure if you noticed, but I'm a girl," I say, easing him into the craziness that my brain has become over the last few years.

"Yes. I noticed. You let me see your very nice melons, remember?" he says in a serious tone, and I laugh.

"Right. Well, there are not very many women who do this job

right now. I mean there are some, but it's not like the men. For example, in that fire camp of, say, five hundred men, there were probably fifty of us women. I like that I'm a part of the group that's blazing the path, you know?"

"Sure, yeah. I'm super impressed by you if I haven't already told you that."

I smile and say, "You have said that, and thank you. But because I'm in this trailblazing group, I put pressure on myself. Does that make sense?"

"Yes. It does."

"Well, on this fire we were on, I ran into this guy who was on the engine crew my first year. I, um..." I stop, as a knot forms in my stomach.

Patrick just smiles at me and nods, and I smile too, realizing suddenly that I can tell him anything. His genuine interest in what I'm about to say and the look in his eyes calms all the nerves. I put my hand over his.

"Well, this guy and I got together a few times, and while guys do that kind of stuff all the time and think nothing of it," I say, and he stops moving his hand. I glance over at him, and he blinks and goes pale.

"Oh God. You are trying to tell me you discovered you still have feelings for this guy? Oh, man. I'm so dumb. Sorry, Kenny. I should've talked to you more instead of just..." Patrick is rambling and has tried to stand up, but I put my hand firmly on his leg.

"Patrick, no. That isn't it. Please listen. I'm not done."

"Okay. Can I listen with my head between my knees, or is that too lame? No. Too lame. I know. I'm okay, Kenny. Go ahead," Patrick says.

I chuckle and continue, "As I was saying, we used to get together, and I was always ashamed of that."

"Oh, does he have a horse face? Big teeth, long nose, flat forehead? In my head he is hideous, just so you know," he says, and I bark out a laugh.

"Well, he isn't a handsome professor type with dark hair and blue eyes that make my knees feel funny."

"Good answer. Wait, Professor?" he asks.

"It's the pen you usually have tucked behind your ear. It makes me think of you like a professor." I give a one-shoulder shrug.

"Is that hot or like I'm that teacher you complained about to your friends?"

"Hot, for sure. Can I finish my story?"

"Yes, please." He motions with his hand for me to continue.

"Okay, so no one really knew that Jeff and I were sleeping together except Luke, because he is like a wizard or something, you know? But at the fire when I saw Jeff, I blew him off and ducked into my tent. Luke ran into him and lied, saying he didn't know where I was. I never saw Jeff again after that, and I was hanging my head and complaining about what an awful choice Jeff had been. Luke kind of read me the riot act about it. He pointed out that guys sleep with girls and don't think twice about it. It was always very clear to both Jeff and me that we were only blowing off steam. It was just sex, you know? I didn't have feelings for him beyond that physical attraction, and he obviously felt the same way about me. So no harm, no foul." I scan Patrick's face to make sure he's understanding.

"Okay. Besides forcing me to realize that you have had other men in your life, I'm not sure why you are telling me this. Is it because you want me to know he had a tragically small penis? I'm okay with that. You could tell me that," Patrick says, shifting more in his seat.

I shake my head and laugh again. I need to get this out. I want him to understand the pressure I put on myself.

"Right. Sure, we can say that is true if it helps. Patrick, I felt bad not because I had sex with him but because I didn't want people to think I took this job to be around guys so I could sleep with them. I want people to take me seriously." I'm a little better once the words are out.

"I can understand that. Kenny, I promise to never be a firefighter and work on your engine crew." He holds up two fingers in a scout salute.

"Thank you. I appreciate your sacrifice." I roll my eyes.

"You're welcome. I was well on my way. Right after cowboy, I had firefighter on my to-do list," he says as he squeezes my leg.

"Okay. Again, thanks. So I realized that I was putting all kinds of pressure on myself to be this perfect person. Like in all aspects of my life, you know? I didn't want anyone to be able to say I couldn't do this job because of x, y, or z." I glance at him to see if he is following me.

"Okay." He nods as if I am making sense.

"So, when I was on this last fire and I couldn't stop thinking about you, about Adin, and how much I wanted to be here, I felt the same way I did when that happened with Jeff. Ashamed." I stare into those sky-blue eyes, searching for any indication that he is about to run screaming to the truck.

He rubs his chin and runs his hand through his hair. "Like, because there was a small part of you that didn't want to be there, you didn't deserve to be there?"

"Yeah," I say on an exhale, my lungs deflating like balloons.

"I get it," Patrick says, and he leans back into the rickety couch. He puts his hand back on my thigh and gives it a little squeeze.

"You do?"

"Well, sure. I got published at twenty years old. Then I had a whirlwind twelve years of doing nothing but hammering out Kent Price novels. Lived and breathed 'author.' I loved it, but I was also very aware of how others saw me. It was as if I had stopped being human to some of them. I was just a writer, or worse, I was like Kent. They thought I was putting him on paper because that's who I really was." He shakes his head, then continues. "I know it's not exactly the same, Kenny, but I understand what it's like to expect certain things from yourself because you assume that is what others expect." A dark cloud crosses over his face, and he reaches up and rubs it away with a swipe of his hand. "I get it," he says again, with a nod.

"Do you? Did you ever feel like someone was going to tell you that you can't write anymore?" I ask.

"Kind of. For me, it was like I was worried a book would flop. It was like not being able to breathe as the new book hit while simultaneously writing the next book. It was too much, but I couldn't stop. I had all these stories in my head, and I needed them to get out."

"Did you start writing after your parents were killed?" I ask, remembering what I read on his biography page of his first book.

"Nah, I had written a lot of the first Kent Price book before they were killed. They knew about the ideas I had for a series. I had also written a few short stories and things like that in high school. I just never thought I would make money as an author."

"Is that why you have a degree in geography?" The question that has been bothering me for a while pops out.

He laughs. "No, that was just an easy path. It helped my writing, too. Kent travels a lot in the books, and I had a pretty good grasp of the cultures and topography of different regions thanks to my degree." He moves his arm over my shoulder and pulls me into his chest.

"Kenny, I don't think missing me, or this town, or whatever you want to call it makes you less good at your job. It just makes you human. Don't the guys who have wives or girlfriends miss them when they go off on these fires?"

"Well, yeah, I guess so. I mean, Luke said he misses Zia when he's gone," I admit.

"So why aren't you allowed to be the same way?" he asks, and I shrug.

"It seems to me that you hold yourself to an unreasonable standard."

"Maybe. Yes. I do. That's true, but how do I stop? I'm going to the Joint Apprenticeship Committee Academy in January, and I know there won't be a lot of other women there. There will be guys who will look at me and think I was handed this job because I'm a woman. I hate that."

Patrick moves his hand up and down my leg. He's looking at me with such kindness that my heart does a little flip. It's so good to have him touching me like this. I glance at his hand, then up at him, giving him a small smile.

"Kenny, I bet it takes people all of five minutes of working with you to see that you were not hired for anything but your skill and badassery." he says, and I laugh.

"Well, yeah, but it's that initial reaction, you know? Like guys don't ever have to deal with that, do they?" I ask, putting my hand over his. I love having this connection again.

"No, I'm sure that happens to guys in all lines of work. I went to a big convention once after my third book, and I was placed next to this older woman who wrote romance novels, like a million romance novels. I don't know when that woman slept because, seriously." Patrick shakes his head and continues, "Anyway, she was very condescending toward me and actually complained that I was next to her. She said there was no way I was old enough to be a writer. That writing requires not just a good imagination but 'world experience,'" Patrick says, making little air quotes with his fingers.

"She sounds horrible." The thought of anyone being unkind to this man makes me a little feral.

"Yeah, I was pretty sensitive back then. You know, not tough and rugged like the cowboy I am now. It really bothered me. I mean, she hadn't read any of my books. She just assumed I wasn't any good based on my age."

"Wow. You do get it." The final bit of tension I had been holding onto unravels inside me.

"Yeah, I really do." Patrick reaches for me, pulling me onto his lap. The couch makes another creaking noise, and we freeze.

"My stuff should be here this week sometime. Then we can come back out here and sit on a comfortable couch that isn't trying to kill us."

I smile leaning in to kiss him.

COWBOY POETRY

UNPUBLISHED WORK

Fear and love wrap
around and through
The feelings I have
are nothing new
My heart knows
the way she moves
My soul knows
and it tries to prove
I am worthy
~By Patrick Smith 1988

TWENTY-SIX
PATRICK

It's so hard to believe she is here, in my arms. I had to pull her onto my lap because having her next to me on this rickety thing masquerading as a couch is just too much. I want to run my hands over every inch of her beautiful body so I can make sure she is real.

"In case I haven't mentioned it, Kenny, I'm really glad you're back," I say. She smiles and kisses me again, pressing those perfect lips to mine. I can taste the beer she chugged and her mint Chap-Stick. She smells of wood-smoke and something fruity. My lips travel over her cheek to her neck, then down her shoulder in a hungry path.

"Are we still taking it slow?" she asks, and my brain goes a little haywire.

"I don't want to," I start to say, but she interrupts my next thought by immediately straddling me, pressing herself into me. My next words were going to be, "but I think we should," however they never made it past my brain.

My mouth is too busy enjoying every inch of her lips and neck. Her tank top is off, and I don't honestly know if it was me or her because our hands are desperate and quick. My shirt is next, and I pull her close to me so I can have her skin against mine. I groan, and she responds by moving her hips in small circles on my lap.

"Jesus, Kenny, I'm not going to last long if you keep moving like that." I grab her hips and try to hold her still. She throws her head back and tosses her long brown hair around. She runs her fingers through it, and I feel myself grow harder. It's like melting chocolate waves cascading around her face and shoulders; my resolve slips away just as smoothly.

She lowers her gaze to meet mine and says, "I don't care if you don't last long the first time, because it won't be the only time, and I don't want to wait any longer. I need you."

I press my forehead against hers and take a ragged breath. Wanting some control, because I want to make this good for her. I scoot to the edge of the couch with her in my lap and stand up, holding her. She wraps those strong legs around my waist, and I kiss her deeply, enjoying having her hanging onto me like a lifeline.

It's so nice to be needed, and right now, it feels like she needs me as much as I need her. I walk us down the short hallway into the tiny bedroom. The moon is full, and the window in here has no coverings, so it's brighter than the main room. Thankfully, I put new bedding on the bed here. I toss her onto the bed, and she laughs.

"God, Kenny, you are so beautiful," I say as I stare down at her. In nothing but a white lace bra and short denim shorts, she is my teenage dream. Her skin is tan, and her muscles are toned to perfection. Her hair spills over the pillow, still wavy and silky-looking, and I long to run my hand over it, through it.

She reaches down and unbuttons her shorts, then lifts herself up, sliding them down. One flick of her leg and the shorts are gone. She is staring at me, but I'm frozen, unable to do anything but watch.

I swallow hard and clear my throat. "Your underwear matches your bra."

"Yep. I did that for you. Do you like it?"

"Yes. So much. Damn, you are perfection. Do you know that?" I say. My voice sounds gravely to me, and I rub my hands roughly over my face.

"Lose the shorts, Patrick," she says, and my fingers listen, quickly undoing the button and zipper. I drop my shorts and kicked out of my shoes in one move. When I crawl onto the bed, I lay next to her instead of on top of her. If this is going to happen, I want it to last. I want to worship her.

She turns onto her side and runs her hand down my chest, pausing to dance her fingers through my chest hair. I push her hair behind her ear, then I cup her face and lean in to kiss her. The sudden realization that the entire box of condoms I purchased on my shopping trip is in my nightstand back at the ranch hits me like a bucket of ice-cold water.

Damn.

"Kenny, I can't do this," I blurt out like the idiot I am.

"What? Why?" She props herself up on one elbow, looking at me like I've lost my damn mind.

Which I have.

"I don't have condoms here." My hands move to my face and I groan. "I was going to wait, make sure you felt comfortable. I didn't want to rush you, and you just got back."

"I'm on the pill, Patrick," she says with a little eye roll. "Any other concerns?"

"Oh. Oh, well, I, um..." I stammer.

"I just had a physical before I started work and I'm healthy, you know?" She raises an eyebrow at me, then adds, "I don't have anything, and I haven't been with anyone in like a year." She trails her fingers over my cheek.

"Okay, well, I have never had sex without a condom," I'm overwhelmed at the thought of doing just that tonight.

"Really?" She sits up and looks down at me.

"Really. I am or have been really safe," I say, wondering if this is a good thing in her eyes. "It's also been a while for me, too." I added because, damn, I liked hearing that from her.

"God, that is so hot. So, I get to be your first experience bare?"

"Yeah, if you still want to. I mean, I would really like that if you—"

She cuts me off with her lips as she climbs over me, pressing me into the mattress. "I've never been happier," Kenny says breathlessly against my lips.

All I can do is smile and cover her mouth with mine, kissing her with all the passion I have held for the past few weeks. My hands slide down to grab her ass, pressing her into my hardened length. I'm immediately rewarded with a sweet moan from Kenny, and I roll us so I'm on top. I move down to her chest, wanting to get rid of that bra. The moonlight is bright enough for me to see the front clasp, and I flick it with my fingers, springing the bra open. Her perfect, round breasts appear with small, pink nipples pointing at me, begging for attention. Even if I want to dive right in, I take my time, tracing my thumbs over the top of her breasts, trailing down and grazing those tight rosebuds. I lower my mouth, unable to wait any longer, pulling one nipple with my lips, sucking and tugging gently. I use my other hand to worship her other breast, then switch, enjoying her moans and gasps.

I help her remove the bra, and as she lies back down, I smile and say, "I have never in my life seen tits so perfect."

"Thank you," she says, smiling up at me.

"Are you sure about this, Kenny?" I ask as I trail my hand down her stomach. I tease along the top of her white lace thong, giving it a little tug. It barely covers her, and I cannot focus on anything else.

"I'm sure, Patrick." Her gaze finds mine, and with an intensity matching my own, she says, "I want you." She kisses me. "Missed you." Her hands find my face, and she holds me with her gaze and her grip. "I need you," she says, and it's that last part that has me on my knees yanking that indecent lace underwear off her body. My hands slide up from her ankles, pressing her knees apart. I began my slow path of kisses to her center. She moans as I get closer, and I let my lips trace softly over her arousal.

"God, Patrick, you are driving me crazy."

"Good," I say, and I take a long and slow lick up her seam, slipping one finger in, testing her.

"Is this all for me? You are so wet." My voice is gruff as I peer up at her, enjoying the way her face is flushed, her expression desperate.

She squirms and whimpers, "That's so good, Patrick," so I add another finger. I slowly move in and out, curling my fingers up, hoping I'm hitting that spot. I want to see her fall apart, to crumble at my touch, to be the one who she is vulnerable with.

I dip my head down, then move my mouth over her, finding her clit and sucking as I twist my fingers. She grabs at my head, running her hands into my hair, pulling a little.

"Do you like that, Kenny?"

She looks down at me with her eyes half closed, licks her lips, and says, "It's so good. Please don't stop. I'm so close."

I resume my feast, licking and sucking every part of her, thrusting my fingers in and out until she yells out my name and clenches her thighs, lifting her ass off the bed. I draw out her orgasm, taking all of it. All of her.

When she finally lowers herself back to the bed, I slowly remove my fingers and sit up, wiping my mouth and smiling down at her.

"Oh my God. I have never had an orgasm like that. You need to give me a minute," she says, dropping her arm over her eyes.

"You're very good for my ego, Kenny." Crawling back up her body, I kiss a path that I want to memorize, map like it's my way home. My mouth finds her breast and I suck gently on her nipple before continuing on. When I finally make it to her lips, I place mine gently over hers, swallowing her sigh.

My emotions pour into this kiss softly, with each slide of my tongue I am taking my time to show her what she does to me. This could go on for hours, and I would be a happy man. Her soft lips and rewarding moans are igniting my blood in a way I've never experienced. I want to be everywhere all at once, over her, in her. The desire to consume every bit of her spikes as she reaches down and places her hand over my length, giving it a firm squeeze.

"Patrick, you need to get rid of this underwear. It's in my way."

I stand and pull them off quickly, moving back over her, settling on my forearms. I kissed her again, allowing my weight to settle on her fully, overwhelmed by the sensation of all of me touching all of her. She pushes at me, so I stop and look down at her.

"Roll onto your back, Patrick," she says in a seductive whisper.

Reluctantly, I rolled off her, pulling her with me. It was nice having her caged beneath me, trapped by my body. I liked the feeling that I could protect her.

She kisses my lips, then down my jaw to the pulse point at my neck. She peppers kisses all over my chest and moves down my stomach, causing my breathing to stop.

She chuckles. "It's going to be okay, Patrick. Just breathe. Can't have you passing out now when it's just about to get good."

She wraps her hand around my length, squeezing a little. "Well, Mr. Smith, you have been hiding this from me." She lowers her head and gently kisses around the tight skin at the base of my erection.

"I didn't mean to. It's yours now. You can have it," I huffed out, barely able to speak.

She runs her tongue up my cock, swirling it around the tip before going back down. My hips thrust up as if they had a mind of their own. "Jesus, sorry," I mutter, trying to catch my breath.

"God, you have an amazing dick, Patrick," she says, and before I can thank her, she takes my cock in her mouth, farther back than anyone has before. I know I'm not a small guy. Women have commented before on my size. The few times I have had a woman use her mouth on me, it was more of a tease. Don't get me wrong, it's all good, but I don't think I have ever had a real blow job until this moment.

Holy hell.

The tip of my cock hits the back of her throat and she swallows, taking me even deeper. My vision goes a little hazy, and I gasp as she starts to suck and move her tongue. She bobs her head, and I look down to see the most beautiful woman on earth looking up at me, watching my reaction. The sight of her lips wrapped around my cock and her hands moving up and down my length is so erotic I almost shoot off like a rocket.

"God, Kenny, I'm going to come if you keep doing that," I say, thinking that she will stop, but it seems to spur her on. She moves her hand a little faster and sucks a lot harder, moaning as I grab her hair.

Its building, the tingle at the base of my spine, the tightness in my balls, but the release comes so fast that there wasn't time to warn her. As I unload in her mouth, and she gulps and swallows, moving her hands to my thighs as I pump into her it seems she got what she wanted. Never in my life have I experienced anything like this. Stars, no, entire galaxies are exploding behind my eyes as my orgasm seems to go on forever. When the final shudder of my release subsides, I grab her and pull her up to me. Kissing her as if she holds the air I need to live, I realize that is true.

"Kenny," I finally manage to say. My breathing is still coming out hard and fast.

She just smiles down at me and tucks herself into the crook of my neck, making little circles across my chest and down my stomach. My cock twitches and jerks every time her hand gets close because I want her again. It doesn't seem to matter that I just had the best orgasm of my life. My dick is rising to the feathery touches of her hand.

Rolling us so I'm on top of her, she snakes her hand between us. Her hand wraps around me as she guides me to her entrance. I don't know how it's possible so soon, but I never went completely soft. My cock is thickening, growing stiffer again, so I pause, hold my breath and pray I will last longer this time. She is wet and tight and perfect. As the tip slips past her opening I groan, taking my time and allowing her to get used to my size.

"Hold on," she says, breathing a little harder. She shifts her hips a little, allowing me to slide in further, and we both groan.

"That's better," she says and kisses my lips softly.

I pull back and look down at her. "God, Kenny. You feel incredible."

"You're, um, bigger than I'm used to, give me a second."

I press my forehead to hers. "Am I hurting you?"

"No," she says, and she kisses me softly again, causing my cock to throb and beg for more. I want to be so deep in her she forgets all those other guys.

"I need to move, Kenny. I'll go slow," I say, and I squeeze my eyes shut for a second.

"Okay, I'm ready," she says, and she tilts her hips again, driving me even deeper. I groan at how tightly she is squeezing me.

I push slowly in, pulling back out a little, then pushing in further until there is nothing between us. The sensation of her around me, hot and wet, is heaven. This is where I want to be for the rest of my life. Right here. I pull back slowly, then move in all at once, enjoying the way her lips part and a small moan escapes.

"Oh God. Just keep doing that."

I lean close to her ear and whisper, "I couldn't stop if I tried."

That gets a laugh, and she moves with me, scraping her fingers across my back. Chills run down my body from her touch, and I'm caught between fire and ice. I want this to last longer, so I grab her and roll her over so she is on top of me.

"I want to see you," I say, my voice coming out more demanding than I intended.

Kenny smiles and leans forward, placing her hands on my chest and moving her hips in slow, steady circles. She lifts, and I see her glance down, watching me slide back into her. She reaches behind her and finds my balls, gently rolling them as she rides my length.

"Oh God. I'm going to explode if you keep doing that, and I want to see you come again. I need you to fall with me," I breathe out, and she smiles.

"I'm close too. Just fuck me, Patrick. Tell me what you need to get there and I'll do it."

This girl is absolutely perfect. I growl and grab her hips, holding her in place as I slam into her from below. Her eyes flutter and her head tips back at the same time I feel her pussy flutter and contract around me. There is no longer a sense of myself; where I stop and she begins is the same. Bright spots erupt in my vision as I strain to keep my eyes open to watch her fall apart on my cock.

It's too much. My balls tighten as I empty everything I have left into her. Her name bursts from me as I pin her in place, needing to be as deep as possible. Her shudders continue as well, and we both freeze, unable to look away from each other. She leans forward and places her lips on mine, and I wrap her in my arms, rolling us so we are on our side. I kiss her gently, thoroughly, and with as much passion as my heart can allow as it tries to regain its normal rhythm. The only thought going through my mind is how long I will need to wait before we can do that again.

COWBOY POETRY

BEYOND THE FENCE LINE~ PUBLISHED 1950

Her head dips low,
a slow smile spreads
Out here where there are only
us two
I capture parts of her
that I share with
Only the cabin, the meadow,
the mountains and the sky
~By M.S 1918

TWENTY-SEVEN
KENNY

I can't really say that I fell asleep. It was more like I lost consciousness.

After the first time, he held me like he thought I might escape, his big, warm hands exploring my body gently while he told me how beautiful I am. I felt drunk on his affection. It was overwhelming in the best way, and I couldn't keep my hands off him either. It didn't take Patrick long before he was moving again, sliding down between my legs, worshiping every inch of my body until we were trying to merge our bodies into one. I think it was around the third time that I floated off into another place, feeling loved and cared for.

I wake up with my leg draped over Patrick and his arm cradling me. His eyes are still closed, and his mouth is slightly open. I dragged my fingers through his hair so many times last night that it's sticking up everywhere in the most adorable way.

God, he is so handsome. He has these crazy, long, black eyelashes that rest on his perfect cheeks. His beard stubble is sexy as hell, but I think if he tried to grow a beard, it would be a little patchy. There are parts of his jaw that still have smooth skin, not a bit of stubble. I reach up and trace my finger down his cheek to his jawline, lightly running my thumb across his lips. Without warning, he opened his mouth and nipped at my thumb, earning a yelp from me. He throws his other arm around me and quickly rolls me onto my back, peppering my face and neck with kisses.

"Good morning, you beautiful thing," he says, and I smile up at him.

"Good morning. Any idea what time it is?"

"I don't even know what year it is anymore," he says, nuzzling into my neck.

I sigh and arch into him, wrapping my legs around him.

"Kenny?" Patrick asks as he tries to pull back a little.

I move my feet to his ass and pull him in. "Yes, Patrick?"

"There is no food here, and my stomach has started to reabsorb the rest of my body. I burned more calories last night than I have all month. I need to eat." Patrick gives me one quick kiss on my lips before jumping off me and grabbing his clothes.

"Okay. I'm actually pretty hungry too." I smile and stand, looking for my underwear. When he bends to pick up my shorts, bra, and thong, he looks at them, handing me only the bra and shorts. He stuffs my thong in his pocket.

"Hey! Those are mine!" I say, reaching for him.

"No. They belong to me now. I earned them. Do you not remember the things you said to me? You're mine, therefore I get to keep this sexy scrap of fabric you call underwear," Patrick says, pulling me close to him. He kisses me softly, moans and says, "Damn it. Why do I need to eat?"

"I'm sure that after breakfast there will be opportunities." I kissed him quickly before pulling away. When I walk into the main room, I find my tank top, get dressed and wait for Patrick. I glance around the room. In the daylight, it's even more charming. The fireplace is incredible, and I run my hand along the wooden mantel.

"It figures that is what you would be drawn to first," Patrick says, and I turn to look at him.

"Yeah, this is gorgeous. When was this cabin built?"

Patrick rubs his chin and says, "I think Rusty said around the 1800s. I'm sure there is something in the paperwork at the ranch. The house on Country Road W was built in 1950, Rusty said Mitchell lived out here full time until it was complete."

"There is no electricity! Is there running water?" I ask, and Patrick nods.

"According to Rusty they have a pipe from the creek that supplies water. The generator that was here is old, so I got a new one."

"Well, I'm sure we can make this place very livable."

Patrick smiles and says, "I'm so glad I met you." He pulls me in for a kiss, then grabs my hand and leads me out to the front of the cabin. I look around the meadow and the creek and sigh. This place is really a slice of heaven. I close my eyes and imagine Mitchell standing here in this same spot, and I feel connected to my old friend in a way that I haven't in a long time.

A little while later, when we pull up to the ranch house, Patrick stops at the big blue mailbox and gathers his mail before we go down the driveway. He set the pile of mail on the seat between us, and I glanced down at the envelopes.

"Your middle name is Russell?" I ask with a smirk.

"Yeah? Why? Is that a funny middle name?" He puts the truck in park, hops out and comes quickly to open my door.

"No, it's just interesting is all," I say, still smiling.

"Interesting?" He shrugs and says, "It's a family name, I guess. Meant something to my grandpa because my dad's middle name was Russell too."

"Really?" I stop him, placing my hand on his arm. My eyes were wide and eyebrows raised.

"Why are you looking at me like that?"

"How old would your dad be today if he had lived?" I ask.

"Let's see, he was born in 1925, so I guess he would have been sixty-three. Why are you asking me that?" Patrick unlocked the door and held it open for me. I walk through, trying to piece it all together before I say anything.

"I'm sorry. It's probably a coincidence, you know? Probably nothing. Hey, how old is Rusty?" I ask.

"Actually, I do. He was born in 1920. The same year Mitchell lost Helen," he says. He follows me as I walk into the kitchen. I put the mail on the table, and he goes to the fridge to pull out the eggs and some cheese, and peppers.

"Omelet okay?" he asks, and I nod.

He cracks the eggs into a bowl and adds a little water before whisking them all together. I step next to him to chop the peppers, still trying to figure out if there is anything worth mentioning.

"I guess I have a question if you don't mind," I finally say.

"Sure, I have no secrets."

"Well, so Rusty is short for Russell, and—" I start, but Patrick cuts me off.

"It is? Wait, really?" He has poured the egg mixture into a pan but turns toward me.

I finish chopping the peppers and slide the cutting board to him.

"Well, yeah. I remember I asked Mitchell once how long they had been friends because Rusty is a surly asshole most of the time, and Mitchell was, well, really sweet. Soft-spoken, kind," I say, then tilt my head and look at Patrick. "He was a lot like you."

"Oh, yeah. Rusty scares the crap out of me most of the time. Hey! Did you know he and Jenny are married?" Patrick says as he dumps the peppers into the eggs. He lets the whole thing bubble a little before scraping the eggs toward the middle, allowing the uncooked portion to spill onto the hot skillet.

I laugh and say, "Yes! But to be honest, it shocked the hell out of me when I found out too."

Patrick adds cheese to the eggs, then expertly folds them in half, creating a restaurant-quality omelet. He sprinkles a little more cheese over the top, then slides the whole thing onto a plate and starts the process all over again.

"There is hot sauce in the fridge if you want, or you can eat it like that. You don't have to wait for me. This won't take long," he says, and I shake my head.

"It's okay, I don't mind waiting. It has to cool off anyway," I say, then blurt out, "Hey, so are you secretly related to Rusty somehow?"

Patrick just laughs. He finishes his omelet and slides it onto a plate, then brings both plates to the kitchen table.

"Sorry if that was rude, but when I asked Mitchell how long he knew Rusty, he said as long as Rusty had been alive. A part of me assumed he was his son or something, like maybe Helen died in child-birth, but I didn't want to pry. I figured the only person that would put up with that grumpy-ass Rusty would be his family, you know?" I take a bite of my omelet. It's wonderful; just the right amount of salt and butter, and the cheese and peppers are perfect.

"Nah, Rusty explained it to me. I guess Mitchell was good friends with Rusty's dad. He was killed in a logging accident in the first year of Rusty's life. Mitchell had just lost Helen, so he kind of took on the role of father, but there is no blood between them."

"Oh, wow. That explains some, I guess. I could tell Mitchell thought the world of Rusty, even when Rusty was stomping around here grumbling about the cattle or something like that."

Patrick makes a noise in his throat as if he knows exactly what I mean about Rusty. He's finished his breakfast and is now leafing through the mail. A very thick envelope catches his attention, and he opens it and scans the first page, then flips to the very last page and gasps.

"What's wrong, Patrick?"

He shakes his head and puts his face in his hands. I'm not sure what to do, so I wait. He groans and leans back in his chair, blowing a puff of air up to the ceiling.

"I guess I better get to work," he says, and he stands, gathering our plates to take to the sink.

"Work? What are you talking about?"

"My next book. I have to get started on it because they think I have almost finished it. I guess I told them I was close to being done, so of course they think that. It's not like they are sitting there in their enormous glass building making shit up. Like, 'Oh, Patrick must have almost finished his first book in his new series. We better send him a boatload of money!'" he says, pacing and pulling at his hair. "But have I finished it? No. Have I even written one single fucking word of it? Also, no." Patrick lets out a groan that isn't the sexy kind I heard earlier. This one has pain behind it, and I stand and wrap him in my arms.

"It's going to be okay. You are a very talented writer. I'm sure you can do it," I say as I rub his back. "How long did it take you to write each Kent Price book?"

"About six months, but I had all the ideas. There were timelines and characters written out. I had locations I wanted him to visit in each book, outlines for all twelve books before the first one was even published. I learned his voice as I wrote, you know, so they got easier. But now? I have none of that. I just have some lame idea that I threw out in desperation when I met with my agent," he says, and he rests his chin on my head.

"Oh, well, that's... Oh," I say, understanding now why he is stressed out.

"Do you want to tell me about your idea? If you talk about it, I bet more will come to you. What was it?" I ask, pulling him by the hand into the living room.

We sink into the couch, and he puts his hands over his face and leans back into the cushions. He takes a ragged breath, then he says, "It was about a rancher who suddenly had a lot of money and the train that ran through his property was always getting robbed."

"Oh. So the rancher was a robber?" I ask.

"No, that would be lame and obvious and no. That can't be it. But do I know what it actually is, Kenny? No. No, I do not. Because it's a stupid, stupid idea. I went in there with no idea, talked about my poetry, and then when my agent looked like he was going to throw up, I came up with that! I don't understand what the hell I was thinking. There is no way to make that into something. It has dead end written all over it! I mean, seriously, what is wrong with the publishing company? Do they have no standards? It's horrible!" Patrick says.

"Poetry?" I ask, and he just sighs and presses his hands into his eyes a little harder.

"Yes. I was inspired by Mitchell. I've been writing poems since one night when I was on a drive and saw the stars. Saying it out loud makes me sound really, really lame, but that is how it happened," Patrick says with a sigh.

"Can I hear one of your poems?"

He drops his hand and cocks his head at me, his eyes twinkling with delight. "You want to hear my poems?"

"Well, sure. I really liked the book of cowboy poetry. I love that one of Mitchell's, but that entire book was really neat. I like to think about these rough-as-sandpaper ranchers sitting under the stars and writing beautiful words to describe their surroundings. It speaks to me."

"Okay, well, I have one committed to memory. The others I wrote down, and I'll show you someday, but"—he clears his throat and continues—"bright like I had never seen, leading me to you. The arch of the Milky Way, mirrored in the soft curve of your hip. I trace my fingers along the path, leading me to you." He stops and looks over at me with a vulnerable smile.

"Is that about me?" I ask, my question catching in my throat.

"Yes. I wrote it the first time you kissed me," he says.

"I love it," I say, feeling suddenly very overwhelmed by the man sitting next to me.

"I'm glad. To be honest, I wasn't ever planning on sharing it with you, or anyone really. I have written a lot of poems, but they are really just for me right now. It's like a salve for my soul. Those Kent Price books took all I had. They laid me bare and ruined me. To be honest, I didn't think I could write again. I mean, I wanted to. I came here hoping a change of scenery would inspire me, give me my next great novel, you know?" he says, turning to face me on the couch.

"Yeah, I can understand that." I placed my hand on his knee, hoping I could provide a bit of comfort.

"Well, I looked at the people I met here, trying to find a main character that could tell a story. Like when I first met Ryan, I thought, 'Okay, macho fire guy. He could be a main character, hero type,'" he says, and I instantly go stiff.

"I get that you don't like him, and now I get it, but I was just explaining that when I first met him, I wondered, you understand right?" Patrick seemed to sense my shift.

"It's okay. I get it. But that guy? He's a fucking douche. A jailbait-dating, know-it-all, probably-small-dick, two-pump chump. I hate him." I can feel my anger bubbling up in my chest.

"I really do understand, Kenny, sorry," he says, then pauses and asks, "Wait, did you say jailbait dating?"

I groan with irritation and say, "Yeah, he is fucking around with Bonnie at our ranger station, and she is only seventeen. Ryan is twenty-one. I overheard him telling her to sneak out and meet up with him, and she was making sure he'd bring condoms. God, he's so gross."

"What? Oh my God! Kenny, that isn't just gross, it's illegal!"

I put my head in my hands and say, "I know. I mean, I know what I heard, but it's not like I can prove it, and after he got away with going through my red bag in my tent, I didn't want to bring up another thing."

"What?" He shakes his head, then asked, "What's a red bag, and why was he in your tent?"

I explain about the bag we use for off-forest assignments and how I caught Ryan in my tent, and how he had pulled out my underwear from my dirty clothes. I tell him about how I went to the captain and nothing came of it. There's an uneasy feeling in my stomach as I recount the story, like I did something wrong. I try to shake it off and tell Patrick to forget about it.

"Listen, the season only lasts until October or November, and then he will go away and probably won't be back next year. I don't want to cause anymore conflict on the engine this year."

"Okay, but Kenny—" Patrick starts, and I cut him off with a wave of my hand.

"Seriously, Patrick. Let it go. There is nothing we can do about it, and I don't want him to be even more of an asshole to me than he already is."

Patrick lets out a long breath and closes his eyes. He stays that way for longer than I like, but he finally raises his head and looks at me. "Okay. I think you should tell your captain about the thing you overheard about that Bonnie girl, but I respect your decision. It's not my place."

"Thank you. Maybe she will break up with him, and I won't have to worry about it anymore."

"Yeah, maybe," he says, his voice tinged with sadness.

COWBOY POETRY

BEYOND THE FENCE LINE~ PUBLISHED 1950

Watched you walk away
When you knew it was wrong
Watched you take my heart
And I didn't know for how long
Would I die alone here
In the place where we came apart?
~By M.S 1922

TWENTY-EIGHT
PATRICK

After I drop Kenny off at her house, I go into the little store to grab a few things I'm out of, and run into Rusty. He is buying a bottle of wine, and I think, There's one more thing I didn't know about this guy. I figured he just drank whiskey and that black sludge he calls coffee. I would like to pretend that I don't see him, but this store isn't that big, and there is only one checker.

"How are you, Rusty?" I ask, and he looks over his shoulder at me. He grunts and looks back, waiting his turn at the register.

"Did you know your name is short for Russell?" I ask because I clearly have a death wish.

"Yeah, I'm familiar with my name, you ninny," he says without turning around.

"Well, Kenny pointed that out to me because, well, my dad's middle name was Russell, and take a guess what my middle name is?" I say, leaning too far into his personal space for my own safety, but I'm committed now. Might as well go for it.

Rusty turns slowly, and I step back a little, clutching my loaf of bread and my toothpaste. I attempt a laugh, but it sounds strangled and comes out more like a burp.

"Your middle name is Russell?" he asks, narrowing his eyes at me.

"Yep, just like my dad. Isn't that interesting?" I ask, and Rusty grunts, then turns around and goes back to ignoring me.

"I didn't know anything about it, except that it was a family name. I thought maybe it was on my dad's mom's side, but yep, I'm a Russell too in a way. Long line of Russells. You, my dad, me." I pause. Rusty steps up to the cash register and sets his wine on the counter. As the clerk rings him up, he stares straight ahead, handing over the cash when he's given the total. He turns on his heel and walks out without a word.

Sighing with defeat, I step up and pay for my things. When I go back out to my truck, I try to think of a way to bring this up again without getting punched. I'm surprised to see Rusty leaning against my truck with his arms folded across his chest.

"My father's name was Russell," he says matter-of-factly.

"Oh. Oh? So were he and my Grandpa Wallace friends too? Mitchell and your dad were friends, did they all know each other?"

"Yeah, Mitchell, his brother Wallace and my dad were all best friends. I couldn't get Mitchell to tell me very much over the years except that after my father died, he and your grandpa had a falling out. I wish I knew more now, knowing Wallace gave my name to his boy," Rusty says as he pushes himself off my truck.

He tips his head back, sighs, then says, "I think back on all the years I was around Mitchell, all the things he taught me, told me, and sometimes I wish I had a recording of it all. So I could play it back, go over it again and again." He is standing with his hands on his hips, and he levels his gaze at me. His expression is different now, but I can't put my finger on why.

"We don't always understand what lessons are important until after the teacher is gone. Now it's too late," he says with a shrug and walks over to a big motorcycle. It has fat tires and a large leather seat. The gas tank is a shiny silver with an American flag painted across the side. A black skullcap helmet hangs from the handlebars, and I can see the wine bottle sticking up from the leather saddlebag. He grabs the helmet and slips it over his bald head. Then he slings his leg over the huge street bike and kicks once to start the engine. The loud rumble makes me smile. Of course Rusty rides. He can pretty much do anything. I toss the groceries into my truck and walk down to the Frosty to get a milkshake. I don't want to go home yet. My things are due to arrive tomorrow, and that means my desk and my typewriter will be available to me for the first time in months. I feel my stomach twist at the thought of sitting down to write a story about a train-robbing rancher.

"Well, hey there, sweetie. How ya doing?" Jenny says as she leans on the windowsill.

"I'm good, Jenny. How are you?" An easy smile spreads across my face. Jenny is one of the nicest people I have ever met.

"I'm alright now, but will be better when I get home. I heard Rusty rumble by on the hog, so I'm betting he bought my favorite red wine," Jenny says, waggling her eyebrows at me.

"Oh yeah, I saw him," I say, then add, "He definitely had red wine with him."

"Good. He's such a romantic man. Sometimes I wonder how I got so lucky."

I look over my shoulder, wondering if I'm being pranked. When I glance back at her, she's wearing a dreamy smile that makes her look years younger.

"What can I get you?" she asks, ignoring my confusion.

"I would love a chocolate milkshake." I reach back for my wallet, but she stops me with a wave of her hand.

"It's on me, honey," Jenny says, ducking back into the restaurant. She reappears a minute later with a large shake topped with whipped cream, just how I like it. God, this woman is a saint.

"Would you tell me about how you and Rusty met someday?" I ask. I'm very curious about how someone as grumpy as him could be married to such a ray of sunshine.

"Not much to tell. We were in school together, he left for war, came home, and asked me to marry him," she says, ticking off each thing with a finger like she is counting.

"Oh, come on. No way that is the whole story!" I lick the whipped cream off the top of my shake and point to the door, telling her I'm coming inside. She rolls her eyes and smiles.

"Listen, you expect me to believe a sweet, kind woman like you just got swept off her feet by a guy like Rusty?" I say as soon as I walk into the small indoor seating area. There are only three tables, and I've noticed since moving here that most people choose to eat outside even if these are available. I sit on the chair that faces the kitchen and place my shake on the table.

"Well, you see one side of him, and I see another," she says with a wink.

"You're killing me. I was with him for a week, chasing cattle and fixing fences. He has two sides, and neither one of those has me understanding this. When we went to Seattle together, I guess I saw a little softer side, but make me understand, Jenny." I lean toward her with an expectant look on my face that makes her laugh.

She pours herself an iced tea and comes over to join me at the table. She pulls her apron off and drapes it over the chair before she sits.

"Patrick, people are more complex than characters in a book." She pauses and smiles, knowing I'm not going to let this go.

"Rusty and I have known each other since we were about eight years old. There were times that I hated him, and there were times we were friends." She runs her fingers over the outside of her cup, removing the condensation in trails.

"In high school he developed quite a crush on me, but I wasn't interested. By the time we were seniors, those feelings had flipped. I thought he hung the moon, and he wanted nothing to do with me. Then, his mom signed a letter so he could join the Air Force at seventeen. He wanted to go to war. He wanted to 'fly for freedom,' he always said." She pauses and blinks slowly, and I can see on her face she is back there, watching a seventeen-year-old boy leave for war.

She sighs and says, "He told me if he came back we would get married. He said that to me as he climbed into his friend's truck, like it was an afterthought, or maybe he wanted to give himself hope, you know?" She stops, and I nod, fully invested in this story.

"Mitchell was devastated. He was so mad at Mary for signing that letter. He told her she had just signed his death certificate." Jenny shakes her head and goes silent.

I'm not sure what to say. My father was too young for the war to end all wars, but he went to fight in the Korean War. My mom didn't think he'd come home. I was born in 1956, three years after that war ended. That was a background story in my house as I grew up. I wish I would've asked more questions about that time in my father's life. When I was younger, I wasn't interested in my dad's experiences, except for things I wanted to use in my books. I feel a pang of guilt at the memory of my asking very specific questions, never letting him just talk and tell his story.

Jenny clears her throat and says, "Rusty had flown some in high school. Mitchell taught him." Jenny mentions this as if it's something I would know about my great-uncle.

"Mitchell flew airplanes?" I'm shocked.

"Oh yeah, he was quite the daredevil. Anyway, since Rusty had a few hours under his belt, they fast-tracked him to fly. I try not to think about that. I am forever grateful that my sister and I were too dumb to understand what was really going on when the boys left the valley for war. It was all very romantic, you know, going off to fight against the Nazis. But when David Franco's family got a telegram that David was missing, then about a week later a black government car pulled into town." She stops and takes a breath before continuing. "Well, that is when it all started to get very real."

A customer comes to the window, and Jenny excuses herself to take the order as I sit with the weight of her words. There is so much I want to know, so many questions I wish I had asked. I miss my parents a lot, and I have gone through the stages of grief, but no one really explains that new things will pop up that start the process all over again.

I pinch the bridge of my nose and fight the tears off as I wait for Jenny to return. Taking my notepad out, I write some key points that she said, things that stuck with me. Mitchell is like an onion, and I'm sure I haven't made it through very many layers.

Jenny comes back and sits down, giving me a sweet smile. I put my pen behind my ear and tucked my notebook away, wanting her to see that she has my undivided attention.

"So how long was Rusty away at war?"

"Almost two years. He flew his allotted twenty-five missions and was set to go home, but he opted to stay a little longer. A friend of his was in the hospital, and he didn't want to leave him. He volunteered to fly two more so he could stay."

"That was brave."

She shoots me a look and says, "No, it was stupid. It was a miracle he made it through those twenty-five flights. Most airmen didn't come home."

"Well, he made it though. He came home in one piece."

"His body was in one piece, Patrick. But his mind? That is a whole different story." Jenny's expression has turned completely somber, something I have never seen.

"I'm sorry. A lot of the guys who made it home left their hearts and souls on the battlefield. I shouldn't have ever called Rusty a grumpy bastard. He has every right." My stomach sinks thinking about all the assumptions I've made.

Jenny takes a deep breath and sighs. "Patrick, Rusty is a grumpy bastard. He was that way when he was eight years old. The war didn't do that to him."

"Really?" I fight off a laugh because in my head, eight-year-old Rusty had a long, white beard.

"Yeah, that's just one side of him. No, the war took away his sense of humor. Rusty was the class clown, if you can picture it. Like a deadpan, dry sense of humor kind of guy. He was so quick and funny and, well, when he came back, that was gone."

"Rusty was funny?" I ask, completely perplexed.

"Oh, honey, he was so funny. His comic timing rivaled Bob Newhart's. It was one of the things that made me love him." She cocks her head at me and smiles before asking, "Why the sudden interest in our lives?"

I lean back in my chair, trying to put into words what I'm feeling. My overwhelming need to understand my roots. Even though Rusty isn't my blood relative, Mitchell thought of him like a son. I'm still confused why Mitchell left the ranch to me and not Rusty. Then there is the mystery of what happened between Mitchell and my grandfather. Now I also want to understand why my father and I have the middle name of Russell. I can't ask her all those questions now, because more will follow, I'm sure.

"Why did Rusty buy a bottle of wine?" I ask instead.

"Today is the anniversary of when he came back from the war. Today, forty-three years ago, I heard a motorcycle roll through town, and I stuck my head out that window,"—she points over her shoulder to the order window of the Frosty—"and a handsome nineteen-year-old man in military dress pulled into the driveway. He hopped off the bike and sauntered to the window." Jenny throws her head back and laughs. "I asked him what he wanted, and he didn't say anything. He just pulled me through the window and kissed me senseless." Jenny blushes and looks away.

"I was so mad. I pushed away from him, then I stormed out the door to tell him he had some nerve kissing me like that, but when I made it out the door, he was down on one knee with a ring in his hand, and I couldn't see through my tears to tell him anything but yes."

"So, there is significantly more to your story, Jenny." I chuckle, then ask, "Why are you waiting to go home when you have an airman waiting for you?"

"I like to make him wait. I wish I had made him wait that day, to be honest. Each year I think he waits at home a little bit longer for me to come. It's all I have against the force of his love," she says with a huge smile. "He overpowers me in the best way, Patrick."

I smile because I understand that for the first time in my life.

"Patrick, can I ask you a question?" Jenny asks, leaning forward in her chair.

"Of course."

"Is Kenny the reason you wanted to move here permanently?" She pins me with her bright blue eyes.

I freeze, unable to move or answer. Pretty sure I stopped breathing while I considered this question. Was it the reason? If there were no Kenny in Adin, California, would I have sold the ranch and the cattle and moved on? Would I have bought four books on how to raise and care for cattle? Would I have? I know the answer but am too ashamed to admit it to myself, let alone Jenny.

COWBOY POETRY

BEYOND THE FENCE LINE~ PUBLISHED 1950

When they ask who,
I will tell them it was
you
They will know by the blood on
your hands
And the guilt in
your eyes
But it will be me
That turns you in
~By M.S 1949

TWENTY-NINE
KENNY

I stare into my cupboards and refrigerator, hoping a balanced meal will appear.

It doesn't. I need to go to the store, but I'm so tired. A bowl of cereal is the best I can come up with, and I carry the bowl to the couch and get comfortable. My book rests on my lap while I eat. I need to read Misery before I visit my dad again, or he will be seriously mad. I glance over at Patrick's novel on the table and think about sending it to my father. He would probably enjoy it.

I take a huge spoonful of cereal and open the book on my lap. The premise makes me a little uncomfortable since I'm kind of obsessed with an author, but I assure myself my situation is different. I'm about ten pages in when I finish my cereal. After I put the bowl on the coffee table, I dive back into the book but only get a few pages when I hear a knock at my door. I glance up, not really positive that is what it was. I wait and it comes again, louder this time.

"Just a second!" I yell and grab my bookmark. I pad to the front door and pull it open, totally surprised to see Bonnie standing on my front porch with tears in her eyes.

"Kenny, can I talk to you?" she says, and I nod, stepping aside so she can come in.

"Hi, Bonnie. What's up?" I'm trying to sound casual, but she is literally the last person I expected to show up on my porch.

"Well, I would like to say this is a social call, but I'm here to ask you to please stop hitting on my boyfriend," she says, and I can tell it's a sentence she has practiced in the mirror. It kind of hurts my heart a little.

"I'm sorry?" I blink a few times, trying to register what she said.

"You heard me. Ryan said you are hitting on him at work, and it makes him uncomfortable. He wants you to stop," she says, and she puffs her chest out a little.

I blink again and shake my head because I've clearly fallen into a wormhole or something.

Bonnie pushes past me and goes to the couch, moving my book out of her way. She sits and levels her gaze at me as she says, "He's really handsome, I get it. But Kenny, we are in love. You can't keep trying to get him to go out with you."

"Sorry, Bonnie. I'm trying to understand what you are talking about." I walk toward her slowly with my hands up, like I'm approaching a crazy person, because I am.

She pulls out a pair of underwear from her pocket and drops it on the table, then points at them. "These, Kenny. Ryan said you left them in his room when he was gone, like you were trying to lure him or something. It's just sad. You can't do stuff like that." She tries to sit up straighter. If it were any other person accusing me of this, I would have already punched them right in the face.

I pick up the pink cotton thong and immediately recognized it as mine. There is the black mark from my soot-covered fingers when I pulled them off that night. The seam on the left is coming undone where I yanked the price tag off. My stomach drops, and I fight the urge to cover my mouth. He must have taken these from my red bag when he was in my tent. I'm going to kill that little fucker.

"I'm not sure how he got these, Bonnie, but I promise you I did not leave them in his room. I don't even know where he lives," I explain, and she shakes her head.

"He said he saw you leaving last night, and he thought you were maybe just leaving a note or something. Kenny, please, I really like you, and I don't want to have to fight you over a guy," she says, and I choke back a laugh, folding my lips together.

"Bonnie, last night I was on a date with Patrick. We went to The Bar and had a drink, then he took me out to Mitchell's cabin. I stayed the night out there with him," I say, really wanting to add something about the amazing sex I had, but I refrain.

"But that isn't possible," Bonnie says slowly, the wheels in her head spinning, trying to find a way to still believe her piece of shit "boyfriend."

"Well, you can ask Patrick if you don't believe me. We were together. I doubt I would make a pit stop at Ryan's house while on a date with the guy I'm seeing," I say, throwing my hands in the air.

"You and that new guy are dating?" Bonnie asks, and I laugh. Only in a small-ass town would that be something uttered by a local.

"Yes. We have been for a while now." I sit down next to her on the couch. This is the first time I've said that to anyone other than Luke.

"Well, why does Ryan have your underwear then? I don't understand," Bonnie says in a sad, small voice. She looks around my little government-issued house, and I can see her eyes sparkling with tears.

I rub my hand down my face, wishing I was better at stuff like this. Truth is, I'm horrible at stuff like this. I have exactly one female friend. The rest of my friends are guys. I don't really do girl talk or comfort or whatever the fuck this is about to be.

"Bonnie, Ryan is an idiot," I start, and immediately realize this is not what she wants to hear.

Her head whips towards me, and she is immediately defensive. "I love him, Kenny."

"I understand. I do, but I see a different side of him than you do.

You get that, right? Like at work, he's different. We don't get along at all, Bonnie. I have to fight off the urge to punch him right in his boys every day. Trust me, I'm not flirting with him."

She twists her hands in her lap and chews on her lip. She isn't saying anything, so the need to fill the uncomfortable silence tugs at me.

"Bonnie, I want you to realize there are always going to be guys like Ryan. Guys who are good at hiding their worst side to get what they want." There is more I want to say, but she interrupts me.

"He loves me. He told me that. We were each other's firsts. He said he waited for me when he didn't even know me. Like he said, he felt like I was why he waited."

"Oh, Bonnie, no." I shake my head, trying to figure out how to tell this young, naive girl that she gave her virginity to a lying sack of shit. I look up into her eyes, and I can't do it. I can't be the one to break her heart.

"Okay, well, how about this? I'll ask him where he got these and find out why he's telling you these things. It doesn't make any sense, and I'm sorry you are hurting. I'd never do that to you, Bonnie. I knew you guys were dating," I say, and I choke a little on the word dating. That is not what Ryan is doing. God, he is such a pig. I hated him before, but now I want to kill him.

"You'd do that? Gosh, Kenny, that is really nice of you. My Uncle Rusty said you are a good person. I should have known you wouldn't do the things Ryan said. I just don't get why he would make up such a story." Bonnie put her hands over her face and takes a breath or two before lowering them and standing.

She turns to face me as I stand up too. I reached my arms out, awkwardly pulling her into a hug complete with weird back pats.

"I'll get to the bottom of this, Bonnie. I promise."

Her eyes brighten suddenly, and she says, "Maybe they fell out of your red bag that day you guys got into town, and Luke thought it would be funny to mess with you two. I bet that is it. Ryan said that he and Luke are always playing pranks on each other. Guys in fire are like that," she says, apparently forgetting I'm a "guy in fire."

"Sure, yeah, I guess that could be it." My underwear on the coffee table is making me uncomfortable, so I grab the pink thong and shove it into my pocket.

"Well, I'm on my lunch break, so I'd better get back. Thanks, Kenny. I appreciate you talking to me. You're so mature and cool and stuff," Bonnie says, and I give her a tight smile. My blood pressure must be off the charts. My eye is twitching and the vein in my forehead throbs. I follow Bonnie out and walk toward The Bar as she veers off to return to the ranger station. I need a beer and a plan.

When I push through the door of The Bar, it takes my eyes a moment to adjust to the dark room. I pause in the entryway and blink a few times. When the room comes into focus, I see Luke and Zia at the pool table. She lifts a hand and waves me over.

A huge smile crosses my face. "Hey, Zia! I haven't seen you in a long time. How are you?" Zia is the most beautiful woman I have ever seen. She has jet-black hair and eyes to match. Her wide cheekbones and big eyes are alluring and feminine, but also a little intimidating. She has perfect, full lips and a big smile that lights up her face.

"I'm great, Kenny. Ma wants me to see if you'll come by soon. She wants to add to that deck in the front. She won't let any of my cousins work on it now that she knows a woman carpenter." Zia's laugh is as beautiful as she is.

"Of course I will! I told her that she needed to run it all along the front of the house. I'm not surprised she wants that. If I tell you the supplies I need, can you get them before I come out? Luke and I could knock that out in an afternoon." I kick at Luke, who is trying to make a shot.

"Hey! I would have made that," Luke says as the cue ball bounces off the edge of the table.

"No, you wouldn't have," I say and turn toward the bar. I need that beer, then I'm going to kick Luke's ass at pool.

Jimmy is behind the bar, wiping glasses and setting them on a rack. He's staring out the front window, squinting as if he's trying to make out who someone is from a distance. I glance over my shoulder, Ryan is walking past on the opposite side of the street. He turns up Aspen Avenue, and Jimmy and I watch him until he is out of view.

I clear my throat and place my hands on the bar, telling myself to breathe. No good will come from me running out of here and kicking Ryan right in his twig and berries. Even if I can practically feel my foot connecting with his junk. I glance up at Jimmy, who seems to be thinking the same thing. Interesting.

"Can I get a Coors Light, Jimmy?"

"Bottle or draft?" he asks without taking his eyes off the window.

"Bottle. Your tap always has too much foam for me," I say, hoping to get a laugh or at least eye contact.

Jimmy reaches under the bar to the small fridge there and pulls out a bottle, popping the top before handing it to me. He never takes his eyes off the window, so I glance back too, sliding onto a stool.

"You watching Ryan?"

"Yep," he says, popping the p at the end.

"Can I ask why?"

"Don't like that kid. Want to make sure he knows it," Jimmy says, twisting his rag into another glass and setting it on the rack before grabbing one more to do the same.

"I can feel your glare from here, so I'm sure all the hairs on his stupid head are standing straight up."

"Hope so," he says.

I take a long drink of my beer and can hear Zia and Luke laughing behind me over a terrible shot that Luke made. That guy sucks at pool, even when he's not stoned.

I study Jimmy, then glance down at my beer. Digging my nail into the top of the label, I pick at it, hoping to get a clean pull. There is something very satisfying about ripping the label off an ice-cold longneck. My nails are too short, so I just manage to make a mess.

I'm trying to gather the courage to ask Jimmy why he hates Ryan. Not like I care what his beef is; more like I want to know if it's the same reason I hate that greasy little fucker. Jimmy would see how Ryan is with the local women.

He finally looks away from the window and sighs. "How is he on the engine crew, Kenny? You have any problems with him?"

"Me personally? Yes. The guy is a fuckwad," I say without hesitation, and Jimmy laughs.

"I like how you tell it like it is, Kenny."

"Well, he is. You know the deal. Most guys think I don't know my shit because I'm a girl or whatever."

Jimmy chimes in. "You are a better firefighter than most of the guys I have seen come through here, Kenny, and I haven't been on the line with you. I just know."

"Thanks, Jimmy."

"So you don't like him?"

"No."

"What about the surfer boy over there?" Jimmy asks.

Without missing a beat, Luke yells, "Fucking hate that loser."

We both laugh, and I yell back, "Thanks, Luke."

"So why do you hate him, Jimmy? Don't see you disliking many people," I say, finishing my beer. He grabs the empty and tosses it behind him, landing it in the trash without having to look. He raised his eyebrows in question. I nod, and he hands me another beer before answering.

"Can't put my finger on it. I've seen him in here, and he's just slimy. I can see the way women react to him, like all on edge. Do you understand?"

"Yeah, I mean I can see how he would creep the women out. He hits on all the women on the fire line. It's just gross."

"I was at the ranger station the other day getting a burn permit, and he walked in to talk to Bonnie. Gotta say it made me very uneasy how excited she was to see him. Sweet girl, that Bonnie. But man, I don't think she has all her chickens in the coop, ya know?"

I spit out my beer and clamp my hand over my mouth. I've never laughed and growled at the same time. God, I think I have beer in my lungs. Coughing a few times I pound my hand on my chest.

"Jesus, Jimmy. You can't just whip out the funny small-town sayings like that." I wipe my hand down my face and smile at him.

"Well, it's true. If she wasn't Jenny and Rusty's niece..." He shakes his head and stopped talking.

"Yeah, I think she is pretty sweet on him," I say, not giving up any more.

"She needs to focus on school and just graduate high school. I saw her last year at the Fourth of July parade, and I asked her if she was excited to see the fireworks, and she looked up at the sky. It was the middle of the day, Kenny." Jimmy shakes his head in disbelief.

I laugh and shift on my stool, suddenly very aware of my pink thong I have shoved in my pocket. I pat the bar and tell him I'm going to play a round of pool. Jimmy just nods at me, and I slide off the barstool and head over to Luke and Zia.

"Hey, can I show you guys something?" I say, slipping my hand into my pocket.

"Five ball in the corner pocket," Zia says, expertly hitting the cue ball into the five, zinging it off the bumper and right into her pocket. Luke groans, and I laugh.

"Okay. Sure, Kenny. What's up?" Zia says, leaning her stick on the table. Luke picks his up and walks around, looking for a shot he can actually make. I pull the underwear out of my pocket and drop it on the felt.

"Listen, I like you, Kenny, I really do, but Zia and I aren't into sharing," Luke says, looking at my underwear.

"Gross. No thanks. Not what I was going to say."

"What's with the thong?" Zia asks, raising her perfect eyebrows at me.

"They're mine. Bonnie brought them over to my house. She said they were at Ryan's," I explain. I lean with both hands on the green felt of the pool table and rub my thumbs across it, contemplating the ways I want to hurt Ryan.

"Why the fuck did he have your underwear?" Luke says, slamming his pool stick down. Jimmy looks over at us but doesn't say anything. I don't know if he heard me, so I lowered my voice.

"Well, he told Bonnie that I left them at his house because I'm hitting on him all the time and I want to date him."

Luke barks out a laugh, but Zia's eyes darken. Her nostrils flared as she breathed in deeply.

"What?" The word comes out as a snarl.

"Yep. Apparently I am so hot for him I am breaking into his house to leave him my underwear."

She places her stick calmly on the table and spins to look at Luke. "Let's go."

"What? Where?" Luke asks, putting his pool stick next to hers.

"We're getting my brothers, and then we are going to pay that little mullet-wearing white boy a visit." Zia looks fucking terrifying. Her eyes go even darker, and she is grinding her teeth.

"Babe, no. We can't just call in the Mountains," he says, using their widely known nickname. "Let Kenny finish. I'm sure she has a plan for how to handle this."

Truthfully, I don't, and the thought of Zia's six foot-four twin brothers rolling up to Ryan's front door makes me unreasonably happy. I met them once and almost wet my pants, and they were smiling at me. Don't want to imagine what them angry would look like. I'm guessing about ten times more terrifying than how Zia looks right now.

I clear my throat and say, "I'd like to talk to Ted again. I want him to know there's more, you know?" My heart sinks because that is a way weaker option than the twin mountains.

"More?" Zia asks, and I fill her in on the things that have happened. I can't help but notice that she is looking at Luke as if she is disappointed in him for not sharing this information with her.

"Okay, well, I guess that is a place to start, Kenny. You need to be careful, though. Guys like Ryan aren't just creepy. He could be dangerous." Zia arches an eyebrow.

"Nah, he's afraid of me," I say, and I scoop up my underwear and put them in my pocket. I take a deep breath and blow it out, frustrated that I have to deal with this.

"Well, if you need anything, just let me know. My brothers are back for the summer, and I have a feeling they would love to kick the shit out of that idiot," Zia thinks about it for a minute before adding, "I would too."

COWBOY POETRY

BEYOND THE FENCE LINE~ PUBLISHED 1950

Thunderclap, lightning boil
Wide eyes on the range
Fear scurries through the herd
As driving rain pelts the soil
They hunker down under the oaks
Folding ears and lowered head
The storm will pass
But the fear lingers, soaks.
~By M.S 1923

THIRTY

KENNY

As I walk into work the next morning, I steel myself for a tough day. I'm going to talk to Ted, preferably first thing. I toss my backpack into the engine bay near the desk and glance around.

Luke comes in and gives me a nod. "Want me to come with you?"

"Nah, I'm good. I'll see if he's in the office. I thought he'd be out here."

Luke crosses to me, placing a hand on my shoulder. "Kenny, I would've kicked his ass if I had known."

"I know, I would've too. Oh, so you know, he told Bonnie that you and he are best buds and play jokes on each other all the time."

Luke rolls his eyes at that. "Tell me what Ted says, okay?" He gives me a little shake, and I nod.

Ten minutes later I come back out frustrated and angry. I slam my foot into the desk and curse.

"Well?" Luke asks.

"What the fuck do you think? He said he would look into it." I make air quotes.

"Well, that won't do." Luke stands up and crosses to the phone. I realize what he is about to do and step in front of him.

"No. Don't call Zia. I will deal with him." My body is vibrating with anger.

"Okay. I'll give Ted some time too but, if this isn't handled soon, we'll have to fix this."

"I know."

"Fix what?" Ryan says, walking over to us and dropping his bag. "The pump out at Rice Creek busted again?"

I spin on my heels and take a step toward him, anger spilling out of me like waves breaking on a beach.

"You are an asshole," I spit out, and Ryan leans back as if I had hit him.

"Hey there. Settle down, Kendra. Are you on your period or something? Jesus, I only asked a question." He jerks his thumb towards me and says to Luke, "Chicks, am I right?"

I lunge before I can even think about it, grabbing Ryan by his shirt, as Ted walks into the engine bay.

"Kenny!" Ted's voice echoed through the room like a gunshot, making me freeze.

"She attacked me, Ted! I asked if the pump was broken out at Rice Creek, and she called me a name and grabbed me. I can't work with her! She is crazy!" Ryan has his hands up in the air in surrender, and I glance down at my clenched fists. To calm my breathing, I take slow, purposeful breaths through my nose. I'm sure I appear crazy because at the moment I am.

"Kenny, I told you I would look into this. You shouldn't be taking this into your own hands, literally. Step back and give me a minute," Ted says.

I pull the pink thong and toss it at Ted. "Ask him why my underwear was at his house. Oh, and while you're at it, Ted, ask him why his underage girlfriend Bonnie was the one to tell me he had them."

Ted snaps his head toward me, then immediately back at Ryan, who looks down at his shoes. Ted's face gets red, and his eyes narrow.

I tried to tell him in his office, but as soon as I said I was having problems with Ryan again, he didn't want the whole story. The only part I was able to get out was that Ryan said I was hitting on him at work before he shooed me away. I guess I should have led with the Bonnie thing, because Ted looks pissed.

"Is that true?" Ted says, eyes burning holes in Ryan.

"What part?" Ryan asks. He steps back a little and widens his stance.

"The part where you're dating a seventeen-year-old, and the part where she found your co-worker's underwear at your house. Those parts, Ryan." Ted puts his hands on his hips and waits.

Ryan doesn't blink or move. He just says in an even tone, "Bonnie is just a friend. I don't know why she would say those things."

"Well, why did she have my underwear? She came to my house yesterday on her lunch, accusing me of trying to steal her man by leaving my underwear at your house!"

"Well, what if you did? How should I know how they got there?" Ryan asks, and Luke reaches over to grab me before I can lunge forward.

Just then the overhead speaker crackled, then a tone filled the room, quickly followed by another tone. Dispatch saying, "Engine four, medical aid Hwy 299, mile marker twenty-three, motorcycle down, two injured, ambulance en route."

I spin and run to the engine, yanking the door open so Ryan can climb in. Ted and Luke are right behind us, and Chuck is climbing in. Ted radios dispatch to say we are on our way.

I lean back in the seat and go over the possible injuries in my head, trying to focus on the task at hand instead of how I want to reach over and rip Ryan's face off.

The accident is bad. An older gentleman and his wife, returning from a poker run in Reno, took a turn too fast and went down hard. The female has a broken leg, but the man suffered a laceration to his abdomen. Ted sent me in the ambulance to the hospital in Fall River

Mills so I could help the EMTII with care. Crashes out here are always worse because we are so far away from any type of hospital care. That "golden hour" gets eaten up just driving the patient to the hospital.

When I finally get back to the ranger station in Adin, everyone else is off work since it's past seven. I go into the engine bay to grab my bag and head home, looking forward to a quiet evening. I want to call Patrick and see how he is doing. His moving truck was due today, so I imagine he was pretty busy.

I have no idea what happened after I left the crew to go to the hospital, but I hope like hell that Ted spent some time talking to Ryan and got some answers. I trudge up the hill toward my house, suddenly feeling how tired I am. We grabbed dinner before heading back up the hill, so at least I don't need to cook a meal when I get home.

I push into my house and drop my bag, heading to the fridge to get a cold beer. As soon as I open the door, I hear a creak behind me. I freeze and take a breath. It's weird, but I've felt on edge ever since Bonnie came over. I reach in, grab a beer, and turn around slowly, holding the bottle in my fist by the neck.

There are heavy boots on the wooden floor in the hallway, and I take a step forward cocking my head. Maybe it's Patrick. Maybe he came to surprise me; he's like that. I want to believe this, but every fiber of my being knows it's not Patrick.

"Took you long enough." I hear the voice before I can register where it's coming from. I spin and look at my couch, then back down the dark hall toward my bedroom. There, silhouetted in the archway, is a man's frame. I know immediately who it is. I moved the bottle behind my back and stepped into the living room.

"Why are you in my house, Ryan?" I ask, and I hate how my voice is shaking. I clear my throat, but it feels like I just ate a peanut butter sandwich. My throat clogged and thick.

Words swirl through my mind, like I'm strong; don't be afraid. I can kick his ass. I can defend myself. As these are spinning through my head, trying to land and gain traction, my feet have become glued to the floor.

"Waiting for you, baby," he drawls, and my stomach turns.

I take a breath, fighting the pain and fear rising in my chest, and say as calmly as I can, "Get out of my house, Ryan."

"I might get fired because of you. Why are you such a bitch, Kendra?" Ryan steps forward toward the living room where I'm standing. The bottle is still behind my back, so I put my other hand on my hip, hoping he doesn't notice what I'm holding.

"Get out of my house, Ryan," I say again, calmer this time. I blink and try to count to three, but he moves closer quickly. I step back and run into the wall, the bottle clanking against the doorjamb.

"What do you have behind your back, Kendra?" he asks as he takes another step toward me. He isn't much taller than I am, and not much bigger. I'm strong. I have muscular arms, strong legs, and I can defend myself. I can. Except I can't move. Him being here and coming out of my bedroom—my personal space—has me so fucked up. I swallow hard and wait for him to take another step. Just as he does, I swing the bottle at his head, but he ducks and grabs my wrist, twisting it quickly. The beer flies free of my grip and falls to the floor with a crash. The bottle doesn't break, but the beer sloshes out onto the wood as he kicks it away. He holds my wrist at an angle that is so painful I see stars.

"Get out of my house, Ryan," I say for the third time, but it sounds so weak. I squeeze my eyes shut for just a minute and try to squirm free. I manage to kick him, my boot landing just above his knee. He yells out in pain and twists my wrist harder, moving it quickly up and behind me. I cry out in pain, and it seems to encourage him more. He spins me by twisting my arm and slams me into the wall face-first, then pushes himself against my back.

I can smell beer and cigarettes on his breath as he whispers, "I better not get fired because of you, Kendra. You shouldn't even have this job, you fucking little bitch. Stealing jobs from men who deserve them? That's not cool, Kendra." His breath is hot and stale on my cheek. He shoves my wrist up higher, and this time I refuse to make a noise. He reaches around, grabbing at my shirt just above my breast where our engine logo is, and he yanks it. As the shirt rips, Ryan snickers.

"You shouldn't get to have this shirt. It's a man's shirt. Girls should wear pretty things, Kendra." He lets his hand trail over my breast where he tore my shirt, and I shudder.

Closing my eyes, I count again to calm my nerves. I need to spin, need to throw him off me. I understand these things, but my body won't cooperate. As I sag against the wall and whimper, he kicks my feet apart. It's now or never, so I shift to the right as I lift my left leg and stomp down with all my strength on the top of his foot. The only reason it works is because I caught him off guard. He thought I was giving up. Ryan drops my wrist, and I spin and grab his shirt, pulling him into me as I bring a knee up into his groin. He grunts but doesn't drop like I expect. Instead, the last thing I see is his fist barreling down on my face. I hear a crack, and the darkness spreads through my consciousness like oil across a pond.

COWBOY POETRY

BEYOND THE FENCE LINE~ PUBLISHED 1950

The clouds roll in blocking the sun
Casting shadows over my land
I see the patterns in the tall grass
As I ride.
Can I hide in the shadows
Like I did as a child
Will she find me
like she did back then?
~By M.S 1940

The ambulance returned a little past six, so I know she's home, but since I'm not a needy boyfriend, I decide to finish my beer before going to see her. Luke filled me in on the accident they went to, explaining why Kenny wasn't back, and introduced me to his girl-friend, Zia. She is lovely. A tall, thin girl with thick black hair that goes to her waist in a braid. She has the darkest eyes I have ever seen, and I was compelled to write a quick note so I could use a description of her in the future.

All of my things arrived from Seattle, and I found a home for my furniture, then led the moving truck out to the cabin with some of Mitchell's furniture that had been at the ranch house. It was a very exhausting ordeal, but it had to be done.

I had walked into the front bedroom of the ranch house, the one I turned into my office, and had zero inspiration to write. I even tried sitting at my desk and threading a piece of clean, white paper into my typewriter, hands poised, but nothing came to me.

I knew better than to fight writer's block, so I headed into town to see Kenny.

Now, after two beers and a lovely cheesesteak sandwich Jenny whipped up for me, I'm ready to go to my girl. I stand and wave at everyone walking out of the propped-open door. With my head down, the night I left the bar with Kenny comes to my mind. She was such a funny drunk. The memory tugs at my lips, a smile forming. When I see the patch of grass where she had lain, I turn, remembering how she said you could see her house from here. Yep, you sure can. There it is right on top of the hill, although now it's still light out, and that night it'd been much later. The whole town looks pretty in the fading sun, and I take a deep breath in, closing my eyes for a moment.

When I open them and step forward to cross the street, I hear dogs barking and catch a glimpse of what looks like Ryan jogging across Kenny's little lawn area. He turns and heads up the hill away from me and the road. An uneasy tingle creeps up my spine. My feet move faster, unsure if I'm chasing him or trying to get to Kenny. When I reach her house I can't see him anymore, so I run up the stairs and knock on the door. My knuckles rapping on the wood causes the door to creak open, so I poke my head in and call out, "Kenny?"

When there is no answer, I push the door open the rest of the way, spotting a beer bottle on the floor in a puddle. I call out again louder this time, "Kenny?"

I walk all the way in and let my eyes adjust to the dark, long enough to find the light switch. I flip the switch up and glance around, seeing nothing out of place in her small kitchen. As soon as I turn the corner into the living room however, my heart stops.

Kenny is lying on the floor, her face covered in blood. Her shirt torn at the neck, exposing her left breast. Quickly, I'm at her side on my knees, desperate to see if she is okay. I feel for her pulse on her neck with two fingers, a wave of relief floods me when the strong, stubborn thumping of her heart presses back against my fingertips. I say her name softly at first, then louder. "Kenny?" She doesn't stir at all. Glancing around, I'm unsure what to do first. I need help; that much is clear. I run to the phone in the kitchen and call the Frosty.

Kenny had explained how they don't have 911 up here yet, so if there was ever an emergency, I should call the Frosty. After hours, the phone is rerouted to all the first responders in town via a party line.

"Fire phone, Ted speaking. What's your emergency?"

"Ted? This is Patrick. I'm at Kenny's house. She's hurt." I pinch the bridge of my nose and blow out a breath. My voice is shaky as I say, "Um, she has a pulse, and she's breathing, but she's not answering me. She has blood all over her face."

"I'm on my way," Ted barks, and I hear several other people on the line say the same thing. I hang up and hurry back to Kenny. Kneeling down, I grabbed her hand and notice the bruising along her wrist. It's swollen and red, so I lay it back down gently and move to her other side. It's hours, my heart will tell you, before Ted and Chuck come running in with Luke and Zia right behind them.

"Shit." Ted comes up to Kenny on her right side. He kneels down and opens his medical bag, grabbing his stethoscope and a few other things.

"Her wrist looks like it's hurt," I say lamely.

I wish I knew what to do, how to help. Since I don't, I move out of the way and let Chuck come over to her left side. I sit on the couch, unable to take my eyes off her. Watching as Ted moves his hands over her body and down her arms and legs, gently but with purpose.

He turns to Chuck and says, "Her belt isn't undone. Her shirt is still tucked in. I don't think—" He stops himself, and Chuck nods. When Ted is done with his search for injuries, he snaps a small white package and waves it under her nose.

Kenny groans, and the reverberation hits me from across the room. It rattles my heart inside my chest, and I have to tell myself to breathe.

"Easy, Kenny. Hold still now. Can you open your eyes?" Ted says. He's leaning forward, gently pushing on her face with his thumbs. He starts at her jawline, then works his way inward toward her cheeks and nose.

"This orbit might have a fracture. Chuck, let's get her in a C-collar just to be safe. I want to take her down to Fall River Mills for some X-rays. Her nose looks broken, and I don't like how her wrist felt on palpation, there's already a lot of swelling."

Luke steps closer to Kenny, but Zia comes to sit next to me on the couch. Her eyes are wide, and having her next to me makes me feel better. I'm not the only one overwhelmed by this scene playing out in Kenny's living room.

"Luke, go get the ambulance. I ran up here, wasn't thinking straight," Ted says as he stands. He pulls a set of keys from his pocket and tosses them at Luke. "And get Henry. I want him to drive so I can be in the back with her. Chuck, you stay here. We can't all be gone if the engine gets called out. Neil or Rick can take Kenny's spot."

Luke turns to go just as Ted says, "Oh, and call Ryan. Let him know what happened."

At that, my memory of seeing him jogging from the house snaps into focus, and I shout, "Ryan was here! I saw him running up the hill that way." I pointed in the direction he went, no more than ten minutes ago.

Zia stiffens next to me, and she and Luke share an unspoken sentence. She nods and says, "Time to go to the mountains." She stands and follows Luke out the door.

Kenny groans again and tries to move her head, but Chuck has put a rigid collar around her neck. She lifts her left hand to touch her face, and I step over so I can look down at her. Dropping to my knees, I lean over and gently press my lips to her forehead.

"Hi," she says weakly.

"Hi. Are you okay, Kenny?"

"Probably not. Ryan attacked me, and now I'm going to murder him. I'll be going to jail soon, Patrick," she says, and Chuck comes back over, kneeling down next to her.

"Ryan did this to you?" he asks, his jaw grinding and his nostrils flaring.

"Yeah, he was in my house when I came back from that call.

Little fucker. I need to get up, Chuck. I'm fine. Don't make me go all the way back to Fall River Mills tonight."

Chuck shakes his head. "Ted isn't going to take no for an answer. You need to get some X-rays, and we need to get law enforcement involved. Our L-4 is out of town. We will talk to the sheriff or the highway patrol."

This time the groan that escapes Kenny's lips is one of frustration rather than pain. Ted and Luke came back in with a backboard, and they positioned it next to Kenny, who started to curse and complain. I move out of the way and watch as the three men carry their friend out to the ambulance. My heart must be strapped on that board too, because I can feel it being pulled away from me.

I've followed them down the stairs to the ambulance, but I can't let them take her away, can't bear to have those doors close from the outside. The words tumble out, "Can I go?"

"That is the only part of this that sounds like a good idea. You better let Patrick come with me!" Kenny yells into the night.

Ted looks at me and nods, so I climb in, grateful I can be with my beating heart. Watching it drive away would have killed me.

The drive down to the small hospital in Fall River Mills takes forever. Kenny tells us everything she can remember about what happened, but it isn't very much. She remembers coming home, getting a beer out of the fridge, and then getting punched in the face. I'm sure more happened, but try as she might, she can't remember. She isn't sure what happened to her wrist; she doesn't know how her shirt got torn, and she isn't sure how long Ryan was in her home. Ted takes notes, writing everything down and then asking her again but phrasing it in a slightly different way. I'm sure he's hoping she will remember more.

After an hour and a half at what I would call a clinic, not a hospital, we all loaded back into the ambulance. This time Ted drives and Henry rides in the passenger seat, allowing Kenny and me to sit in the back. She has a hairline fracture on her wrist and in her eye socket. Her nose is broken, and the doctor had to set it. I almost threw up when he explained to Kenny what he was going to do. She took it like a champ. Well, a champ who was offered morphine. In my head, and when I retell this story years from now, I'm sure I'll say she reset her nose herself. She is that much of a badass.

There's a soft cast and bandage wrap on her wrist, and a large butterfly-shaped brace on her nose. The doctor said she would probably continue to swell and bruise. I don't know how it could get worse. She already has two black eyes, and her lips look puffy.

I'm holding her good hand as she closes her eyes to rest. I can't keep my eyes off her. My heart has cracked wide open, and I want to pull her inside me to protect her.

An officer had met us at the emergency room, and Kenny recounted the attack, and Ted filled in the information about what had happened leading up to tonight. I learned Ryan had a pair of her underwear, and Bonnie confronted her about it. This is all so messed up. I've never been so wrong about a person as I was about Ryan. When I met him in the store that day, I thought he was so cool. My eyes close with the weight of the day and the guilt of not being there for her. I lean back against my seat, not letting go of Kenny's hand.

I must've dozed off because I'm startled when Ted opens the back door of the ambulance. Kenny opens her eyes too and looks out at her boss blinking a few times.

"Where are we?" she asks.

Ted nods over his shoulder. "Back at your place, Kenny."

"No. No, thank you," she says, and she slowly shakes her head, wincing in pain as she does. I had unbuckled and stood up, but stopped when I saw her.

"Kenny, are you okay?"

"I'm not staying here. No. Nope." She is still shaking her head.

"Okay. Well, we can stay out at the ranch. My truck is at the Frosty. I'll go get it," I say, but Ted climbs in the back with us and sits down in front of Kenny.

"Kenny, do you want to stay with Patrick? I can check your

house, you know, make sure it's safe before you go in," Ted says, and she shakes her head again.

"Nope. Not staying here. Please, Patrick. Get your truck."

"Henry?" Ted calls. "Take us back down the hill to the Frosty, please."

Ted pulls the door to the ambulance shut, and we ride down the short hill to where I parked. They helped get her out and into the cab of my truck, and I'm finally in charge of what happens next. I thank them both and climb behind the wheel, glancing over at Kenny. She has her eyes closed and is cradling her wrist with her other hand.

"We'll be home soon, Kenny," I say softly, and she just nods. I can't be sure because it's dark in the cab of my truck, but I swear a tear ran down her cheek.

COWBOY POETRY
UNPUBLISHED WORK

Glass all at once
Colorful
Strong
Beautiful
Shattered
~By Patrick Smith 1988

I don't want to open my eyes.

There is a horrible throbbing in my face and wrist, and my body thinks I worked twenty-four hours straight. I want this to be a bad dream, but as I move to adjust my head, I know it's not a dream; it is a fucking nightmare. I let out a small whimper, and Patrick is here, touching me lightly and grabbing my hand.

"I'm here, Kenny. What do you need, honey?" he says close to my ear. His breath is soft and warm, and I wish I could wrap myself in it like a quilt.

"I hurt" is all I can manage, and he is gone. My throat works as I try to swallow, but it's so dry. I must've slept with my mouth open all night. It's like I ate sandpaper.

"Here, I brought you some juice and your pain pills. There is a straw," he says, as it touches my lips. I take a long drink of gloriously sweet, pulp-free orange juice because this man is absolute perfection.

"Thank you," I rasp out.

"You need to take these pills too. The doctor said every four hours, but you have been asleep for about eight hours. I didn't want to wake you, but seeing how much you're hurting, I guess I should've.

I'm sorry, Kenny," Patrick says as he puts two chalky pills in my mouth.

I take another drink of juice and swallow the pills. "Thank you, Patrick. I needed sleep, and honestly, I wasn't in pain until I woke up."

"Here, let me help scoot you up," he says, and he climbs over me, straddling my body without touching me. He slips his hands under my arms, and in one smooth move he lifts me so I'm more upright. The change in position causes my face to throb, but it stops pretty quickly.

"Thank you. Thanks for letting me stay here." I glance around his room with my one good eye, noticing a beautiful painting that wasn't here before, and I realize I'm in a king-size bed that must've been stitched together in heaven. The sheets are a cool cotton that I crave on a hot summer day.

"I like your new bed," I say, attempting a smile.

"Well, I've had it for a while. It was in Seattle. All my stuff came the other day and I..." He trails off and looks down. I reach over and grab his hand.

"Patrick, what's wrong?"

"I should've come to town sooner, gone straight to your house when I saw the ambulance return. God, I could've stopped him, Kenny. If I had been there sooner, I could've stopped him," he says, as a tear drops on my hand.

He tilts his head back and sniffs before leveling his gaze at me. His eyes are red-rimmed and swollen. "I was so scared when I saw you there on the floor. You had so much blood on your face. I was so scared." His voice hitches, and he shakes his head, forcing out a breath. "I was afraid I had lost you when I had only just found you."

"Oh, Patrick." My emotions clog my throat before I can continue. This man, this sweet, caring, sensitive man. How on earth did I get so lucky? Does he have any idea what he brings to my life? Probably not, because I have never told him. I should, but I learned something about myself when Ryan broke into my house. I'm a chicken.

"Patrick, I'm so glad you came when you did. It's okay. Ryan isn't going to get away with this. All this will heal. I'll be fine." I wonder if I say that enough if I will believe that.

"I know. Ted called earlier to check on you, and he said they went to Ryan's place last night, but no one was there. Maybe he will show up today."

"Hopefully. Can I come out to the living room? I'd love to sit on a couch and eat something."

"Of course. I can make scrambled eggs or pancakes, whatever you like." He holds out his hand for me and helps me up. Walking out into the living room, a sense of safety and peace washed over me. Unfortunately, being upright makes me realize my nose weighs 800 pounds. If I ever see Ryan again, I'm going to kick his ass.

After I eat, Patrick brings me the cordless phone and encourages me to call my parents. It is the hardest phone call I've ever made. I don't want to appear weak, and I hate making my parents worry, and with one phone call I'm forced to do both things. It takes an hour to convince my dad that they don't need to come up. When I finally hang up, I'm so tired I can't keep my eyes open. Patrick put a pillow on my lap to support my wrist and adjusted my legs on the coffee table with a cushion under my feet. I want to say thank you, to tell him how much I appreciate him, but I'm pulled under into a thick but blissful sleep.

THE NEXT FEW days pass by both quickly and painfully slow. Painful when I'm awake, then medicated sleep, skipping time forward in leaps and bounds. Patrick makes sure I have my medication, food, and something to drink. I never have to ask for what I need; he just seemed to know. He even went to my place in town and gathered more clothes for me so I don't have to wear the ripped shirt. It was just my crew T-shirt, and I have a couple of them. I glance down at my chest, and a memory scurries past my eyes.

"Hey, I think I remember when he ripped my shirt," I blurt.

"Really?" Patrick leans out from the kitchen, holding a jar in his hands. He quickly puts it down and joins me on the couch in the living room.

"Yeah, Ryan was mad that I had a spot on the engine crew. He grabbed at my shirt and said I didn't deserve to have this job, that I was stealing it from a guy. He pulled on the neck of my shirt, and I remember hearing it rip."

"Jesus, Kenny. I'm so sorry that happened to you," Patrick says. "They still haven't found him. I checked in with Ted when I got your things. Bonnie was there at the office, and it was obvious she had been crying. I'm guessing the shit really hit the fan after that night."

"I'm so glad I missed it all. Well, not all of it, I guess," I say, waving at my face. The swelling has gone down quite a bit, but the bruising looks terrible. I really don't know how Patrick looks at me with such love in his eyes when I look like a monster.

"I'm glad you agreed to stay here with me. I wasn't going to be okay if you wanted to be alone at your place. There's a chance I would have curled up on your front steps," he says, and I laugh, picturing his tall frame folded on the little cement steps that lead up to my house. The house I don't want to be in anymore. The house I'm currently avoiding.

"I have a project I'm working on, and I was wondering if I could bring it in here and sit with you? Are you still feeling sleepy?" he asks.

"No, and my pain is better so I probably should start taking less of the medication. I can switch to just an anti-inflammatory now and see how I do. It would be nice to be awake more," I say, then add, "What are you working on?"

"Well, I have all the things from my place in Seattle, and I have been going through my boxes. That part is simple." Patrick pauses and rubs his hands on his legs. "What I'm struggling with are the boxes that came from my parents' house. I haven't been able to go through those. I guess I would just like some company while I do that."

My heart squeezes in my chest at the thought of him sitting alone with all that's left of his family—boxes of papers and pictures triggering memories, good or bad, tugging him under.

"I would be honored to sit with you. I can help as long as I don't have to bend over. My face is still not a fan of that position," I say, and Patrick smiles and comes over to gently kiss my lips.

"I'm going to go get you some Advil first, then I will grab some boxes out of the office." He stands and walks out of the room. I lean back into the couch and close my eyes. How is it possible that I feel lucky while I sit here with a broken face and wrist?

"Okay. Here, take these, and here's some water." He hands me the pills and a glass of water, then quickly leaves the room again to retrieve the boxes. When he returns, he has four bank boxes he sets at my feet, then goes back for a bigger box marked "photos." He puts that one on the couch next to me and smiles.

"Here. You can reach in and pull out any number of embarrassing pictures of me from my childhood. That should keep you entertained while I go through the boring papers." Patrick gives me a warm smile.

"That sounds perfect. It's like a grab bag. I'm seriously excited about this," I say and reach my hand in, pulling out a handful of pictures.

"Do you want me to sort these or just admire how cute you are in your little bunny suit?" I wave a picture at him.

"Just enjoy yourself. No need to add a job to your fun." He squints at the picture and says, "That is actually not a bunny suit. I was Eeyore. See, it's gray, and I'm trying to look depressed." He points at the picture, and I glance at his face.

"That's you trying to be sad? You have the biggest grin on your face." I laugh.

"Yeah, I was so excited to be my favorite character, I couldn't help it." He shakes his head and smiles at me. My stomach does a little flip, something it has been doing a lot since I started staying out here. I watch as he settles onto the rug and pulls a box toward him. Lifting the lid, he lets out a sigh.

We settle into a comfortable silence, broken only when I hold up a picture demanding an explanation or asking who someone is. They seem to be kind of in order, with the pictures toward the bottom being mostly in black-and-white. I reach in and pull out a picture of Mitchell and who must be his brother, Wallace. They both have on work jeans and long-sleeved button-up shirts. There is a young man next to Mitchell, and I think it might be Rusty. All three of them are standing in front of a nice black sedan. My finger traces over Mitchell's face, missing his deep voice and gravely laugh. I wonder how old he is in this picture. I don't notice that Patrick has stood and come to sit next to me on the couch until he's peering over my shoulder.

"What's that? I haven't seen that picture before. That is my grandfather. Wait, is that Mitchell?" He gently pulls the picture from my hand and squints at the faces.

"I think so. Do you know that young man in the picture?" I ask.

He looks closer and shakes his head. "No, I don't know that person, but that is my grandpa's car. He was still driving that when I was born!"

"Wow. That is a fancy car! He must have come up here. That's a dirt road they are on," I say.

"Wow, yeah. So who is the young guy? He looks about eight or nine." Patrick's eyes go wide. "Wait, is that Rusty? Holy crap, that is Rusty!" Patrick says, and he stands with the picture in his hand.

"Did you know his father was named Russell? He was named after him. I guess my father's middle name was in his honor. I carry the name as my middle name too, and I know nothing about the man. It was important to these men to carry on the name of their friend, and I'll never know the story," Patrick says, sitting back down. He doesn't return the picture to the box. Instead, he places it on the coffee table.

I reach back in and pull out another stack of black-and-white photos, and this time Patrick leans in and watches as I flip through them.

"This is Mitchell. He looks young here," I say and flip the picture over, seeing a faint date written on the back.

"1919." When I say that, Patrick sits up.

"That's a year before Rusty was born and a year before Mitchell lost Helen. Do you think there is a picture of Helen?" Patrick's voice has a hopeful edge to it.

"Maybe. We can keep looking."

I pull out another stack. After flipping through a few pictures of cattle and what must have been Adin in the 1920s, I get to a picture of three men and two women. I recognize Mitchell, and next to him, tucked under his arm, is the most beautiful woman I've ever seen. She has short hair falling just below her ears, and she is thin. She has on a dark-colored dress that has a wide belt. Her face is turned up a little so she can see Mitchell. She has the sweetest half-smile on her face, the love apparent in her eyes. Next to him on the other side is his brother, Wallace. Between Wallace and a man who must be Russell is a woman with blonde hair. She is a little taller than Helen and has a pleasant face with rounded cheeks and full lips. She is wearing a floral-print dress that hangs just below her knees. It looks like both Wallace and Russell have an arm around her. I flip the picture over, and it says, "1918 the best friends a guy could have," written in a man's scrawl.

I hand the picture to Patrick and watch his eyes travel the same path mine had. He lingers on Helen's face, and his eyes light up.

"God, she is just like I imagined. She looks like a movie star. Look at her jawline and her perfect nose," he says, running his finger lightly over her face.

"Hey, I'd really appreciate it if you didn't talk about perfect noses in front of me," I joke, but he's lost in the picture.

"This must be Rusty's mom. Mary, I think, is her name. God, Rusty looks just like his dad. This is two years before Rusty was born," he says and opens his mouth to say more. He stops because that is also two years before Russell and Helen passed away.

The room falls silent, and I'm not sure what to say. I reach into the box and feel something that isn't a bunch of pictures. I pull out a bundle of letters that look familiar.

They're tied with a leather strap, and I run my finger along it, wondering where I have seen this before. I close my eyes and hold the letters up to my nose. There is a faint smell of Old Spice, and I tug at the strap and pull the first letter off the stack. It is in Mitchell's handwriting and is addressed to his brother in San Francisco. The memory that danced along the outside edge of my brain snapped into focus.

"Patrick, stand up and do me a favor," I say, and he looks at me and what is in my hands.

"What's that?" he asks, reaching for them, but I pull away.

"I'll show you in a second. I want you to do something first. Go to the bookcase over there." He walks over and stands there, looking at me like I've lost my mind.

"Okay, now see the third shelf there? Run your hand under that. There is a lever. If you pull it, the panel will open." The confusion on his face makes me laugh a little.

"I built it, remember? Trust me."

He drags his hand under the shelf. I built a trapdoor of sorts and a hidden compartment. I hear the lever slide, and the shelf moves a bit.

"Now pull the shelf toward you. There is a small space behind it. Reach in there." Patrick sticks his hand into the recess, pulling out a bundle of letters just like the ones I hold.

"What are these?" His voice laced with awe and excitement as he steps toward me.

"Letters. These are from Mitchell to your grandpa, and those must be your grandfather's to Mitchell. I knew I'd seen a stack of letters like this before. When Mitchell and I drew up the plans for the bookcase, he was pretty obsessed with having a secret hiding place. I thought it was for his will or something, but I saw him put these letters back there before closing the shelf and loading it with books."

"But these are my books. My books are hiding his letters?" Patrick asks, and I nod.

"Makes sense to me, and it must have made sense to Mitchell," I say.

Patrick brings the letters over to me and sinks into the couch. For the first time since I met him, I can't read his expression.

"Are you okay?" I gently place my hand on his leg.

"What? Oh, sure, yeah. It's just a lot, you know?" he says. He reaches his hand out, so I give him my bundle of letters. I also hand him the leather strap that was tied around his grandpa's letters, and he runs his finger along it, lost in thought. I suddenly feel like I'm intruding, so I feign a yawn and ask him if he would mind if I take a nap.

"I'm just not used to being upright for so long, I guess," I say, and he nods and walks me back to his room, helping me into bed.

"Sorry if I wore you out. Do you need anything, Kenny?" he asks, and I shake my head.

"Just a nap. I'll be okay. You can wait to go through the rest of that stuff till after my nap if you want." This time the yawn that escapes is real.

"Yeah, I probably will do that. If you are going to nap, I might go for a run. I need to...I don't know what I need. I need to clear my head, I guess."

He pulls the covers up over me and leans in to kiss me, making me wish I felt better. I wanted to give him space, but now that I'm lying down, I can see a nap might be a good thing.

"Sleep well, my love," he says as he places gentle kisses all over my face, the last one lingering on my lips. My eyes flutter shut, and in my head only I say, "I love you too."

Muddled thoughts wrap around
My mind
My heart
My soul
Where do I belong?
The city
The fields
The town
Who am I now?
Author
Rancher
Lover
~Patrick Smith 1988

THIRTY-THREE
PATRICK

My feet pounding the pavement allows me the reprieve I need. The last few days have been so crazy. With all my things here, it solidifies that this corner of California is my home. Then there is the pressure of a book hanging over my head, Kenny getting hurt.

God, Kenny.

When I walked in and saw her there, covered in blood, looking fragile and broken, it almost killed me. I should've gone to her house once she was home. I could've gotten there sooner to catch Ryan in there.

That night plays over and over in my mind, and I think about all the scenes I have written about assaults. Kent Price always comes to the rescue, just in time, of course. I got it all wrong. The hero doesn't make it in time, and the scene isn't like a piece of fabric stained with fear. It's terrifying. It's an unexplainable, unimaginable fear that grips your heart when you see the woman you love lying helpless.

The familiar guilt of the past few days rises in my chest. I'm reminded yet again, that I am nothing like the hero I created. My feet stopped on the gravel road, and I bent at the waist, breathing deeply.

There's a terrible pain in my side, and my chest is being gripped in a vice.

I need to make this right. Ryan needs to be found and brought to justice. I need reassurance that he's going to pay for what he did. It's the least I can do for Kenny. I lift my hands above my head and walk around, trying to get my heart rate down so I can continue my run. My mind wanders to the pictures and letters. I plan on reading them, putting them in order, layering the first one, then the response, going back and forth to get the whole story. Does Rusty know about them? That makes me wonder if he has ever seen the pictures.

About an hour later, I made my way back to the house. I'm resolved in my new plan: find Ryan and read the letters. Taking care of Kenny all the while, of course. God, it's been so nice having her here. I wonder if she would move in with me. Is it too soon? We get along so well, and the realization that I'm in love with her has settled in my heart. I wish I knew whether she felt the same way. Of course, I could ask her, rip the bandage off. If she doesn't feel the same, then I need that information. I can't keep fooling myself that this is the start of something great.

When I push through the front door, I can hear singing, terrible singing. A smile spreads across my face, and I follow the sound back to my room. Steam is pouring out of the bathroom, and the singing is louder. Something about a red rose on a front porch. I laugh at how off-key she is and wonder what I should do. Not wanting to startle her, I yell, "Hey, Kenny! I'm back. Do you need anything?"

"Just you."

I strip off my shirt and shorts faster than a man who fell ass-first into an anthill. I step into the bathroom and see her behind the shower doors, something big and bulky on her arm.

"What is that on your arm, Kenny?" I ask with a chuckle.

"I had to cover the cast, so I borrowed a garbage bag and some tape. Get in here and I will show you my handiwork!"

I slide the door open and step in, taking in the most beautiful woman I have ever seen. Her hair is slicked back from the water, and her garbage-bag-covered arm is hanging at her side. She's trying to soap herself with one hand, so I take the bar of soap from her.

"Here, let me help. You did a great job on this," I say, nodding my head toward her broken wrist, which she has wrapped in a small white bag and sealed with tape.

"Thanks. I guess I could have waited, but when I woke up I was hot and sticky." She makes an adorable face scrunching up her nose. "It's been days since I had a shower." She peers at me with narrowed eyes. "I can't believe you didn't say anything about the odor."

I lather the soap between my hands and start at her shoulders, going down her arms then back up to her shoulders, taking time to massage the tense muscles.

"You don't smell bad, Kenny." My voice sounds different, and she notices too.

"That feels really good, Patrick."

I lean in and kiss her gently, and continue to wash her stomach, dropping to my knees before her. My finger traces across her tattoo, and I notice the goosebumps rise as I move along. There's a yellow bruise at the bottom of her ribs on that side, and I wonder if that is from something Ryan did, or if she got that at work. I don't ask. I don't want to bring him up now.

"Were you able to wash your hair?" I ask, and she shakes her head no. I stand, and she looks up into my eyes.

I pour some shampoo into my hand, and tell her to turn around. My soapy hands gather up her hair, rubbing her scalp gently as I go.

"Is this okay? I'm not hurting you, am I?"

"No, it's amazing."

I can't help myself. I step back, watching the white suds slide down her back, trailing across her firm, round ass. The suds finally make their way to her ankles, and I reach out and run my fingers through the trail they made. She shivers, and I know I should ask if she's cold, but I can't. I can't take my eyes off her. She spins slowly and tips her head back into the shower stream, sending the suds down across the front of her. They arch over her firm breasts and trail down her stomach, and I'm mesmerized. I reach up and help her get the last of the soap, gently tracing around her breasts, lightly grazing her nipples. Bending, I kiss her breast softly, and she moans. One nipple, perfect and hard, finds my lips, my tongue, and I am rewarded by another sweet moan. I'm suddenly very aware of how hard I am. I straighten and kiss her softly.

"Let's get you out of here and dried off."

"Okay, but only if we can continue this in the bedroom." Her eyebrows raise and lower, but slower than one would for a waggle. I try not to laugh.

"Are you up for that? I don't want to hurt you."

"Yes, I'm fine. I want this. I want you, want to feel normal again." The last part coming out a little choked.

"I want you, Kenny. I always want you. Let me wash off quickly."

I step into the shower stream to rinse myself off before we climb out of the shower. Her eyes roam over my body and settle on my rock-hard cock. It twitches at her as if it's waving hello. She reaches out and wraps her hand around me. I groan and move closer to her, kissing her lips softly.

I take her hand gently off me and lead her out of the shower. I help her dry off, enjoying the slow process of caressing her with a plush towel. When I have no more reason to be rubbing her with a towel, I help her dry her hair. She runs a comb through it, looking in the mirror at herself.

"God, I look so awful," she says. She had removed the nose splint to shower, and I'm finally able to see the slight bend in her nose and the bruising under each eye. It's fading to a nauseating green and yellow shade, but the swelling has gone down, so I know it is healing, but it also marks the time. It's been almost a week since the assault. She catches my eye in the mirror and looks down.

"You are still the most beautiful woman I have ever seen, Kenny."

"I know. I'm pretty hot. If you like the Rocky Balboa type," she says, and I laugh.

"I have always thought Sylvester Stallone was a good-looking guy, so this works out well for me." I follow her into the bedroom and watch as she climbs into the bed, then I unwrap the bag she used to protect her soft cast.

"We're going tomorrow for the follow-up X-ray on this. Hopefully you can just have a removable splint," I say, and she nods.

"It doesn't even hurt anymore. It was such a slight crack they almost didn't put me in this, but when the doctor talked to Ted and learned about my personality, they decided to cast it." She laughs.

"I think if that was your only injury, you'd be out there using your saw." I climb in next to her.

She shrugs. "Probably. I believe you were running your hands all over my body very seductively a few minutes ago. I'm not sure how we ended up discussing normal, everyday things."

"Oh, right, sorry. Kenny?" I move in a little closer.

"Hmmm?" She lowered herself onto her back, gaze locked onto me.

I drop my towel as I rolled over her, careful not to hit her arm. "The hardest thing I have ever done is lie next to you these last few nights and not touch you."

"You've touched me, held me, rubbed my feet, my shoulders, my neck. You have been wonderful to me, Patrick."

"I didn't want to be wonderful to you. I wanted to grab you and pull you on top of me, letting you sink down on top of my rock-hard cock." My husky voice is low as I nip at her neck and ear.

"Oh, my!" she says as she fans herself with her one good hand.

"Is that better or still boring, everyday things?" I ask with a gentle kiss on her lips.

"Oh, I think I like what you just said. That kind of talk is way better than talking about broken wrists or doctors. Tell me what you would have done to me," she says, fluttering her lashes at me.

"You like that, huh? Okay." I clear my throat, suddenly very nervous. I've never really done the whole dirty talk thing; I kind of just winged it with the rock-hard cock comment.

"I would have pulled your pants down... Wait, no. I would've lifted your shirt, then lowered your bra. Um, I would have unhooked it, helping you take it off, because really, who wants to have some tight bra wrapped around them while they are having their breasts played with."

"Patrick?"

"Yes, Kenny?"

"How about you just show me."

"Okay. You sure?"

"For someone who is really good with words, you are surprisingly bad at dirty talk." She laughs then, her eyes twinkling with delight, so I kiss her softly.

She grabs the back of my head and kisses me with more pressure, so I allow her to set the pace, moving my mouth over hers. She opens her lips for me, and I slide my tongue along hers, enjoying the sweet moan that escapes. I pull back and yank the towel loose, exposing her perfect breasts. Sliding down, I kiss my way to each nipple, taking my time sucking and pulling them with my lips. My tongue flicks out, lavishing one while my fingers gently pinch and roll the other.

"You like that?"

Her entire body is squirming as she pants out, "God, yes. So good, Patrick."

I lie on my side next to her, sliding my hand down between her legs. She parts them easily, and I dance my fingers back up to her stomach and down her legs, circling but never quite touching where she wants me to.

She arches her back and moans, "Patrick, please."

"Please, what, Kenny?" I kiss her breasts, then move down to kiss along her stomach and hips.

Her breath hitches, and she says, "That. Please do that."

I look up at her. "You aren't very good at dirty talk either, Kenny."

She laughs, and I slide my fingers through her slick, wet center, pulling her wetness up, circling around her clit, then diving back in. She gasps and pulls my hair as she arches up off the bed.

"Oh, that. That is what you want."

"Yes, please," she panted.

God, I'm a superhero when I get her making those sounds. My fingers roam, slipping one inside her, then another. As she writhes and squirms, I slide two fingers in and move my mouth down, kissing as I go. The soft, barely there kind of kisses, flicking my tongue out occasionally to taste her. I'm in no hurry. I want to worship her, make her feel loved, wanted, and safe.

"God, Patrick, I love how you can turn me on. I love your hands on me, your kisses, your tongue," she says breathlessly, and I stop what I'm doing and look up at her. I thought for a minute she was going to say she loved me.

"I am so obsessed with you, Kenny. You make me so happy." I position myself between her legs, allowing just the head of my cock to rest at her entrance. She changes position, trying to bring me closer, but I hold back.

"You are so beautiful." I tilt in a little more, stopping when just the head slips in.

"You are so smart and funny." I pull back out, the head of my cock tapping gently on her clit. She whimpers in complaint.

"I love spending time with you," I say, sliding back inside a little more than before.

"I love your laugh." My words tumble as I pull back out. I grab my cock and rub it through her center, moaning at how wet she is. Probably not a good idea to tease her like this, since it's torture for me as well.

"Patrick, you are driving me crazy," she whines, arching her back.

"Yes, I know, but I'm talking. I need you to know these things, Kenny." I slide a little further in, and she contracts around me, trying to pull me further into her hot, wet center.

"I think your body is incredible," I say, pushing in further, and we both moan this time. She is so tight and wet I don't know how much longer I can withstand this torture.

I pull back out slowly and say, "I think I might be falling hard for you, Kenny."

Her eyes snap to mine, and for a brief moment I wonder if I'd said the wrong thing. She wraps her legs around me, using her heels to push my ass down, forcing my cock all the way into her in one thrust.

"Jesus" I arched into her, all thought of teasing erased in one motion.

"Patrick, I know I'm falling for you. Hell, I have fallen. Please move. I am so close."

That's all it takes. I unleash on her, thrusting my hips in firm, unrelenting strokes until she screams out my name as she falls apart.

One more thrust, and my balls tighten as I unload all I have into her. I continue to pump my hips jerkily until I'm empty and panting. I collapse on her, kissing her lips before I lie on her with all my weight, unable to hold myself up.

We are both breathing hard. My heart is leaping out of my chest pounding against hers, matching her rhythm with every happy thud. When I finally calm down, I pull out of her and roll to her side. I prop myself up on my elbow and let my gaze drop to her face. She is smiling at me, and suddenly I can't breathe.

"I love you, Patrick. Is that what you wanted to hear?" Her eyes have a sheen of unshed tears, and her voice is soft.

"You do?" My words come out a little more pathetic than I intended but she's still smiling.

"Yes, I'm so obsessed with you. You are so funny and smart and, God, you have the best dick."

I burst out laughing and kissed her a little too hard. She squeaks, and I pull back. "Sorry. I'm just so happy. If you'll excuse me, I need to run out to County Road W and yell 'Kenny loves me' at the top of my lungs."

"Maybe put on some pants first."

I waggle my eyebrows at her and climb over her, peppering her with kisses again.

"Maybe later. I think I want to show you how much I love you. Do you know that?"

"Yes, but I think I need you to show me again." She tilts her head up so I can kiss her neck.

COWBOY POETRY

UNPUBLISHED WORK

New to me, but old to you
The line of cattle winding down
Grazing here, grazing there
Safe within the fold
~By Patrick Smith 1988

THIRTY-FOUR
KENNY

I promised the doctor not to hit anyone or lift anything over ten pounds with my right hand, so he didn't keep me in a full cast. He was happy with how my nose was healing too, so I'm out of the splints and allowed to go back to light duty at work. No one has seen Ryan since the night of the attack. Ted has called everyone he listed on his emergency contact form, and only one number belonged to an actual person. She said there had been no word from Ryan in years and was surprised to learn she was his emergency contact. He listed his last address as a place in Sacramento, California, so law enforcement is going to pay a visit.

There is an uneasiness I can't shake, like my skin is too tight. I braided my hair in a low braid so I wouldn't have to turn my wrist for my usual French braid. I tried to get Patrick to help me yesterday, but we ended up laughing so hard at his twists and yanks to my hair that I didn't want to ask again.

As he drives me into town, he keeps his hand on my thigh and occasionally looks over at me. At the stop sign before turning onto Main Street, he leans in and kisses me, letting his lips linger over mine in the most delicious way.

"I love you," he says against my lips. It's my favorite way he tells me. To hear the words and feel them at the same time makes all the butterflies take flight in my stomach. He's not content until I confess my love as well, so I do, pulling him by the neck so he is closer to me.

"You're lucky there's not a lot of traffic in this town." He looks to his left and pulls out onto the main road, and we're at the back lot of the ranger station before I know it. I crane my neck, looking for Ryan's truck.

"He's not here. Ted told me. I wouldn't have brought you if he were," he says, squeezing my leg.

"Okay, yeah." I take a deep breath that does nothing to calm my nerves.

"You ready? I'm going to walk you in, then hide under your desk all day. Just get me some water now and then, and perhaps unfold me at lunchtime," he says so casually I think he's serious. I burst out laughing and leaned over to kiss him. His lips melt into mine, and he cups my face with his hand, growling a little.

"Sorry, I didn't mean to get you all riled up," I say with a wink and a smile.

"Kenny, I'm always riled up around you. I have had a semi since that day you kicked me in the shoulder."

"That is so not true! Stop." I unbuckle my seatbelt and climb out. Patrick must know how nervous I am, how hard it will be to face everyone.

I'm wearing my Nomex pants and boots and fire shirt, even though I know I can't go out with the engine. No one tells you what to wear on your first day back after such a thing. To be honest, it's like I'm walking around in another person's body. I'm not sure how to do this. My breathing is weird, and I lean against the truck. I press the heel of my hand into my good eye and force myself to breathe deeply.

"You don't have to come in today. Ted said you can have more time." Patrick is standing close, shielding me with his body. He has his hands on my shoulders, and he's waiting for me to look at him. I finally lower my hand and look up at him.

"I don't want to let him take this from me. This is where I work. It's my job, my joy. I love it here," I say weakly, and he gathers me in his arms.

"You are strong. You can do whatever you set your mind to, Kenny. I'll walk you in, then I'm going to the Frosty to wait for Jenny to open because I have a milkshake addiction. Don't worry, I'm not going to leave Adin today. I'm here. I was only partly joking about hiding under your desk," he admits.

"You are so good to me," I whisper as he rests his forehead against mine.

"Will you have lunch with me?"

"Patrick, you packed me a lunch, remember?"

He smiles and says, "I packed myself one too. I want to know if you'll eat with me or if I have to sit alone? Lunch is at noon, right?"

I laugh and shake my head, about to tell him how ridiculous he is, when he grabs my hand and pulls me toward the building. I didn't realize until that minute how much I needed that push to move forward.

My day is spent going over maps and making copies of random pieces of paper. I swear people are just trying to give me something to do. I also answer the phones because apparently Bonnie's parents don't let her work here anymore. It all came out that she was dating Ryan, and that they were having sex. I guess Luke told her about all the girls that Ryan had slept with since coming to the Big Valley Ranger District. I'm sure she is hurting, and I feel terrible for her. None of this was her fault.

At lunchtime Patrick is there waiting, and we sit out back at one of the picnic tables beside the engine bay to eat. He brought me a milkshake that was only about half-full. Apparently he drank his and started on mine on the walk over. He really does have a problem.

"How are you doing?" Patrick asks, and I shrug.

"Okay, I guess, but they haven't gotten any calls today. If I have to sit here when they go off to a fire, it's going to be hard," I admit.

"Yeah, I understand. I thought about that. You are on light duty for only what, two weeks?"

"Yes, the longest two weeks of my life." He leans in and kisses me, and I smile against his lips. "You can't fix this with your magical mouth, Patrick," I say, and he scoffs.

"You don't know that. Let's try." He waggles his eyebrows at me.

I continued the next day, the same as the first, on repeat for the next two weeks. Patrick is there every day to drive me in, meet me for lunch, and pick me up. We never talk about my house, or about me going there. The first day I was at work, Patrick gathered all my clothes and belongings and moved them to the ranch house. I always imagined that if I moved in with a boyfriend, there would be at least a conversation about it, but no. I just live at the ranch house now.

Not that I'm complaining. I wonder, though, if I should go back to that government-issued house with the tumbleweed couch and the memories of hot, stale breath in my ear. That I can't bothers me more than anything. I loved that house, loved the sense of security it gave me. I have a permanent position on the engine, in the ambulance and in the community. It's not like I owned the property, but it felt like home—safe and, well, mine. What has become clear to me is that even if he hadn't assaulted me, that sense of ownership dissolved the moment I saw his shadowy form in the doorway.

If he could get in, it wasn't really mine. That is the thought that has clung to me, kept me up at night. He broke into my home, but I let him into my mind, let his words seep into my brain and my heart. I didn't deserve this job. I stole it from a man who deserved it.

I asked Patrick to take me to the house on the hill so I could get my truck. I didn't go in; just climbed into my truck and drove off, not even looking back to say goodbye.

Patrick decided we needed a night out when the last of my light duty came around, so we went to The Bar before heading home.

All the bruising on my face is gone, and my wrist seems totally normal, so I guess I'm ready to get myself back out there. I've dealt with all my co-workers and a few of the locals, but I haven't gone back to The Bar. It's too exposed, too vulnerable for some reason. I don't know if Ryan sat in here, drinking and plotting his attack, but that's what I've been picturing.

As we walk in, the jukebox is playing Brown Eyed Girl, Luke and Zia are at the pool table, and I immediately relax. I turn and grab Patrick, pulling him down for a kiss.

"Not that I'm complaining, but what was that for?"

"For normal."

"Anytime, my love." He kisses me slowly, as if we aren't in the middle of a bar.

He pulls back and inhales sharply, pressing his forehead to mine. "Also, whenever you want to leave, just give me the signal. I'll drive you home."

"What is the signal?" I ask, trying not to laugh.

"You know, just give me that look." His eyebrows raise to his hairline as he emphasized the last word.

I giggle, "What look, Patrick?"

He lowers his mouth to my ear and says, "The one you give me as I'm making my way down to bury my face between your legs."

My entire face turns red as my body heats at the thought. "Oh," I say. "That look."

He presses his lips against mine again, my face cupped between his hands. My legs weaken, and I'm about to say we should go when Veronica stomp past us.

"Get my beer ready, Rusty! I'm coming in!"

I laugh and pull back from him to watch the show.

Jenny comes out of the kitchen to watch as well, and the whole bar cheers when Rusty slides the full beer mug in front of Veronica's barstool a second before she sits down.

"Damn, I thought she had you that time," Jenny says and turns to go back to the kitchen. She catches sight of me and winks, giving me a little smile.

Rusty glares at us, and all is right with the world.

I make my way to the pool table as Patrick goes to the bar to order us some drinks.

"Has anyone seen or heard from Ryan?" Luke asks as I chalk my cue stick.

"Nope." I wait for him to rack the balls. My stomach a little twisty at the mention of Ryan's name.

Zia leans in and says in a quiet voice, "I hear the mountains are very dangerous this time of year. Maybe he wandered off."

I snap my gaze to Luke, who lifts the triangle off the felt, then leans down to inspect the balls. "Perfect," he says. "You want first shot, Kenny?"

I glance at Zia, whose normal blank expression has returned.

Luke waits a beat, then shrugs and says, "Okay, I'll break."

He lines up and smacks the white ball into the neatly ordered ones, sending them scattering like the thoughts in my mind.

COWBOY POETRY

BEYOND THE FENCE LINE~ PUBLISHED 1950

Brother
Friend
One and the same
Two by three
By four and me
She loves
She chooses
Tearing us apart
~By M. S 1924

THIRTY-FIVE
PATRICK

Now that Kenny is back at work and settled in a little, I can get back to the task of writing, going through the boxes, and most importantly, reading the letters. I called my publisher and asked for an extension, explaining about my girlfriend getting injured at work. It felt weird to say to someone that I have something more important than my writing. Not bad, just weird.

They told me they understood and were excited to see what the train-robbing rancher was up to in books one and two. Good lord, I had forgotten I promised them a short series.

I rub my temples as I sit at my desk. I've threaded a clean sheet of paper into my trusty typewriter and have even pounded out the first sentence: "The wide-open range hid only those who had no secrets."

I bang my head on the desk after that, then groan and walk out of my office and into the living room, plopping myself on the couch. I grabbed the first letter from Uncle Mitchell to my grandfather. It's dated March 1923, probably right after Wallace left the valley for San Francisco.

Wallace,

I wish I could change your mind. It is not the same without you here. Rusty is growing like a weed, and Mary has started to work part-time at the school. I ride into town for groceries and I still think I will see her. I think I will see you, but it hurts more that you left. You had a choice.

Mitchell

THE REPLY WAS JUST as harsh, and I feel like I'm watching a heart break in real time.

Mitchell,

She made her choice four years ago. I can't change that. I have a good job here with the construction company. There is a lot of building happening, and I'm proud to be a part of something bigger. The tall buildings and the fancy clothes had me out of sorts at first, but now I'm exhilarated. I don't want to come back to the place where I lost my heart. I figured you of all people would understand.

Wallace

THE LETTERS CONTINUE LIKE THIS, back and forth, with my grandfather trying to get Mitchell to understand and Mitchell trying to get his brother back. I almost gave up reading because it's just sad, but then my grandpa started to tell a story, reminding Mitchell about something that happened when they were boys. All three of them—

Wallace, Russell, and Mitchell—racing across the big valley on horseback, being chased by an angry rancher. They broke through the trees, him hot on their tails, and ditched the horses, jumping down into a creek. They hid in a washout where the creek had cut into the bank, providing a little overhang. Breathing hard and trying not to laugh, they heard the rancher ride on past, cussing them out for cutting his fence line. He had better fishing on his land, and they had been too lazy to walk around so they took the horses and rode on through. Wallace said they were all ten years old.

An image comes to me as clearly as a movie of three barefoot boys with rolled-up pants riding like the wind across the plains. My heart surges, and tumbles in my chest. Without a doubt this is the story.

I read through the rest of the letters, delighting in more tales of the three best friends. Some were told by Wallace and some by Mitchell. The only voice missing was Russell's. This was their grief, their way of finding a path back. The letters stop when Rusty would have been in high school, just after Mary would have signed the letter permitting him to fight in the war. The last one to write was Mitchell, and it provides the answer to what happened that caused the rift.

Wallace,

I did try. I told her not to sign the damn letter. You can sit there in your big fancy city with your son who isn't old enough to serve and cast judgment on me? I did all I could. I will never forgive you for blaming me. My heart left my body for the second time in my life when that boy climbed into the truck that took him off to war. I'm in pieces, but you know that. Well, you would know that if you hadn't left me too.

Damn you, Wallace, damn you to hell.

Don't write me, don't return. We are done.

Mitchell

. . .

MY HEART SHATTERS into a million pieces. It's as if the loss of my parents, an uncle I never met, and my grandfather have all been tossed into a blender. I struggle to take a breath in, suffocating in the grief that had been poured out in the letters, the grief I had hidden away in the boxes, and the grief I thought I had driven away from when I came here.

I do the only thing I know how to do. I stand up, walk back to my typewriter, and rip out the page I started. After I thread a new page in, my hands hover over the keys. In a flash my fingers began to move, starting before the sentence is formed in my mind, words pouring onto the page as I watch. I'm a spectator only; this story isn't mine. It belongs to them, but it deserves to be told.

The crunch of tires on the driveway causes my head to snap up from the typewriter. I have a stack of papers upside down next to me, and I have to force my hands down to my lap. I blink, and I wonder if it's been hours since I last did that.

Jesus, what time is it?

"Patrick? You in here?" Kenny yells, and I arch my back and stretch my hands over my head.

"I'm in the front bedroom, or my office now," I say, and Kenny peeks around the corner.

"Hi! What are you doing?" She walks up behind me and puts her hands on my shoulders. I groan.

"Wow, you are tense. What are you working on?" She peers at the typewriter in front of me.

"My new book."

"Oh? The train-robbing rancher?" Her nose scrunches up as she says that.

"God no. I had an inspiration. It's something else. Something much better." It's slowly dawning on me how long I have been sitting here.

She glances over at the pile next to me and asks, "Is that all from today?"

I nod. My stomach rumbles. Kenny puts her hand on her hip and cocks her head at me. "Have you eaten today, Patrick?"

Sheepishly, I answer, "Probably not. Unless you have come home early from work. I sat down about an hour after you went in this morning."

"Patrick! That was nine hours ago! I'm actually late getting home. We had a call around three that kept us." She grabs my shoulders and turns the swivel desk chair around to face her. She places her hands on my knees and bends forward to kiss me.

"Does this happen when you write?" she asks when she pulls back.

"I guess it's been over a year since I've written anything." I blink at her, feeling that pull back into reality. My surroundings solidify around me, the story I had been lost in fading away. I clear my throat and gaze into her eyes.

"I love you, Kenny," I say, because that is all I can think when she is this close to me.

She climbs onto my lap, straddling me, dropping her lips to mine. She places a hand on either side of my face and kisses me so slowly and softly that I moan.

"You need to stand up and come out to the living room. I brought you a milkshake and some chicken strips from the Frosty."

At the word milkshake, I stood abruptly, holding her to me. She wraps her legs around my waist, and we walk to the front of the house, kissing and bouncing off walls. I pull my lips off hers long enough to eye the counter so I can put her down, then quickly grab the milkshake and take a long pull from the straw.

"God, you are perfection. You know that?" I say, and she laughs.

"You're an easy man to please, Patrick." She hops off the counter and grabs a plate from the cupboard, and the ranch from the fridge. The Tupperware container with leftover macaroni salad comes out, then a bowl of cut-up chicken is next. The last one she grabs has some fruit. I marvel that this was all in the fridge only a few feet away from me all day. She quickly arranges a plate, and my mouth waters.

"That looks so good." She walks past me to the small table by the window and sets the plate down. Going back to the fridge for two beers. I sit and wait for her.

"Dig in, Patrick. I've eaten already." She winces and says, "Sorry, beer after a milkshake is probably kind of gross. I should've held the milkshake back, like dessert."

"Don't ever do that to me. God, it's like you don't even know me, Kenny." I shoveled the food into my mouth. I didn't even realize I was hungry, and now I feel like I will never get enough.

She pops the cap off her beer, then mine, and leans back in her chair, letting out a big sigh. "I'm glad I came home when I did. You would have starved to death."

"You saved me, that's for sure. When I was writing my first book, well, and my second, I would go way too long between meals. It's easy to get trapped in the story." I take a few more bites before finishing that thought. "I learned to set timers or alarms so I would be forced to get up and walk around, or eat or drink something."

"Didn't you have someone..." she starts, but then stops and takes a drink instead. "Sorry, I shouldn't pry like that."

"No, it's okay. I had a girlfriend as I was writing the last book, but she wasn't around much while I was writing. She and I would go out on dates and stuff, but I get kind of focused. Our relationship got better after I finished the book," I say, and Kenny shifts in her seat.

"Oh, well, that doesn't bode well for me," she says with a tiny laugh, then asks, "What happened with you two?"

I rub my hand down my face and wipe the crumbs off. I think back to all that was wrong with Tricia and my relationship. Do I tell her that or the thing that made me end it?

"Well, to be honest, I should have probably never started dating her. She was a fan. I met her at a book signing."

"Oh my God!" Kenny says, and she leans forward like she can't wait to hear more. That kind of surprises me, so I cock my head at her and say, "Uh, yeah. Probably not the smartest thing I have ever done."

"Did she take you to a cabin and lock you up? Did she break your ankles?" Kenny asks with a twinkle in her eye.

"Jesus, no! What is wrong with you?"

She shrugs. "I just read a book by Stephen King called Misery. It was like that."

"Oh my God. No. More like she thought I was like Kent. Or rather, I think she wished I was more like Kent," I explain. She looks puzzled.

"What? Wait, like she thought a fictional character that came from your imagination was somehow a secret version of you?" Kenny asked with delight in her voice.

"Yeah."

Kenny pauses for a moment, then leans her head back and lets out a booming laugh. Her shoulders are shaking, and she is making a noise like a braying donkey.

"Had she met you? Like talked to you?" she says when she finally regains her composure. "I have only read the first Kent Price book, but Patrick, you are nothing like Kent!"

"I know!" I say, throwing my hands in the air. "Thank you for noticing. Yes, of course we talked. We dated for a few months."

"So when did you realize she was hoping you'd morph into Kent Price, man of action?" Kenny asks.

"Well, we were having sex, and she called me Kent."

"Holy shit! Patrick, that's awful. Was she crazy?" Kenny reaches for my hand and gives it a squeeze. I've told no one the reason for my breakup with Tricia; it was just too embarrassing. It feels good to say it out loud. It also makes me realize how ridiculous it was.

"No, she wasn't crazy. She understood I wasn't him. She told me right then and there that she wished I were more like him, though."

"While you were having sex?"

"Yes."

"What a bitch."

Now it is my turn to laugh. "Yeah. You know what? She really was a bitch."

The next few weeks went by faster than a train speeding away from a robbing rancher. Kenny calls the house on her lunch break to make sure I'm eating and getting up from my typewriter. I'm so excited about the way my book is coming along I can barely pull myself away from writing. Kenny is proving to be so good for my mental and physical health that I have no clue how I wrote twelve books without her in my life.

Last night when she came home, she grabbed the stack by my typewriter and curled up to read. She has been doing this every day, circling typos and making small suggestions here and there. But last night, she got to the pivotal point of the story, the part where everything changes for the three friends.

Mary.

"Is this really what happened?" she asks, and I look up, startled.

"What do you mean, Kenny? It's a fictional story."

"Well, yeah, I get that." She levels her gaze at me. "But this is about Mitchell, Wallace, and Russell, right? I mean that is always what I thought. Am I wrong?"

"Yeah. It's based on their lives, but I hoped I had changed enough of the details so that no one would see that."

"Patrick, everyone in Adin will know who this is about. You called the town in the story Albin. You describe the bar and the restaurant that was there before the Frosty. Rusty is for sure going to know you are talking about his father."

"Shit." I lean back from the typewriter.

"It's a really good story, Patrick. Like so good, I can't wait to get home every day and see what happens next. But I do think you need to tell him."

"I guess I was thinking the book is about people who are no longer here. Helen and Mary and the three boys are now all gone," I say, then sigh. "But this is Rusty's story too. Fuck, I need to tell him, get his permission to tell it, don't I?"

"Probably should give him a heads-up at least," she says with a little shrug.

I drop my forehead to the desk and moan. Great. A grumpy man who hates me on most days needs to be okay with me telling the story of how his mom and dad's love for each other tore a group of friends apart.

Cool.

COWBOY POETRY

BEYOND THE FENCE LINE~PUBLISHED 1950

Spilling out
To the open field
Grateful to be home
The cattle call to one another
Remembering the journey
Over hills
Through streams
Across the plains
Home opens before them
Shelter of the barn
Wrapping them in safety.
~By M.S 1949

THIRTY-SIX
KENNY

I promised Patrick I'd go with him to talk to Rusty. I also suggested we enlist Jenny's help. As we walk into The Bar, however, my stomach tightens. Maybe this wasn't a good idea. Rusty is already glaring at Patrick. I hold up my hand in a little wave and tug on Patrick's hand to get him to follow me.

"Hi, Rusty!" I say a little too brightly.

"Kenny," he says, looking me and Patrick up and down. His eyes pause on our joined hands, and he grunts.

"Hello, you two! Come sit. I made some cheesesteak sandwiches. I'll get them from the kitchen now." Jenny scrambles out of the booth.

Patrick lets me slide in first, then sits next to me, reaching for my hand under the table. Rusty has a bottle of whiskey on the table and four glasses. He pours himself and Patrick a glass, and waits for Patrick to pick up his glass. This time, instead of angrily drinking his shot, he clinks the glasses together and says, "To Mitchell."

Patrick nods and says, "To Mitchell." They both drink, setting their glasses back on the table at the same time.

Jenny comes out with four plates balanced expertly and sets

down each one. She climbs in next to Rusty, leaning in to kiss him before turning to us.

"Did you toast already?" she asks, and Rusty grunts.

"I told you to wait for me," she says, and rolls her eyes. "Did you get any?" she asks me.

"No, not yet," I say, quickly adding, "It's okay. I figured you and I could make our own toast."

I'm sure Patrick doesn't know that today is Mitchell's birthday. I hoped Rusty would think that's why we wanted to meet, and Jenny agreed.

Jenny pours some whiskey for me and her, then raises her glass.

"To Mitchell. Happy birthday, you old coot. I miss you something fierce," Jenny says, and I clink her glass with mine.

"Same here." I drink and glance over at Patrick, who looks like he is going to be sick.

Jenny talks about her favorite memories of being out at the ranch and the way Mitchell sounded when he laughed. Then I share a few stories of when I first met him and how he wouldn't let me leave his house once because he learned I could build things. I was trapped looking over plans for bookcases and side tables for hours. I'd initially gone out there as a favor to Ted to drop off a burn permit. It was a good thing it was my day off, or they would have been worried.

Rusty even shares some stories of his childhood, and what Mitchell was like back then. I nudge Patrick under the table, and he glances over at me. I nod toward Rusty, like now would be a good time to tell him. Patrick just blinks at me and shakes his head.

I nod again, and he shakes his head more obviously.

We both look over when Rusty grunts and see Jenny smiling sweetly.

"Patrick, it's okay. Tell him," Jenny says.

"Tell me what?" Rusty barks out.

"I, um, well, I found some things that were in the boxes from my parents' house." He reaches into his shirt pocket, pulling out the photo of the three men and two girls, and putting it on the table in front of Rusty.

Rusty looks down and leans forward to peer at the picture before gently picking it up.

"I've never seen this photo." His voice was softer than I had heard before.

His eyes traveled over the group of friends, lingering on his parents. He turns the photo over and looks at the date on the back. He flips it back over and clears his throat.

"Can I make a copy of this?" he asks, and Patrick shakes his head.

"Take it. I found another one that must have belonged to Mitchell," Patrick says, then clears his throat. "Uh, I also found letters written between my grandfather and great-uncle. I learned why they fought, what tore them apart, and well, I got inspired by their story. Not only my family, but your dad too. The three of them were such good friends, Mary and Helen too, later on. It just has so much to it. I gave it my own spin, of course."

Rusty holds up his hand, stopping Patrick. "Are you saying you are writing a book about them?"

"Yes. I am. I'm about halfway through. I only have two sides of the story, so I'm creating the other parts. It won't be accurate or even recognizable to you."

I cough and nudge Patrick with my leg.

"Okay, well, Kenny knew right away that I was writing about Adin and Mitchell, but most people won't." The words are spilling out of him; it's obvious how nervous he is.

"I see," Rusty says and hands the picture to Jenny so she can see. She has tears in her eyes as she traces her finger over the picture.

No one says anything for too long, so I chime in. "I've read it, Rusty. It's really good. I think you will like it."

"Why did they fight?" Rusty asks.

"What?" Patrick squeaks.

"You heard me. Why did they fight?" Rusty says, his anger apparent. "I don't want to learn by reading it in a damn book. I want to know."

"That's fair," Patrick says, then takes a long, deep breath and starts to explain all he learned from the letters.

"Wallace and Russell were both in love with Mary, but Mary only had eyes for Russell. They vowed not to let a woman come between them, but when Mary finally chose, it tore Wallace apart. He spent weeks out on the range with the cattle and stopped hanging out with the group. When Helen got sick, he came around a little more to support his brother, but things were strained. Once Rusty was born, they all gathered around Helen's bed, one life new to the world and one on its way out. They vowed to Helen to stay friends and help each other because it was all she wanted. She wanted the group to be back together." Patrick pauses and looks around to ensure everyone is following along. He hasn't gotten to the hard part yet.

"Shortly after she passed, Russell was killed in the logging accident, and Wallace assumed he would step in and care for Mary and you. Mary was so grief-stricken, losing her best friend and then her husband, that she pushed Wallace and Mitchell away. Wallace gave up and moved to San Francisco with his broken heart. Mitchell refused to give up. He kept going around until Mary realized it was a promise they had all made. They were all that was left, Mitchell and Mary, but they had you, Rusty. You helped bridge that gap for them."

"Okay, but why did your grandfather and Mitchell fight? If it was just a broken heart, why did the brothers stop talking?" Rusty says, shaking his head.

"Well, that happened when you left for the war. Did you know that Mitchell tried to stop your mom from signing that letter allowing you to enter the war at seventeen?" Patrick asks.

"Yeah, I learned that later when I got back," Rusty says. "I told Mitchell it was none of his damn business if I went to war or not."

Jenny shakes her head and says, "It was the only time they fought."

"Well, I guess my Grandpa Wallace and Mitchell fought about it too. Wallace was furious at Mitchell for not stopping you," Patrick says. He looks down and trails his finger across the grain of the wooden table. I know he's worried about how Rusty will take this news. I'm worried too. Jenny said it would be okay, that Rusty can handle it, but when he stands and walks away from the table without a word, it's Jenny's turn to be worried.

"Well, damn," she says.

"Should I go after him?" Patrick asks, but Jenny shakes her head. "Not unless you want to get punched right in the teeth. No, let him sort it out." She reaches for the whiskey bottle and pours some into each glass.

"To men, stubborn and mean. They love you rough and they leave you keen," Jenny says, and we all throw back the whiskey.

"That's a great toast," Patrick says, and she nods.

"Mary used to say it all the time. Now I know more of the story behind it, I like it even better."

"It is a really good book, Jenny. I think he'll like it when he reads it," I say. Patrick squeezes my hand and gives me a weak smile.

"Well, he loved all those Kent Price novels, so I'm sure he will like this one too. I don't think the book is why he's upset. He is just out there blaming himself for the brothers fighting. He's gonna stew on that for a while, I imagine," Jenny says with a shrug.

I guess you don't stay married to a guy like Rusty for this long by being sensitive about his moods.

We sit and talk about other things for a while as The Bar fills up with locals. Jimmy is tending bar tonight, so Veronica stomps in without her usual threat of a kiss, and someone drops a quarter in the jukebox. Hank Jr.'s "Family Tradition" comes on, and Patrick smiles at me, pulling me into a kiss.

"This is my favorite memory of the night I met you," he says, and I push him away with a laugh.

Luke and Zia walk up to the table to say hello, and Jenny smiles and winks at Zia. I cock my head, wondering what that is about when I remember her comment about how the "mountains" are dangerous this time of year. I excuse myself and grab her by the hand, pulling her toward the bathroom.

"What?" she says, laughing, but I have a feeling she knows exactly what I'm going to ask.

"Where is Ryan?" I ask as soon as we are in the girls' room.

"Don't know. Don't care." Her shoulder lifts in a shrug.

"Zia, did your brothers have something to do with him going missing?" My stomach turns at the thought.

"All I'm going to say is you don't have to worry about him anymore, Kenny. Rusty knows. Jenny knows. You don't need to know." She smiles and pats my cheek, then walks back out to the bar.

Jesus.

After splashing some water on my face and taking a few deep breaths, I walk back out to find Rusty and Patrick at the pool table. Patrick gives me a little thumbs-up, so I smile and slide in next to Jenny.

"Someday I want to hear the story, Jenny."

"Okay, Kenny, someday you will," Jenny says, then throws back another shot of whiskey.

EPILOGUE
PATRICK

It took a year to get the book into print.

I did all the edits and rewrites out at the cabin after Kenny made a few improvements to the place. She made me promise to take breaks and eat or stretch. Walks outside to the creek helped clear my head and connect me to the characters in the book. It was a relationship that grew deeper than the one I had with Kent Price.

The day it's released, we throw a huge party out at the ranch with everyone from town. Jenny and Rusty helped with the food and drink, and Kenny handled all the invitations. Somehow, in her spare time, she also managed to build a ramp for her father's wheelchair. I had met her parents before down at their home in Chico, but this is the first time they have been here since Mitchell passed. They spent a long time admiring Kenny's work, like the beautiful bookcase she had built in the living room and the bedroom.

Once everyone is gathered in the backyard under the bright, big valley night sky, I clink my glass to get their attention.

"I'd like to make a toast!" I yell, and everyone turns. Kenny stops talking to Neil and Ted and turns toward me with her big, beautiful smile.

"Two years ago I came into town lost and alone." The crowd lets out a collective "aww," then laughs.

"I was sad and pathetic, I know. But I met someone who made sure I knew that. Rusty, will you come up here, please?" Everyone laughs and claps, pushing Rusty toward me. I drape my arm over his shoulder, and he turns to me like he could kill me with one blink.

I chuckle and drop my arm. "Not quite there yet? Okay, cool. Well, anyway, Rusty made sure I understood that I wasn't a big deal. Not that I thought I was, but he seemed to be under the impression that because I was an accomplished writer, I must also be an asshole," I say, and everyone laughs again.

"Rusty has taught me so much, not just about cattle or the proper way to drink whiskey, but about love." When I say this, everyone goes wild. Rusty grunts at me and tries to walk back into the crowd, but I stop him.

I reach into my pocket and pull out an envelope. Holding it up, I say, "That's why I want to give you this." I hand it to him and watch his eyes scan over the information on the front.

"I haven't told Rusty this, but I gave him credit in my book and insisted that he get a portion of the royalties for each copy sold. This is an advance on your share of the first-year royalties. You can expect a check next year, and the year after that. Hopefully, for just as much, though I'm not sure how well the book will do."

Rusty tears open the envelope and pulls out the check made out to him. His eyes go wide, and he looks up at me.

"What the hell did you do?" he says angrily.

"I told your story. You deserve that."

"Damn it," he growls and pulls me in for an angry side hug with another signature Rusty grunt.

I laugh, then turn back to the crowd, seeing the faces of people who have become family to me. People that I didn't know I needed and now can't imagine my life without.

"Kenny, can you come up here too?" She hands her beer to Ted and walks up next to me.

"I want to thank you in front of all these people for kicking me in the shoulder and passing out on the lawn. You are the most incredible woman I've ever known, and I'm forever grateful that Mitchell lived here in this place, because you are here. I couldn't have written Big Valley Brothers without your help. Literally, I would've starved to death." People snicker, so I pause. "There is only one way to tell you," I pull a box from my pocket before dropping to one knee to recite the line from the poem she has on her hip. "And I love her still," I continue with my own words. "I love her in her strength, her fear; I love her with her saw, her axe. I love her in the day and in the night, and I love her most with my name. Kenny, will you marry me?"

I open the box, and she gasps and punches me in the shoulder. I hear the laughs and hoots from the crowd as I stand, rubbing my arm.

"Yes! Of course I will! I love you so much, Patrick."

I grab her, pull her into my arms, and wait for her to meet my gaze. "I love you too, Kenny. Today and always."

ABOUT THE AUTHOR

Pamela Dean lives in Northern California with her husband and their very spoiled golden retriever. She was a wild land firefighter in the early 90's and worked on engine 4 out of Adin. While she never achieved the level of badassery of Kenny, she was proud to be a part of the group of women who forged the way. After suffering a career ending injury, she went on to work in a variety of fields, gathering characters for future books along the way.

She is currently working on more heartwarming romantic comedies, so follow her on Facebook to get the latest updates. She can be reached via email at PamelaDeanWrites@gmail.com or through her website www.pameladeanauthor.com